WHISPERS FROM THE MOUNTAINS

A West Virginia Legacy

A NOVEL

DARLENE A. WILLIAMS

This book is inspired by true events as told to me by my Native American (Shawnee) great grandmother, my mother, and a friend's recurring dream. Names, characters, and locales have been changed. Some incidents are based on personal experience and others are strictly fiction.

WHISPERS FROM THE MOUNTAINS: A West Virginia Legacy by Darlene A. Williams

darlenew_is@yahoo.com
ISBN 13 – 979-8-218-71367-6
Cover by Darlene Williams
Excerpt from the *Virginia Gazette* (December 14, 1769)
PRINTED IN THE UNITED STATES OF AMERICA

DEDICATION

To my friend, Tommy Wyatt—this book would not exist without your persistent dreams, our deep conversations, and the incredible friendship we share. I am profoundly grateful.

I also want to honor my Native American grandmothers and my mother, who shared with me cherished family events that have inspired this writing. I love and miss each of you dearly.

ACKNOWLEDGMENTS

I thank God for giving me the wisdom and courage to try my hand at writing.

I would like to express my gratitude to my father for his unwavering support and guidance. I will always remember the final words he shared with me before his passing in 2021. He stated, "I believe that God will bless your books; don't stop writing." Dad, your encouragement motivates me to persevere. I hold you dear in my heart and miss you profoundly

I want to thank my editor Sandy Tritt of Inspiration for Writers Inc. (www.InspirationForWriters.com) for her patience and attention to detail.

I'd like to give credit to *Virginia Gazette* for the article on page 379. *Transcription Source: Virginia Gazette*, December 14, 1769, 2.

Finally, I'd like to thank my readers.

I appreciate each of you.

TABLE OF CONTENTS

CHAPTER ONE

LEAVING FLORIDA

May 2024

It was a warm spring morning in early May when Sarah finished loading the last piece of luggage into her already packed car. She tended to overpack for trips, but this wasn't a vacation—it was a trip to West Virginia to take care of her grandmother. Sarah had always shared a close bond with her grandmother. A recent phone call, during which her grandmother hinted at her declining health, had filled Sarah with anxiety. The thought of "Sarah, please come home. Your room is as you left it." replayed in her mind, adding urgency to her worry. *What if something happened to her? Why didn't I visit more often?*

She shook off the unsettling thoughts and got into the car, starting the engine. There were still a few loose ends to tie up today before her departure in the morning. She made up her mind, she was moving back home to West Virginia, a decision she hadn't yet mentioned to her grandmother. She knew her grandmother would try to persuade her to stay. *Oh, who am I kidding*? Grams would likely be the first to hop on a plane to help with the packing. A smile crossed her face at the thought. Pulling her phone from her purse, she checked her messages and noticed one from her best friend, Stacy, sent late last night, asking if she had already left.

Sarah rolled her eyes. “Typical Stacy,” she whispered. “I tell her I’m leaving tomorrow; she messages today asking if I made it there safely.”

Six years ago, Sarah learned her boyfriend of two years was cheating on her. Hoping to take Sarah’s mind off things, her grandmother rented a beach house, and they went to Florida for a much-needed vacation. They were walking along the beach when a dog broke free from its owner and jumped on Sarah, knocking her flat on her back. He then proceeded licking her face.

A woman rushed toward them yelling the whole way. “Max, Stop! She grabbed the dog’s leash and pulled him off.

Sarah’s grandmother helped her stand, brushing the sand off her back. She drew her eyes down at both the lady and the dog. “You need to keep control of your dog.” Her grandmother said firmly.

“I’m sorry. Max has never done anything like this before. Are you all right?” She clutched the dog’s leash in both hands.

“I’m fine.” Sarah managed to smile and patted Max on the head. “He’s beautiful. Golden retriever, right?”

“Yes, that’s correct. My name’s Stacy Boyd, and you’ve already met Max.” Stacy motioned at her dog.

“I’m Sarah McMillan and this is my grandmother, Grams for short.” Sarah placed an arm around her grandmother’s shoulder and gave it a little squeeze. It was her way of telling her grandmother to be nice. Grams took the hint and nodded.

Stacy spent the next three days giving Sarah and Grams the grand tour of Florida. Sarah fast became Stacy’s best friend. She even grew on Grams. That is, until a year later, when Sarah announced she had a job offer and was moving to Florida. That was five years ago, and Sarah always managed to visit her grandmother every summer and Christmas.

After Sarah's parents had abandoned her, her grandmother had taken her in. The only thing Sarah knew about her father was that he rejected his role as her dad, moved to Maryland, and started a new family. As for her mother, Sarah had heard conflicting stories; her aunt claimed she had passed away, while her grandmother's neighbor insisted she was living on the streets and battling addiction. Confused, Sarah found it hard to decide whom to believe. One thing she did know was if someone had wronged her grandmother, it took a lot to regain her trust. Sometimes she was so sweet you could almost see honey dripping from her lips. That's what her grandfather used to say.

Sarah felt a warm smile spread across her face at the memory of her grandfather and his wise words. He had left this world when she was just twelve, and his absence left a deep void in her heart. She recalled his insight into her grandmother's cunning nature, how she could be quite relentless in pursuing what she desired. It wasn't that her grandmother meant any harm; she simply preferred to have things her own way. As a tear trickled down her cheek, Sarah hoped her grandmother hadn't lost her feisty attitude. It was her indominable spirit that she loved and missed most.

Sarah shook the memory from her thoughts and walked back inside, dialing her grandmother's number as she looked out the window at the children playing across the street. "Come on, Grams, pick up," she whispered.

"Hello." Grams answered on the fifth ring.

"Hi, Grams, it's me, Sarah."

"Hello, dear. How are you?"

"I'm fine. How are you feeling?" Sarah hated small talk, but she went along with it for her grandmother's sake.

"I'm not doing so well; this may be the end for me," Grams said in a frail voice.

"You're going to be fine." Sarah crossed her fingers. "Think positive."

"I'll try." Grams' voice became shaky. "It'll be better once you get here." She paused. "You are coming, aren't you?"

"Yes, Grams. I'll be leaving at four in the morning."

"All right, sweetie, I love you. Have a safe trip."

"I will. I love you, Grams." Sarah smiled. "I'll see you when I get there."

"Okay, dear. I'll have dinner ready and waiting."

The line went dead, but Sarah couldn't shake the nagging feeling that her grandmother was faking illness. Her grandfather's words echoed in her mind: "That woman's an ornery little spitfire who always gets her way." It wouldn't be the first time her grandmother faked an illness to get her way. Instantly, a wave of guilt washed over her for harboring such a thought. After all, she knew her grandmother better than anyone else. Grams cherished honesty and was always straightforward about her likes and dislikes. She never shied away from expressing her feelings to Sarah.

After showering, Sarah climbed into bed but struggled to fall asleep. The heat in her bedroom made her uncomfortable. She got up to turn on the air conditioner and returned to bed. Despite her efforts—shuffling around her pillow and attempting to read—her mind was consumed with worries about losing her grandmother. Eventually, she rolled over, embraced her pillow, and finally succumbed to sleep.

She woke up early the following morning. Choosing to forgo breakfast, she planned to pick up something on her way. After a final check to ensure she hadn't forgotten anything, she got into the car and carefully backed out of her driveway. *Hold on, Grams. I'll be home soon.*

CHAPTER TWO

HOME IN WEST VIRGINIA

The twelve-hour drive seemed to fly by. Before she knew it, Sarah was pulling into her grandmother's driveway.

The massive old house still looked the same as the day Sarah moved out. It was the oldest, most beautiful home in the neighborhood, with its huge front porch and an expansive balcony above. The balcony, Sarah's go-to spot, opened from her former bedroom. Whether she was working on school assignments or lost in a captivating book on warm summer nights, the balcony was the perfect retreat.

She exited the car and then opened the trunk to retrieve her suitcases. She set them at her feet on the pavement and glanced around her old neighborhood. *If only I can make it in the house before Mrs. Stevenson sees me.*

She closed the trunk and reached for her luggage when something caught her attention. It was Mrs. Stevenson, the neighborhood gossip.

"Oh no, I hope she didn't see me," Sarah whispered. She grabbed her belongings and attempted to hurry into the house, but it was too late. Mrs. Stevenson rushed across the street, frantically waving her hands while shouting.

"Sarah! Sarah! I need to have a word with you."

Shoot, she saw me. Sarah put on her best fake smile. "Hello, Mrs. Stevenson. It's so nice to see you," she lied.

"Oh, goodness." Mrs. Stevenson placed a hand on her chest and paused to take a breath. "I need to talk to you about your grandmother."

"Look, Mrs. Stevenson, I just arrived, so if you don't mind, I need to check on Grams." Sarah turned to walk away. Mrs. Stevenson followed.

"I tried to warn her, ya know."

"Warn her?" Sarah made it to the foot of the stoop.

"Yes." Mrs. Stevenson rushed up the steps, blocking the way. "I warned her not to enter her pie in the baking contest." She leaned forward, her hands on her hips.

"Baking contest, seriously?" Sarah rolled her eyes.

"You know, at the county fair." She crossed her arms over her chest. "Geez, Sarah, you haven't been gone that long."

"Mrs. Stevenson, I don't mean to sound rude." Sarah walked around her and put the luggage next to the front door. "That's between you and Grams. You'll have to take it up with her."

"That's what I'm trying to tell you." Mrs. Stevenson spoke through gritted teeth. "I tried to reason with your grandmother, but she wouldn't listen. Do you know what she did this morning?" She crossed her arms and patted her foot.

"No, but I'm sure you're going to fill me in." Sarah peeked through the door window for any sign of Grams.

"She was watering her plants and threw a glass of water on me. That's what she did," Mrs. Stevenson said angrily.

"Oh, only a glass?" Sarah snickered.

"I'm glad you find this amusing." Mrs. Stevenson scoffed. "You tell your grandmother that I'm winning the contest this year." Her eyes narrowed as she pointed her finger at Sarah's face.

"If you truly believe that, then why are you here?" Sarah's gaze met hers.

"To warn her not to waste her time entering." Mrs. Stevenson fidgeted with her apron. "I mean, I'm just trying to protect her from the disappointment of losing." She smirked.

"The only one who'll be disappointed is you." Sarah stepped towards her.

"Oh, really?" Mrs. Stevenson stared at Sarah wide-eyed.

"Yes, really. Grams passed all her secret recipes to me." Sarah glared at her.

"What are you saying?" Mrs. Stevenson stepped back.

"When the good Lord calls my Grams home, I'll continue her tradition. Except I'll enter her pies in every contest from here to Virginia." Sarah snatched her luggage.

"Oh!" Mrs. Stevenson gasped. "You wouldn't dare." She slammed both arms down at her sides.

"Have a good day, Mrs. Stevenson." Sarah opened the door, entered the house, and shut the door before Mrs. Stevenson had a chance to retaliate.

"Sock it to the Ol' Biddy," came a voice from behind Sarah.

She jumped and turned to find her Grams standing there in a boxer's stance, as though ready for a fight.

"Grams, you nearly frightened me to death." Sarah placed a hand on her chest.

"Sorry, dear." Grams stepped past her and looked out the window. She watched as Mrs. Stevenson made her way across the street and back to her own yard, arms flailing and grumbling all the way. "The next time ol' sourpuss Stevenson comes in my yard, I'll have the water hose ready for her."

Grams closed the blinds and turned to face Sarah.

"Grams, I thought you were sick." Sarah pursed her lips. "You have some explaining to do." Sarah was the only one who'd ever gotten away with speaking to her grandmother that way.

"Oh, dear, I need to check on dinner." Grams hurried into the kitchen. She put on her oven mitt and pulled a roast out of the oven. She spooned broth over the roast, all the while refusing to make eye contact with Sarah.

"Grams, you led me to believe you were on your deathbed." Sarah leaned her back against the counter. "I'm glad you're all right, but I can't keep coming up here at the drop of a hat." She crossed her arms and stared at the floor.

"So, are you saying that you wouldn't have come unless I was on my deathbed?" Grams crossed her arms over her chest and glared at her. She had a way of turning the tables and making Sarah feel guilty for questioning her.

"Grams, that's not what I meant, and you know it." Sarah's stomach rumbled. She hadn't eaten since breakfast and was feeling the effects of it. She leaned toward the steaming food and breathed in the delicious aroma. "That smells wonderful." Sarah hugged her grandmother. "You're forgiven." She winked.

"Me, forgiven? Whatever for?" Grams teased.

"I'm happy to see you still have your sense of humor." Sarah kissed her grandmother's cheek. "I'll take my things to my room." She strolled into the living room to retrieve her luggage and ascended the stairs leading to her old bedroom. Everything was just as she had left it. She placed her suitcases on the bed, unpacked them, and put her things away. She was just finishing when her grandmother made her way into the room.

"I was just finishing up." Sarah hung the last few items in the closet.

"Take. . . your. . . time, dear," Grams said between breaths. Sarah closed the closet door and turned to find her grandmother holding onto the foot of the bed with one hand, the other on her chest. Her face was ghostly white.

"Grams!" Sarah rushed to her side, "Are you all right?" She grabbed a chair next to the closet and helped her grandmother sit down. After a few minutes Grams' breathing eased.

"I'm fine." Grams patted Sarah's hand. The color slowly returned to her cheeks as her breathing became normal. At that moment, Sarah knew she had made the right decision to move back home.

"How long has this been going on?" Sarah gently rubbed her grandmother's back.

"Oh, a few weeks or so." Grams stared at the floor.

"What did Doc Brown say?" Sarah suspected her grandmother hadn't seen the doctor when Grams shifted in her seat. "Grams, you did see the doctor about this, didn't you?" Sarah knew the answer before she even asked the question.

"I didn't feel the need to." Grams stood while holding onto Sarah. "You know how I hate waiting at a doctor's office just for them to tell me what I already know."

"What would that be?" Sarah questioned. "That you're a stubborn old woman, or that you're a hardheaded stubborn old woman?"

"I may be old and stubborn but remember the McMillan blood flows through your veins." Grams slowly made her way toward the bedroom door.

"What's that have to do with anything?" Sarah asked.

"It means that you're just as stubborn and hardheaded as I

am." Grams paused in the doorway. "Are you going to help me downstairs, or am I going to have to slide down the rail?"

"Don't you dare try it," Sarah gasped. She wanted to believe her grandmother was joking, but she wasn't about to find out. "I'll help you." They locked arms and descended the staircase. Once her grandmother was safe at the bottom, Sarah pulled her phone from her jeans pocket.

"Who are you calling?" Grams eyed Sarah suspiciously.

Sarah took a few steps back. She wasn't taking any chances on Grams grabbing the phone. After a few rings, the receptionist answered.

"Hello, Dr. Brown's office, Lanie speaking How may I direct your call?" came a cheerful voice on the other end.

"Hello, my Grandmother Florence McMillan needs to be seen as soon as possible." Sarah avoided making eye contact with her grandmother, who clearly wasn't thrilled about going to the doctor. She paced back and forth grumbling to herself. "I'm a grown woman. I can make my own decisions," Grams muttered.

"Thank you, have a good day." Sarah placed her cellphone in the back pocket of her jeans.

Grams stopped pacing and turned to face her. "I'm not going." She flung her arms in the air. "End of story." She turned and walked into the kitchen, followed by Sarah.

"Grams, you're going to the doctor in the morn—"

"Nope, I'm not doing it," Grams interrupted.

"Your appointment is at ten, and you're going if I have to drag you kicking and screaming," Sarah said firmly. "Look, Grams." Sarah softened her tone. "Please go. I need to know you're all right."

Grams walked to the kitchen sink and stared out the

window. "All right, I'll go, if it will shut you up." She turned to face Sarah.

"Yes!" Sarah looked toward heaven and whispered, "Thank you."

"Afterwards, we can go shopping and have lunch." Grams winked.

"That sounds like a plan." Sarah hugged her.

Sarah helped set the table. She set the roast in the center of a platter, then placed potatoes and carrots around it. Grams brought a basket of homemade hot rolls and a bowl of seasoned green beans to the table.

"Goodness, you cooked enough to feed the neighborhood." Sarah giggled. "We'll be eating leftovers for a week." She took a seat across from her grandmother.

"I must say, it smells delicious," came a male voice from the kitchen.

Sarah tilted her chair back, hoping to see who was at the back door. She caught a glimpse of a handsome gentleman. She gasped; her breath caught in her throat. She leaned back a little too far. The chair and Sarah both hit the floor.

"Sarah! You're not hurt, are you?" Grams rushed to her side.

"Just my pride." Sarah's face reddened.

"Here, let me help you up." The gentleman held out his hand.

Sarah refused his help. "I'm fine, thanks." She stood.

Grams set the chair upright, "Hello, Jimmy, you're late." She patted him on the back as she stepped around him and headed back to the kitchen. She removed three glasses from the cabinet and placed them on the counter and then retrieved a pitcher of sweet tea from the fridge. She filled the glasses to the brim. Sarah helped bring the drinks to the table and then quietly took her seat.

"I'd like you to meet Sarah, my beautiful granddaughter." She motioned toward Sarah. "My beautiful, single granddaughter." She smiled mischievously. "Sarah, this is Jimmy, but I guess you can say you already fell for him." Grams chuckled.

"Grams, Stop it." Sarah blushed.

"It's nice meeting you." Jimmy smiled. His pale green eyes were mesmerizing. Sarah found it hard to look away. There was something familiar about those eyes. Sarah picked up her glass and took a huge gulp.

"Yeah, it's not every day you first meet someone on their back with their legs stuck in the air," Grams chimed.

Sarah spit sweet tea everywhere. This time it was Grams whose face reddened upon realizing what she had said. "Oh, dear, I... Uh. . . Oh dear, that's not at all what I meant. I'll get a towel." Grams got up from the table and went to the kitchen. It was the first time Sarah had seen her grandmother so embarrassed. She looked at Jimmy who was trying his best not to laugh, but when Sarah placed a hand over her mouth to stifle a giggle, he could no longer contain himself. They both burst into laughter and were soon joined by Grams.

"I must say, that's the hardest I've laughed in a very long time." Grams placed a napkin on her lap. "Now, let's dig in.

After dinner was over, Jimmy helped Sarah load the dishwasher. "That was a delicious meal." Jimmy took Grams' hand and gently placed a kiss on the back of it. "Thank you for inviting me." He smiled.

"Thank you for coming, both of you." Grams looked from Jimmy to Sarah.

"It was my pleasure," he replied.

"Sarah, would you mind showing Jimmy the house?" Grams turned her back and poured herself another glass of tea.

"Uh... Sure... I guess," Sarah stuttered, a confused look upon her face. She led the way to the living room and then upstairs to the bedrooms.

Sarah watched as Jimmy inspected every nook and cranny with professional precision.

Sarah's curiosity got the better of her. "I'm sorry, but what exactly are you doing here?" she asked.

"Your grandmother hired me to inspect her house for home repairs." He rubbed his hand down the hand-carved molding along the bedroom doors. "Gorgeous handiwork," he whispered.

Sarah looked around the immaculate room. "What could possibly need repaired?" She walked to the window and pulled back the curtains. She could see the Stevenson's house across the street.

"I'll let you both know as soon as I get through with my inspection." Jimmy's tape measure snapped shut. He began taking a few photos.

"Well, then, I'll leave you to it." Sarah turned on her heel and went back downstairs to check on her grandmother. She found her sitting on the back porch swing. Sarah strolled across the porch and took a seat on the swing next to her.

"It's such a beautiful day." Grams stared toward the blue sky. "Don't you think?" She turned and smiled at Sarah.

Sarah looked up at the huge puffy white clouds slowly floating by. The sun kissed her darkly tanned skin. Her long auburn hair glistening in the sunlight as though on fire. She patted her grandmother on the hand, closed her eyes, and smiled. "Yes, it sure is a gorgeous day." A noise upstairs reminded Sarah of the reason she left Jimmy alone. She had questions she wanted answers to.

"Are you planning on selling the house?" Sarah stopped the swing and turned to face her grandmother.

"What are you talking about?" Grams looked surprised. "This house has been in our family for generations—two hundred sixty-two years to be exact."

"I know, it's just that . . . ."

"I'm not selling my home, and if you are wondering about Jimmy, he's offered to do a free inspection in exchange for a homecooked meal. End of story." Grams stood and looked toward the roof of the porch.

"I'm sorry, I thought he was inspecting the place in order to give you an appraisal." Sarah stood next to her grandmother.

"Do you see that?" Grams pointed at the roof.

Sarah looked up. "It seems you may have sprung a leak."

"Exactly, and that's why I asked Jimmy to inspect the rest of the house." Grams patted Sarah on the arm. "This house has stood for generations. I'm not about to let it fall apart now."

"Let's go find him and see how it's going." Sarah placed an arm around Grams' shoulder.

They met Jimmy as he was descending the staircase. He stopped midway on the stairs, glanced around the room, and smiled. "You have a lovely, well-kept home here, Ms. McMillan. The hand carved wood is exquisite." He gently ran his hand over the stair rail as though it were a delicate flower.

"Thank you. Sarah and I were just discussing how it's been in our family for generations." Grams looked around the room, smiling proudly. "When the good Lord calls me home, I'm passing this house down to Sarah." She slid an arm around Sarah's waist.

"Thanks, Grams. Hopefully, that won't be for a long time to come." Sarah hugged her.

“Should you ever find yourself in a financial situation, you can always turn the place into a bed and breakfast or a museum,” Jimmy suggested.

“I’ll not have strangers running around in my home, banging up my woodwork or spilling stuff, thank you very much.” Grams never bothered hiding her annoyance.

“Calm down, Grams. I’m sure he was only trying to help.” Sarah gave her grandmother’s shoulders a little squeeze.

“I just meant that this house is such a gorgeous piece of history that it should be shown off.” Jimmy motioned around the living room. “Sorry if I offended you.”

“No, I’m the one who should apologize.” Grams took his hand and patted the back of it. “I get a little defensive when it comes to my home or my granddaughter.” She turned and started toward the kitchen. Sarah and Jimmy followed. “I know that my neighbors talk,” she continued. “They say things like I should sell. This house is too big for an old lady to keep up with, but I pay them no mind.” She slapped the air as though swatting at an annoying fly.

“It’s okay, Grams.” Sarah rubbed her grandmother’s back. “You have every right to feel aggrieved.”

Jimmy’s phone alerted him to a text message. “I should go. Thanks again for the incredible meal.” He headed for the back door, stopping dead in his tracks when Grams spoke.

“Hold on a second.” Grams picked up a to-go tray from the counter. This is for you. It’s leftovers from dinner.” She handed it to him.

“This is the best tip I’ve ever gotten.” Jimmy’s eyes lit up. “Well, it’s the only tip I’ve ever received.” He chuckled.

“I hope you enjoy it.” Grams winked.

“Yes, ma’am, I sure will.” Jimmy bowed playfully. “It’s not

often that I get a home-cooked meal." He closed his eyes and sniffed the container, taking in the wonderful aroma. "Aww, it smells like heaven." He grinned.

Grams straightened her shoulders and stood a little taller. She smiled proudly. "We'll have to do it again sometime. Sarah is an excellent cook." She nudged Sarah with her elbow.

"Really! Beautiful and can cook. That's a perfect combination." His smile sent chills down Sarah's spine.

"Thank you," Sarah whispered.

"Your boyfriend's a lucky man." He turned to walk away.

"She doesn't have a boyfriend." Grams shouted a little louder than she had intended.

Sarah cocked her head sideways toward her grandmother. "Grams!" Sarah whispered through gritted teeth. Her grandmother ignored her annoyed expression.

"I'm sorry about that, but Grams doesn't seem to know when to bite her tongue." Sarah glared at her grandmother, who once again ignored her.

"I'll get back with you in a few days to discuss everything, and we'll take it from there." Jimmy held up the container of food. "Thanks again."

"It was my pleasure." Grams patted him on the back of the arm as he turned and walked out.

"What a nice young man." Grams turned to face Sarah, who stood with her arms crossed over her chest.

"Grams, what are you up to?" Sarah tapped her foot to show her annoyance.

Grams smiled slightly and patted Sarah's arm. "You'll thank me later, dear." She walked to the counter and noticed a container which held a huge piece of homemade chocolate cake. She picked it up and handed it to Sarah. "If you hurry, you can catch Jimmy and give him this dessert." Sarah opened her mouth to protest, but before she could say a word, her grandmother turned her toward the back door and gave her a little shove. "Hurry!" she shouted.

Sarah rushed outside. Part of her hoped to catch him in time, while at the same time she didn't want to face him so soon after her grandmother's embarrassing comments. As she rounded the corner of the house, she found him parked behind a huge Rhododendron bush talking to someone on his cellphone.

"It's a beautiful home. It just needs a few minor repairs." He paused. "No! I can get more out of it than what the buyer's proposing." He paced back and forth in front of his truck. "Just tell them it'll be ready in three weeks. . . Yes, I'm sure." He hung up the phone and stood there, rubbing the back of his neck.

Anger boiled in the pit of Sarah's stomach. She had no idea what game he was playing, but she was going to make sure he lost. She straightened her shoulders and tried to compose herself. She was about to alert him that she knew of his plans to sell her grandmother's house. She took a deep breath and stepped around the bush, startling Jimmy when he turned and saw her standing there. She forced a smile and handed him the container.

He looked confused as he gently took it from her hand.

"Grams wanted you to have a slice of her homemade chocolate cake." She looked him in the eyes. She once again found it hard to look away. *Get a grip, Sarah. Behind those gorgeous eyes stands a man full of deceit.*

"Hello." Jimmy waved his hand in front of her face. "Are you all right?" he asked.

"Huh . . . Oh yeah, I'm fine." She knew if she didn't leave

quickly, she might lose her temper. She turned and walked away.

"Thank your grandmother for me," Jimmy shouted after her.

Sarah threw her hand up. "She only invites people she trusts to have dinner in her home. Have a good day." She continued walking without looking back. She heard the truck door open and close, and he drove off as she was entering the house. Sarah furiously headed upstairs, taking them two at a time. *The nerve of him trying to take advantage of an old lady.* She made up her mind that she wouldn't leave until she got everything straightened out. *This man's handsome, I'll give him that, but if he thinks he can charm us out of our home, he's got another think coming.* She lay across her bed fuming.

"Sarah! Are you up there?" Grams shouted from the foot of the stairs.

Sarah sat straight up. "I'll be down in a minute." She rushed into the bathroom, splashed cold water over her face, and stared at her reflection in the mirror. "Okay, buddy, that handsome face doesn't disguise your ugly motives," she whispered to herself. She grabbed the hand towel off the rack and dried her face before rushing out of her room. She met her grandmother on her way upstairs.

"Grams, if you don't mind, I would rather you not climb these stairs." Sarah placed her hand around her grandmother's forearm. "At least not until you see the doctor."

"Oh, fiddlesticks." Grams waved a hand in the air. "I'm fine." She pulled a tissue from the box on a stand at the bottom of the stairs and dabbed her nose.

"Grams, are you taking a cold?" Sarah's brows furrowed.

"No, dear, it's allergies." She sniffed. "My nose runs like a sugar tree this time of year." She grabbed a fresh tissue from the box and placed it in her apron pocket.

Sarah snickered at her grandmother's choice of words. She wondered if everyone spoke that way back in the day.

They sat on the back porch swing talking about old times until darkness began to fall.

"It's been a long day." Grams stood. "I think I'll turn in for the night."

"Me too." Sarah stood, stretched her arms above her head, and yawned. She walked her grandmother to her room, which was located off the living room and down a short hallway. After tucking her grandmother into bed, Sarah made her way upstairs to her old room. She was taking a shower and getting ready for bed when her phone rang. She answered on the second ring.

"Hi, Stacy, what's up?" Sarah asked nonchalantly.

"Well, since you asked." Stacy sounded annoyed. "You were supposed to call me as soon as you arrived."

"Sorry, I was going to call before bed."

"How is your grandmother?" Stacy asked in a gentler tone.

"She had an episode with her heart, I think." Sarah's voice trailed off.

"Oh no!" Stacy gasped. "That doesn't sound good. What happened?"

"When she exerts herself, her heart races and she can hardly breathe." Sarah sighed as she lay across the bed.

"Has she seen a doctor?" Stacy said softly.

She pushed herself up, swinging her legs over the edge of the bed. "She has an appointment tomorrow morning."

"Hopefully, she receives a good report," Stacy said. "Sorry to cut it short, but I must go. Call me as soon as you find out something."

"I will." Sarah stood.

"Talk to you then." Stacy hung up before Sarah could say another word.

Sarah hated that but also understood Stacy's fear of saying goodbye to friends and loved ones. She admittedly had always been superstitious. Sarah went back downstairs and found Grams sitting in the living room.

"Come sit down and watch a movie with me." She patted the couch cushion next to her.

"I thought you'd be fast asleep by now." Sarah sat next to her and placed her head on Gram's shoulder.

"I couldn't sleep, so I figured I'd see what's on Netflix." Grams pressed the power button on the remote.

"What are we watching?" Sarah drew her feet upon the couch.

"How about this one?" Grams scrolled through a list of movies, stopping on a picture of a little girl and her dog standing in front of a darkened house.

"That's *Guarding Angel*, the new movie I've been wanting to watch." Sarah sat up. "Stacy has all three books in the series."

"Well, then, *Guarding Angel* it is." Grams scooted to the edge of the couch. "Right after I make popcorn and sweet tea."

"I'll help." Sarah leapt and then helped Grams off the couch. "I'll make the popcorn while you make the tea," Sarah said. "You know how much I love your sweet tea." She winked.

"Oh, well that's easy enough." Grams opened the fridge, pulled out a pitcher, and set it on the counter. "There you go, fresh sweet tea." She smiled proudly. "I made it while you were in your room."

"That's even better. Sarah grabbed two large glasses from the cabinet and filled them with tea. The microwave dinged an alert that the popcorn was ready. Grams carefully opened the hot bag of popcorn, poured it into a bowl and carried it to the living room with Sarah close behind, tea in hand. They took their seats and for the next hour and a half they watched the movie. By the end of it, they were both wiping tears from their eyes and smiling at the same time.

"Whoa, that's a good movie. It brought out every emotion," Grams said as she dabbed her eyes with a tissue she held in her hand throughout the movie.

"I agree." Sarah motioned toward her own face. "Look at me, I'm a blubbering mess." She pulled a tissue from the pocket of her robe and wiped her eyes.

"We have an early day tomorrow." Grams stood. "I'm turning in for the night." She hugged Sarah. "Thanks for the lovely evening."

"We should do this more often." Sarah walked her grandmother to her bedroom door.

Grams turned to face her. "I'll see you in the morning. Have a good night." She turned and shuffled the last few steps to her bedside.

"Goodnight, Grams, I love you."

"Goodnight, sweetheart, I love you too."

CHAPTER THREE

GRAMS' DOCTOR VISIT

The next morning Sarah found her grandmother sitting at the breakfast table. It was her favorite spot in the house. The table sat in the corner, surrounded by windows. The yellow floral curtains gave off a warm, peaceful vibe. A cool breeze carried with it the myriads of fragrances from trees and flowers beginning to bloom.

"Ahh, I love springtime." Sarah leaned into the breeze and breathed in the sweet aroma.

"It's a lovely time of year." Grams continued staring out the window. Sarah detected sadness in her voice.

"Grams, is something wrong?" Sarah's brow furrowed and she straightened.

"Everything's fine, honey." Grams forced a smile.

"You know, if there's something on your mind, you can confide in me, right?" Sarah rubbed her grandmother's shoulder as she sat in the chair next to her.

"I know, dear." Grams smiled sweetly. "I was just daydreaming about your grandfather. He was a pip." She giggled slightly.

"That he was." Sarah smiled.

"He loved you more than life itself." Grams turned her head

to hide a tear escaping her eye.

Sarah pretended not to notice. Her grandmother hated anyone to see her cry. Grams placed her hands on the table and fidgeted with a tissue she had pulled from her apron pocket.

"He loved us both." Sarah looked out the window. "He told me several times about how the two of you met. I loved the way he stared off in the distance, his eyes sparkled, and his face lit up." She placed her hand over her grandmother's. "The love he held for you was unprecedented."

Grams dried her eyes. "All right, that's enough reminiscing." She stood. "Let's get out of here and get this doctor's appointment over with. I have things to do and a contest to win," she said cheerfully. She grabbed her purse and headed out the door.

The drive to the doctor's office was quick and the wait was even shorter. Before long, the nurse opened the door and called them back. "Ms. McMillan, the doctor will see you now." She led them down the hall, stopping and motioning to a room. "If you'll step in here, I'll get your weight and vitals before showing you to the exam room."

Grams stepped in, but before getting on the scales, she handed Sarah her purse. "Here hold this." She then slipped off her shoes. "Don't say a word." She glared at Sarah. "I am not allowing those things to say I weigh an ounce more than I do."

"I thought I was the only one who did that." Sarah laughed.

"Actually, most all our female patients do that." The nurse chuckled as she led them to the exam room. "The doctor will be with you in a minute."

"Ms. McMillan, it's good seeing you." Dr. Brown stepped into the room, closing the door behind him. He took a seat on the stool and flipped through the medical files he held in his hands. He wasn't your typical doctor. He believed in doing things the ol' fashioned way. Sarah questioned him about it a few times, and his answer was always the same. "If it ain't broke, don't fix it." He finished reading and spun around on the stool to face Sarah and Grams.

"Well now, Ms. McMillan, have you been following my instructions since your last visit?" He slid his glasses to the end of his nose and looked at Grams over the top of them.

"I . . . uh. . . well, yes, I would say that I have." Grams held her purse on her lap and fidgeted with the strap.

"Grams! What is he referring to and why didn't you tell me?" Sarah gave her a sideways glance. "What instructions would that be?" She raised a quizzical brow before turning her attention back to the doctor.

"He advised me not to overexert myself." Grams stared at her folded hands. "I have followed the instructions fairly well."

"Fairly well isn't good enough." Sarah placed a loving hand on her grandmother's arm. "You almost passed out climbing the stairs."

"That's what I was afraid of." Dr. Brown closed the files and took Grams by the hand. "I told you, Florence, there may be a problem with your heart." He released Grams' hand and faced Sarah. "I made her an appointment with a heart specialist last month, but she refused to go." His eyes darted from Grams to Sarah and then settled on Grams. "I can't help you unless you're willing to help yourself."

"Set up another appointment and I'll see to it that she goes," Sarah said firmly. She gently rubbed her grandmother's shoulder. "Please go, if not for yourself at least do it for me," she said softly.

Grams nodded and stood. "Set up the appointment, Doc, and

make it soon because I have a contest to win this fall."

"Now, that's the Florence McMillan we all know and love." Dr. Brown jotted a few things in his notes. "I'll have my nurse call you with the appointment."

"You're not doing any bloodwork?" Sarah asked.

"Hush your mouth." Grams gave Sarah a stern look. "He didn't say anything about poking me with a needle, and you don't need to remind him." She pointed her finger at Sarah's face.

"Don't fret, there's no need for bloodwork today." Dr. Brown chuckled. But if you don't slow down and keep this appointment, you may end up in the hospital, and I don't think you'd want that. Would you?" He tilted his head, looking over the rim of his glasses.

"Is it that bad?" Sarah already knew the answer, but she was trying to convey the seriousness of the situation to her grandmother.

"If I had my way, I'd admit her for a few days for observation," Dr. Brown suggested.

"You'll do no such thing," Grams snapped. "I'm going home to my own bed." She headed toward the door. Dr. Brown stood.

"Does a hospital stay seem necessary?" Sarah placed a hand on her grandmother's shoulder.

"If you make sure she gets plenty of rest and doesn't overexert herself, then I think she would do better at home." He tilted his head and looked over the rim of his glasses yet again. Sarah noticed he had a habit of doing that. "No climbing stairs," he said sternly.

"Thank you. I'll make sure she follows your instructions." Sarah shook Dr. Brown's hand.

"If she has any more episodes take her to the ER

immediately."

"I will." Sarah nodded.

"Give these to the receptionist." Dr. Brown handed Grams some papers.

"Thank you, Doc." Grams took the papers and turned to leave.

"One more thing, Ms. McMillan," Dr. Brown said.

Grams turned to face him.

"If you would like, I'll stop by later to check on you." Dr. Brown smiled and patted her on the shoulder.

"There's no need to trouble yourself." Grams adjusted the weight of her purse from one arm to the other. "I appreciate the offer."

Sarah followed Grams out of the exam room, stopping at the front desk. She handed the receptionist the papers.

"All right, Ms. McMillan, the doctor wants to see you in a month." The receptionist stared at the computer. "Is morning or afternoon better for you?"

"Either is fine with me." Grams placed her purse on the desk in front of her.

"Here ya go." The receptionist handed her an appointment card. "We'll call you as soon as we set up an appointment with a cardiologist."

"I'll see you then." Grams placed the card inside her purse and turned to leave. There in the waiting room sat Mrs. Stevenson. "Oh, great, it's too early in the day to put up with ol' sourpuss," Grams whispered to Sarah.

"Imagine meeting you here, Florence." Mrs. Stevenson wore a huge toothy grin. "You're not sick, are you?"

Grams ignored her and headed for the door. Mrs. Stevenson grabbed Sarah by the elbow, stopping her. "Is she going to drop out of the contest?" Excitement rang in her voice.

"I don't have time for this Mrs. Sourpuss—err, I mean, Ms. Stevenson." Sarah's cheeks grew pink. Her grandmother burst into laughter. Sarah locked arms with her and quickly rushed her outside. Mrs. Stevenson turned to her husband. "What did she just call me?" Her husband shook his head and continued looking at a magazine.

"Oh, my goodness that's the funniest thing I've heard all day." Grams continued laughing. Before long, Sarah joined in and they were both holding their sides by the time they made it to the car.

"What do you say we grab a bite to eat and do some shopping?" Sarah asked as she started the car.

"That sounds wonderful. Tonight, we can order pizza and watch a movie," Grams said excitedly. She reminded Sarah of a little girl, giddy with excitement for her first sleepover. It was moments like this Sarah savored and would cherish long after her grandmother was gone.

The two of them spent the day shopping at the local boutiques. They later planned to have lunch at a little place called Serenity's Café, a quaint little restaurant on the outskirts of town. As they were leaving Jacqueline's Boutique, they met Jimmy coming out of the hardware store.

"Hello, Ms. McMillan," Jimmy said. "How are you ladies today?"

"Hello, Jimmy," Grams replied. "We're enjoying a lovely day of shopping."

"Are you having a nice visit?" Jimmy asked Sarah. She hoped he wouldn't strike up a conversation with her. She has no desire to speak with him.

"Yes, I am," she said flatly.

"So, Jimmy, when do you plan on getting started on the repairs to my house?" Grams interrupted.

"I'm hoping to get my crew out there tomorrow, if that's good for you." He smiled.

"That's wonderful." Grams glanced at Sarah. "We're looking forward to it. Right, dear?"

"Sure, I suppose." Sarah looked away.

"What brings you to town today?" Grams asked while giving Sarah a sideways glance.

"I came for supplies, and I couldn't help admiring the buildings here." Jimmy turned, facing the hardware store. "The architecture is incredible."

"Yes, yes, it is." Grams looked at the building. "Did you know it's one of the first and oldest stores in town?"

"No, I didn't know that." Jimmy took a few steps back to get a better look.

"It was built in eighteen eighty-five by the Johnson family and passed down from generation to generation. They kept the original design of the storefront as well as the inside." For the first time, Sarah realized the town was like stepping back in time, from the cobblestone streets to the old storefronts with mannequins in the windows wearing the latest fashion.

"I've never noticed how gorgeous this town truly is, until now." Sarah pulled her phone from her purse and snapped a few photos. She sent them to Stacy in a text message and slid her phone back into her purse.

"I suppose a person doesn't notice such things until you've been away for a while," Jimmy said. He looked around admiring the beauty of the surrounding area. He turned to face Sarah. "What are you doing this evening?" He shifted from one foot to the other.

Sarah, being caught off guard, glanced from Jimmy to her grandmother. "I . . . uh . . . ." She found herself drawn to Jimmy, and that frightened her more than anything. She no longer trusted men and she didn't want to let Jimmy get close enough to use her to scam her grandmother out of her house. She gave her grandmother a pleading look. When she didn't take the hint, Sarah said, "I'm sorry Jimmy, but I have plans with Grams tonight. Right, Grams?"

"Nonsense girl, go on, get." Grams shooed Sarah with the back of her hand. "You two go have a good time." She took a seat on a bench outside the little shop.

"I would love to see more of your town." Jimmy took Sarah by the hand, sending a bolt of electricity through her body. Stunned at what she felt, she jerked her hand away and turned her head in hopes he hadn't noticed. She turned toward her grandmother when she realized she was taking deeper breaths than usual and clutching her chest.

"Grams, are you all right?" Sarah knelt in front of her.

"I don't know about you, but I'm pooped." Grams smiled faintly.

Sarah stood. "Thanks for the invite, Jimmy, maybe another time." She smiled.

"I understand." He nodded and then gently rubbed Grams' shoulder. "I hope you feel better soon, Ms. McMillan." Jimmy's eyes shone with concern.

"Thank you, Jimmy." Grams patted his hand.

"I need to take her home so she can rest," Sarah stated.

"I should get back to work myself." Jimmy turned to leave.

"Jimmy!" Sarah shouted.

He turned to face her, hoping she'd changed her mind about spending the day with him. "Sorry, but would you mind waiting here with her?" She nodded toward her grandmother. "Just long enough for me to get my car." Her expression was hopeful.

"Oh, sorry, where are my manners. I'd love to keep Ms. McMillan company." His green eyes sparkled when he smiled.

Sarah felt an unfamiliar sensation course through her body. She looked away. *What is it about him that makes me feel this way?* She straightened her shoulders and ran her sweaty palms down the side of her jeans before speaking.

"Luckily, I parked just over there." She nodded across the street before hurrying off. A few minutes later she pulled the car in front of the store.

Grams was already on her feet waiting with Jimmy by her side. He opened the car door and helped her take a seat. "You two have a lovely evening." Jimmy closed the car door and waved goodbye before walking away.

"Let's go home." Grams placed her purse at her feet.

"Grams, I could've helped you to the car," Sarah scolded.

"Ah. posh." Grams waved her hand in the air like a cat swatting at a string. "When you get to be my age, you'll accept all the attention you can get from a handsome young gentleman." She pulled the seatbelt over her shoulder.

"Whatever you say, Grams."

"Someone needs to show him some kindness," she continued. "Since you're too stubborn and won't give him the time of day."

Sarah rolled her eyes. "Look, this has nothing to do with Jimmy. Dr. Brown said not to overexert yourself."

"I know you're only looking out for my best interests." She fidgeted with the seatbelt, trying to fasten it. "I appreciate that." The seat belt locked with a click. "But you worry too much."

"I know, Grams." Sarah looked straight ahead. "It's just that. . . ." She cocked her head toward her grandmother. "You're all I have left in this world." She swiped at a tear with the back of her hand.

"I'm not going anywhere." Grams took Sarah by the hand and gave it a gentle squeeze. "I'm too stubborn for that." She released Sarah's hand. "Besides, I have too much to do—not to mention a contest to win." She winked.

"Grams, you're one of a kind." Sarah shook her head, a slight smile spread across her lips.

"Don't you forget it." Grams chuckled.

Sarah pulled onto the street and headed home.

CHAPTER FOUR

REMINISCING

Sarah busied herself with laundry while Grams relaxed on the patio swing. She loved watching the hummingbirds flutter from one flower to the next collecting its sweet nectar before flying off. One little bird landed on the bird feeder next to the swing.

"Well, hello there, little fellow." Grams spoke softly so as not to frighten it away.

The hummingbird fluttered toward her and hovered in front of her face. "I see that I'm not the only one who loves the myriads of colors and fragrances coming from my flower garden." She smiled.

"Grams, who are you talking to?" Sarah asked as she stepped out the kitchen door, scaring the hummingbird in the process. It quickly flew away.

"Have you ever seen anything so beautiful?" Grams' eyes lit up as she watched the rest of the birds scatter, only to return a few moments later and zip in and out amongst the flowers.

"Just look at how trusting these little things are." Grams never took her eyes off the birds.

Sarah took a seat on the swing next to her and sat quietly. "They trust me to take care of them." Grams continued. "They have faith that the nectar I place for them is safe; they don't hesitate to take it." Grams glanced at Sarah and then at the birds still fluttering around the flowers. "If only I had half as much faith." Sadness swept over her face, causing her to look every bit her age. In Sarah's eyes, her grandmother was a beautiful lady. She held her looks well. Sarah hoped she looked as good at that age.

"I know you're scared," Sarah said softly. "I'm sure everything's going to be fine." She got no response from her grandmother. Sarah swiped at a tear before it escaped her own eye. "We'll pray about it." She smiled.

"That's exactly what we'll do, pray about it." Grams laid her head on Sarah's shoulder. "You know, no matter what happens —" Grams paused. "Either way, I'm in a win-win situation." She looked toward heaven and smiled.

"How so?" Sarah tilted her head, placing her cheek against the top of her grandmother's head.

"I've lived a good life," Grams said thoughtfully. "Should God choose to take me home, I'll be with your grandfather and the rest of our loved ones." She sat straight and looked Sarah in the eyes. "Should he decide to let me stay, I'll be here with you, my beautiful granddaughter." Tears welled in her eyes before spilling over and running down her cheeks. They hugged and cried together for several minutes.

"All right, that's enough of that." Grams pulled away and rubbed her eyes with the back of her hands.

"It never hurts to have a good cry occasionally." Sarah sniffed. "Isn't that what Grandpa used to say?" She dabbed her eyes with her fingertips.

"Yes, he did say that." Grams smiled while continuing to wipe the moisture off her cheeks with a tissue she pulled from her apron pocket.

"Well, I'm going to make this the best summer we've ever had." Sarah stood and paced back and forth.

"What about work?" Grams shifted in her seat.

"I'll get a job here."

"Sweetie, I don't want you putting your life on hold because of me." Grams shook her head.

"I'm not leaving you alone ever again." Sarah stopped pacing. "Besides, I've made up my mind and I'm here to stay.."

"Are you pulling my leg?" Grams stood.

"No, I'm serious." Sarah hugged her. "I wasn't going to say anything until later, but now's as good a time as any."

"What about your belongings in Florida?" Grams slowly lumbered to the kitchen door.

"Stacy has been wanting to come for a visit. I'll send her a list of the things I need and the rest she can keep or give to someone in need."

"It's wonderful having you home for good, as long as you're doing it for yourself and not because of me." Grams searched Sarah's face for some sign of regret about her decision.

"When I crossed over into West Virginia and saw those beautiful mountains, I knew I was home, and I knew this is where I want to be." She stared up at the huge maple trees with their branches stretching toward the bright blue sky and breathed in the fresh mountain air. "I belong here."

It was at that moment that Grams was certain that Sarah was telling her the truth. She remembered coming home from a vacation in Texas and having that same feeling upon seeing the lush green West Virginia mountains after passing through Charleston. She too realized she would never leave these mountains. Nicholas County was her home.

"It's in your blood." Grams looked toward the mountains standing high and proud. "The beauty of these ol' mountains is captivating, especially in autumn."

"That reminds me. This fall, we'll be sure to enter your pies in the Fall Festival baking contest." Sarah gave a little smirk.

"I know what that smirk is all about." Grams pointed a finger at Sarah. "We're going to show ol' sourpuss a thing or two." She could hardly contain her excitement.

"Ah, Grams, we're so bad." Sarah snickered.

"Yes, we are, but we're so good at it." Grams giggled.

"You look tired, and I have laundry to finish." Sarah stood, crossing her fingers behind her back. "Let me help you to your room. The rest will do you good."

"I am a little tired," Grams admitted.

Sarah saw her grandmother safely to her room and helped her into bed.

Sarah stood in the doorway. "If you need anything, pull the string next to the head of the bed." She pointed. "I have a bell attached to it that will ring in the basement if I'm doing laundry."

"Oh, my goodness." Grams glanced at the string. Sarah had tied a metal ring on the end to help her grandmother get a better grip on it. "All this fuss over one old lady." Grams shook her head.

Sarah knew her grandmother enjoyed the attention, and she was more than happy to give it to her.

CHAPTER FIVE

SECRET BENEATH THE STONE

Sarah descended the basement stairs and placed another load of laundry in the washing machine. She took the clothes out of the dryer and put them in the laundry basket. A loud noise startled her. She jumped, knocking over a large toolbox that belonged to her grandfather. It hit the wall, with a loud bang.

A raccoon scurried across the floor and then up the steps of the basement door which led outside.

"Whew, it's only a raccoon. I'm glad it found its way out," she whispered. "Hopefully, Jimmy will help fix the door," she said aloud as she picked up the old toolbox.

"What, my dear lady, could you possibly need help with?" came a male voice behind her.

Sarah, startled, turned to find Jimmy standing there with his hands in the front pockets of his jeans. His short chestnut brown hair was neatly combed to one side—except for one strand that had fallen over his forehead. Sarah found him even more attractive. The dark red button-up shirt brought out his emerald green eyes. Sarah once again found them captivating. It sent a shiver down her spine.

"What are you doing here?" Her voice cracked.

"I dropped off a few supplies." He glanced around the room. "Your grandmother said you were down here. Are you all right?" He stepped closer and was now standing in front of her.

"Oh, yes, I'm . . . ." Sarah stared at the floor. "A raccoon frightened me." Her eyes met his, and she quickly turned away. *Get a grip, Sarah. Remember, he's up to no good.*

"Excuse me, are you sure you're all right?" Jimmy placed a hand on her shoulder.

"Wh... what? I'm sorry, what were you saying?" Sarah's cheeks grew pink.

"I asked, which way did the raccoon go?"

"He went that way." She pointed.

Jimmy inspected the area but found nothing. He peered up the steps leading outside. A single ray of sunlight revealed a hole in the door and provided enough light to see that the space was empty, and the door needed replaced. He pulled a small notepad out of his shirt pocket and jotted something down.

"If you ask me," he said as he turned to face Sarah. "I believe you scared that coon more than he did you." He placed his notepad back in his pocket.

"Yeah, well, he caused me to make a huge mess." Sarah strolled over and picked up a few tools.

Jimmy helped set the toolbox upright.

Sarah realized that the heavy box of tools knocked a huge stone loose. It was part of the original foundation. Sarah tried pushing the stone back into place.

"It's too heavy." She continued trying to move it.

"Let me help you with that." Jimmy placed both hands around the stone, trying to wriggle it into place. "Something's blocking it." He pulled the stone free and rolled it aside. Sarah peeked into the opening.

"I found something," Sarah announced. She reached into the cavity and emerged with a steel strongbox. She placed it on the worktable and tried opening it to no avail.

"Allow me." Jimmy flipped the strongbox upside-down. On the bottom was a slot that held a huge key. After several attempts, he managed to dislodge it. He then worked on the lock until the strongbox finally clicked open. Inside, nestled within the steel casing, was a wooden box.

Sarah's excitement grew as she lifted the wooden box from its hiding spot. She gently placed it on the worktable next to the strong box.

"Wow! I wonder how long this has been down here, and what's inside?" She blew some of the dust off, revealing exquisite scenery carved into the box. It was beautifully detailed, with hand-carved flowers on each end. The top and sides revealed a meadow, trees, and a river with a fish leaping out of the water. Upon closer inspection, she saw a girl sitting under a tree, holding a book.

"The craftsmanship is gorgeous." Jimmy ran his fingers over the top of the box.

Sarah was in awe of such an amazing find. She ran her fingers over the rusty latch.

"I wonder what's inside," she whispered.

"I'm not sure, but we're about to find out." Jimmy studied the latch.

"I don't see a key; how can we open it without destroying the latch?" Sarah searched the strongbox but found nothing.

"Let me have a look." Jimmy picked up the wooden box and began running his fingers over it. He pressed one of the flowers on the end and a secret compartment dropped from the bottom. An old key fell out.

"Oh my gosh!" Sarah threw her arms around Jimmy. "You're amazing." She blushed and stepped back.

"Hmm, if you're that thrilled to find the key, I can't wait to see your reaction when we find out what's inside the box." Jimmy chuckled.

"Ha, ha, very funny." Sarah picked up the key and tried unlocking the old rusty latch.

"Wait!" Jimmy placed a hand over Sarah's.

"What's wrong?" she asked.

"How about the two of us going out to dinner to celebrate whatever treasures are inside?" He studied her face as she gently set the wooden box on the table.

"One, we have no idea if there's anything in there." She pulled her hand away. "And two, that's low, even for you." She smirked.

"What's that supposed to mean?" Anger flared in his eyes.

"Never mind, it's nothing." Sarah realized she knew nothing about him. "It's just . . . I haven't had the best luck with men."

Jimmy ignored her last comment. "Maybe it's best that I leave." He took a step back.

"Jimmy, wait." Sarah stepped towards him. "I'm sorry. She stared at the floor. Please stay. we found this box together and I'd like you to be here when it's opened." He nodded, relief washing over him. He wanted to see what the box contained, but more than that, he didn't want to leave on bad terms. He picked up the old steel box and examined its handiwork.

"We know it's very old. It's the smallest one I've seen." He ran his hand over it. "It has a nice patina. Its surface shows filing and pounding by hand." He lifted it up and further inspected the bottom. "There you are," he whispered. "It has a date in the corner. 1775." He placed the steel box on the table next to the wooden box.

Guilt began to eat at Sarah as she watched him. She felt horrible for jumping to conclusions. She wanted to make it up to him. "I would like you to have the honor of unlocking it." She motioned toward the wooden box.

"You sure you want to trust someone like me?" Jimmy turned to face her.

"I didn't mean it that way." Sarah felt her face and ears grow hot from embarrassment. She wished she hadn't said anything.

"Lighten up." Jimmy nudged her. "I'm joking." He gently took the wooden box from her hands along with the key. He placed the key in the rusty keyhole and wriggled it a few times until they heard the lock click.

"Oh my gosh! You did it." Sarah resisted the urge to hug him again.

"Let's see what you're hiding." Jimmy slightly raised the lid to the box.

"Wait!" Sarah shouted louder than she intended as she slapped her hand over Jimmy's, causing the lid to slam shut.

Jimmy stared at her like she'd lost her mind. "What's the matter?" He waited for her to answer.

"I owe you an apology." She wrung her hands and stared at the floor. "If you still want to, we'll celebrate whatever's inside."

"And, if there's nothing in there?" he questioned.

"Well then, I have a beautifully hand-crafted antique box." She smiled at him.

"Hmm, with your temper, I'll need to think about it," Jimmy teased.

"I said I was sorry." Sarah pretended to pout. "I'll show you my secret fishing spot," she said in a sing-song voice.

"Secret fishing spot, huh?" Jimmy playfully tapped a finger on his chin. "How could I possibly turn that down?" He chuckled.

"Yes!" Sarah did a fist pump in the air. "You may open the box now." She motioned.

"It's yours, so you should have the honor." Jimmy bowed playfully.

"Oh, good grief." Sarah stepped next to him. "If we keep going back and forth like this, we'll never find out what's in there." She shivered when his arm brushed against hers. She hoped he hadn't noticed. Unbeknownst to Sarah, Jimmy felt the same.

"What are you waiting for? Open it already." He nudged her.

Sarah slowly lifted the lid and they both peered inside.

"It looks like a diary." Jimmy blew the dust off the cover.

Sarah gently picked it up. She carefully opened the cover and silently began reading. "It's not a diary." She stared, her mouth agape. "It's a handwritten book." She placed it on the table.

Jimmy ran his fingers over the first page. "It says it was written in the year 1775." He stared at the book in awe. "It's a true story, based on the life of the McCullough family," Jimmy read aloud.

"It has to be one of our relatives." Sarah placed the book back in the wooden box. "Let's show it to Grams." She headed for the basement stairs leading to the kitchen. Jimmy followed.

They found Grams piddling around the kitchen, singing softly to herself.

"Grams, what are you doing out of bed?" Sarah scolded.

"I may be old, but I'm not an invalid," Grams shot back. "Tell her, Jimmy." She waved her hands in the air.

"I believe I'd better stay out if this." Jimmy glanced at Sarah.

"I'm concerned for you, Grams," Sarah reasoned.

"Don't worry, I'm fine. Now, what do you have there?" Grams nodded toward the box.

"I almost forgot, I . . . I mean we." She motioned at Jimmy. "We found this in the basement." Sarah set the box on the kitchen table. "It was hidden behind a huge stone that was part of the original foundation."

"How wonderful." Grams clasped her hands together. "Oh, my goodness. Let me see." She looked over the box. "It's beautiful," she gasped.

"Wait until you see what's inside," Jimmy said.

"Show me." Grams' eyes danced with glee.

Sarah opened the box, revealing the book inside. "It's a handwritten book."

"What kind of book do you suppose it is?" Grams reached for it.

"Careful, it's very old and delicate," Sarah warned. "It says it's based on the McCullough family."

"Does it say who wrote it?" Grams inquired.

"Yes, Anna Carlin. Have you heard of her?" Sarah looked at her grandmother.

"Why yes, yes, indeed." Grams' face lit up. "She's my great, great grandmother. What an incredible find."

"I know, exciting, isn't it?" Sarah placed the book on the counter. "We could read it together tonight if you like."

"I would love that." Grams ran her trembling old fingers over the cover. "I'm not so sure the pages can take much handling."

"She's right," Jimmy said. "The pages are incredibly old and delicate."

"I have an idea." Sarah pulled her phone from the back pocket of her jeans.

"What do you have in mind, dear?" Grams inquired.

"I'll take photos of each page and print them out," Sarah said as she took a picture. "This way the pages aren't disturbed any more than necessary."

"What a wonderful idea." Grams clasped her hands together.

"I'll help." Jimmy gently turned the page and waited for Sarah. She'd take a snapshot and send it to the printer. They continued until the entire book was printed.

"What do you say we celebrate?" Grams picked up a glass of sweet tea off the counter.

"Didn't we have a celebration date planned?" Jimmy reminded Sarah.

"A date, how lovely," Grams said.

"Yes, we did . . . uh, I mean do." Sarah nodded at Jimmy before turning to face Grams. "It's not a date." She glared at Jimmy as she brushed past him.

"Sorry," Jimmy stated. "I wasn't thinking. Would you like to come, Ms. McMillan?"

"Goodness, in all the excitement I forgot that I have company." Grams peeked around Jimmy toward the living room.

"Who's here?" Sarah's eyes followed Grams' gaze.

"Mrs. Stevenson," Grams whispered. "If she thinks I'll give up my secret recipe, she has another think coming."

"Would you like us to stay?" Sarah glanced at Jimmy and then back to Grams.

"No, I'll be just fine." Grams placed a hand on Jimmy and Sarah's backs. "You two go, have a nice time. If ol' sourpuss messes with me, I'll put pickle juice in her sweet tea." Grams snickered.

"Grams!" Sarah gasped. "I'd better stay."

"I'm kidding. I'll be on my best behavior." Grams grinned mischievously at Jimmy.

"We won't be long, I promise." Jimmy placed a hand over his mouth to hide a smile.

Sarah apprehensively followed Jimmy out the back door, stopping on the porch.

"I'm not so sure about this." She turned back toward the door.

"I'm sure she'll be fine." Jimmy took her by the arm. "I believe your Grams can handle this."

"I suppose, but I'm not so sure about Mrs. Stevenson." Sarah hesitantly left with Jimmy and climbed into the passenger seat of his pickup truck.

"Where would you like to go?" Jimmy fastened his seatbelt and waited.

"How about Serenity's Café and then to the river?" Sarah pulled the seatbelt over her and after several attempts, it finally clicked.

"Sounds like a plan." Jimmy started the truck and pulled out of the driveway.

For the next ten minutes they drove in silence. Jimmy knew Sarah had a lot on her mind, but the deafening silence got the best of him. The only time she spoke was to tell him which direction to go or when they were approaching their turn off. Sarah, on the other hand, knew her grandmother could take care of herself. The thing that weighed heavy on Sarah's mind was wondering about the story the book held within its tattered old pages—and the strange feeling that she'd met Jimmy somewhere before. She just couldn't put a finger on where.

"You're awfully quiet." Jimmy broke the awkward silence.

"Are you worried about your grandmother?"

"Not really. Well, maybe a little," Sarah corrected. "I was just thinking about the book. You know, wondering what life was like back then."

"It had to be a hard life for some, I suppose." Jimmy answered.

"I suppose." Sarah sat straight. "We're here." She nodded toward the café.

Jimmy pulled the truck into the parking lot. "This is a popular restaurant," he said as the truck rolled to a stop in front of the quaint little café.

"Yes, it is." Sarah looked around at all the parked cars.

"I can see why it's called Serenity's Café." Jimmy stared at the place in awe. The whole place was decorated in a myriad of colors, from the purple walls that faded to blue to the purple, pink, and blue flowers lining the front of the building. A fountain sat to the right, surrounded by foliage and bright orange, yellow and red flowers.

"It isn't your typical café, I presume." Jimmy stepped out of the truck and took in the beauty of the surroundings. "It's lovely. It should be called Paradise Café."

Sarah nodded in agreement. "This place was aimed at kids and the younger generation, but older folks love it as well." She strolled over and stood next to him.

"I can certainly see why." He could hardly take his eyes off the water fountain. It stood tall next to the building with beautiful colored lights built into the sides of the fountain base, reflecting the different colors in the water. Lights behind the waterfall caused the same effect. "This is gorgeous."

"Yes, it is. It's Grams' favorite."

"Well, I can certainly see why." Jimmy turned and headed for the front entrance, with Sarah at his side.

Once inside, they noticed the place was packed. Jimmy took in the beauty of the café from the greenery hanging from shelves overhead that lined the whole room to the polished woodwork on the counters and door frames, oblivious to several ladies who stared in his direction. Sarah noticed and stepped closer to Jimmy. One lady smirked and turned back to her meal. They stepped up to the counter and were approached by a waitress.

"Oh, my goodness, Sarah McMillan, is that you?" The waitress bounced excitedly. Her long blond ponytail swung back and forth. "I haven't seen you in, well, forever." She giggled. "How have you been? How's your grandma? Who is this handsome gentleman?"

"Calm down, Gina." Sarah laughed. "Grams is fine. I moved back to care for her, and this is Jimmy." Sarah motioned at Jimmy.

"Boyfriend?" Gina inquired.

"Oh, no. He's doing repairs on Grams' house." Sarah blushed.

"So, you're available?" Gina leaned over the counter toward Jimmy.

"Darlin', I know you don't want to spoil our surprise." Jimmy placed his arm around Sarah. "But I think we can trust Gina to keep our little secret."

Gina could hardly stand still. "You can trust me. My lips are sealed." She motioned as though locking her lips and throwing away the key.

"What?" Sarah looked at Jimmy quizzically.

"You know, sweetie." Jimmy winked. "The engagement." He placed one hand to his mouth, as though trying to keep a secret while purposefully speaking loud enough for Gina to hear.

"How exciting!" Gina squealed. She furrowed her brows. "Why would you want to keep that a secret?"

"Well, we. . . Uh. . . We . . . ." Sarah stuttered. "You explain it to her." Sarah cocked her head at Jimmy. "I'm going to the lady's room." She turned on her heel and headed in the direction of the restroom.

"Honey, what would you like me to order?" Jimmy called after her.

"Whatever you like." She waved a hand over her shoulder and hurried to the restroom. Once inside, she pulled her phone from the back pocket of her jeans and called Stacy.

"Hello," Stacy answered groggily.

"Hey, it's me, Sarah. Wait, were you sleeping? It's the middle of the day. Are you sick? Oh lord, I sound like Gina."

"Who's Gina?" Stacy interrupted.

"Never mind. I'm with Jimmy at Serenity's Café."

"You mean, like a date? Don't tell me he's married," Stacy grilled.

"No, it's nothing like that." Sarah replied. "We're celebrating. We found an old, handcrafted box containing a book written by my grandmother's great, great grandmother."

"How exciting." Stacy sounded more awake now. "Then what's the problem?" She yawned.

"Nothing," Sarah said softly. "He's funny, handsome, he has gorgeous eyes, and he's . . . perfect."

"Oh, no!" Stacy breathed in. "You have it bad."

"Wait, what are you talking about?" Sarah looked in the mirror and ran her fingers through her hair.

"You have a major crush. That's what."

"No, I don't," Sarah said defensively. "I mean, he's cute and all, and there's something familiar about him—"

"Admit it, you like him," Stacy interrupted. "Don't forget, he's trying to scam your grandmother out of her home," she added before Sarah could reply.

"What if I'm wrong?" Sarah reasoned.

"Then it's your job to find out," Stacy answered softly. "I'll call you later. I have a few errands I need to run."

"Talk to you then, bye." Sarah hung up and stood staring in the mirror. "What if I'm wrong?" she whispered to herself.

CHAPTER SIX

JIMMY'S RECURRING DREAM

Sarah stepped out of the ladies' room and made her way back to the dining area. As she rounded the corner, she saw Jimmy standing at the register with Gina, who continued talking non-stop. He rubbed his temples. His expression was one of relief upon seeing Sarah returning. He rushed to her side like a child trying to get away from a bully.

"Hey, babe." Jimmy slid his arm around Sarah's waist. "I placed our order to go." He held up a bag containing the food.

"It was nice seeing you again, Sarah. Enjoy your lunch." Gina turned and hurried away.

"You looked like you were in need of rescuing," Sarah said in a low voice.

"Thank you," he whispered. "Let's get out of here before your friend gets back." His eyes scanned the room.

"It serves you right for teasing me." Sarah laughed as she nudged him with her shoulder.

"Guilty as charged." Jimmy chuckled. "In my defense, you seemed to enjoy it."

"Maybe a little," she admitted. "Especially the look on Gina's face. It was priceless." She snickered.

"I hoped I didn't make you uncomfortable." Jimmy glanced at her.

"Not at all." She shook her head, refusing to make eye contact for fear he could read her mind. She didn't want him to know how much she loved the attention.

"Where are we going?" He turned on the radio and scanned the stations. It stopped on a song titled, "A Thousand Years." Sarah listened to the words, smiling to herself. The song reminded her of Jimmy. She had no idea why.

"Earth to Sarah." Jimmy broke the silence.

"Sorry, I forgot you don't know your way around this town quite yet." She stared straight ahead. "Turn right, just ahead."

Jimmy took the next right onto a single-lane dirt road. He wondered why a park was located on an old dirt road, but he said nothing. After driving for another ten minutes, his curiosity got the best of him. "Why would anyone place a park out here?" He took in his surroundings.

"The park isn't out here." Sarah leaned forward to get a better look at where they were. "Turn here." She pointed to the left. "I promised to show you my favorite fishing spot." She smiled.

They pulled down the little side road which led to a large open area. The truck rolled to a stop. Sarah quickly unbuckled her seatbelt and exited. She ran around the front and met Jimmy on the other side. They strolled to the edge of the clearing to the riverbank. They watched the river gently flowing. Fish could be seen swimming near the river's edge in the crystal-clear water. A largemouth bass leapt out of the water to catch its prey.

"This is a beautiful place." Jimmy stared at the water. "It's like listening to nature's lullaby." He looked up into the branches of the huge maple tree. "No wonder you love it here." He turned to find Sarah texting on her phone.

"Nature's lullaby, I love that." She continued typing. She glanced at Jimmy, then back at her phone. "That's a lovely way to say it. Sorry, but I just had to jot that down before I forget it." She turned and headed to the truck. He watched as she retrieved the food and pulled a blanket from the bag she had brought with her. She laid the blanket on the ground underneath the huge maple tree which stood tall and proud on the riverbank. Next she placed the food on the blanket and sat down.

"Come on, have a seat." She patted the spot next to her. "Let's eat."

Jimmy's heart raced when she looked up at him. He took in every detail about her. From the sparkle in her hazel eyes when she smiled to the way her red hair framed her face, complimenting her tanned skin. *Why does she look so familiar?* He made his way over and took a seat on the blanket. "I thought redheads burn easily." He picked a blade of grass, placed it between his thumbs and blew on it, making it whistle.

She tossed a stone in the water. "It's a good thing I'm not a redhead." She winked.

"What is your true color?" He blew on the blade of grass again.

"Dark blonde." She peeked inside the bags. "I wanted to try something different."

"It looks good on you, but I would love to see your natural color sometime." He picked up a twig and began drawing lines in the sand.

"You will, as soon as this color starts to fade." She sniffed one of the containers.

He watched in silence as she removed the remaining

containers of food, along with two plates and utensils.

"You thought of everything, didn't you?" she asked as she opened the container. "Yes! Fried chicken. Serenity's fried chicken is the best. Even better than Grams' . . . Shh." She placed a finger on her lips. "Don't tell her I said that."

"It's that good, huh?" Jimmy leaned his back against the tree. As he quietly watched her, an overwhelming feeling washed over him. No matter how hard he tried, he couldn't shake the feeling he'd been here before.

He loved the way she excitedly opened each food container to find what surprises they held. She reminded him of a kid on Christmas morning.

"I made a plate for you. I hope you don't mind." She held a plate of food in front of him. She realized he was deep in thought and hadn't heard a word she said. She set the plate next to him, picked up a roll, then broke off a piece and threw it at him, striking him between the eyes. He jumped. Looking down, he found the culprit laying on his lap. He directed his gaze toward Sarah. She sat with her knees drawn to her chest staring up at the tree branches, pretending to be innocent.

"Did you just throw bread at me?" He sat straight, holding up the evidence.

Sarah averted her gaze and began whistling a tune. Jimmy chucked the piece of bread at her. It bounced off the tip of her nose. She gasped and grabbed a drumstick from one of the plates she had prepared. She held it above her head.

"Lucky for you, I love this chicken." She grinned, leaned over, and pressed the drumstick to his lips. He playfully took a bite. His eyes grew wide.

"Mmm, . . You're right, it's delicious, although I'm more of a breast man myself." His eyes moved downward, and he realized he could see down the top of her shirt. "Ahem." He cleared his throat and looked away.

Sarah quickly sat up, pulling her shirt up higher than intended. "I'm sorry about that." Her cheeks grew pink. "We should eat while the food's still warm." She picked up the plate she prepared and handed it to him. They ate in silence, listening to the gentle flow of the river.

Finished with their meal, they lingered, absorbing the sounds of nature. It was as though the world put on a show just for them. Birdsong filled the air, punctuated by the distant bark of a dog. A chipmunk scampered up a nearby tree, and gold trout shimmered in the crystal-clear river as they swam.

"This looks like a lovely place for a swim." Jimmy never took his eyes off the water.

"Yes, it is. When I was a little girl, I used to come here with my grandparents. We'd have a picnic, go for a swim, or camp during summer."

"That sounds like a nice memory." Jimmy picked up a pebble and threw it into the water. Sarah pulled her knees to her chest, wrapping her arms around them. "Sometimes my grandfather and I spent the day here, fishing." She sighed. "I miss those days."

"I'm sorry about your grandfather." Jimmy set his empty plate beside him.

"Thank you, but now it's just me and Grams. She's all I have left." She watched a bird land on the tree branch above her. It cocked its head from side to side as though waiting for her to finish her story. "Sometimes, I come here to be alone and write." She smiled faintly.

"I didn't know you're a writer." Jimmy shot her a surprised look. "Have you published anything?"

"Actually, I used to write for our local paper. I also have four novels published."

"Wow! I'm impressed." Jimmy stared at her as though he was seeing her for the first time. "You never cease to amaze me." He shook his head.

"It's no big deal." She waved her hand in the air. "I love writing, and this is my favorite place. That's why I take a stroll here a few times a week during summer and fall."

"Wait, are you sure this is the same spot?" Jimmy motioned all around him. "It's a long way for a stroll."

"Actually, my house is about three quarters of a mile through the woods." She pointed at a wooded area across the road.

"Are you serious?" Jimmy stood, truly baffled, as he stared in the direction she pointed.

"We drove the long way around." She stood next to him.

"I suppose so." Jimmy ran his fingers through his hair.

"Next time, we'll walk." She watched him pick up a flat stone and skip it across the water. "Well, what do you think?" she asked when the stone stopped and then sank to the bottom of the river.

"Huh?" Jimmy turned to face her. "Oh. . . sure, I'd love to." He slid his fingers into the front pocket of his blue jeans. "I can't shake the feeling that I've been here before." He shifted from one foot to the other.

"Do you mean like déjà vu?"

"I don't know, maybe." He took her by the hands. "Can I trust you with something? I mean, without you thinking I'm crazy?"

"Yes, of course you can." She smiled warmly.

He released her hands, and then he began pacing back and forth. He stopped and stared toward the wooded area leading to Sarah's home. He turned to face her once again, contemplating whether he should say anything.

"You don't have to tell me if it makes you uncomfortable," Sarah said soothingly.

"No, I want to tell you." He bent to gather the paper plates and napkins, and Sarah joined him. Together, they quickly finished cleaning up the picnic area. Sarah gave the blanket a brisk shake before folding it and stuffing it into her bag.

"Want to sit in the truck?" he asked, tossing a final rock across the river. "It's cooler and more comfortable."

"Sure, we can talk on the way home." She watched the rock skip across the water.

After they were satisfied the area was clean, they headed for the truck. Once they were settled, he paused, took a deep breath, and slowly exhaled.

"Here goes nothing," he whispered. "I've had a recurring dream since I was fours-years-old." He glanced at her. He had her full attention. "I dreamed I lived in a cabin with my wife and children during the Revolutionary War." He shifted in his seat. "I was woken in the middle of the night and rushed off to fight. I barely had time to kiss my wife and children goodbye." He gazed up at the tree. "The last thing I remember is getting shot and lying on my back in an orchard beneath an apple tree." He turned to her. "I believe I died there, staring into the branches of that old tree," he said sadly.

"What happened? I mean, is that it, or is there more to the dream?" she asked, shaking her head slightly.

"There was someone with me, a friend, perhaps." He bowed his head. "I asked him to relay a message to my wife."

"What was the message?" Sarah whispered.

Jimmy raised his head, eyes locked with hers. "I vowed to come back to her, if not in this life, then in the next." He averted his gaze and stared blankly out the window.

"When did you last have this dream?" Sarah placed her hands on her lap.

"Last night, only this time—" He paused. "This time I saw my wife's face." He gazed into Sarah's eyes. "It was you."

"Me?" Sarah placed a hand on her chest. "I don't understand. What's that supposed to mean?"

"I can't comprehend it myself." Jimmy pulled his seatbelt around him and fastened it.

"Are you saying that you believe in reincarnation?" Sarah fastened her seatbelt and crossed her arms over her chest. "Because if you are, I don't believe in that stuff."

"No, I don't believe in it either. Or at least I didn't until I met you." He hoped she didn't think he was making it up to get her attention, but her actions told him otherwise.

"I can't believe this," she whispered. "I must admit, I thought I'd heard it all, but you take the cake." She spoke through gritted teeth.

"I'm telling you the truth." He started the truck and placed both hands on the steering wheel. "Everything feels familiar to me, including this spot, here, by the river." He turned his head toward the river, then looked back at Sarah. "Whether you believe me or not, it's up to you," he said softly. He started the truck and pulled onto the dirt road.

Sarah didn't tell him she had the same feeling of familiarity about him. It was as though she'd known him her whole life. *Stacy's right,* she thought. *If he is a con-artist, he's a darn good one.* She refused to look at him. "Let's just focus on the lovely day we had." She smiled faintly.

"I agree, but I will say this. If God wants to recycle souls, that's his business." He shrugged. Sarah had never heard it put quite that way. She stared out the window, wishing he'd never said anything.

"I'll take you home to check on your neighbor."

"My neighbor? Don't you mean my grandmother?" Sarah corrected.

"No, I mean your neighbor. After all, your grandmother did threaten to pour pickle juice in her tea." Jimmy let out a loud chuckle.

"You're right. A few days ago, she threw a glass of water on her." Sarah chortled.

They were still laughing when they pulled into the driveway. Jimmy and Sarah exited the truck and rushed inside the house, relieved to find Grams and Mrs. Stevenson sitting at the kitchen table having a nice chat. Sarah exhaled the breath she hadn't realized she'd held until that moment.

"Whew, Mrs. Stevenson, you're okay. I mean, you're fine," Sarah blurted without thinking.

"Excuse me!" Mrs. Stevenson placed a hand to her chest and glanced from Sarah to Grams.

"I . . . Uh. . . I meant you look great," Sarah stuttered. She gave Jimmy a pleading look, to which he caught on quickly.

"She's right, my dear lady." He took Mrs. Stevenson by the hand. "You look stunning."

"Well, I did have my hair done today." Mrs. Stevenson proudly brushed a hand over her hair.

Grams rolled her eyes as she stood and placed the dishes in the sink.

"You look lovely as well, Ms. McMillan." Jimmy playfully bowed.

"Ah, posh." Grams threw a dish towel at him. "Save it for the young naïve gals." She turned back to the sink to hide a smile that slowly spread across her face.

Sarah could tell her grandmother loved the attention. Jimmy had a way with the ladies, and he knew it. That's one of the things she liked most about him. She also enjoyed seeing her grandmother blush, even though she thought she hid it well.

"I need to check on my crew." Jimmy turned to leave. "It was nice meeting you, Mrs. Stevenson." He stepped past her.

"I'll walk you out." Mrs. Stevenson leapt from her chair and locked arms with Jimmy before he had a chance to protest. She grabbed something off the counter and slipped it into her pocket.

"I enjoyed our picnic." Jimmy glanced over his shoulder at Sarah as Mrs. Stevenson rushed him out the door.

Sarah couldn't help laughing at such a comical site. Grams, on the other hand, wasn't amused. She vigorously scrubbed the sink.

"Grams, you're going to scrub a hole through the sink." Sarah placed her hand over her grandmother's. "What has you so upset?"

"The nerve of that woman." Grams gripped the edge of the sink so tightly her knuckles turned white.

"Mrs. Stevenson? What has she done now?" Sarah placed an arm around her grandmother to try to calm her.

"She's a married woman, acting like a floozie," she grumbled. "You should have been the one to walk your date out the door." She spun around, pressing her back against the sink.

"Grams, it wasn't a date. We're just friends." Sarah said softly.

Her grandmother placed a hand to her head while holding the back of the chair with the other.

"Grams! Are you all right?" Sarah helped her to the chair and stooped down in front of her.

"I'm fine." She sucked in a breath and slowly exhaled. "I spun around so fast; I made myself a little dizzy.

"Let me help you to bed." Sarah stood, waiting for her grandmother to feel confident enough to stand.

"All right, I am a little worn out from my visit and from baking today. Grams' voice sounded weak.

Sarah knit her brow, wondering if she heard her grandmother right. She hoped she didn't let Mrs. Stevenson sweet talk her into giving up her secret recipe. Sarah decided it was best not to inquire about it until her grandmother was feeling better. She helped her to bed and tucked her in. She checked the time and was surprised to find it was only seven o'clock. They still had a couple of hours before dark. *Grams never goes to bed before nine.*

Sarah called the doctor's home phone. He answered on the first ring.

"Hello."

"Hello, Dr. Brown. This is Sarah, Florence McMillan's granddaughter."

"Hello, Sarah. What can I do for you?"

"I'm sorry to bother you. It's Grams." Sarah choked back tears. "Would you mind coming over?" She paused. "I. . . I'm worried about her."

"I'll be right over. Just keep her calm." Dr. Brown hung up the phone, grabbed his medical bag, and left.

Sarah nervously paced the floor, awaiting the doctor's arrival. She peeked in on her grandmother and found her clutching a bible to her chest, praying. Tears pooled in Sarah's eyes. She quietly pulled the door shut to give her grandmother some privacy. A knock at the front door sent her running to answer it. She was surprised to find Jimmy standing there.

"I thought you were the doctor." She opened the screen door wide.

"Doctor! Is it your grandmother?" Jimmy stepped in.

"Yes." She nodded. "After you left, she had a dizzy spell or something. I'm so afraid for her." She placed her hands over her face and sobbed.

Before Jimmy could respond, there was another knock at the door. They turned to find Dr. Brown standing there with his medical bag in hand. He opened the screen door and let himself in.

"Thanks for coming. She's lying down." Sarah wrung her hands. "She had a dizzy spell."

"Stay calm and take me to her." Dr. Brown shifted hands with his medical bag and, with his free hand, he ran his fingers through his thinning gray hair. Sarah turned and led the way through the living room to the short hallway leading to her grandmother's bedroom. "She has no idea that I called you," Sarah whispered before tapping gently on the door.

"Come in," Grams said. Her voice sounds weaker than before. She tried sitting up, but she realized Sarah wasn't alone.

"David. Er. . Dr. Brown, what on Earth are you doing here?" Grams asked although she knew the answer.

"Just lay still, Florence, while I take a listen to your heart." She laid back and waited patiently. Dr. Brown sat on the bed beside her. He pulled a blood pressure cuff and a stethoscope from his bag and placed it to her chest "Uh huh," he said as he listened. "Uh hem." He drew his eyes down as he glared at Grams, who then flashed him a look of warning. Dr. Brown shook his head. "Florence, are you going to tell her, or should I?"

"You'll do no such thing." Grams crossed her arms over her

chest.

"Florence." Dr. Brown raised his eyebrows and cocked his head.

"Fine. I have an appointment with the cardiologist on Thursday." Grams snapped.

Dr. Brown stood and stared at her over the rim of his glasses. "Have it your way Florence."

"Is she okay? What's wrong with her?" Sarah placed her fingers under her eyes and wiped the tears that threatened to spill down her cheeks.

"It appears that your grandmother has had a little too much to drink." He looked sternly at Grams and shook his head.

"What! She's drunk?" Sarah's voice unintentionally came out as a high-pitched squeal. "She doesn't drink, so how can she be drunk?" she demanded.

"Uh . . . Sarah," Jimmy started.

"What?" She spun around to face him.

Jimmy covered his mouth to stifle a laugh. "Ahem." He cleared his throat. "Mrs. Stevenson was about three sheets to the wind herself."

"Grams, were you and Mrs. Stevenson drinking?" Sarah could hardly grasp the idea.

"The old battle axe spiked my tea," Grams said defensively.

"Why would you let her get away with it?" Sarah sat on the bed next to her. "You had to have noticed alcohol in your tea."

"Oh, I noticed, and I knew what she was up to." She crossed her arms. "That old biddy was trying to get my secret recipe."

"Oh! She's got some nerve." Sarah patted her grandmother's leg. "What did you do?"

"I gave it to her," Grams said smugly.

"Tell me you're joking." Sarah gasped.

"I told her my secret ingredient was salt; it heightens the flavor of the fruit." Grams stared at the ceiling.

"That's true." Sarah took Grams by the hand.

"Yes, it is, but only a pinch of salt, not a whole tablespoon that I added to the recipe that she took." Grams grinned mischievously.

"She stole your recipe!" Sarah stood.

"Not exactly," Grams said nonchalantly. "I pre-mixed my ingredients in a couple of baggies, one of which I let her taste." Grams giggled. "The other I added extra salt to, a lot of salt." A huge grin spread across her face.

"It serves her right for being so conniving." Sarah crossed her arms.

"Yes, it does," Grams agreed. "One of two things will happen. She'll either taste the ingredients and know she was duped, or she'll use it, unchecked, to make a pie for the contest." Grams and Sarah burst into laughter.

Dr. Brown shook his head and turned to leave. "Get some rest, Florence, and I'll check on you in the morning." He patted Jimmy on the back as he left the room. "Looks like you have your work cut out for you son."

"Thank you for coming, Doctor." Sarah walked him to the front door and Jimmy followed.

"Make sure she keeps her appointment with the cardiologist." He switched hands with his medical bag. "She's still the same ornery gal I dated in high school." He smiled and shook his head.

"Wait, you must be mistaken." Sarah held up a hand in front of her. "You couldn't possibly have gone to school with my grandmother, let alone dated her."

"No, there's no mistake. We dated for one summer when

we were sixteen." Dr. Brown looked Sarah in the eyes. "I can't believe she never told you about it."

Sarah stood in stunned silence. "I don't understand. She's ninety-two years old."

"Ninety-two! What in the world?" Dr. Brown studied Sarah's face. "I have no idea what's going on, but your grandmother is seventy-two, not ninety- two."

There was an almost imperceptible pause as Sarah tried to digest the information. "I'm sorry, Doc. I'm just shocked and confused. I mean . . . ."

Dr. Brown gave a half-hearted smile as he looked at Sarah sympathetically. "It seems you and your grandmother need to talk." He stepped onto the front porch and paused. "I'd talk to her before she sobers up. The truth has a way of coming out when you're inebriated."

"Yes, Doc. We will have a talk." She closed the door and turned to face Jimmy. "Sorry you had to witness that." She smiled faintly.

"I find the whole situation hilarious." Jimmy took her by the hand. "Your grandmother is a force to be reckoned with." He placed his hand over his mouth to stifle a laugh and cleared his throat.

"Yes, she is." Sarah glanced toward the hallway leading to her grandmother's bedroom. "I can't believe she's twenty years younger than I was led to believe."

"Look at the bright side," Jimmy said.

"And what would that be?" Sarah crossed her arms over her chest.

"You have another twenty years with your grandmother before she turns ninety-two."

"That's one way of looking at it." Sarah tapped a finger on her chin. "So, why are you here? Did you forget something?"

"Mrs. Stevenson whisked me away so quickly, I didn't have a chance to say goodnight. Plus, I wanted to check on your grandmother." Jimmy gazed into her eyes. For a moment, Sarah thought he was going to kiss her. She was a little disappointed when he turned to leave. "I'll see you both in the morning, provided your grandmother feels up to having my crew working on her house. You know, loud noise and a hangover isn't a good combination."

"I'm sure it'll be fine. Sarah reassured him.

"Tell her goodnight for me." He opened the door and left.

Sarah pressed her back against the door and placed her fingers to her lips. She wasn't sure how she would have reacted had he kissed her, let alone what he was thinking. Questions whirled through her mind. She shook the thoughts from her head. She has more important things to think about. Her grandmother was her main concern.

She tiptoed across the living room and down the hallway to her grandmother's room. She opened the door slightly, just enough to peek in to see if her grandmother was sleeping. She wasn't and motioned to Sarah.

"I'm awake, come in." She patted the bed next to her.

Sarah stepped in and took a seat next to her. "How are you feeling?"

"A lot better, thanks." She placed her hand on Sarah's and gave it a little squeeze.

They chatted amiably about sundry things. Sarah couldn't stand it any longer. She stood. "Grams, how old are you?" she asked bluntly.

"I'm seventy-two. Why? Who wants to know?" She ran her hand over the soft blanket.

“Why did you allow me to believe you were ninety- two?” Sarah crossed her arms.

“Ninety-two!” Grams sat straight up in bed. “Do I look that old to you? Never mind, don’t you dare answer that.” She seemed to sober up quickly.

At a loss for words, Sarah stared at her in silence. “I’m sorry, I don’t know how I could have made such an awful assumption.” She sucked in a huge gulp of air and slowly exhaled. “I’m delighted you’re much younger than I thought.” She hugged her.

“Well, that makes two of us.” Grams looked around the room.

“What are you looking for?”

“A camera. For a second there, I thought I was being pranked.”

“That’s funny, Grams, but I’m not pranking you. I do hope you live to be ninety-two. No, she corrected, make that, one hundred and two.”

“You and me both.” Grams laughed.

“Would you like me to read to you from the book we found?”

“That would be wonderful,” Grams said cheerfully.

“I’ll be right back. I need to get it out of the printer.” Sarah left the room and came back with the printed copy in hand. She sat on the bed next to Grams, who anxiously awaited, and she began to read.

CHAPTER SEVEN

THE OLD BOOK

The year was seventeen sixty. King George II of England died and was succeeded by his grandson, George III. Talk of an impending war circulated through town. The men gathered in front of the tavern, their weekly meeting place to discuss the latest news and events.

Eleven-year-old Anna had no interest in politics, nor did she care to hear of war coming to her home in Virginia. She was the youngest in her family of six—a rambunctious girl who preferred fishing and hunting rather than learning to cook and sew like her sister Virginia.

Anna would rather spend her days outside gathering eggs, feeding the chickens, slopping the hogs (as her father called it), and tending the horses and cattle. She enjoyed it. It made her feel as though these animals depended on her for survival, and she loved that. Unbeknownst to Anna, her brothers James and Adam stopped Pa on the back porch and complained to him.

Thirteen-year-old James confronted his father. “Pa, you need to do something about Anna,” he insisted, referring to his eleven-year-old sister.

Their father sighed, placing a hand on his hip and raking the other through his hair. "What's she done now?" he asked, his gaze fixed on the floor.

After glancing around, making sure Anna was out of earshot, twelve-year-old Adam piped up, “She’s always getting in the way.”

“She’s slowing us down, making it harder to complete our chores on time,” James added.

“Very well, I’ll speak with her.” Pa turned on his heel and headed toward the house in search of Anna. Little did he know, she had gotten up early, fed the chickens, gathered the eggs, and placed the basket on the kitchen table before rushing off to the barn. She wanted to get there before her brothers. She made up her mind she was going to show them she could do their chores better than the two of them put together.

This morning, she decided that she was going to try to milk the cow. How hard could it be? She watched her brothers and father do it a thousand times. She set the stool next to the cow, grabbed the bucket off the hook, and placed it under the cows’ udders. “All right, Miss Bessy, just hold still while I milk you.” She gently squeezed one of the teats. Nothing happened. She bit her bottom lip in frustration.

“Anna! What do you think you’re doing?” James shouted, scaring the cow, who kicked the empty bucket, sending it flying. Anna jumped and fell backwards into the hay.

“Now look what you did!” She stood, brushing straw from her hair with her fingers.

“You’re doing it wrong.” James snatched up the bucket and placed it under the cow, took a seat, and easily began milking Miss Bessy.

Anna watched carefully and soon realized what she was doing wrong, although she’d never admit she had erred. “I could have done it, if you hadn’t scared the daylights out of us.”

She continued watching her brother's skilled hands at work. Miss Bessy flipped her tail, smacking Anna across the face. She stumbled sideways into James, practically knocking over the half full bucket of milk as well as James, who luckily managed to brace himself and held onto the bucket.

"Anna! Move out of the way." He stood, bucket in hand. "Here, take this to Mother." He handed her the bucket of milk. She took it, turned around, and bumped into Adam.

"Anna, get out of here." Adam rolled his eyes.

"I'm only trying to help." She choked back tears. The last thing she wanted was for her brothers to see her cry. To her it was a sign of weakness, and she refused to give them the satisfaction.

"Go help Mother and Virginia in the kitchen." James picked up a rake and began cleaning one of the horses' stalls. "I'm sure they've started breakfast by now." James kept his back to her as he worked.

"That's right," Adam agreed. "Your place is in the kitchen with the womenfolk, doing sissy work." He leaned toward her, grinning sarcastically.

Anna flew into a rage. "You better take that back, Adam McCullough, or else." She placed both hands around the bucket handle and glared at him.

"Or else, what?" Adam challenged. "Are you going to hit me with your broom?" Adam glanced at James, and they burst into laughter.

"You're both full of it!" Anna shouted.

She turned to leave, but stopped when Adam shouted back at her, "Full of what? Wisdom or truth?" He snickered. "Wisdom enough to know a woman's place or for speaking the truth about it?" Adam turned and began shoveling horse manure into a pile.

Anna gently set the bucket of milk on the ground and picked up an old bucket she found sitting next to the barn door.

"I'll show you what." She scooped up a bucket full of manure and dumped it on Adam's head. "That's what!" She yelled and stormed out, taking the bucket of milk with her.

"You better run!" Adam screeched. He sprinted after her, tripped over the old bucket and fell face first into a pile of fresh cow manure. He sat up, spitting and gagging. He wiped his face with his shirttail.

"She's right." James chuckled. "Not only are you full of it, but you smell like it too." He doubled over laughing hysterically.

"Oh, shut up! Adam leaned forward, shaking the manure from his hair. "I'm going to the creek to clean up." He stomped across the barn floor.

"You should take a bar of Ma's lye soap with you," James teased. "You better make that two, because you stink." He chuckled.

"What's going on here?" Pa asked as he met Adam on his way out of the barn.

"Ask Anna!" Adam spoke through gritted teeth as he stormed out.

Pa shook his head and looked at James.

"You don't want to know." James tried to compose himself.

"You're right, I don't." Pa looked around the barn. "Finish up here and then come to breakfast" He turned to leave, pausing at the door. "Never mind, just take your brother a change of clothes." He stifled a laugh.

"Yes, sir." James saluted playfully and followed his father to the house.

Anna stood at the kitchen sink grumbling about her brothers

to her mother and sister. She deliberately left out the incident in the barn. She knew her mother would scold her for doing such a thing. *It's not lady like.* She could hear her mother's words playing in her mind.

"Outside chores are for the men." Her mother looked at her sternly. "You need to be—"

"Ma, please don't say it." Anna covered her ears. "I've heard enough from Adam and James." She looked up to see James and her father standing in the kitchen doorway. James began snickering.

"James, fetch your brother's clothes." Pa cast him a sideways glance. "Then both of you come to breakfast."

"What's going on, and why would Adam need clean clothes?" Ma asked, eyeing Anna suspiciously.

"I'll bet Anna knows," Virginia said as she continued setting the food on the table. "Don't you?" She smiled mischievously.

"Oh, I know a lot of things, Virginia. Hmmm . . . should I start with what I know about you?" Anna placed her hand on her hip and glared at her sister.

Virginia fidgeted nervously. She didn't like the way Anna said her name. Long and stretched out. Nor the way she looked at her when she said it. She usually called her by her nickname, Ginny. She was unsure of what Anna was referring to, and chose not to find out, at least not in front of everyone. She felt relieved when Ma changed the subject.

"Anna, what did you do now?" Her mother stared at her from across the table.

"Sorry Ma, but they were making fun of me. Adam said I belonged in the kitchen doing sissy stuff," Anna said defensively. "So, I dumped a bucket of horse biscuits over his head."

"You mean horse manure." Ma corrected. "What would possess you to do such a thing?" Ma crossed her arms and tapped her foot. She often did that when she was upset and waiting for an answer.

"He was covered in more than horse manure." James chuckled as he strolled back into the kitchen, Adam's clothes draped over his shoulder. "After you left—" He looked at Anna. "Adam tripped over the old bucket and fell face first into a pile of cow manure."

Everyone burst into laughter. Ma placed a hand over her mouth and giggled.

"I'm glad y'all find it amusing." Adam shouted through the open kitchen window.

"Now, now, son." Ma peeked out the window. "We weren't laughing at you, not really."

"Yes, we were." Anna smirked. She decided to take her seat at the table when Ma shot her a dirty look.

James stepped next to Ma and playfully covered his nose as he handed Adam his clothes through the open window. Adam snatched them from James' hand. He grumbled to himself as he headed to the barn to change.

"Just leave the dirty clothes next to the outhouse," Mother called after him. "I'll wash them after breakfast."

Adam waved a hand over his shoulder, acknowledging that he heard her.

"All right." Pa rubbed his hands together. "Let's have breakfast."

"Yes, let's eat." James patted his stomach. "I'm famished."

They took their seats at the table and began filling their plates. Adam strolled into the dining room and quickly took his seat. He refused to look at anyone, especially Anna. He knew if he did, it would turn into a huge quarrel, so he thought it was best to finish breakfast and get his chores over with.

"After breakfast, I'm riding into town. Would you like to come?" Pa glanced at Ma between bites of scrambled eggs.

Ma ran her fingers over her hair, making sure to tuck any loose hair under the bun, which was also coming loose. Pa called it a bird's nest. Ma hated that. "Well, I suppose I could." She smiled. "I'll go change." She ran her hand over her apron.

"May I go too, Pa?" Adam looked hopeful.

"I don't see why not." Pa placed the glass on his lips and chugged the remaining milk. "How about we all go to town today?" He set the glass down next to his empty plate before pushing himself away from the table.

"That would be wonderful." Virginia clapped her hands and giggled.

"Pa, would it be all right if I rode my horse into town?" Adam looked from Ma then back at Pa, a pleading look in his eyes.

"He wants to ride past Elizabeth's house. He's smitten with her, ya know." Anna smirked.

Adam's eyes shot daggers at Anna, but he said nothing. He was relieved that Ma hadn't heard Anna's snide remark.

Pa stood and kissed Ma on the forehead. "Ask your Ma." He placed his hat on his head and strolled out the back door.

"Can I Ma? Please."

"Does this have anything to do with being upset with your sister?" Ma's eyes darted from Adam to Anna, who sat playing with her food, oblivious to the conversation.

Adam glanced at Anna and then back at his mother. "No, I'm over it," he lied. *I'll get her back one way or another.* He rubbed the back of his neck, refusing to look his mother in the eyes for fear she could read his mind.

"Very well then." Ma stood and began clearing the dishes. "James can ride his horse and go with you." She smiled slightly as she put the scraps in a bucket to feed the hogs later that evening.

James shoved a huge spoonful of food in his mouth and nodded in agreement before finishing off his second serving of scrambled eggs and biscuits. He stood, grabbed a biscuit, and placed it in his pocket. "Let's get the horses." James motioned for Adam to follow him, to which he gladly complied.

"Anna, eat your breakfast and then help Virginia with the dishes." Ma looked at her sternly and placed the bucket of scraps on the countertop. She decided it was best to feed it to the hogs before leaving for town, otherwise it would attract flies.

Anna emptied her plate into the bucket. She contemplated sneaking out but figured it best not to press her luck.

"I'll wash while you rinse." Virginia took the water off the heating stove and poured it into the dishpan. Ma always kept water heating in the woodstove reservoir for dishes or baths. In summer, everyone bathed in the creek. Pa dug a huge hole in the creek bed. It made a perfect size pool to swim and bathe in. Everyone referred to it as "The Run," due to water continually running into the creek from somewhere up in the mountains.

They finished their chores, then everyone except for James and Adam climbed on the buckboard and headed into town. It was an unusually warm day for October, making the ride to town an enjoyable one. Upon arriving, everyone went their separate ways. Pa went to Farabee's Blacksmith to catch up on the latest news. Virginia and Ma visited Collin's Mercantile, while Anna waited on a bench outside the mercantile. She soon grew bored and decided to visit the new woodworking shop.

The sign above read *Carlin's Woodwork.*

Just as Anna rounded the corner of the mercantile, she bumped into someone, which knocked her backward. Anna fell flat on her buttocks. She quickly straightened the skirt of her dress before attempting to get up.

"Sorry, miss, may I help you to your feet?"

Anna, grumbling all the while, took the outstretched hand. "You should watch where . . . I'm . . . walking." Anna said breathlessly as she gazed into the face of the most handsome boy with piercing green eyes that she had ever seen.

"It's not where I'm walking, it's your," he corrected.

"What?" She could hardly take her eyes off him.

"Never mind, but you ran into me." He stepped back and gave her the once over.

"Excuse me. You're the one who knocked me down." She stomped her foot and crossed her arms over her chest.

"I apologized, even though it was your fault." He placed his hands on his hips. "I'm Johnny Carlin. What's your name?"

"I'm not telling you anything. Just go your way." She motioned for him to move.

"Fine, I will," he snapped. "I can't believe such a beautiful girl has such an awful haughty attitude," he mumbled as he brushed past Anna.

"Anna!" Pa hollered. "Bring the buckboard and help me load this." He pointed to something that Anna couldn't see from where she stood.

Johnny turned and continued walking backwards. "Anna, is it?" He bowed playfully. "Beautiful name for a young hoyden girl."

"A hoyden!" Anna screeched. "You call me rude. I'll show you rude." She picked up a clump of dried horse manure and threw it at him. He dodged it and laughed as he turned to walk away. She grabbed another one and smacked him in the back of the head with it. "Next time, Johnny Carlin, it'll be a horse biscuit between the eyes."

Johnny turned toward her. It was all he could do not to pick it up and throw it back at her. He knew that he could hit her from this distance, so he decided against it. "You just proved my point . . . hoyden." he shouted, then turned and continued on his way.

Anna stood there fuming. Never in her life had she ever been so angry at a boy, not even Adam. The next few years she avoided Johnny like the plague.

CHAPTER EIGHT

A CHANCE ENCOUNTER

July 1762

It was a hot summer day with little rain. The creek had run dry, so everyone decided to wander down the path behind the house that led to the river. Anna cherished these family outings; they were some of the rare moments when James and Adam could be civil with her. Virginia pitched in to help Ma prepare a picnic lunch. After taking a cool refreshing swim, Pa and Ma settled onto a blanket underneath the sprawling branches of a giant maple tree, enjoying several hours of relaxation and a much-needed break from everyday life.

Anna relished outings at the river alone. She'd take a quill and parchment along for writing. She spent as much time at the river as possible. Most days she sat on the riverbank and daydreamed about whatever crossed her mind.

After finishing her chores today, Anna ventured into the woods, eager to reach her favorite spot by the river. She settled down, her eyes fixated on a frog perched on a rock. Suddenly, it took a leap, splashing into the water. As it paddled in small circles, Anna couldn't help but smile at its antics before it climbed back onto the rock, poised and waiting for its next meal to swim or flutter by.

Nearby, the squirrels were in full swing with their playful games. One chased another across the ground, only to scamper up a tree trunk. They twirled around each other in a dizzy race before scaling higher into the branches. Sometimes, they'd freeze on a limb, gazing into the distance, and at other times, one would take a bold leap, landing precariously on a thinner branch that swayed dangerously beneath its weight. Anna's thoughts drifted to whether that branch had ever snapped, sending a squirrel tumbling. The image made her chuckle—the idea of a branch flinging a squirrel into the air was too funny to resist. "Now that's something I'd love to witness!" she exclaimed, laughing at the thought.

"What, my dear lady, would that be?" came a male voice from behind Anna.

A startled Anna looked up to see Johnny standing on the riverbank next to a huge bush. She leapt, placed her hands on her hips and glared at him. "Johnny Carlin! What are you doing here? Are you spying on me?"

"Whoa! Slow down and give a guy a chance to answer." He stepped away from the bush.

"Make it quick. I don't have all day." She crossed her arms over her chest.

"First, I came here to swim, and second, No! I'm not spying on you." He picked up a rock and threw it across the river. He watched it skip and then slow to a bounce over the water before sinking. "Besides, your life isn't that interesting." He turned back to face her.

"If my life is so uninteresting, then why are you following me?" She retorted.

"I'm not following you!" He shouted as he turned on his heel facing the direction he came.

"Look around, Johnny." She stood with outstretched arms motioning toward the water. "There's a huge river here, yet you decide to come to my spot."

"For your information, this," he motioned all around him, "is not your river."

Anna quietly stood there staring at him. After a moment of silence, she said, "Fine. I never said this is my river." She stared at him defiantly. "I said this is my spot, and it wouldn't kill you to go somewhere else."

"That's the best idea you've had all day." He threw his arms up in frustration and turned to walk away. He took a few steps, stopped, and turned to face her.

"What are you doing?" Anna spoke through gritted teeth. "Go away!" she shouted.

"I will go away." He kicked off first one shoe and then the other. "After I do what I came here for." He pulled off his shirt.

"Don't even think about it, Johnny Carlin." Anna stepped back.

"What?" A confused look crossed his face. "Oh, my lord." He rolled his eyes. "You're daft, I wouldn't touch you with a ten-foot pole." He walked to the edge of the riverbank and jumped in.

Anna felt relieved. Her face flushed upon realizing how she must have sounded to him. She watched Johnny disappear underwater and held her breath waiting for him to resurface. Several moments passed, no sign of him. She rushed down the bank, her eyes darting back and forth scanning the area. He was nowhere to be found. In a panic, she raced along the water's edge and tripped over a huge rock.

Johnny popped his head up in the middle of the river, just in time to see her tumbling face first into the water.

"Are you all right?" He swam toward her.

She stood, angry and dripping wet. "I'm fine, I just thought —"

"You thought what?" He got out of the water and stood next to her.

"Never mind." She lifted her dress to her knees and squeezed out as much water as she could. *It's no use.*

"You need to remove your clothes in order to dry them." He grinned mischievously.

"Oh, you'd like that, wouldn't you?" she snapped.

"Just trying to help." He skipped another rock across the river. Anna watched in amazement as the rock skipped and hopped across to the other side. She quickly looked down at her wet dress. She didn't want Johnny to know his flair for skipping rocks impressed her.

"Well, I don't need your help. She twisted her dress and gave it another good squeeze. Water splashed from it and onto the rocks at her feet. "In fact, I'd like you to leave," she added.

Anna wasn't about to undress, especially not with him there. She gathered the wet material and held it off the ground. She climbed the embankment and sat on a huge rock where she continued wringing out her clothes.

"How old are you anyway?" He picked up his shirt and put it on, leaving it unbuttoned.

"Why do you want to know?" She stood.

"Does your Ma know you're out of the yard?" he asked sarcastically.

"If you must know—" She placed her hands on her hips. "I'll be fourteen next month." She turned to walk away.

"Yeah, well you're infantile for your age." Johnny smirked,

stopping her.

She spun around to face him. "Oh! Is that so?" Anger flashed in her eyes. "How old are you?" She crossed her arms over her chest.

"I'm fifteen as of last week." He plucked a blade of grass, placed it between his thumbs, pressed them to his lips, and blew a high-pitched whistle that reverberated across the water.

Anna watched in awe. She wondered how he did that, but didn't dare ask. She didn't want to give him the satisfaction.

"Well, you act as though you're two." She smirked. When he didn't respond, she turned and walked away, a triumphant smile upon her face.

Johnny watched as she made her way down the well-worn path through the woods leading to the field behind her home. There was something about her that irritated yet intrigued him at the same time.

"Females," Johnny groaned. "They're a pain in the rump." He tossed a twig into the river. A fish swam to the surface, nipped at it several times before giving up and disappearing back underwater.

Humph, must be a female fish. Johnny grumbled. *Nip, nip, nip. That's what they do before giving up and going away*. He buttoned his shirt, slipped on his shoes, and headed home.

Anna rushed through the front door of the house hoping she could make it to her room without getting caught, but no such luck. Adam met her on his way out.

"Anna, you know you're not allowed to go swimming alone." He yelled as he ran past her. Any other time he would have stayed and picked an argument out of her, and normally she would have obliged, but all she wanted was to get out of her wet clothes. She wondered what had gotten into Adam lately.

He'd been rushing to get his chores done, then running off to God knows where. Anna shrugged her shoulders. She had her own problems; she didn't have time to worry about anyone else's.

CHAPTER NINE

SECRETS

That night Anna lay in bed and reflected on the events of the day. She couldn't get Johnny out of her mind. Every time she closed her eyes; she pictured him without his shirt on. His tanned muscles flexed each time he skipped a rock across the river. His gorgeous green eyes and perfect smile. Anna's eyes flew open. *Stop it, Anna. Don't forget how annoyingly cocky he is.* She flipped her down and feather pillow over and punched it before settling her head into the luxurious cloud-like softness. The pillow molded to her head, neck, and shoulders like a mother cradling her newborn baby.

"Anna, would you please go to sleep!" her sister Virginia, at seventeen the oldest of the siblings, scolded.

"Sorry, Ginny, I'll try." Anna rolled over. Ginny was the nickname Anna had given her older sister Virginia when Anna was a wee thing just learning to talk, and it'd stuck ever since.

"What's weighing so heavy on your mind that has you fretting so?" Virginia placed her hand over her mouth and yawned.

"It's nothing, really," Anna said groggily. She closed her eyes and soon fell fast asleep.

Virginia didn't press the issue; she knew if it were something important that Anna would have confided in her. Besides, Virginia had a few secrets of her own that she didn't dare share with anyone, at least not yet.

The next morning, Anna awoke to the sound of a rooster crowing outside her bedroom window. She placed her pillow over her head to block out the noise. It was no use. The rooster crowed again. Anna rolled onto her back and stared at the ceiling.

"Quiet, Jack!" she yelled.

"Anna, how many times have I told you to stop naming the animals?" Pa said as he strolled past the bedroom door on his way to the kitchen.

"Sorry, Pa." Anna threw both legs over the side of the bed and sat for a few minutes before getting up.

"Breakfast is ready," Ma called from the kitchen.

"Ya better say goodbye to Jack." Adam poked his head through the bedroom doorway. "He's going to be dinner tonight." He giggled and ran when Anna threw her pillow at him.

"That's not funny, Adam!" she shouted after him. She leapt and pulled the curtains closed over the doorway. "I can't wait till Pa makes a real door for our room," she mumbled to herself. She quickly combed her long dark blond hair, pulling it back into a ponytail and securing it with a powder blue ribbon. She usually wore it in braids twisted and fastened at the back of her head, but not this morning. She wanted to look her best today. She planned to sneak off to the river, hoping to find Johnny there. She stared at her reflection in the looking glass. Wisps of hair framed her lovely face. The natural curls on the ends of her hair rested against her back just above her hips. She loved the way her hair felt against her bare skin and bounced from side to side when she walked.

It dawned on her that no one had seen her hair that way. Not wanting to cause suspicions, especially from her loudmouth brother, Adam, she quickly gave her hair a twist and pinned it on top of her head, making sure to hide the ribbon. She glanced once more into the looking glass just as the ribbon poked out.

"Well, that's definitely going to attract attention," she whispered. She pulled the ribbon from her hair and shoved it in the waistband of her skirt, quickly braided her hair, then twisted and pinned it against the back of her head before heading to the breakfast table.

"Anna, breakfast!" Her mother shouted as she set a platter of fried eggs on the table.

"I'm here." Anna made her way around the table and took a seat next to her sister. "Good morning, Ginny." Anna smoothed out her skirt before placing her hands on her lap. "You could've woken me when you got up."

"I could've, but it's more peaceful to let you sleep," Virginia answered sarcastically.

"I don't know how you'd think Anna sleeping is the least bit peaceful." Adam grinned sheepishly at Anna. "You snore."

"I do not," Anna argued.

"Yes, you do," Adam and Virginia said in unison. "You sound like an old bear," Virginia said.

"More like a grumpy old boar." Adam began snorting like a pig.

"Pa, make them stop." Anna stood and scooped a spoonful of scrambled eggs and fried potatoes onto a biscuit.

"All right, you two, that's quite enough," Pa scolded.

"Apologize to your sister." Ma looked sternly at Virginia and Adam.

"Sorry," they said in unison.

"Anna, sit down and say grace." Pa made a praying gesture, closed his eyes, and waited.

Anna reluctantly took her seat, crossed her hands in prayer, and said grace.

She'd hoped to use the teasing as an excuse to leave the table. No such luck. Pa wasn't having it. He had a rule that the family must eat meals together. Anna would have to think of another way to get out of the house. She secretly hoped to find Johnny at the swimming hole. She thought of picking a fight with Virginia or one of her brothers but feared it would only get her grounded. Her face lit up when she came up with what she thought was a brilliant idea.

"What are you smiling about?" Adam nudged her with his elbow.

It was then Anna realized he had taken a seat on the other side of her.

"None of your business." She elbowed him back.

"If the pair of you don't start getting along, I'm going to pin your shirttails together until all the chores are finished." Ma crossed her arms and drew her eyes down at them.

"He started it," Anna said in her defense.

"Ma, you wouldn't dare." Adam stared at her wide-eyed.

"Don't try my patience." The look in Ma's eyes told them she wasn't joking.

Neither Adam nor Anna could think of a worse punishment.

The room grew silent. The only noise was the sound of silverware scraping against the ceramic plates.

"I need you to take a ride with me after breakfast." Pa broke the silence and sat staring at Ma. "Ahem, Mary Lou."

Ma glanced at Pa as she took a sip from her glass of milk. Her expression changed to a look of surprise. "Oh, are you talking to me?"

"Who else would I be talking to?" He smiled.

"Should I wear my Sunday best?" Her eyes sparkled with excitement. She stood and ran her fingers through her hair, pinning back any loose strands.

"No darlin', you look as beautiful as the day we met." Pa took her by the hand and spun her around. Ma placed one hand over her mouth and giggled. "Oh, Daniel, not in front of the children." She blushed.

Anna loved these playful moments between her Pa and Ma. she hoped one day to marry a man just like her father. Someone who was strong and protective of his family, yet gentle and loving. A God-fearing man, that's how Ma described him to the ladies at the church social last year.

"Where are you taking me?" Ma's curiosity was getting the better of her.

"Well, now, if I told you, where's the fun in that?" Pa kissed Ma on the cheek. "I'll hitch up the horses to the wagon and meet you at the front of the house." He smiled and tipped his hat.

"I wonder what in heaven's name your Pa is up to now?" Ma could hardly contain herself.

"Whatever it is, you best be hurrying along," Virginia said as she stood looking out the front door. "Pa's entering the barn now."

"Oh, goodness, this is thrilling." Anna clasped Ma's hands in hers.

"You girls clean the kitchen, and I'll tell you all about it when we get home." Ma rushed out the front door and anxiously waited on the porch. She ran her hands down her dress and realized she forgot to take her apron off. She quickly untied it and handed it to Virginia.

"Here, hang this on the hook in the kitchen, please."

"Yes, ma'am." Virginia draped the apron over her arm.

A few minutes later, Pa pulled up on the horse and buggy, jumped onto the ground. Dust stirred in the process and was carried away by a gentle breeze. He helped Ma up into the seat and then sprinted around the back of the buggy, climbed into the driver's seat, and off they went. "We'll be home later," Pa shouted over his shoulder.

"Oh, my goodness, I wonder what Pa's up to?" Anna said as she followed Virginia into the house.

"I suppose we'll find out soon enough." Virginia walked into the kitchen and hung Ma's apron on the hook. She grabbed a dish towel and removed the cover off the reservoir on the stove. Anna placed the dirty dishes on the counter while Virginia dipped water from the reservoir and filled the dish pan.

"How can you be so calm?" Anna crossed her arms and leaned her back against the counter. "Aren't you the least bit curious?"

"Not particularly." Virginia pursed her lips.

"What's wrong with you?" Anna turned to face her. "You've been acting peculiar the past few days."

"That's none of your concern," Virginia snapped.

"You don't have to be so crabby," Anna scoffed.

"It's a secret that I'd rather not discuss." Virginia reached into the dish water and vigorously began scrubbing a plate.

"Are you and Patrick quarreling?" Anna blurted out.

"How do you know about Patrick?" Virginia stared at Anna, astonished.

"I've known about Patrick for the past two months." Anna grinned mischievously.

"What else do you know?" Virginia crossed her arms and glared at her.

"I know about your secret meetings at the swimming hole," Anna said smugly.

Virginia turned and continued washing dishes. She stated, a hint of defensiveness in her voice, "I'm the same age as Ma when she met Pa." without turning, she asked softly. "Have you mentioned it to anyone?"

"Not a soul." Anna smiled proudly. "See, I can keep a secret. Please trust me with whatever it is you know." Anna clasped her hands in a pleading gesture.

"Oh, all right." Virginia dried her hands on her apron. "I suppose it'll help to get it off my chest." She breathed deeply and peeked out the window, making sure her brothers weren't nearby. She exhaled when she spotted the two of them working in the field. She grabbed Anna by the hands, her eyes searching her face, contemplating whether to trust her with something so surreptitious.

"Why are you so hesitant? Just tell me." Anna tapped her foot impatiently.

"I'm not sure I should let the cat out of the bag." Virginia looked away.

"What does that even mean?" Anna knitted her brow.

"Never mind." Virginia drew in a deep breath. "I saw Pa coming out of the widow Baker's house." She blurted out.

"That's it, that's the big secret?" Anna's disappointment was apparent.

"Clearly, you don't understand." Virginia began washing the dishes. "Pa's been acting strange and spending a lot of time away for months." She glanced at Anna to see her reaction, but Anna stood there, a confused look on her face.

"They were laughing," Virginia continued. "Pa acted like a child with a new toy—or, in this case, mistress." She stared at a dish in her hands.

"What a dreadful thing to say!" Anna shouted. "You take that back." She placed her hands on her hips.

"I wish I could." Virginia tilted her head back. A tear trickled down her cheek.

"Are you serious?" Anna whispered.

"Yes, unfortunately." Virginia nodded.

They finished the dishes in silence.

James and Adam strolled through the back door carrying buckets filled with potatoes, green beans, and carrots fresh from the garden. Without a word, they set them on the table and headed back out to finish their chores.

"I've never seen Ma more excited," Anna said, breaking the silence.

"Nor have I." Virginia dried her hands and retrieved the roasting pan from the cabinet. She washed the vegetables, placed a beef roast in the center of the pan, and surrounded it with the vegetables. She slid it into the oven.

"I trust Pa. Maybe it's not what you think," Anna said.

"Not what I think!" Virginia screeched. "Have you seen the way the women in town stare and snicker at Ma?"

"No, I haven't." Anna stared at the floor. "I'll give them a piece of my mind." She paced the floor angrily.

"Calm down. Ma mustn't know." Virginia lowered her voice.

"I reckon Pa's feeling mighty guilty." Anna stormed across the kitchen floor, grumbling with each step. "I can't believe this, surprising Ma with a buggy ride to hide his infidelity."

"Keep your voice down. Your brothers will hear," Virginia said softly.

"What infuriates me most—" Anna turned to face Virginia. "Is that the whole town knows or at least suspects something." She crossed her arms over her chest.

"I'm just as upset as you are, but—"

"Upset!" Anna shouted. "Surely you jest," she added sarcastically.

"This is between Pa and Ma. I'm sure it's just a misunderstanding," Virginia said.

"When I go to town, those ladies are getting a piece of my mind," Anna stated through gritted teeth. She grabbed the broom and began sweeping the floor, grumbling to herself.

A while later, Pa and Ma pulled up in front of the house. They were both smiling. Anna wondered why Ma didn't get down from the carriage or why Pa didn't bother helping her. Instead, he rushed into the house.

"Virginia! Anna! Stop what you're doing and come with me." he shouted excitedly.

Anna crossed her arms over her chest and refused to budge until Virginia scowled at her. "Anna, please." she whispered. Pa either didn't notice or was too happy to care what was going on.

"Fine!" Anna stomped her foot and followed Pa and Virginia outside. They both climbed into the back of the wagon and off they went.

"Where are we going?" Virginia inquired.

"You'll see." Ma looked back at Virginia and Anna. A huge smile spread across her face. Her excitement was contagious. Anna could hardly sit still. She scooted up behind Ma and placed her arms around her neck.

"I just love surprises," she said in Ma's ear.

They drove a mile up the road, turned left, and followed the newly formed road. Anna noticed each side of the road was lined with freshly planted sugar maple saplings. She imagined what it would be like to travel this road with Johnny in autumn when the leaves changed to gorgeous hues of reds, oranges, and yellows, and the leaves fell from the trees and covered the road. She closed her eyes and could almost hear the rustling and crunching of the leaves as the carriage slowly rolled over them. She was brought back to reality when someone shouted, "Here they come!"

She opened her eyes to see the whole town. Everyone was clapping and cheering. James and Adam had managed to beat them there. They were standing on the steps of a magnificent house.

"Oh, goodness!" Anna gasped. "I wonder who lives here?"

"We do, or we will soon," Pa said proudly.

"Surely you jest!" Virginia exclaimed. She got up on her knees and slid closer to the front of the wagon to get a better look. It was gorgeous. She stared at the house in awe.

"How can we afford such a thing?" Anna glanced at Pa and then went back to the house.

"A lot of hard work—I built it." Pa never took his eyes off the place. "Well, that is, me and your brothers, as well as help from a few of the town's folk."

"It appears even bigger than when I first laid eyes on it." Ma leaned over and laid her head on Pa's shoulder.

Everyone lined the dirt driveway leading to the front porch. They were hooting and hollering as Pa steered the horse between them. A huge grin was plastered on his and Ma's faces.

"Whoa!" Pa shouted, pulling back on the horse's reins. The

horses slowed to a gentle walk and the wagon rolled to a stop.

Anna immediately jumped to the ground. Patrick hurried to help Virginia.

"Did you tell them?" Patrick whispered in her ear.

Virginia gazed into his eyes for a brief second and then quickly looked away. "Not yet." She stared at the ground and then ran her hand down her dress to smooth it. She watched Ma and Pa and longed for the day that she and Patrick would wed and have a home of their own. She knew she had to tell them about Patrick, but not today. She figured this was Ma's special moment.

"What better time to ask your pa's permission than now, while they're in a wonderful mood," Patrick coaxed.

Virginia watched her parents. She had never seen either of them so happy. Ma's face glowed; her eyes sparkled when she smiled. Pa had a twinkle in his eyes watching Ma. It was apparent the love they had for each other.

"All right, we'll tell them after everyone leaves." Virginia smiled slightly. Deep inside, she felt like she would burst with joy. She wanted nothing more than to throw her arms around Patrick and announce their courtship at once.

Anna raced into the house with James and Adam leading the way. They ascended the staircase, located off the living room, two steps at a time in a rush to pick out their rooms. Adam and James chose a room next to one another at the front of the house, while Anna preferred the room on the opposite side facing the back. She stood looking out the window at the meadow below and the wooded area beyond it.

Ma was downstairs showing the ladies the kitchen before giving them the final tour of the rest of her new home. Afterwards, everyone met in the front yard for a picnic.

Virginia helped Ma spread a blanket on the ground underneath the huge sugar maple tree. Anna watched from afar. She knew by the look on Virginia's face that she was going to tell Ma about Patrick, but before she had a chance, Ma sat on the quilt and handed Pa a plate of food the ladies from town had prepared earlier in the day.

"So, Virginia, when are you going to tell us about Patrick?" Ma smiled sheepishly.

"How'd you know?" Virginia drew her eyes down at Anna.

"Don't look at me. I didn't say a word," Anna said defensively as she sat on the blanket next to Ma.

"Anna's telling the truth." Ma patted Anna's knee. "She never said anything to me."

"I told you I could keep a secret, just like the one about Pa." Anna grinned proudly.

Ma gasped and Virginia's face turned three shades of red. "Anna! Be quiet!" Virginia screeched.

"Are you two talking about the new house or the stove?" Ma asked curiously.

"Neither. She thought Pa was stepping out on you with the widow Baker," Anna shouted over the music that a few men had begun to play.

Pa, who hadn't previously been paying attention to the conversation, spit coffee everywhere. He jumped up and wiped his shirt and trousers with his hands.

Virginia stood, fuming. "That does it, Anna. I shall never trust you again." She frowned and looked at her father. "Sorry, Pa. I made a wrong assumption." She glared at Anna and then stormed off.

Anna sat there, her face sullen. "I didn't mean to upset her." She lowered her voice. "I'm sorry, Pa. I didn't believe you were doing anything wrong." Anna's eyes filled with tears, and she ran off in the opposite direction. To make matters worse, she saw Johnny talking to Sally.

"I need to have a word with Virginia." Ma stood and kissed Pa on the cheek. She found Virginia sitting with her back against a tree at the edge of the woods and took a seat on the ground beside her.

"Oh, Ma, I should have listened to Anna. She tried to tell me that Pa would never. . . ." Virginia's voice trailed off as she sobbed.

"There, there, don't cry." Ma placed Virginia's head on her shoulder and stroked her long brown hair. "I have a confession to make." Ma sighed.

"A confession?" Virginia sat up, her brows knit. "What could you possibly have to confess?" She sniffled.

"I also thought your father was being unfaithful," Ma admitted.

"You did?" Virginia rubbed the moisture from her eyes.

"Yes. Don't you think I saw the ladies in town pointing and snickering at me?" Ma placed a stray hair behind Virginia's ear. "I saw your father leaving the widow Baker's house more than once."

"Why was he there so much?" Virginia asked.

"I'm ashamed to admit it, but do you remember the day I took a long walk?" Ma stared at her hands folded on her lap.

"Yes, I remember. That's the day you asked me and Anna to make soap."

"I wanted you and Anna to busy yourselves while I rode the horse into town."

She now had Virginia's full attention. "Were you spying on Pa and the widow Baker?"

"Actually, I went to visit the widow Baker." Ma paused before continuing. "I asked her what was going on between her and your Pa."

"What did she say" Virginia whispered.

"Did you see the beautiful hutch in the dining room of the new house and the New Ben Franklin stove in the kitchen?" Ma fidgeted with her skirt.

"Did she give those things to Pa?"

Ma smiled half-heartedly. "The widow . . . um, Mrs. Baker, needed some repairs done to her home. Your Pa offered to do it for free, but she insisted on paying him. She no longer wanted the hutch and offered to give it to your Pa, but—"

"Knowing Pa, he refused to take it unless he could work for it. And what of the stove?" Virginia asked.

"The widow Baker's son works for James Mitchell of Yorktown, Virginia." Ma looked up and saw Anna disappear into the woods. *Hmmm, I wonder where she's off to.*

"Who is James Mitchell? Is he a relative?" Virginia interrupted Ma's thoughts.

"No, he makes Pennsylvania fireplaces, or, as we call them, Ben Franklin stoves," Ma clarified. "The widow Baker's son brought her one, but due to her failing health, she took her son up on his offer to move to Yorktown with him." Her gaze drifted towards the wooded area where Anna went.

"Let me guess." Virginia shifted positions. "Pa worked for the widow Baker as payment for the stove."

"That he did." Ma nodded.

Virginia placed her hands over her face. "Oh, Ma, I'm so ashamed for thinking such awful things of Pa," she said through tear-filled eyes.

"It's all right. Even I thought the same thing," Ma said

soothingly. "Now, enough with the tears. We have a lot of packing to do starting tomorrow, and you have a handsome young man searching for you." She pointed at Patrick walking through the field behind the house.

"One thing before I go." Virginia shifted onto her knees. "How did you know about Patrick?"

"Mother's instinct." Ma placed her hand under Virginia's chin. "Besides, you've always hated going into the woods alone, then all the sudden you began making regular trips every evening." Ma pulled a piece of tree bark from Virginia's hair.

"Did you ever think that maybe I changed my mind about the woods?"

"I might have, if I hadn't seen Patrick step out of the woods with you one evening." Ma smiled. "Now, get going, don't keep Patrick waiting." She nodded toward Patrick, who was now heading their way.

"I love you, Ma." Virginia kissed her cheek before racing to Patrick. She threw her arms around his neck and hugged him. Patrick threw a hand up and waved at Ma as she made her way back to her picnic spot where Pa sat patiently waiting.

Patrick, his heart pounding, braced himself as he approached Pa about courting Virginia. Pa, a towering figure beside Patrick's five-foot-eight frame—a mere three inches taller than Virginia—stood waiting.

"S . . . s . . . sir," Patrick stammered, his nervousness palpable.

Pa, sensing the young man's apprehension, decided to have some fun. "What are you hem-hawing around about, son?" he boomed. "If you have something to say, spit it out."

Patrick's face drained of color. "Sir, I'd like permission to court your daughter, Vir . . . Virginia."

Pa's eyes narrowed. Though a smile played on his lips, his

voice remained stern. “What makes you think I’d allow her to court the likes of you?”

Patrick struggled to articulate his worthiness. “Well, sir, I . . . uh . . . .” he stuttered.

Pa chuckled, then slapped Patrick on the shoulder, turning to Ma with a wide grin. “What do you think, darlin’?”

“I think you should stop jesting with the boy and answer him before he faints,” she replied, a hint of concern in her voice.

Virginia, her cheeks flushed, stepped beside Patrick and offered a supportive hand.

“Well, since Virginia seems fond of ya, I suppose we can give you a chance,” Pa conceded, a hint of amusement still in his voice.

Virginia’s eyes lit up. “Thank you, Pa!” she squealed, hugging him tightly, before turning to Patrick and embracing him with equal enthusiasm.

“You ornery ol’ cuss,” Ma whispered to Pa. “You nearly frightened him to death,” She covered her mouth with her hands and snickered.

Pa roared with laughter, pulling her close. He watched Patrick and Virginia stroll down the road hand in hand, a proud smile spreading across his face.

Anna had no problem finding her way to the river. She sat on a huge rock that stretched out into the water. “What’s the matter with you?” she grumbled to herself. “Ginny will never trust me, and I will never trust Johnny.” Tears spilled down her cheeks. She picked up a flat rock and flung it across the river. It skipped on the water’s surface and didn’t stop until it reached the other side.

“That’s the best rock skipping I’ve ever seen,” came a voice behind her. Startled, she jumped and turned to face the intruder. Tears blurred her vision. She rubbed her eyes with the sleeve of her dress and stared into the face of Andrew Chapman. He and his brothers were known for causing trouble around town. His Pa was an abusive drunk and his Ma left them when Andrew was nine. According to the rumors, Andrew had been bitter ever since.

"My, oh my, ya sure have growed and gotten mighty purdy." Andrew spat brown tobacco juice on the rock at her feet.

Anna grimaced. "What do you want?" she snapped.

"A purdy girl such as yourself shouldn't roam these woods alone. Ya's needs a strong man to take cares of ya's." He stepped closer, and before Anna had a chance to react, he placed a hand around her waist and pulled her close. She struggled to free herself. The fowl stench of body odor mixed with rotten tobacco breath made her nauseous. She managed to pull free and slapped him hard across the cheek. His face grew red with anger.

"Ya's gonna regret that, ya stupid wench." He drew back to strike her. Anna covered her head with her arms and awaited the awful blow.

"You no good pig. I ought a beat the tarnation out of you!"

Anna looked up. To her surprise, Johnny had Andrew with one arm pinned behind his back and the other around his throat.

"I didn't hurt her none. I's jest tryin' to steal me a kiss is all." Andrew kept his eyes to the ground. "I mean, jest a look at her, she's a purdy thing."

Johnny turned him loose and spun him around to face him. "If you so much as look at her, I'll—"

"Ya's a gonna do what, Johnny Carlin?" Andrew spat tobacco juice on the ground. "Ya's ain't a-gonna do nuffin'."

Johnny stepped toward him, anger flaring in his eyes. Anna had never seen him so mad. "Don't test me, Andrew. I'm warning you."

"I know that yer Pa will disown ya's if'n ya gets in trouble wif the law." Andrew grinned, showing half decayed tobacco-stained teeth.

"What's that supposed to mean?" Anna retorted.

"It means Johnny will lose his inhabitance."

"It's inheritance, you moron," Johnny corrected. "I could care less about my Pa's business."

"Then you won't care if me and my brothers burn it to the ground." Andrew's eyes narrowed.

"If you or your brothers come near my Pa's business or Anna, I'll hunt you down like the dogs you are." Johnny stepped toward him. His fists clenched at his sides.

Andrew backed up. His gaze fixed on Anna. "Next time ya's won't be so lucky."

Johnny grabbed him by the throat. "Let me make this clear. Keep your mouth shut or your father will be burying you next to your Ma." Johnny instantly regretted saying such a thing upon seeing the hurt in Andrew's eyes. He turned him loose.

The feeling was short-lived when Andrew retaliated. "I ain't skeerd of ya's, Johnny Carlin." His voice quivered. "I do what I want, to who I want."

"Is that so?" Anna stepped in between Johnny and Andrew.

"Yeah, that's so." Andrew sneered.

"Well, I have nothing to lose, and I can fight my own battles." With that, Anna stomped Andrew's barefoot. He yelled in pain. Before he knew it, she gave him a hard shove, sending him flying backward off the rock and into the river.

He began flailing his arms and shouting. "Help! I's can't

swim."

"Stand up!" Johnny and Anna shouted in unison.

Andrew stopped thrashing about and stood to find the water waist deep. "Ya's could've kilt me!" he yelled.

"Think about that next time you get the stupid notion to try anything with me again!" Anna shouted over her shoulder as she turned to walk away. "Oh, and my Pa is going to hear about this."

"Go on, tell 'em!" Andrew shouted, still standing in the water. "Wait! Who's yer Pa?"

"Daniel McCullough. I'm sure you've heard of him," Johnny answered.

"Oh, bull butter. Not Big Dan. Ya's an idiot," Andrew mumbled to himself. He smacked his hand across the water as he trudged out and hurried home.

Johnny and Anna walked slowly along the path leading to the new house. Anna's mind wandered to what could've happened had Johnny not shown up. Johnny knew what she must be thinking from her worried expression.

"Don't fret, I'll make sure that Andrew never bothers you again." Johnny picked up a stick. He snapped it and threw the pieces toward the woods as they walked.

"Thank you. I don't know what I would have done if you weren't there." Anna stared at the ground as she continued walking.

"You're very welcome, my lady." Johnny stepped in front of her and bowed playfully.

Anna giggled, but her smile soon dissipated when she looked up to see Sally strolling toward them.

"Johnny, can I have a word with you, alone?" She barely looked at Anna.

"Anna, I'll see you in a little bit." Johnny walked away with Sally, leaving Anna standing there. Her heart was broken. She ran toward the house. She didn't want to face anyone. She saw Adam's horse tethered to a tree. She untied him, climbed on, and raced back toward their old home place.

Adam chased behind her yelling, "Anna! You get back here. That's my horse."

She ignored him. She looked back and saw Adam angrily throw his hat to the ground. Salty tears streamed down her face and onto her lips. Once out of sight, she slowed the horse to a trot. "Who does Sally think she is, demanding to talk to Johnny? And what's worse, he obeyed," she grumbled to herself.

The horse whinnied as though he understood her.

"Tomorrow's my birthday. Some birthday this is going to be." Anna made up her mind to forget about Johnny. "If Sally wants him, she can have him," she said softly to herself.

That night as she snuggled under the blankets, the events of the day played over and over in her mind. She tossed and turned half the night. Finally, exhaustion overtook her, and she drifted off to sleep. The next morning when she awoke, an idea came to mind and her excitement grew at the very thought. The autumn harvest dance was in October. Which was two months away, and that gave her just enough time to make herself a new dress.

Anna's excitement grew at the very thought of showing up at the dance wearing a beautiful new dress. That excitement was short lived upon realizing she had no idea how to sew, let alone make a dress. She sank to the floor with her back against the bed, knees drawn to her chest, and sulked.

"What's wrong with you?" Virginia placed an armload of

laundry on the bed and began folding it.

"Ginny." Anna fidgeted with a long curly lock of hair that hung to the front of her waist. "May I ask you a question?"

"I suppose." Virginia continued folding laundry.

"Would you mind teaching me to sew?" Anna stood and avoided making eye contact.

Virginia briefly stopped what she was doing. She gave Anna a quizzical look, opened her trunk, and pulled out an old dress and tossed it on the bed. "We can use this one as a pattern." Virginia finished folding laundry and put it away. Anna was relieved she didn't ask questions. She wasn't in the mood to discuss her personal life.

Virginia picked up the dress and handed it to Anna, who eagerly tried it on. Virginia circled her, carefully examining the fit. Anna removed the dress and placed it on the bed. She turned to Virginia. "So, what do you think?" "It's a perfect fit," she whispered. "Here ya go." She draped the garment over Anna's shoulder. "Start by taking it apart and come to me when you're finished." She walked out of the bedroom. Anna followed.

"Wait! Anna shouted.

Virginia turned to face her.

"How do I take it apart?" Anna hated asking what she felt was an ignorant question.

"Oh," Virginia snickered. "I forgot you've never sewn before, let alone prepared a pattern." She took the dress from Anna and searched along the hem until she found what she was looking for. A thread with a knot on the end.

"Do you see this?" She showed Anna the knot before breaking the thread. She then pulled on it. Anna watched in amazement as the threads unraveled.

"Oh, my goodness!" Anna exclaimed. "What if it unravels like that while I'm wearing it?" She knitted her brow.

"Trust me, it won't." Virginia laughed.

"Ginny, thank you." Anna's eyes locked with her sister's. "I just . . . Uh . . . ."

"Don't fret, there's no need to explain anything." Virginia smiled. "I'm just happy you've taken an interest in sewing."

"One more thing." Anna held out the dress. "Would you help me choose the material?"

"I'd be delighted." Virginia looked the dress over. "Let's see, we'll add a ruffle here, some lace there. Hmm."

Anna became lost in thought. She wondered what Johnny would think seeing her in a beautiful new gown. Would he ask her to dance, or would his attention be on Sally McAlister?

Sally was the same age as Virginia. She was beautiful and from a rich family. Her father owned half the town.

"Anna, I'm speaking to you." Virginia snapped her fingers in front of Anna's face.

"Oh, I'm sorry. What were you saying?" Anna shook the thoughts from her head.

"I said, I think it will be pretty, don't you?" Virginia hugged the dress to her chest. She often did that when she grew excited about something or when she daydreamed.

"Yes, I believe it's going to be lovely when it's finished." Anna took the dress and continued taking it apart.

"If you have any problems, there's a small paring knife in the kitchen. It works perfect on stubborn threads."

"Thank you, I'll keep that in mind." Anna pulled on a thread and it slowly unraveled.

"I'll leave you to it." Virginia headed back to the kitchen.

Virginia hoped to become a teacher one day. Her love for

children was obvious. Each time they went to town, the children gathered around her and she would sing to them or tell them a short story she'd thought up at the spur of the moment. Virginia was the one who stirred within Anna her love of writing. Anna kept a journal of her family's lives and planned to become an author. She hoped to be as good as Charlotte Lennox.

Virginia never told Anna, but deep down she believed her sister would be efficacious at whatever she chose to do.

CHAPTER TEN

PREPARING FOR WINTER

Summer soon turned to fall, bringing with it the beautiful autumn foliage. The amber, gold, auburn, and crimson-colored leaves clung to the huge maple tree next to the house as though dreading the end of summer. Finally, the last leaf would give up as the cold fingers of fall winds ripped it from its resting place and it slowly floated to the ground. Winter would soon follow. Winter. The name itself didn't sound as bad as it truly felt. It was a time everyone dreaded. A time when most people in town walked around dragging their feet, looking as cold and dead inside as a chilly winter day.

It was everyone's least favorite season. At dinner each night, the family held hands and prayed for an easy winter. This time of the year wasn't just hard on people, it was tough on the animals as well. Pa, James, and Adam stored hay and corn to feed the animals. They threw fresh straw on the barn floor in hopes of keeping them warm, should it be a bad winter. There was only one cow, four horses, several chickens, and twelve goats, and each one was important in its own way.

Anna and Virginia helped Ma make fresh butter and cheese

with the milk from the cow as well as cheese from goat's milk. They gather eggs from the chickens, but sometimes during cold winter months the family settled for porridge for breakfast. For lunch and dinner, they made stews from garden vegetables and whatever meat they had on hand. Rabbit, deer, wild duck, turkey, bear, and, on occasion, they would have chicken, but chickens were kept mainly for their eggs.

Come Spring, Pa allowed a couple of hens to set. Anna looked forward to seeing new baby chicks running around the yard. She especially loved baby goats. Pa repeated the same thing every year. "Anna, do not name the animals." He knew he was fighting a losing battle yet felt obligated to remind her. Those words played over in Anna's mind, yet she couldn't help herself. She always chose the runt of the bunch and secretly named it. At least, she thought it was a secret, but Pa and Ma knew. They figured if they said nothing to Anna, then she couldn't protest much when it came time to slaughter the poor animal.

Ma also knew Pa had a big heart and would never hurt any animal that Anna named. Each year, Pa hunted, and they ate whatever he brought home. This year, he and his friend Nathaniel Wright were going hunting, along with James and Adam. Whatever game was brought home would be split between the two families, although it was just Nathaniel and his wife Gracie. They never had children of their own.

Last year, Gracie came to visit just before her twenty-sixth birthday. She told Ma she had given up hope of having children.

"Come now, Gracie, don't feel that way," Ma had said.

"I'm sorry." Gracie shook her head. "I can't help it." She took a seat at the kitchen table. "I fear I'm getting too old; I'll be twenty-six next week." She stared at her hands folded on her lap.

"There's still time." Ma handed her a glass of apple cider.

"Nathaniel and I have prayed for a child every night for seven years," Gracie said sadly. "I don't think God is listening." Her tear-filled eyes met Ma's.

"He's listening, I'm sure of it." Ma took a seat next to her, choking back her own tears. "I'll be praying for you both." She handed Gracie a handkerchief.

Gracie gently took it and placed her hand on top of the table. "Thank you. You always have a way of cheering me up." She forced a smile.

"Just have faith. God will see you through." Ma squeezed Gracie's hand.

Gracie nodded as she dabbed the moisture from her eyes. "Thank you. You're a wonderful friend."

Ma and Gracie kept in touch over the summer. Ma always made it a point to stop for a visit whenever she and Pa went to town.

CHAPTER ELEVEN

WOUNDED BEAR
October 17, 1764

The Wrights came to visit. Pa and Nathaniel were excited about their hunting trip with James and Adam. Gracie and Nathaniel arrived just before dark and were spending the night so the men could get an early start the next morning. It was unusually warm for October —at least during the day. Mornings were a bit chilly, but no one complained. Well, no one except the men. They hoped for snow, as that would make it easier to track deer.

Warm days like this allowed the ladies more time to catch up on things around the house. Ma had made sure the house got an extra good scrubbing to prepare for Gracie's visit. She'd be staying until the men returned, and Ma was ecstatic about it. It wasn't often that she had visitors.

Early the next morning, the men awoke and gathered provisions for the hunting trip.

"Well, ladies, we'll be home in a couple days." Pa hugged Ma and she kissed him for luck.

Nathaniel took Gracie by the hand and led her outside onto the front porch. The cold morning air cut through her. She shivered, holding her shawl tight around her. Nathaniel pulled her into his arms. She snuggled against him, taking in the warmth of his body. He placed two fingers under her chin and tilted her face up. He gently placed a kiss on her lips. "I'll see you in two or three days." Her eyes reflected sadness. He hated being away from her.

"We'll be back sooner if we get something. Until then, enjoy your visit." Gracie nodded and gave him one last hug.

As they stepped back into the house, they were met at the door by an anxious Adam and James. Sixteen-year-old Adam could hardly contain his excitement; this was his first real hunting trip, complete with camping alongside the men. He'd hunted with his father in the woods behind their house, but this was different. They would be staying in Nathaniel's hunting cabin on top of Blackburn Mountain.

Nathaniel built the cabin as a wedding present for Gracie, but she didn't want to live so far from town. She feared being in the mountains alone while Nathaniel worked. Nathaniel wanted to make his new bride happy, so he purchased property near town and built a cabin there. They enjoyed having a mountain getaway when they needed a break from all the hustle and bustle in town.

The men gathered their guns and provisions and off they went. They decided to go into town for a few extra supplies before leaving for the cabin. Upon arriving in town, Nathaniel noticed a flyer nailed next to the tavern door. He ripped the flyer off the wall, folded it, and slipped it into his pocket. James noticed that whatever was on that paper irritated Nathaniel greatly, but he said nothing. James figured that whatever it is, Nathaniel would reveal it when he's ready.

After making their purchases, they met the sheriff on their way out of the mercantile.

"Hello, Daniel." The sheriff nodded. "Nathaniel. Where are you boys off to?"

"Hunting trip. We'll be staying at my cabin," Nathaniel answered.

Daniel placed a hand on Adam's shoulder. "This will be Adam's first hunting trip," he said proudly.

"Good luck, son." The sheriff nodded at Adam before turning his attention to Pa and Nathaniel. "Where's your cabin located?" he glanced around as though it were a secret.

"Top of Blackburn Mountain. Why?" Nathaniel asked curiously.

The sheriff pulled off his hat and ran his fingers through his thinning gray hair before placing it back on his head. "Listen, Daniel, ya'll be careful up there." He lowered his voice. "There's a wounded bear on the rampage."

"Did you say wounded bear?" Nathaniel stepped closer to the sheriff, hoping that he misunderstood.

"That's right. It mauled Ben Wilson this morning." The sheriff glanced in the direction of the doctor's office. "His brother brought him in."

"Is he all right?" Pa asked.

"I'm not sure, Daniel," the sheriff said sadly. "Doc Burns is working on him now." The sheriff pulled his hat off and held it in front of him. "It's not looking good," he said sadly.

"He's a good man," Pa said soothingly.

"Yes, Daniel, he is," the sheriff agreed. "If it weren't for the natives, he wouldn't be here."

"Natives?" Pa's head shot up.

"The Shawnee tribe. They mended his wound and placed a piece of bear skin over it." The sheriff shook his head. "Of all things, a bear tried to take his life, and now the skin of another may save it."

Pa and Nathaniel removed their hats and placed them to their chests as a gesture of respect. "I'll keep Ben in prayer," Pa said softly.

"As will I." Nathaniel nodded in agreement. "May God be with him."

"Thank you both. I'm sure his family would appreciate it."

"We'll pray as well." James had overheard the conversation; he motioned toward Adam as he stepped next to Pa.

Adam was talking to one of the local boys and was oblivious to the conversation. He strolled over and stood next to James.

"What'd I miss?" he asked nonchalantly.

"God bless you all." The sheriff tipped his hat. "Be extremely careful up there." He looked toward the mountains.

"We will. Thank you, sheriff." Nathaniel turned to Pa. "What do you think? Should we take a chance with the boys?

"Chance what?" Adam knitted his brows. "What's going on?"

"There's an injured bear roaming the mountain." Pa spun his hat around and around in his hands, contemplating what he should do.

"If the bear's injured, then we have a better chance at killing it." Adam thought it was a brilliant assumption.

Pa shook his head. "No, son. A wounded bear is far more dangerous. You both will stay close to me." He turned his head and looked at Nathaniel.

"You're Pa is right. We won't be taking any chances."

"If there's anything we can do to help, just let us know." Pa turned to face the sheriff.

"Thanks, Daniel, the men are getting a hunting party together." The sheriff shifted position. "That bear must be killed before anyone else is hurt."

"Let the hunters know they're welcome to stay with us at my cabin. There's plenty of room." Nathaniel stared in the direction of the doctor's office. "They'll be a lot safer there."

The sheriff patted Nathaniel on the shoulder. "That's very kind. You can tell them yourself, if you like." He pointed down the road. "They're meeting at the church as we speak."

They made their way to the church and met several men who were geared up and ready for a bear hunt. Once inside, they took a seat in the back pew. The church had twenty-four voracious men. The sheriff lumbered in and stepped up behind the pulpit.

"All right, everyone please take a seat." The sheriff motioned with one hand. The few men left standing found a seat and sat down. "As you all know," the sheriff began. "A bear attacked Ben this morning. His brother Billy Bob shot it, and now we have a wounded bear on the loose."

"I can take it down single-handed," one man yelled.

"Now, Sam, we don't need anyone else hurt. No one needs to be a hero." The sheriff glared at him. I want everyone to divide up into groups of five, and for God's sake, stay together."

"I'm going with Sam," another man shouted. "He's the best bear hunter around." A few other men agreed, and soon Sam had five men in his group. Everyone else decided amongst themselves until there were four groups of five, not including Pa, Nathaniel, James, and Adam. "That leaves the four of you." the sheriff said. "We need one more man to even it out."

"I'll go," a voice spoke as the church door opened wide. Everyone turned to find Johnny Carlin standing there with his hands in the front pocket of his trousers.

"I'm not sure about this. You're awfully young, son," the sheriff replied.

"I'm sixteen, same age as Adam," Johnny reasoned.

"Let the boy go," Sam shouted. "If he causes trouble, we'll feed him to the bear."

"This is no time for jesting. My husband's fighting for his life because of that vicious beast." No one noticed Ben's wife standing behind Johnny. He stepped aside, allowing her to enter. She swiped at a tear that escaped her eye and rolled down her cheek. "I want that bear dead," Mrs. Wilson spoke through gritted teeth.

"I'm truly sorry," Sam stated. "We'll not come back until that bear has paid for what he's done to Ben."

Johnny's hands remained deep in his pockets. He began rocking on his heels, waiting for an answer.

"Do you have your Pa's permission?" Daniel inquired.

"Yes, he does." Mr. Carlin hobbled through the door of the church. "I'd go myself if I didn't have this bum leg, and I trust Johnny's judgment."

"It's settled, Johnny. You'll ride with us," Nathaniel answered.

"I best be getting back to check on Ben." Mrs. Wilson turned to leave.

"Mrs. Wilson." Adam ran after her. She stopped at the foot of the steps and turned her head. her eyes welled with tears.

"Tell Ben . . . Uh, Mr. Wilson, he's in my prayers."

Mrs. Wilson smiled faintly, gently nodded her head, and then walked away. Adam slipped back inside the church and stood next to Pa. Pa smiled proudly and placed a hand on Adam's shoulder.

"Everyone, settle down." The sheriff knocked on the pulpit with his knuckles. "Nathaniel has an announcement to make." He held his hand high and motioned for Nathaniel.

Nathaniel sauntered up next to the sheriff and shook

his hand. "Thank you, Sheriff." He then turned to address everyone. "I have a cabin on that mountain," he said loudly. "There's room for everyone, but make sure to bring your own bedroll." He stared out at the crowd. "I figure we'll be safer inside, especially at night."

Everyone agreed, and the church filled with chatter. "He's right," said one man to the guy next to him. "Very generous of him to offer," said another.

"I suppose that's all." Nathaniel took a step back, turning the meeting back over to the sheriff.

"Is there anything else you'd like to say before I close the meeting?" The sheriff cocked his head.

"No, sir." Nathaniel shook his head.

"Thank you for your generous offer." The sheriff shook Nathaniel's hand before continuing. Discuss the details when you reach the cabin." He patted Nathanial on the back. "You men can decide amongst yourselves which group hunts first. Agreed?" He scanned the group for confirmation.

The men agreed that it was a good plan and were grateful for the offer of the cabin. Everyone except Sam. "I came to hunt that beast, not sit in a cabin gossiping like an old woman," he grumbled as Nathaniel approached.

"You, being the best, your group should hunt first." Nathaniel stopped next to Sam. It was then he noticed how much taller his six-foot-two frame was to Sam's five-eight.

Sam was a stocky man with a long gray beard. He was the oldest of the group, but with age came wisdom and experience.

Sam looked up at Nathaniel and nodded. He ran his fingers over his beard, smiled, and spoke. "You've grown to be a fine young man."

Nathaniel stared into the gray eyes and the tired, wrinkled

face of the man, who once was his father's best friend. His mother said life took the two friends in different directions. His father told him differently. Sam secretly fell for his mother and couldn't handle the idea of her choosing his best friend over him. They argued and harsh words were spoken before each went their separate ways. Nathaniel couldn't imagine holding a grudge for so long.

"Alrighty, men, saddle up. Time to hunt us a bear," Sam shouted.

Everyone headed out the door hooting and hollering as they went.

Ben's wife left to check on his progress. The worry and stress made her appear much older than her forty-four years.

"God be with her," James said as he watched her cross the street on her way back to Doc Burns' office.

"I feel bad for her." Adam watched her step into the doctor's office, closing the door behind her. He wondered how ol' Ben was doing.

The men stopped their horses in front of the doctor's office. They took their hats off and placed them over their chests. Daniel led everyone in prayer for Ben's recovery.

"Dear Lord, you see our friend Ben. Lord, he's in a mighty bad way, so if you could see fit to heal him and allow him several more years here with his family, we'd be mighty grateful. We ask you in Jesus' name. Thank you. Amen." Daniel placed his hat back on his head.

"Let's find that bear!" Sam shouted.

Everyone began hooting and hollering yet again. They turned their horses and rode in the direction of Blackburn Mountain, each man secretly hoping to be the one to take down the bear.

CHAPTER TWELVE

STACY ARRIVES

"We'll stop here for now." Sarah laid the book on her lap. Running her fingers over the pages, she imagined what life must have been like then. "We'll pick up where we left off tomorrow."

"I hate to stop now." Grams yawned. "I am getting sleepy, so I suppose I'll have to wait."

Sarah kissed her cheek. "Goodnight. I love you."

"Goodnight, sweetie. I love you too." Grams rolled over onto her side and closed her eyes.

Sarah turned off the light, leaving the door slightly ajar. She made her way to the kitchen and finished cleaning up. She settled into a long hot bath and called Stacy.

"Hey, girlfriend, what's up?" Stacy answered on the first ring.

"Not much. Just missing my bestie." Sarah ran her toes over the bar of soap sitting on the corner of the bathtub.

"Good, I'm glad you said that." Stacy paused. "Because . . . I'm on my way to visit and I'll see you tomorrow," she said excitedly.

"Are you serious?" Sarah squealed with delight. She sat up, accidentally knocking the bar of soap in the water.

"Would I lie to you?" Stacy shook her head. "On second

thought, don't answer that."

"Wait! did you say you're on your way?"

"Yes, I'm at a hotel in North Carolina," Stacy said drowsily. "According to my GPS, I'll be there in four and a half hours."

"Call me in the morning when you leave the hotel."

"I will, bright and early." Stacy yawned. "Have a good night."

"Goodnight." Sarah stared at the phone for a moment before climbing out of the tub. She grabbed a towel from the rack, dried herself, and then slipped into her nightgown. She brushed her teeth and quickly ran a comb through her hair. She lay in bed and closed her eyes hoping to fall fast asleep, but no matter how hard she tried, sleep wouldn't come.

Although she was excited to see Stacy, her mind kept wandering to the book. She considered reading a few more chapters but decided to wait and find out what happened next along with Grams. Sarah had trouble sleeping. The day's events played over in her mind, especially the things Jimmy revealed to her. She refused to believe a word he said—at least, that's what she kept telling herself. She wished she knew why he seemed so familiar to her. She tossed and turned for several hours before sleep finally came.

Early the next morning, Sarah awoke to the sound of tires hitting the pavement. She jumped out of bed, ran to the window, and peered out. Jimmy and his crew had arrived, ready to begin construction on her grandmother's house. Sarah couldn't take her eyes off Jimmy. The blue jeans he wore hugged his hips nicely and the dark blue tee-shirt looked great against his dark skin and hair.

Oh my, he's so handsome. Sarah's heart leapt in her throat when Jimmy looked up at her and waved. She waved and opened the curtains, allowing the warm sunshine to pour into the room. She stepped away from the window and searched through her summer clothes. She slipped on her favorite blue jean shorts and a pink tank top, brushed her hair, and applied a little makeup before hurrying downstairs to check on her grandmother.

Upon reaching the bottom of the staircase, she heard dishes clanging in the kitchen and the smell of bacon wafted into the room. Sarah strolled into the kitchen to find Grams holding a plateful of scrambled eggs and bacon. She took it to the dining room and put it on the table.

"You're up early." Grams hurried back to the kitchen.

"You should've woken me up." Sarah yawned.

"You're a growing young woman." Grams turned with a plate of buttered toast in her hands. "You need your rest." She placed the plate on the table next to the rest of the food. "Besides, I feel fit as a fiddle." Sarah smiled to herself at her grandmother's use of words.

"We have a special guest arriving today." Sarah picked up a stack of plates from the counter and took them to the dining room.

"Let me guess. You've invited the whole work crew to breakfast." She winked.

"No, I was leaving that to you." Grams set a pitcher of orange juice next to the toast. "Well, get going, before everything gets cold." She took a seat at the end of the table. "Wait, did you say we have a special guest coming?" She stood, untied her apron, and hung it on a hook next to the dining room door.

"Yes, Stacy's coming for a visit," Sarah said cheerfully.

"That's wonderful. It'll be nice having you both here." Grams hugged Sarah. "When can we expect her?"

"She's at a hotel in North Carolina. She's supposed to call me before she leaves,"

"What, you don't think she'll call?" Grams asked.

"Don't forget, this is Stacy we're talking about."

"I guess you're right. That girl would forget her head if it wasn't attached." Grams rushed back into the kitchen to get the silverware.

Sarah felt the back pocket of her shorts. "Shoot. I forgot my phone in my room. I'll be right back." She took the stairs two at a time, grabbed her phone, and then hurried back down. She contemplated riding the stair railing down the way she did as a child, but decided it wasn't such a good idea. She jumped over the last two steps and landed at the foot of the stairs.

"Lord have mercy, girl," Grams gasped. "What on earth has gotten into you?"

"Just going to invite the crew to breakfast, like you asked." Sarah turned in the direction of the back door.

Once outside she found the men unloading the work truck. She strolled over to them. Jimmy had his back to her and was giving instructions on where he wanted the crew to begin.

"Hey, guys, sorry to interrupt." Sarah stepped next to Jimmy. Her heart leapt in her throat as his gaze met hers. *Oh my gosh, he's so handsome*. "Uh . . . Grams made breakfast for everyone." She glanced at each one of the crew members, but avoided making eye contact with Jimmy again for fear he could read her mind.

"Well, men, you're in for a treat." Jimmy turned to his crew. "Her grandmother is a fantastic cook."

"Great, I'm starving." Robert jumped down from the back of the truck. Sarah noticed that he was the youngest of the bunch. His red curly hair bounced as his feet hit the ground. "Come on, guys. Grandmothers are the best cooks."

Sarah soon realized that what he lacked in looks he made up in personality. She wondered if he was the class clown in school. He grabbed one of the older men by the head and gave it a good rub with his knuckles.

"Settle down, Robert, if you want to make it to age twenty." The older man chuckled.

"Ha-ha, aren't you funny?" Robert shook his head and took a step back.

They followed Sarah to the back door leading to the kitchen. She stopped on the porch and motioned for them to go inside. "The dining room's through the kitchen on the right." She pointed. "Go on in and have a seat."

The men strolled in, sniffing the air and rubbing their bellies as they made their way to the table. The smell of bacon and sausage filled the air. "Lord have mercy. Is that hot buttered biscuits?" one of the men asked.

"It sure is," Grams said happily. "Hot buttered buttermilk biscuits." She set a plate full of homemade biscuits on the dining room table. She loved having a houseful of hungry people to cook for, and she especially loved the compliments she received. Sarah turned upon hearing a car horn. Stacy's car rolled to a stop behind the work truck. Sarah smiled and ran to meet her.

"You were supposed to call me before you left the hotel," Sarah scolded.

"I left earlier than expected." Stacy exited the car and retrieved a suitcase from the backseat. "Besides, I didn't want to wake you. You need all the beauty sleep you can get," she teased. She set the suitcase on the pavement at Sarah's feet.

"Ha-ha, aren't you funny?" Sarah poked Stacy in the ribs as she leaned in the car to grab her purse. Sarah knew how much

Stacy hated being tickled,

"Aaaah!" Stacy screamed. "Okay, okay, I take that back." She giggled.

"You're forgiven, this time." Sarah hugged Stacy. She noticed a movement out of the corner of her eye. She looked toward the house and saw Jimmy waiting on the back porch. The others didn't waste any time heading to the dining room, with Grams leading the way.

"Oh my, is that him?" Stacy nodded in Jimmy's direction.

Sarah bit her bottom lip and nodded.

"I can see why you're attracted to him." She threw her purse over her shoulder and picked up two suitcases, leaving the remaining two for Sarah. "He's cute."

Sarah gave a quick sideways glance at Jimmy. A chill ran down her spine. She shivered and her cheeks grew pink when she noticed Stacy watching her, but she said nothing. Sarah picked up the remaining two suitcases and made her way toward the house. Stacy followed.

"Behave yourself and don't embarrass me," Sarah whispered.

"Who me?" Stacy said playfully. "I'll do my best, but if he says one word—"

"I'm serious," Sarah whispered through gritted teeth.

"All right, I'll behave." Stacy crossed her fingers behind her back.

"Jimmy, this is my friend Stacy. Stacy, this is Jimmy."

"It's a pleasure to meet you." Jimmy held out his hand.

"Nice meeting you." She shook his hand. "And I happen to be her best friend." Stacy cocked her head toward Sarah.

"We'll see," Sarah said playfully in a sing-song voice as she walked backwards toward the kitchen door.

"Breakfast is getting cold." Grams appeared in the doorway

behind Sarah. "Stacy! It's so good to see you." Grams hugged her.

"I'm happy to see you too, Grams." Stacy took a step back, tilted her head up, and closed her eyes, taking in the aroma. "Oh my, breakfast smells fantastic."

"You're just in time." Grams smiled proudly. "Come on in." She stepped aside.

"I only came to see Grams and for some of her home cooking." Stacy playfully stuck her tongue at Sarah.

"Whatever." Sarah rolled her eyes and then put the suitcase by the kitchen door.

"Come on, Jimmy, better eat while you can, because Stacy eats like a horse." Sarah winked.

"Ha, I could tell you a few stories about Sarah that would make your head spin," Stacy stated.

"Now you've piqued my curiosity." Jimmy smiled at Stacy.

"All right, Stacy, you win. This time," Sarah chortled.

"Speaking of stories," Grams interrupted. "I can't wait to get back to the book." Her brow furrowed. "We are going to finish it tonight, aren't we?"

"Yes, of course we are." Sarah took a seat at the table next to Stacy.

Jimmy introduced his crew before taking a seat. Grams insisted he sit at the end of the table next to Sarah. Stacy grinned mischievously at Sarah, who shot her with a warning look in return. Everyone had a lovely breakfast and listened intently as Sarah and Grams took turns telling the story about the handwritten book found in the old foundation.

When breakfast was over, Sarah and Stacy washed the dishes and cleaned the kitchen while the men began work on the house. Sarah insisted that Grams relax on the back porch swing. She protested at first, but finally gave in.

CHAPTER THIRTEEN

STACY MEETS ROBBIE

"I'd like to join the two of you when you read the rest of the book," Stacy said as she wiped the counter.

"That'd be great. I read to her before she turns in for the night." Sarah finished sweeping. She placed three glasses on the counter. "Would you like something to drink? We have tea, lemonade, or soda."

"Lemonade sounds nice." Stacy took the ice tray from the freezer and filled the glasses with ice.

Sarah chose sweet tea for herself and Grams, then the two ladies headed out to join her on the back porch.

"Here ya go." Sarah handed Grams the glass of tea.

"Thank you, sweetie." Grams scooted over and patted the seat next to her. "Sit down and take a load off."

Sarah and Stacy sat next to her on the swing and began reminiscing.

"How was your trip, dear?" Grams sipped her tea.

"It was a nice drive. It was . . . uh . . . ." Stacy paused as she watched Robert Walk past on his way to the truck. She smiled and turned her head as he fastened a tool belt around his waist.

Sarah nudged her. "Forget it, he's too young," she whispered.

"A girl can look." She fidgeted. "How old is he?" she whispered back.

“I heard one of the men say he’s nineteen.”

“I don’t want to date someone younger than me, so I guess friends it is then.” Stacy made a pouty face.

“I’ve known Robby’s family from the time he was born, and if I’m not mistaken, he’s the same age as the two of you,” Grams said.

“How is it that you know him and I don’t? Sarah asked, puzzled.

“You remember Robby.” Grams turned sideways in her seat. Sarah knitted her brows and slightly shook her head.

“He used to pull your hair in church, and once he stuck gum in it.”

“No way!” Sarah gasped. “That’s rude Robby?” She stood, her mouth agape.

“The one and only.” Grams nodded.

“Why didn’t he acknowledge that he knows me, and why didn’t he say anything when they referred to him as nineteen?” Sarah asked.

“That’s something you should ask him.” Grams set her glass of tea on the table next to the swing.

“I’ll be sure to do just that.” Stacy used it as an excuse to speak to Robert. She stood and raced down the steps, slowing to a brisk walk when she drew closer behind him. He turned around, almost bumping into her.

“Sorry, I didn’t see you.” He blushed and ran his fingers through his curly hair.

“So, Robert, I have a question for you.” Stacy crossed her arms over her chest. She had a habit of doing that when she was serious.

Robert felt his body tense up. He wasn’t used to females

approaching him. He relaxed when Stacy smiled and gently smacked him on the arm. "Lighten up, Robby." She giggled. "I just want to know how old you are." She pulled her hair over her shoulder and twirled it with her finger in her usual flirty way. Robert shifted from one foot to the other. "I . . . I'm twenty-six," he stammered.

"Perfect, do you have a girlfriend?"

"N-no. No one special." He rubbed his palms down his jeans. "Ahem, I mean no, I don't have a girlfriend." He tried sounding more confident.

"You're cute. Maybe we can take a drive after you get off work." Before Robert had a chance to answer, Stacy turned on her heel, slung her long hair over her shoulder, and jogged the few feet back to Grams and Sarah, leaving Robert standing there dumbfounded and grinning to himself.

"I see that went really well." Sarah snickered as Robert rushed stiffly past the three of them, his gaze straight ahead. Stacy watched him until he disappeared. She decided it was best to wait and talk to him alone. She didn't want to embarrass him in front of anyone.

The noise from the sawing and hammering began. The three ladies retreated inside where it was a little quieter. Grams took her drink to the living room and sat on the sofa.

"I'll show Stacy to her room." Sarah picked up the suitcase she had left by the kitchen door and ascended the stairs. Stacy followed. "Your room's next to mine." They entered the huge bedroom. "All the woodwork is original. It's hand carved."

"This is a gorgeous room." Stacy stared in awe. The hardwood floors and the hand carved wood framing the window, doors and walls were polished to a shine. "Wow! This bed is incredible." She ran her hand over the massive headboard. "Is this handcrafted as well?" She sat on the edge of the bed, running her hand over the quilt. "This blue and white quilt makes the room pop. Is it handmade?"

"Yes, it is. Grams made it years ago," Sarah said proudly. "Along with the matching pillow shams and the curtains on the window. It has its own bathroom, as you can see." Sarah opened the bathroom door.

Stacy stepped in and gasped. "Wow, even the bathroom is lovely. You could turn this place into a bed and breakfast." The smile quickly left her face when she saw Sarah's expression. "On second thought, maybe not." Stacy ducked past Sarah. She lifted her suitcase and swung it onto the bed, unsnapped the latches, and flung open the lid before turning to Sarah. "Why are you so touchy about this house?"

"I'm not . . . I mean . . . I'm sorry. It's just . . . ." Sarah paced. "This house is all my grandmother has left and she loves it so," Sarah's voice trailed off. That answer sounded lame, even to her. "Fine, Jimmy mentioned this place would make a great bed and breakfast." She stopped pacing and plopped down on the bed. "This house," she looked towards the ceiling then back at Stacy. "This is all we have left." Her eyes filled with sadness. There are so many happy memories in this place.

"Yeah, not to mention memories from the past." Stacy sat on the bed beside her. "Did you say this house has been in the family for generations?"

"Yes, it has." Sarah nodded. "Since the mid-seventeen hundreds. Which reminds me, I can't wait to get back to the book and find out what happens." Sarah stood.

"I have an awesome idea." Stacy's face lit up with excitement. "We could take Grams to a park or someplace quiet and read from the old book, and we'll just relax."

"That sounds wonderful," Sarah stated. "Let's run it by Grams and see how she feels about it."

CHAPTER FOURTEEN

GRAMS' DAY AT THE RIVER

They raced downstairs and found Grams resting on the couch with a word search book. She loved working puzzles and playing word games, especially when she grew bored. She peered quizzically over the rim of her glasses as the two stood in front of her.

"Grams, how would you like to take a ride to the park or the river, relax, and find out what happens next in the old book?" Sarah asked.

Grams slid the glasses up on the bridge of her nose, closed the word search book, and held it on her lap. "I'd love that." She placed the book on the coffee table. "In fact, I was just wondering about the old book myself." She slowly stood up.

"Stacy, would you mind helping Grams to the car while I grab some lawn chairs from the storage building?"

"No, problem." Stacy placed an arm around Grams. "Come on, Grams, let me help you to the car." Stacy and Grams walked slowly toward the kitchen, out the back door, and toward the car. Stacy helped her into the passenger seat, while Sarah retrieved the printed copy of the book. She placed it on the front seat next to Grams and then rushed off and returned carrying three lawn chairs. She placed them in the car trunk.

She then climbed into the driver's seat. After fastening her seatbelt, she started the car and off they went.

"I forgot to tell Jimmy and the crew that we're leaving." Grams peered out the window.

"It's all right. I told them when I got the lawn chairs from the storage shed," Sarah said reassuringly as she pulled onto the road.

Stacy noticed that something was bothering Sarah. "Okay, spill it." Stacy scooted between the seats and cocked her head toward Sarah.

"Excuse me?" Sarah gave Stacy a quick glance and then turned her eyes on the road.

"Don't play innocent with me." Stacy gave Sarah a little nudge.

"Something's bothering you, and I think I know what—or should I say who—it is. Now spill it."

"I overheard Jimmy having the same phone conversation he'd had before about, you know, selling a house." She nodded toward her grandmother, hoping Stacy would take the hint.

"I may be old, but my hearing is just fine." Grams fidgeted with the strap on her purse. "I deserve to know what's going on, especially if it's anything to do with me."

Sarah looked at Stacy through the rearview mirror. Stacy nodded.

"I believe Jimmy is trying to swindle you out of your house." Sarah snapped her head toward her grandmother to see her reaction.

To her surprise, instead of anger, Grams snickered.

"What's so funny?" Sarah asked.

"He's not trying to swindle anybody." Grams straightened her blouse. "I'm not naïve. I don't sign anything without reading it first. I have a will. Everything goes to you when I'm gone."

"I know, but—"

"No buts about it," Grams cut Sarah off. "If you have a problem with Jimmy, then you need to take it up with him."

"I agree wholeheartedly." Stacy scooted back in her seat and fastened her seatbelt.

"If he's not trying to get his hands on our house . . . ." Sarah paused. "Then whose home is he after?"

They rode in silence for several minutes as they drove past Serenity's café. Grams didn't have to ask where they were headed, but Stacy, on the other hand, had no idea. They pulled to a stop at the campground where Sarah had taken Jimmy for a picnic the day before.

Everyone exited the car. Stacy and Grams walked to the riverbank while Sarah pulled the chairs from the trunk of the car. She sat them next to the tree and helped Grams sit.

They sat quietly, watching the water slowly flow downstream. The crystal-clear water sparkled in the sunlight. They could see every pebble on the river bottom. A couple of rainbow trout swam by, doing a gracefully zigging and zagging as they chased one another upstream.

A gentle breeze blew through the trees, carrying with it the sweet fragrance of Dogwood blossoms. Grams laid back on the lawn chair, breathed deeply, and closed her eyes.

"I've always loved this place." She opened one eye and looked at Sarah. This was your grandfather's favorite fishing and camping spot." She sighed.

"I remember, and it's mine too," Sarah said sadly.

"When you were a little girl—" Grams sat up straight. "You used to dream of this place. You talked in your sleep, ya know."

She leaned back into her chair.

"Oh, I've got to hear this story," Stacy said.

Grams looked over at Sarah for her approval.

Sarah nodded. "I'd like to hear this myself."

"When you were around three- or four-years old, you had a reoccurring dream almost every night." Both their interests piqued, Sarah and Stacy sat on the edge of their chairs. "You dreamed you were a young woman having a picnic by the river with a handsome gentleman. Something horrible happened and he died—shot, if I recall correctly." She sat up in her chair. "I'll never forget those Godawful, gut-wrenching screams." She gazed at the water; her eyes welled with tears.

Sarah and Stacy sat quietly, both choking back the lump forming in their throats.

"That's strange," Sarah whispered.

"How old was she when the dreams stopped?" Stacy leaned forward on her chair with her arms crossed over her lap.

"I believe she was six years old." Grams patted Sarah's knee. "Yes, it was strange."

"No, I mean . . . ." Sarah stared intently at the ground. "I brought Jimmy here for a picnic," she continued. "He said this place seemed familiar to him."

"Maybe he had a dream like yours," Stacy said cheerfully. "Come to think of it," she added, "your dream came true—or at least part of it has."

"Excuse me, that's not exactly how my dream went." Sarah knitted her brows. "At least, I don't think it is."

"Sounds like it to me," Stacy continued. "You know, handsome man, picnic by the river." She tapped a finger on her chin and looked toward the treetops. "Only he hasn't, well, you know." She shook her head.

"How about we do what we came her for and read from the book?" Sarah asked pointedly.

"Okay. I'll get it." Stacy ran to the car and hurried back with the printed pages. She handed them to Sarah.

"Thank you." Sarah smiled as she opened the book and began reading from where they left off.

CHAPTER FIFTEEN

LAUGHTER'S THE BEST MEDICINE

Virginia and Anna were cooking an enormous pot of stew made from venison that Nathaniel and Gracie brought as a gift. Ma started to protest, but Anna insisted that she and Virginia cook while Ma and Gracie relaxed.

"Gracie doesn't need to overexert herself since she's with child." Anna smiled.

"Anna!" Virginia gasped. She grabbed Anna by the arm and led her to the pantry. "What would possess you to say such a thing?" Virginia asked in a low angry tone. "You know she is unable to bear children."

Anna's face grew crimson. She ran back to the living room. "I, I'm terribly sorry." She fidgeted with her apron. "It's just that you've put on a little weight." She fumbled for the right words.

Virginia rolled her eyes. "Quiet, Anna, you're making it worse."

"She's right, I have put on a few pounds." Gracie smiled sweetly. "Nathaniel's an excellent cook, as you can see." She patted her stomach.

"Why has Nathaniel been doing all the cooking?" Anna inquired.

Virginia drew her eyes down at Anna. "That's none of your concern."

"I'm just curious," Anna said in her defense.

"He hasn't been doing all the cooking," Gracie corrected. "He's been helping since I've been ill."

"You've been sick?" Ma's eyes widened. "Have you seen a doctor?"

"It's nothing. I'm much better now." Gracie sat in the rocking chair in front of the fireplace. Ma took a seat in the chair next to her.

"How long have you been ill?" Ma asked.

"It's been about two months, mostly in the evenings." She stared into the fire. "I believe it was stress."

"What could possibly have made you that stressed?" Anna blurted.

"My parents came for a visit," Gracie said in a low tone. "They were here a month and had to return home in Pennsylvania. That was two months ago." She sobbed. "I miss them terribly."

"Anna, Virginia, go check on dinner." Ma shooed them away.

The two took the hint and hurried from the room.

"Gracie, I need to ask you a personal question, if you don't mind." Ma scooted to the edge of her chair and leaned toward Gracie.

"What is it?" Gracie's voice quivered. "Do you think I'm going to die?" She stood.

"No, but it may feel like it later." Ma chuckled. "Sorry." She placed her hand to her mouth.

"What's wrong with me?" Gracie shouted, fear resounding in her voice as she dropped back into the chair.

Anna and Virginia came racing into the room, stopping in the doorway, their eyes darting from Ma to Gracie.

"Well, think about it," Ma said excitedly. "You're putting on weight, you've been sick for two months." She stood and paced back and forth in front of Gracie. "Even though it's an assumption," Ma said to herself.

"Just tell me, please." Gracie pleaded.

"I do believe that you're with child." Ma sat back down and patted Gracie's hand.

Gracie's expression turned from fear to shock. "Pardon? You think I'm . . . having a baby?" she stuttered as she sat back in the rocking chair. "That's a horrible thing to jest about."

"Think about it," Ma reasoned. "When did you last have your courses?" she asked. "Surely you know if you missed your courses each month."

"I've been so distraught over my mother and father leaving that I never paid no mind." Gracie thought about it. A few moments passed, and then her eyes grew wide as she leapt. "I haven't had one for—" She paused. "Well, for at least three and a half to four months."

"That explains the weight gain and the pudgy belly," Anna stated.

"Oh, do you truly believe it so?" Gracie placed a hand on her stomach.

"Well, that's what we're going to find out." Ma turned to Anna and Virginia. "One of you go fetch me some wheat and barley seeds." Both girls hurried to the pantry. Each raced back with the seeds.

"Here ya go. I picked barley because I believe she's having a boy." Anna handed Ma the seeds.

"I chose wheat for a girl." Virginia smiled smugly at Anna.

"All you need to do is put urine on each and whichever one sprouts first means you're with child and will reveal if you're having a boy or a girl." Ma placed the seeds in separate pieces of cloth and tied each with thread. "The long string is barley, and the short one contains wheat." She handed them to Gracie, who nervously took them,

"Where should I do this?" She stood.

"There's a chamber pot in the guest room. Virginia will show you where it is." Ma nodded at Virginia.

"Yes, of course, come with me." Virginia led the way through the living room to the guest room, located on the left. "I'll leave you to it." She pulled the door shut behind her and headed back to the kitchen, where Ma and Anna anxiously waited.

"Well, girls, we'll not get anything done just standing here." Ma stepped in front of the cookstove. She smiled to herself when she thought of Pa and his scheming ways to keep the secret that he had purchased her this new Franklin ten-plate stove.

Benjamin Franklin improved the design of the six-plate stove and created what he called the "Pennsylvania Fireplace"—the stove Ma now owned. In Franklin's improved version, ten plates of cast iron were used. Four plates formed the oven, and he added hinged doors. Smoke passed through the opening on either side and out a pipe. Ma was the first in the area to own one. Ladies came to visit from all over town, just to see it.

Although Ma enjoyed the company, she'd never been one to brag or boast. She taught that to all her children. In Ma's words, *Never brag or boast about anything, for the Lord surely giveth and the Lord can taketh away.*

She opened the stove and poked the embers. Smoke billowed out the chimney like a ghost trying to escape its prison. The fire crackled and popped as she threw in a couple blocks of firewood. Flames danced around the wood, roaring and licking at it like a wild animal attacking its prey. She replaced the cover and turned when she heard Gracie behind her.

"Sorry for taking so long." Gracie apologized. "I was saying a little prayer." She rubbed the palms of her hands down her dress.

"As was I." Ma hugged her. "Please sit." She motioned toward the parlor.

Gracie nodded, stepped into the parlor, and took a seat, followed by Ma and Virginia.

Anna strolled into the room and took a seat next to Gracie. "Have you chosen a name?" she asked excitedly.

"A name?" Gracie fidgeted.

"Anna!" Ma exclaimed. "What has gotten into you?"

"Did I say something wrong?" Anna stood, glancing from Ma to Gracie.

"Even I know not to ask such a question." Virginia glared at Anna.

"I don't understand what the fuss is all about." Anna threw her arms in the air and began pacing back and forth, grumbling to herself. "I mean, my goodness, if I can tell the goat, the pig, the horse, or the cow are having wee ones . . . ." She stopped pacing and motioned toward Gracie. "What makes her any different?" she asked innocently before leaving the room.

To which Ma choked on the cider she was drinking.

Gracie buried her face in her hands bursting into laughter.

Ma thought she was weeping and rushed to her side. "Gracie, dear, are you all right?"

Gracie nodded as she placed her hand on Ma's shoulder and snickered. "That's the funniest thing I've ever heard." She wiped the moisture from her eyes. "I just imagined myself as big as a cow, wobbling to the outhouse." She laughed hysterically.

Ma placed a hand to her mouth and gave a suppressed laugh.

"Can you imagine?" Gracie said between breaths. "Nathaniel hugging something as big as a cow?" She pulled a handkerchief from her pocket and dabbed her eyes.

Anna strolled back into the room and was more confused than before. She looked from Ma to Gracie. "What's wrong with Nathaniel hugging a cow? I hugged a pig once."

Ma could no longer contain herself. She howled with laughter.

Virginia shrieked, then snorted. The three of them sat doubled over holding their sides, cackling like hens, as Pa would say. Anna stared at them like they'd lost their minds. She rolled her eyes, turned, and headed to the kitchen to check on the stew.

A few moments later, Virginia strolled into the kitchen. "I do believe that's the first time I've laughed that hard." She wiped the moisture from her eyes with her fingertips.

"If you ask me—" Anna stirred the stew before replacing the lid. "I think you've all gone mad."

"We were only having a little fun." Virginia opened the stove and poked the fire. She quickly closed the stove door. "It's not my fault. You're too young to understand—and spend more time working with the men," she added flippantly.

"I would much rather be hunting with the men than to be stuck here." Anna flopped down on a chair next to the cookstove.

"I wonder how the hunting trip's going." Virginia leaned her back against the kitchen sink.

CHAPTER SIXTEEN

HUNTING PARTY

Ben's wife stepped out to thank all who prayed. "Ben's condition remains the same." She sniffed and placed a handkerchief to her nose. "It brings my heart joy knowing Ben has friends who truly care." Everyone quietly listened. She paused and dried the tears from her eyes. "I'm sure God and Ben heard your prayers, and for that I thank you all." She slowly backed into the doctor's office and shut the door.

Most of the men cleared their throats, while others refused to make eye contact for fear that one might see a tear they fought hard to hold back. To them, tears were a sign of weakness, and no one wanted to appear weak, especially in front of a group of men during a bear hunt.

They reached the edge of town and started up Blackburn Mountain. Nathaniel, who was still in the lead, stopped his horse and held up his hand. Everyone stopped and waited to see what he had to say. "Listen up, men. My cabin sits atop that mountain." He pointed behind him. "It'll take an hour to get there. Keep your eyes and ears open."

James, Adam, and Johnny rode in the back with Pa. The excitement could be felt throughout the crowd, especially with the three teenagers. Although Adam was quite nervous, he hid it well. He could never allow anyone to know just how frightened he truly felt. He jumped when James poked him with a stick that he'd broken off one of the low hanging tree branches.

"Wake up!" James shouted. "Oh, so jumpy. You're not afraid, are you?" he teased.

"I ain't afraid of nothing," Adam shot back.

"That's enough," Pa said sternly. "There's a savage bear out here, so quit bickering and pay attention."

"Yes, sir," James and Adam said in unison. They both rode for the next several minutes with heads down, staring at the ground. Johnny led his horse between the two of them in hopes of breaking the awkward silence.

"Which one of you boys have hunted bear before?" Johnny asked.

"Neither of us," James admitted.

"What about you, have you hunted bear before?" Adam joined in.

"Nope, can't say I have." Johnny pointed at his gun strapped to his horse. "I've had plenty of target practice though."

"Practice and actually shooting a bear are two different things," James said.

"Yeah, he's right," Adam agreed. "Have you ever killed anything?"

"I have gotten my share of deer, squirrel, rabbit, and even wild boar," Johnny said proudly while sitting a little straighter in his saddle.

"Oh, all right, I suppose practice paid off." Disappointment resonated in Adam's voice. "Let's just hope it pays off this time." He nudged his horse and moved next to Pa.

Everyone grew silent the closer they drew to the top of the mountain and to Nathaniel's cabin. The men were impressed as well as relieved upon seeing the cabin come into view. It was bigger than anyone anticipated. It sat on top of the mountain, just as Nathaniel had said, and the scenery was incredible. The beautiful fall foliage and leaves on the trees painted the mountains in a gorgeous array of colors, which Pa referred to as God's artwork. The cabin's back porch overlooked the river far below. It looked like a tiny stream from the mountaintop.

Once inside, the men discussed which area each group would hunt. Sam, being the oldest and best hunter, took it upon himself to give orders. He was usually an arrogant man who thought he was better at everything, and he liked to brag about it. Not this time. Somehow, he just didn't have it in him. Everyone noticed the difference in Sam, but they said nothing.

Sam looked around the room at everyone. "My group of men will hunt the north side of the mountain. The rest of you can decide for yourselves who will hunt the other three sides." Everyone nodded in agreement and began talking amongst themselves. Once the choices were made the remaining group of five, which happened to be Nathaniel, Pa, James, Adam, and Johnny, were to wait at the cabin and keep a lookout in case the bear came near the cabin. Nathaniel and Pa had no problem with the arrangements. Neither of them wanted to risk one of the boys getting injured.

Pa cleared his throat. "Everyone needs to hunt for three hours and then meet back here."

"He's right. We'll meet in three hours." Sam picked up his gun. "That'll put us back here before lunch."

"Why do we have to stay at the cabin?" Adam questioned. "I want to hunt too."

"Calm down, son," Pa scolded. "We'll be hunting the area close to the cabin."

"Close to the cabin? What kind of hunting is that?" Adam grumbled.

"Adam, come with me." Johnny walked out onto the back porch.

Adam reluctantly followed.

"Look over the edge and tell me what you see." Johnny placed his hands in his jeans pocket and waited.

"I see the mountain side covered in trees. What'd ya think I'd see?" Adam's frustration resonated in his voice.

"Look again." Johnny stepped up next to him. "We can see through the trees to the river below." He gripped the edge of the banister.

"So what? We can see the river," Adam answered sarcastically.

"If that bear comes through there—" Johnny pointed to a huge clearing in the trees. "You have a chance to shoot him from here."

Adam's eyes grew wide as he stared in the direction Johnny pointed. "You're right," he said excitedly. "Let's keep this between the two of us." Johnny slapped him across the shoulder as he walked around Adam and leaned against the porch banister.

"What about James?" Adam asked while continuing to stare at the wooded area. Johnny glanced toward the back door of the cabin and then back at Adam.

"We'll let James in on it, but no one else," Adam whispered.

Johnny nodded in agreement. "We best be getting back inside before anyone comes looking for us."

"True, we don't need the others figuring out what a great

hunting spot this is." Adam and Johnny turned and hurried back inside.

Johnny was thrilled to have gotten Adam to calm down so quickly. He knew the likelihood of the bear coming through the clearing was slim, but if Adam believed it was possible, that's all that mattered. Johnny had always been a peacemaker; he hated conflict. When an argument or fight erupted, Johnny always tried to intervene.

They entered the cabin just as one of the men described the bear attack that Ben endured.

"It was a terrible thing. Poor Ben is suffering something awful." Sam dropped his head and stared at his boots.

"I spoke with his brother; he told me how it happened," Johnny said loudly.

Everyone grew silent. All eyes were on Johnny.

Nathaniel stepped next to him. "Go ahead, son. What did Billy Bob say?"

"He said while hunting the north bend, they came upon a Shawnee hunting party." Johnny paused and looked at Daniel, who rolled his hand in a gesture encouraging Johnny to continue. "The Shawnee were hunting for the bear." Johnny swallowed a lump forming in his throat. "A Squaw and her baby boy were on their way to the neighboring village." Johnny paused. "They ran upon the bear and the baby began to cry." Johnny's face turned pale, he felt sick.

Adams eyes grew wide. "What happened?" His voice cracked.

"The bear stood on its hind legs, looming over the girl and her baby boy," Johnny continued. "She tried backing away but tripped over a log. She . . . She . . . ." Johnny lowered his head and fought back tears. "She dropped the baby, and the bear snatched it up.

"So, she fed her baby to the bear in order to save herself," one man shouted. "It's just like a filthy savage." He made a disgusted face.

"Quiet, Jake!" Pa shouted. "Let him finish."

Jake rolled his eyes. He didn't take too kindly to being told to shut up, especially in front of the other men. He glanced around the room at everyone. They paid him no mind.

"Go on, son," Pa nodded at Johnny.

"Ben and his brother Billy Bob joined the Shawnee tribe to search for the baby." Johnny lumbered to the window and stared out.

"Did they find the baby?" Adam asked softly.

"All they found was the palm of the baby's hand." Johnny turned to face everyone. The room grew quiet.

"What's that have to do with Ben?" Jake asked.

"Ben vowed to get revenge," Johnny continued. "He came upon a cave. His brother begged him not to go inside, but old Ben wouldn't listen. He entered the cave alone." Johnny paused.

"The bear was in the cave, wasn't it?" James whispered.

"Yes, it was." Johnny turned to face James. "Before Ben could take aim, the bear drew back its huge paw and swiped at Ben. It, it slit his stomach open." The color drained from Johnny's face.

"Did you say it slit his stomach open?" Nathaniel placed a hand on Johnny's shoulder and looked him in the eyes.

Johnny stared up at him and nodded. He swallowed hard. "Yes. Ben managed to get away. He stumbled out of the cave, clutching his stomach, trying to keep his innards from falling out." Johnny felt nauseous. He placed a hand over his mouth, hoping he didn't lose his breakfast. "The bear was close behind him and it would have killed Ben if Billy Bob hadn't shot it. The

Shawnee tribe wants revenge for the baby."

"Well, I'm here for Ben." Jake began pacing. "Not for no filthy savage." He stopped and glared at Pa.

"I'm warning you, Jake," Pa said through gritted teeth.

"What are you going to do about it, Daniel?" Jake put his hands on his hips in a sad attempt to act brave. Nineteen-year-old Jake stood five-foot-nine. He enjoyed bullying everyone. Most people avoided him—but not from fear by any means. Jake was a coward and the whole town knew it.

"Are you as stupid as you look?" James' eyes shot daggers at Jake.

Jake crossed his arms and looked at the ceiling. "She tried to feed her baby to that bear to save herself," he whispered.

"A mother and father are grieving; their baby was eaten alive by that beast." Pa's eyes narrowed as he glared at Jake. The room grew deathly silent.

"Ben's fighting for his life." Nathaniel stepped toward Jake, his fists tightened at his side. "Besides you, that bear's the only savage in these mountains. Now, either keep your mouth shut, or I'll use you for bear bait!" he bellowed.

"Sorry," Jake apologized. "I wasn't thinking." He dropped his head.

"All right, men. Let's head out and get us a bear," Sam shouted while holding his gun up above his head.

The men were a little less than enthusiastic after hearing the gut-wrenching story of the baby and learning how serious Ben's injuries truly were. Adam felt a sense of relief that he would be hunting from the safety of the cabin's back porch.

Johnny withdrew from the group and exited to the back porch. He stood gazing at the mountains. *So beautiful, yet so dangerous*. He then thought of Anna. He wished he could have seen her before he left. He didn't hear James behind him.

"The men are leaving now." James stepped next to him, startling Johnny. "You're awfully skittish." James eyed him curiously.

"Who wouldn't be, knowing what that bear has done?" Adam said as he joined them.

Johnny turned his head in the opposite direction. "That poor baby," he said sadly. "I can't imagine what his family's going through.

"If Ben survives, I think the whole town should have a celebration party for him." Adam strolled to the other end of the porch and peered into the trees below. He saw a few hunters making their way down the mountain. He watched until they disappeared. "You wouldn't think a place this beautiful could be so dangerous." He dropped his head.

James and Johnny figured it best to leave Adam to his thoughts. He clearly had a lot on his mind. They went back inside and were met at the door by Daniel. "I think it's best if we hold off on hunting until at least one of the groups make it back." He looked from James to Johnny.

"May I ask why, sir?" Johnny glanced at James.

"It's best not to have too many people roaming the mountains. Someone could get shot," Daniel responded.

"He's right," Nathaniel answered. A few of the men seemed pretty on edge.

"I don't care who gets that bear, as long and someone makes it pay for what it's done," Adam said as he stepped back inside the cabin.

They all agreed. That bear needed to be brought down before anyone else got hurt.

CHAPTER SEVENTEEN

SERENITY'S CAFE

Sarah's phone alerted her to a text message. "That's Jimmy. They're finished for the day." She closed the book.

"Is it that late already?" Grams checked her watch. "Oh goodness," she gasped. "It's five o'clock. I can't believe we spent the whole day here."

"I can." Stacy rubbed her stomach. "I'm starving."

"Me, too." Sarah stood. She helped Grams up and then folded the lawn chairs.

"Let's grab something to go from Serenity's Café," Grams suggested.

"Yes, and maybe we can read a little more from the book after dinner tonight," Stacy said as she sat down in the backseat of the car.

"We'll definitely read more later." Grams stretched her shaky old hand toward the car door.

"Here, let me help you with that." Sarah opened the door and helped her grandmother into the car. She then ran around to the driver's side. She slid behind the wheel and started the engine. "Let's hit the road." Grams stretched her arm out in front of her. She reminded Sarah of an Army sergeant leading his platoon. She imagined her grandmother in such a position. *She would've made a good sergeant in her day.* Sarah quickly looked away to keep from laughing.

Several moments later they pulled into Serenity's Café. The three exited the car. "Whoa! This place is gorgeous." Stacy gasped.

"I forgot this is your first time here." Sarah stopped walking and waited while Stacy snapped a few photos.

"I can't wait to see inside." Stacy rushed up the steps. Stopping at the top, she took a few more photos before going inside.

Once inside, a waitress met them at the door. "May I show you ladies to a seat?" she asked politely.

"No, thank you, we're ordering to go." Sarah picked up a menu from off the counter and flipped through it.

"Just let me know when you're ready to order." The cashier smiled and patiently waited.

"Stacy, you have to try the lasagna." Sarah held up the menu with a photo of lasagna on the front.

"That looks incredible." Stacy's mouth watered. "I'll have that." She placed a hand on her rumbling stomach.

"Oh, my, is that your tummy making all that noise?" Grams patted Stacy's stomach.

"I'm afraid so." Stacy snickered. Her cheeks grew slightly pink.

"In that case we'll take a whole pan." Grams flipped her hand in the air at the cashier.

"Would you like just the lasagna or the meal?" the cashier asked as Grams dug through her purse looking for her wallet.

"Make it a meal. We're celebrating." Grams winked at Sarah. "I have my two favorite girls with me and a wonderful old book that I'm anxious to get back to."

"That will be $51.38." The cashier placed a pan of homemade rolls and a huge garden salad in a to-go bag and set it on the counter. The lasagna will be a while. If you'd like to take a seat, we'll bring it to you when it's ready." She placed three cups on the counter. "Drinks are behind you."

"Let me pay for that." Stacy held up her credit card.

"You'll do no such thing." Grams quickly slid her debit card through the card reader before Stacy could protest. She placed her card back in her purse, handed Sarah and Stacy a cup, and then filled her own with orange soda before leaving to find a table.

"I'm not sure who's more stubborn, you or your grandmother." Stacy whispered to Sarah.

"Hmmm . . . ." Sarah tapped a finger against her chin. "Grams. Definitely."

Stacy playfully rolled her eyes. She brought the camera up on her phone and took photos of the restaurant's interior before taking a seat at the table between Grams and Sarah. "Time for a selfie." She held the phone out in front of her. "Smile, you two." Sarah made silly faces. Grams surprised them by joining in. She crossed her eyes and stuck her tongue out at the camera, unknowingly attracting a few onlookers.

"Hey, Grams, give me one of these." Stacy puckered her lips as though she was going to whistle.

"What on Earth for?" Grams gave her a perplexed look.

"It's a duck face." Sarah puckered her lips to demonstrate.

"Lord have mercy, girls." Grams shook her head. "It looks more like a dog's behind if you ask me."

Several onlookers burst into laughter.

One lady at the table next to theirs spit her drink all over her friend. "That's the funniest thing I've heard all day." The lady handed her friend some napkins. They both continued laughing.

"Well, what have we here?" came a male voice from behind Sarah. She recognized the voice as Jimmy's. Her heart skipped a beat when she looked up and his gaze met hers.

She cleared her throat and looked away upon realizing he wasn't alone; in fact, his whole crew was with him.

"Where are our manners?" Grams motioned for the crew to take a seat at the table next to theirs. "Would you boys like to join us?"

"We wouldn't want to impose." Jimmy responded.

"It's no imposition at all." Grams stood. "Grab that table over there." She pointed. "Slide it over here with ours to make one big table."

The men did just that. Each pulled up a chair, and before long, they enjoyed a lovely meal. Stacy and Robby hit it off. They seemed to have a lot in common. Neither of them ate much, claiming they weren't hungry. Sarah knew better; she saved a plate for them to eat later.

"Would you like to step onto the back deck?" Robby stood with an outstretched hand to Stacy. "They have a lovely view of the mountains back there."

"I'd love to." Stacy took his hand and allowed him to lead her out.

"I would ask if you ladies are getting into trouble." Jimmy glanced around the room. "But from the looks of things, that would be a correct assumption." He smiled mischievously at Grams.

"You'd be correct to assume that." Grams picked up a napkin from the table and shoved one end down the neck of her shirt, making sure the rest covered her blouse. “Someone has to keep these girls in line.” She placed a roll on her plate, pretending to be innocent.

“I agree, and you’re the best person for that job,” Jimmy teased.

“It’s a hard job, but someone has to do it.” She snickered.

“Hey, I’m sitting right here, ya know, and I can hear you both.” Sarah playfully crossed her arms.

“Did you hear something?” Grams nudged Jimmy with her elbow.

“Nope, I didn’t hear anything.”

“Ha, aren’t you two hilarious?” Sarah held up a roll as though she was going to throw it at Jimmy.

“What is it with you and bread?” He chuckled.

Sarah dropped the roll onto her plate. “I’ll just ignore the two of you and enjoy my dinner.” She pursed her lips jokingly.

“Now, don’t start that again.” Gram giggled as she pointed a fork at her.

“Well, ladies, sorry to eat and run, but we have a job to do this evening, so we had better get to it.” Jimmy winked at Sarah before leaving. “See you soon, love.”

Sarah took in everything about this day. She loved watching her grandmother laughing and enjoying herself with not only Jimmy and his crew, but Stacy too. She whispered a silent prayer for her grandmother’s health and many happy years ahead.

It was late when they arrived home. Grams retired to her room to take a long hot bath. Sarah and Stacy decided to watch a movie before bed. By the time the movie ended, Grams was finished with her bath. She strolled into the living room wrapped in a fluffy new robe and a towel around her head.

"How was the movie, girls?" She yawned.

"It was good, but not as enjoyable as the book we've been reading," Sarah answered.

"I agree. I'd rather listen to Sarah read from the book." Stacy nodded.

"Well, if you girls don't mind, I'm turning in for the night." Grams glanced at the book lying on the coffee table. "I'd love to go back to the river tomorrow."

"Sounds like a plan." Sarah stretched. "I'm going to shower and go to bed too." She kissed her grandmother on the cheek. "How about you, Stacy?"

"Yeah, same here. Right after I shower. Goodnight, ladies." Stacy gave Grams a quick peck on the cheek and then raced up the stairs, taking them two at a time with Sarah on her heels.

Early the next morning Sarah was awakened by the sound of her phone ringing. Her heart skipped a beat when she saw Jimmy's name. She smiled as she answered. "Hello, handsome. You're up early."

"Hello, sweetheart." Jimmy said in a deep drowsy voice.

"You sound super sexy in the mornings." Sarah grinned.

"So do you. Listen, the reason I'm calling so early is to let you know that we will be late but tell your grandmother we will get there as soon as we can." He yawned.

"Is everything all right?" Sarah sat up in bed.

"Everything is fine," Jimmy replied. "I'm at the hospital. Bill's father suffered a mild heart attack."

"Oh no! Is he going to be all right?" Sarah swung her legs over the side of the bed.

"Yes, thank God. They got him to the hospital quickly," Jimmy answered groggily.

"It sounds like you've been up all night." She lumbered to

the bathroom, picked up her hairbrush, and ran it through her hair.

"We've been here since two." Jimmy yawned once again.

"You're a wonderful friend and boss, Jimmy."

"I could never allow my family or friends to go through this alone," he said sincerely.

"Listen, Jimmy, take the day off and get some rest." Sarah placed the hairbrush back on the sink. "Grams wants to spend the day at the river. We've been reading from the old book."

"I've been meaning to ask you what the story's about." Jimmy sounded groggier than before.

"Jimmy, I'm coming to the hospital, and I'm bringing Stacy with me." Sarah searched through her clothes trying to find something to wear.

"Why are you coming to the hospital?" Jimmy inquired.

"I'm taking you home," she said flatly. "I'll drive your truck, and Stacy can follow in my car."

Jimmy was too tired to argue and knew he shouldn't drive in his condition. "Thank you, darlin'. I appreciate it."

"Tell Bill his dad is in my thoughts and prayers."

"Thanks, I'll tell him. See you soon."

Sarah hung up and placed the phone on the bed. She slipped on a pair of jean shorts and a dark blue tee-shirt. She decided to let her hair down. It hung to her waist, with huge curls on the ends that bounced with each step she took, which Jimmy loved. She rapped on Stacy's bedroom door and was surprised to find her up and dressed for the day.

"Hey, girlfriend, what's up?" Stacy said cheerfully.

"Bill's father had a heart attack, and I need you to go to the hospital with me to pick Jimmy up," Sarah blurted out.

"Oh my gosh!" Stacy's eyes grew wide. "Is he—"

"He's fine, but Jimmy hasn't had any sleep, and I don't think he should drive himself home."

"Let's go." Stacy pulled a pair of sandals out of her bag and slipped them on.

Sarah turned and headed out the bedroom door. Stacy followed. They met Grams in the kitchen preparing breakfast. Sarah explained everything and assured her grandmother they would be home in time for breakfast and then they'd head to the river.

"I cooked for the whole crew, but under the circumstances, they won't make it today," Grams said sadly.

"I'm sorry, Grams," Sarah said soothingly.

"There's always tomorrow," Stacy stated.

"You know what I always say about that?" Grams looked at Sarah.

"Don't put off until tomorrow what you can do today," Sarah responded.

Grams nodded as she opened the cabinet and retrieved six Styrofoam to-go trays. She filled them with scrambled eggs, bacon, sausage, fried potatoes, homemade buttermilk biscuits, and chocolate gravy. "Here, take this to Jimmy."

"Goodness, Grams, are you trying to fatten him up or something?" Sarah stared at all the food.

"Actually, the second tray is for Bill. The others are for his family and friends." She slung the dish towel over her shoulder, grabbed a plastic bag and filled it with trays of food, extra paper plates, and utensils.

"That was very thoughtful of you." Sarah's stomach rumbled at the delicious aroma. She cut a biscuit in half, slathered it with butter, and then added sausage, eggs, and fried potatoes. She topped it off with a slice of cheese. She handed it to Stacy and then made one for herself before leaving for the hospital.

Once in the car, Stacy placed the huge bag of food on the floor between her feet to keep it from falling over.

Upon arriving at the hospital, they took the food to Bill and his family. "Grams sent plenty of home-cooked food for everyone." Sarah handed the bag to Bill. She looked around but saw no sign of Jimmy.

Bill noticed her disappointment. "Jimmy will be right back; I believe he went to the restroom." He sniffed the bag of food. "Is that bacon I smell?"

"It sure is. There's a little of everything in there," Stacy answered.

Sarah's eyes lit up when she saw Jimmy walking toward her. Although frazzled and worn, he managed to put on a weak smile. She hugged him and handed him a tray. "Curtesy of Grams." She smiled.

"Remind me to thank her later." Jimmy took the tray of food and said his goodbyes. He handed Sarah his truck keys. "I'd rather you drive." Sarah nodded as she took the keys from his hand. He climbed into the passenger seat, anxious to get home and get some much-needed sleep.

Stacy followed in Sarah's car. She pulled into his driveway and stopped behind Jimmy's truck.

Sarah could see how tired he was and thought it best that he got to bed as soon as possible. She walked him to his front door. "I'll say a prayer for Bill's father."

"Thanks. I'm sure he'd appreciate that." Jimmy placed a hand to her cheek and gently kissed her lips before going inside. He put the tray of food in the refrigerator, too tired to eat or shower, He kicked off his shoes, lay across the bed, and fell fast asleep.

Sarah and Stacy drove home in silence. Sarah's thoughts wandered to the old book while Stacy's mind was on Robbie. Upon arriving home, they found that Grams had cleaned the kitchen. She was excited to spend the day at the river once again listening to Sarah read.

"You girls grab a bite to eat, and let's hit the road," Grams said as she dried her hands on a dishtowel and hung it over the oven door handle.

"You don't have to tell me twice." Stacy sat at the breakfast table and began to eat the plate of food that Grams had prepared for them.

"It smells amazing." Sarah kissed her grandmother on the cheek before taking a seat at the table.

After breakfast, Sarah and Stacy cleaned up and packed for a day at the river. The phone rang and Grams eyes sparkled when she saw Doc Brown's name appear.

"Hello, David. I was just thinking about you," she said sweetly.

"Hello, lovely lady," he replied. "I'm calling to let you know your test results are back."

"My test results?" Grams said nervously. "Would you mind giving them to me over the phone?"

"I don't usually give results over the phone, but in your case, I'll make an exception."

"Thank you, David. Should I be sitting down?" Her voice cracked.

Sarah stepped next to her grandmother, worry etched on her face. "Grams, is everything all right?"

"I'm about to find out." She put the phone on speaker. "All right, let's hear it.

"Your heart is good. It occasionally skips a beat, which is

typical at your age." He continued when she didn't respond. "Your vitamin D is extremely low, and you have an underactive thyroid."

"What do we do now?" she questioned.

"I've sent in a prescription to Hometown Pharmacy." He paused. "You do still get your medicine there, right?"

"Yes, I do. What is the name of the prescription?" She stared at the phone.

"It's called Synthroid. I've started you on a low dose and we'll see you in three months." He paused again. "Of course I'll see you later this evening," he said in a flirty tone, causing Grams to blush. She quickly took the phone off speaker before finishing their conversation.

Sarah and Stacy glanced at one another and snickered as they stepped out onto the back porch. Before long, Grams joined them, her face aglow.

"Come, girls, it's a beautiful day." Grams stepped off the porch into the sunlight. "Let's not waste a minute of it."

"It sure is. Let's get this day started." Sarah jumped off the steps. Stacy raced her to the car. Grams even managed to jog to the car. They were on their way.

Upon reaching the river, they spotted a picnic table nestled beneath the expansive canopy of a magnificent oak tree. Its sprawling branches intertwined with a nearby maple, creating a lush cover that extended throughout the area. Dappled sunlight filtered through the leaves, enhancing the serene atmosphere of the area.

"This is amazing," Sarah exclaimed. "I wonder who set up the picnic table?" She grabbed the book as she exited the car.

Grams pointed and said, 'There's a rock sitting atop the table, and it looks like there's a note beneath it.'"

Stacy rushed to the picnic table to investigate. She tossed the rock aside and exclaimed, “It’s definitely a note.” She lifted the piece of paper high for a better look.

“What does it say?” Sarah placed the book on the table.

"It says," Stacy remarked as she opened the note to read it. “Having a picnic on the grass is lovely, but I thought you would prefer this option. Have a wonderful day, ladies. Jimmy.”

"Such a thoughtful young man." Grams beamed as she gently ran her hand over the newly painted table.

“I told you.” Stacy handed Sarah the note. “He’s a keeper.”

"I totally agree. He's a one-of-a-kind guy," Sarah said to herself as she read the note. "Who's ready for a swim?" She tucked the note into her pocket.

Gram was the first to jump up. "I could go for a refreshing dip," she said, making her way to the riverbank. "If I can find a safe path down to the water." Suddenly, she halted in surprise. "Oh, my goodness, you girls have to come see this!"

Sarah and Stacy rushed over to see what had caught Grams’ attention. They were shocked to see that the riverbank had been cleared and filled with mulch. The three of them stared in awe.

“It’s beautiful, but how did they find the time to do this?” Sarah wondered.

“They must have come here after we left Serenity’s Café,” Stacy answered.

“I believe I’m going to pass on swimming today.” Grams strolled back to the picnic table and took a seat. Sarah and Stacy did the same. “I would like to hear more from the book, if you don’t mind.”

“I agree with Grams.” Stacy took a seat next to her.

“Reading it is then.” Sarah sat on the opposite side of the

table, opened the book, and began to read.

CHAPTER EIGHTEEN

BEAR HUNT

Storm clouds gathered on the horizon. The smell of rain lingered on the breeze. A storm was brewing, and no one wanted to get caught in a downpour. The hunters met at the old dogwood tree as planned.

"Men, y'all go on back to the cabin. I'll be along shortly." Sam squinted his eyes, scoping the thick wooded area.

"Did you see something, Sam?" Bob Jones eyed Sam suspiciously. Bob's scraggly hair and graying beard made him appear much older than thirty-four. He was a heavy-set man, and not much of a hunter. He did more falling and grumbling than hunting. He made so much noise that the hope of finding anything dissipated, which perturbed his hunting party greatly.

"The only thing I see is that muddle-head Jake got himself separated from the group." Sam propped a foot on a moss-covered log.

"Want me to go with ya, Sam?" Bob asked half-heartedly.

"No, it's best if you go back to the cabin with your group." Sam turned to face the rest of the men. "Same goes for the rest of ya. Get some rest, and we'll hunt early in the morning."

"Sam, I'm going with you." Dan Woods stepped forward.

"You shouldn't go alone." Burl Miller stood from the tree stump he rested on and picked up his Flintlock Fowler, a gun given to him by his father on his twelfth birthday.

Dan and Burl were both nice-looking, clean-cut men. They had been friends since childhood but felt more like brothers. Burl was twenty-four and Dan was just a few months younger.

"We don't need you going and gettin' yourself lost." Dan stepped in front of Sam. His huge, six-foot muscular frame towered over him. "You're not going alone."

"He won't be alone." Johnny stepped next to Sam. "I'm going with him." He crossed his arms and stared Sam in the eyes.

Sam placed his hands on his hips. He didn't take too kindly to being told what to do, especially not by someone much younger.

His eyes gave Johnny a scathing once over. He placed his hand in his shirt pocket, pulled out a wad of chewing tobacco, and shoved it in his jaw. "I've hunted this mountain ever since I was a boy. I know it like the back of my hand." He spit tobacco juice on the ground at Dan's feet before turning on his heel with Johnny by his side.

Dan looked at Burl. "Did I say something wrong?"

"Where's he running off to?" One man pointed at Sam, who was headed down the mountain.

"I'm gonna find Jake and tan his hide," Sam yelled over his shoulder.

Burl and Dan followed at a distance. They figured they would give Sam some space and then maybe he wouldn't be the wiser. They were wrong.

"Come on, men." Sam stopped, cocked his head in their direction, and motioned for them to catch up.

A few long strides and they were at Sam's side. Twenty

minutes later they reached the river and found an area where huge rocks stuck out of the water like steppingstones leading the way to the opposite side. Once on the other side, Dan and Burl waited for Sam to decide which way to go.

Sam pointed downstream. "The Shawnee Village isn't far from here." He began walking along the riverbank.

Dan and Burl looked at each other before hurrying to catch up.

"Why are we going there?" Burl's long legs stumbling and tripping over rocks made him look like a marionette whose puppeteer had lost control of the strings.

Sam and Dan chuckled at the sight. Burl didn't see the humor in it.

"What makes you think he went this way?" Johnny took in the vast wooded area. The beautiful array of vibrant fall colors painted the entire mountain in hues of red, orange and gold. Leaves continued clinging to the trees as though dreading what was to happen once they fell.

"This beats all I've ever seen," Sam grumbled. "I came to bear hunt, not traipse all over the mountain searching for—"

"Searching for that good-for-nothing Jake," Burl finished.

Sam stopped. "Don't ever let me hear you call him that again." He spun around and glared at Burl. Sam's look softened. "I, I'm sorry. I don't like to hear anyone called worthless." He turned and continued walking. "There's good in everyone—including Jake."

Burl and Dan looked at each other, confused as to why Sam had a sudden change of heart toward Jake.

"He's just tired and possibly hungry," Dan whispered to Burl, who nodded in agreement. They quickly brushed it off.

Johnny, on the other hand, figured there was more to it than that. He wasn't sure what, but he hoped to find out.

The sound of drums intensified, accompanied by the sorrowful wailing of a woman piercing through the rhythmic beats and the heart-wrenching songs of the villagers. They were nearing the Shawnee village. The anguished cries emanating from within were nearly unbearable. The four men stealthily navigated through the dense underbrush and towering Rhododendron bushes. Once they emerged from the foliage, Johnny caught a glimpse of movement on the other side of the brush. He moved ahead of Sam, halting, crouching down and signaling for the others to remain still. Carefully, he parted the branches, and that's when he spotted Jake concealed behind a massive tree trunk, observing the Shawnee tribe.

"What ya looking at?" Burl stopped a few feet behind Johnny.

"Shhh." Johnny placed a finger to his lips and pointed at Jake.

"What in tarnation does he think he's doing?" Sam whispered as he crouched next to Johnny and peered through the bushes.

"Looks like he's trying to get himself kilt." Dan shook his head.

"No one else is dying today." With determination, Sam rose and made his way through the undergrowth, his strides heavy with anger as he approached Jake. Just before he could reach him, a towering, muscular Native emerged from behind a tree, swiftly pinning Jake's neck against the trunk. He spoke in Shawnee, words that remained incomprehensible to everyone except Sam. Raising his hand, Sam responded in the same language. The Native's demeanor softened into a smile, and he offered Sam an amiable slap on the shoulder. The rest of the group entered the clearing, rendered speechless by the scene unfolding before them. "It's good to see you again, Running

Deer," Sam said in English.

"Good see you, my friend," Running Deer replied in broken English. "We knew you come."

Sam stared at his feet and sadly shook his head. "I just wish it was under different circumstances."

Running Deer nodded in agreement.

"Who did the papoose belong to?" Sam swallowed the lump forming in his throat.

"White Lily and Grey Wolf," Running Deer said with a heavy heart. "Come, let's go speak to them." He pivoted and began heading towards the village.

Sam turned to Dan and Burl. "You two head back to the cabin and let the others know we'll return before nightfall." They nodded in agreement and departed. Sam gestured for Johnny and Jake to accompany him to the village.

Johnny noticed Jake's anxiety as he hesitated in place. With a firm grip on his elbow, Johnny coaxed him to move along.

"Lucky for you, Sam's friends with the tribe," Johnny whispered.

Jake pulled his arm back, remaining silent. At sixteen, Johnny was three years younger than Jake, yet he seemed far more mature. His tall, muscular physique overshadowed Jake's short, slender frame.

"He saved your skin, you know," Johnny remarked.

Jake nodded in response. Observing Jake's unease, Johnny figured that Running Deer must have frightened him into silence. Recalling Jake's previous comments about Natives, he decided to teach Jake a lesson.

"You know the Shawnee Tribe are renowned for being fierce warriors, don't you?" Johnny shot a quick look at Jake, who was fixated straight ahead in silence. "Mighty fierce warriors.

That's why the Cherokee team up with them in battle." Johnny pressed on, noticing Jake's lack of reaction. "Sure wouldn't want to find myself on their bad side."

"Shut up!" Jake said through clenched teeth. "You don't understand." He hesitated, then lowered his voice. "I have to make things right."

"What are you talking about?" Johnny pulled Jake by the arm, and they hung back until the others were out of earshot.

"I was there, um . . . I mean, I saw . . . ." Jake looked around to ensure no one was eavesdropping. Johnny's eyes widened as Jake's tale started to unfold. He picked up a stick and began snapping it as he quietly listened until Jake finished speaking.

"Dag nab it, Jake. Why didn't you say something?" Johnny grabbed a branch and hurled it into the underbrush.

"I was skeerd." Jake crossed his arms. "I didn't know nuttin' until I got back to town."

"Come on." Johnny grabbed Jake by the arm.

"Let go of me. I ain't gone nowhere." Jake jerked away.

"You need to make this right. You said so yourself." Johnny poked Jake in the chest.

Jake rubbed the back of his neck and stared at the ground.

"You need to confess. Now!" Johnny shouted.

"I can't. I'll be kilt fer sure." Jake's face was etched with fear as he turned to leave.

"No, you won't." Johnny stepped in front of him. "You have to do what's right."

"What I should have done is kilt that bear when I had the chance." Jake kicked a rock and watched it bounce and roll to a stop. "All right," he said quietly. "Let's be done with it."

"The first thing we need to do is go see Mrs. Winters." Johnny looked down, running his fingers through his hair. "How far away is her place from here?"

Jake's eyes searched the mountains. "I reckon it's a couple miles over yonder on Panther Mountain." He pointed.

Johnny stared at the mountainous terrain. Under normal circumstances he would've taken a shortcut through the woods and over the mountains. For a second it crossed his mind to do so, but after surveying the thick foliage and dense underbrush with a wounded bear roaming these woods, he decided against it. "If you're right, then we should be back right about dark."

"I know what I'm talking about," Jake growled. "I've been there a dozen times." He crossed his arms over his chest and tapped his foot.

"Calm down, Jake." Johnny glared at him. "Stop taking everything the wrong way."

"I'm sorry," Jake said. "It's just that I'm a-feared."

"You mean you're afraid," Johnny corrected.

"Wouldn't you be?" Jake's eyes grew wide. "I told ya, I could git kilt."

Johnny started to speak up to correct him again but then shook his head and decided against it. "Forget it, let's go." He brushed past Jake and took the lead towards the Shawnee Village. Jake hesitated for a moment before hurrying to catch up when he heard a sound behind him.

"I thought we were going to visit Mrs. Winters," Jake murmured, shifting uneasily under the gaze of the Shawnee women observing them. Johnny gave them a smile and tipped his hat as he walked past.

"I don't like this. What are we doing here?" Jake whispered through gritted teeth.

"We need to speak to Running Deer." Johnny kept walking

toward the group of men in the center of the village. Jake stepped in front of him, stopping him.

"What fer?" Jake's eyes darted all around him before settling on Johnny.

"We need him to go with us to Panther Mountain," Johnny said, annoyed. He stepped around Jake and continued walking. Jake hurried to his side.

"Why do we need him when I know the way?" Jake's voice cracked.

Johnny stopped walking and turned to face Jake. "Do you have confidence in your aim or shooting skills?

"Do I have what?" Jake scratched his head. "What does that even mean?

"If we come across that bear, are your reflexes quick enough to bring it down?" When Johnny saw the confusion on Jakes brow, he decided to reword it in a way he could understand. "In other words, if that bear is charging right at you, growling, teeth barred, shaking his head and spit flying, would you run away or shoot it?"

Jake stood there rubbing the back of his neck and staring at his boots.

"Hurry, Jake. I need an answer. That bear is moving fast straight for you." Johnny rushed him.

Jake's eyes grew wide as panic set in. "I . . . uh . . . I don't know. I'd run . . . . No, wait. I'd shoot it."

"Then why didn't you shoot it when you came upon it the first time?"

"Okay, I was skeerd. I told you what happened, and that's the truth." Jake crossed his arms and glanced around the village.

"Sorry, Jake." Johnny looked Jake in the eyes. "You're braver than you think." He proceeded towards the group of men with

Jake trailing behind him. As they approached the center of the village, the sounds of mourning and the rhythmic drumming intensified. Johnny held back, patiently allowing the men to complete their discussion. He observed as Running Deer exited the circle and quickly followed him, reaching him at the woodland's edge, where he explained the situation.

White Lily, the young Indian mother, dashed to the village center, dropped to her knees, and wept uncontrollably. A surge of anguish washed over Jake. He felt as if his heart might burst. He raced towards her but was swiftly intercepted by six male natives. One of them, seemingly around Jake's age, pressed a knife against his throat.

"No! Wait! The baby, the . . . the . . . papoose." Jake motioned toward White Lily.

Running Deer pushed Johnny aside and rushed to Jake. With one swift movement, he disarmed the young native.

Sam raced over, stopping a few feet in front of Jake.

The old Indian Chief Tuscoma, who understood and spoke the English language, followed. All eyes were on Jake as the chief spoke softly so as not to be heard by White Lily.

"Say what you know?" Chief Tuscoma's eyes darted from Jake to White Lily.

"Choose your words wisely." Sam's eyes narrowed.

"I, I was there." Jake paused. His eyes brimmed with tears. The whole village stood watching, all except for White Lily. She was surrounded by several Indian maiden's trying to comfort her.

"Th, the bear attack." Jake placed his hands over his face and trembled.

Sam took off his hat and stepped in front of Jake. His face was just inches from his own. "You saw the whole thing and did nothing?" Sam slapped his hat against his knee. Dust flew from the hat and swirled around his legs before being carried away by a gentle breeze.

Chief Tuscoma placed a hand over Sam's shoulder and shook his head.

"Let him speak," Chief Tuscoma said softly. His golden-brown eyes held wisdom.

Everyone's attention was fixed on Jake, oblivious to White Lily as she approached him and the old chief. It wasn't until she stood beside the chief that her presence was acknowledged. Tears streamed down her face as she gazed at Jake, her swollen eyes reflecting anguish and a deep sense of desperation.

Jake cast a pleading glance at Johnny, who quickly closed the distance and stood beside him, ready to offer moral support. Johnny nodded slightly and offered a faint smile, encouraging Jake to share his truth. Jake's eyes fell upon White Lily, whose long black hair cascaded over her shoulders as she knelt at his feet, her hands covering her face. She brushed away her tears with her fingertips and looked up at him with her large, sorrowful honey-brown eyes.

In that moment, Jake no longer saw the savage he once referred to, but rather a beautiful young mother desperately seeking a miracle. His heart ached for her, and he understood he needed to make amends by being honest. Taking a deep breath, he smiled at White Lily before shifting his focus to Chief Tuscoma. "Please tell her the baby, um, the papoose is alive and well."

Chief Tuscoma stared at Jake, his bewildered gaze searching his face. "If what you say is true, how can this be?" The chief's eyes darted to White Lily and back to Jake.

White Lily stood and took Jake by the hand. "Ni ti mi we lo."

Tears welled in her eyes and rolled down her cheeks.

"What did she say?" Jake asked.

"She's asking you to help her." The chief never took his eyes off Jake.

Jake choked back tears as he looked down at White Lily and nodded. "Tell her the papoose is alive and well." Jake smiled at White Lily as Grey Wolf helped her. They waited for Chief Tuscoma to translate what Jake said. The chief held up two fingers as a signal for them to wait. He wanted to hear what Jake had to say. He turned back to Jake, his old eyes studying his face for any deception. When he saw the sincerity in Jake's eyes, he nodded for him to continue.

"I was hunting for small game early yesterday morning," Jake began. "I was taking them to Martha to cook for me. I always take extra to her as payment." Jake paused.

"What's that have to do with the baby?" Sam sneered.

"I'm getting to that," Jake snapped back.

"Well, then, get on with it." Sam softened his tone.

"I shot several rabbits, skinned them, and then I caught sight of a coon. I watched it for a while before shooting it." Jake stared at the ground. "That's when I heard a woman screaming. I snatched up the coon and raced in the direction of the screams."

"Was it White Lily?" Running Deer asked.

"No." He shook his head. "I mean I don't know." He shifted from one foot to the other. Although Grey Wolf couldn't speak or understand English, his patience was growing thin. He stepped closer to Jake and stared him in the eyes. He said something in Shawnee that Jake didn't understand. Jake's face turned ghostly white. He swallowed the lump in his throat before continuing.

"By the time I got there, I saw a huge black bear sniffing at something on the ground." Jake took a step back from Grey Wolf. "I stood frozen. The bear looked back at me. That's when I saw a baby's hand peek out of the blanket."

"Oh my God!" Sam scrunched his nose and placed a hand over his mouth. He appeared as though he was going to be sick. Chief Tuscoma motioned for Jake to stop talking.

"Wait! The baby is alive," Jake shouted louder than he intended.

"You mean *was* alive," Running Deer said.

"No!" Jake shook his head. "He is alive."

The Chief held up one hand in front of Jake. "Speak only truth. Where is papoose?"

"When I saw the baby, uh, the papoose's hand, I aimed my gun and shot the bear." Jake stared at the ground. "I'm the one who wounded it. I picked the baby up and looked him over." Jake smiled. "He wasn't hurt. He wasn't even crying." Jake dropped his head and placed a hand on his hip. No one spoke. White Lily listened intently and smiled slightly as though she understood.

"Where's the baby?" Sam spoke through gritted teeth.

"I didn't know what to do," Jake continued, "so I took him to Martha Winters up on Panther Mountain."

White Lily turned to Running Deer, desperation in her eyes. He nodded at her and then whispered in Grey Wolf's ear. Grey Wolf's face registered confusion. White Lily grabbed him by the arm and pleaded in Shawnee language. "Papoose?" she asked. It was the only word she recognized in Jake's story. Grey Wolf took her aside and repeated Jake's words. White Lilly knitted her brows. Her eyes were brimming with tears.

Sam grabbed Jake by the arm and pulled him aside. "This

better not be some kind of sick joke." Sam warned.

"It's not, I swear." Jake jerked his arm from Sam's grip.

Johnny strolled over and stood next to Jake and Sam. "What happens now?" He watched the tribe as they gathered around the chief. White Lily shook her head. She was clearly upset. She glanced at Jake with a pleading look in her eyes.

"White Lily is begging for them to take her to get her baby," Sam stated. "The chief doesn't want to take a chance on running into that bear in the dark."

"I'll take that chance." Jake's eyes brimmed with tears. "Tell them that."

"I'll go with him," Johnny volunteered.

Sam nodded his approval. "That's valiant of you both." He smiled slightly. "But I'll be coming with you."

"I don't need a babysitter," Jake said, trying to sound brave. He didn't want Sam or Johnny to know how relieved he was to have them both going along.

"I agree, you don't." Sam kept his eyes on the chief and White Lily. He then turned and stared into Jake's eyes. "You do need an extra pair of eyes who can manage to shoot a bear without panicking."

"He's right," Johnny agreed. "If that baby starts crying, it'll alert every animal in the forest."

"True, I'd appreciate it if you come along." Jake tipped his hat at Sam.

Sam held up his hand, waving it as he made his way to the chief. Johnny and Jake stayed put. They strained their ears to listen but couldn't hear let alone understand the Shawnee language. Several minutes passed and then the crowd parted. The chief led the way to where Jake and Johnny stood. Sam, Running Deer, Grey Wolf, and White Lily followed. The chief stopped in front of Jake and placed a hand on his shoulder.

"We shall speak when you return." The chief studied Jake's reaction for any signs that he was lying about the baby, but he saw truth written in his eyes. A smile touched the corner of his eyes as he stretched up his wrinkled old hand and patted Jake's face. He turned and hugged White Lily before she mounted her horse.

Everyone waited for Jake to lead the way. He climbed on his horse and tipped his hat at the chief. He turned toward Running Deer. "Tell them that if we follow Coon Creek for about two miles upstream and then head up Horse Ridge, we'll reach Panther Mountain in an hour, which will put us back just before dark."

Running Deer relayed the message.

Johnny's brow furrowed with concern upon noticing White Lily appeared weak. After all, she just gave birth a few days ago.

"Don't you think it's better if White Lily waits here?" Johnny glanced away when White Lily's head shot in his direction. "She is weak from giving birth."

Running Deer spoke. "White Lily would rather die than stay here without her papoose."

Johnny nodded at White Lily and then nudged his horse. It trotted alongside Jake. The trip was quiet except for the low chatter of Grey Wolf and Running Deer. White Lily rode stoically, staring straight ahead. Her long black hair that hung to her hips shimmered in the sun and bounced with each trot of her horse. Her honey brown eyes that once cried tears of pain, now held hope and faith.

Johnny's eyes followed Jake's gaze.

White Lily smiled slightly causing Jake to quickly avert his eyes, his cheeks growing pink.

"I sure hope it's her baby." Johnny glanced back at Grey Wolf and Running Deer who were still in deep conversation. "For all our sakes."

"Think about it, Johnny." Jake gripped his reins tighter. "How many Indian mothers and their babies were recently attacked by a black bear?" He nudged his horse with the heel of his boots. The horse galloped ahead.

Johnny turned his head to look back at White Lily. Her face registered confusion. Johnny bit the side of his jaw. He said a silent prayer. He didn't want to think about what would happen if Jake was lying. The chief had a reputation for being an honest man. *According to Sam.* It was Grey Wolf and Running Deer that concerned him most.

They rode the rest of the way in silence. Before long, a cabin came into view. Jake stopped his horse, turned, and held up his hand. "Tell them I need to go alone and talk to her."

Sam relayed the message, but before anyone could reply, a woman stepped out the front door and froze when she saw them approaching. Her golden-brown hair was neatly twisted and pinned on top of her head. She wore a long cream and tan colored dress with an apron tied around her waist. She waved at Jake and nodded at White Lily. "I've been expecting you." She placed a stray strand of hair behind her ear.

It was Sam who spoke first. "Sorry to bother you, ma'am, but Jake here says that you have this woman's baby."

"I, uh, 'tis true I've been caring for a wee one." She smiled nervously at White Lily. *"Pe yi lo."* She motioned for White Lily to follow her.

"You speak Shawnee?" Johnny asked.

"A bit," she replied. "My name's Martha." She opened the door and led the way inside. The cabin's open room consisted of a parlor and kitchen which was nice and neat. All the furniture, including the kitchen table, was handmade. Johnny took in every detail of the woodwork, since he too enjoyed whittling and carving.

Martha strolled across the living room to a beautifully hand-carved cradle. Johnny noticed the cradle was the one piece of furniture with intricate details. There were birds flying, rabbits playing in a field, and a hunting dog standing on its hind legs with its front paws resting on a tree trunk barking at a raccoon whose face could be seen peeking through the leaves. Dogwood blossoms were carved down all four legs of the cradle. Martha noticed Johnny admiring the handiwork

"My husband William made it for our wee one." Sadness overshadowed her face. "If God saw fit to bless us with one." She gently picked up the sleeping baby. He was wrapped snuggly in a blue and white hand stitched quilt. She handed him to White Lily, who quickly unwrapped him and examined him. She turned him over and found what she was looking for. There on his right shoulder was the half-moon shaped birthmark she noticed immediately after giving birth. Tears pooled in her eyes and a huge smile spread across her face.

Sam stepped into the house to hurry things along. He hoped to make it back to the cabin before dark.

Martha stared lovingly at the mother and child. "Tell her that my sister has a papoose about six-months old. She lives just over the hill from me. She has been feeding the baby since I'm unable to."

Sam relayed the message to White Lily.

White Lily nodded and then turned to face Martha. "*Ne yi we,*" she whispered while hugging her baby tight.

"What'd she say?" Jake asked.

"She said thank you." Martha handed White Lily the animal skins the baby was found in, along with the handmade quilt.

"Mi ti." Martha shook her head. *"Ne yi we."* She lovingly brushed a finger down the baby's cheek. "God blessed me with some time with this precious angel." She dabbed her eyes with her apron.

White Lily gently placed a hand upon Martha's shoulder. She didn't speak—her eyes conveyed more than words could say. They both understood the pain of losing a baby. A beautiful friendship was forged that day. Martha spent a lot of time in the Shawnee village. Oft times Grey Wolf, White Lily, and Little Bear (the papoose was so named after surviving a bear attack) visited Martha on Panther Mountain.

White Lily stepped outside and proudly placed the papoose in Grey Wolf's arms. She then mounted her horse. Grey Wolf let out an excited holler that echoed through the hills, scaring the baby in the process. Everyone laughed as Grey Wolf quickly handed the crying baby to White Lily.

Jake took his horse by the reins, but before he could put his foot in the stirrup, Sam caught him off guard when he dismounted his horse. A few quick strides put him next to Jake. Sam rubbed Jake's head and patted him across the back.

"I'm proud of ya, son," Sam said with a big toothy grin.

"Thank you, sir." Jake's face reddened as he averted his eyes.

"How about calling me Pa." Sam placed a hand on Jake's shoulder and looked him in the eyes.

Jake's face registered confusion. "Excuse me, sir?"

"It's a long story son. I only found out myself this morning." Sam smiled at Grey Wolf and White Lily. "Looks like you're not the only ones to gain a son today." He spoke in Shawnee.

Grey Wolf nodded and White Lily hugged her baby tight. She

turned to find Martha standing at the foot of the front porch steps, tears of joy streaming down her face.

"Si li no ke ka no la." White Lily waved at Martha.

"She said, 'See you again.'" Sam hollered as he placed a foot in the stirrup and threw his leg over his horse. Jake and Johnny did the same and off they rode. Sam insisted they see everyone safely to the village. They said their goodbyes before heading back to the cabin.

It was dark by the time they arrived. The smell of Venison Stew filled the night air.

Sam breathed in the delicious aroma. "I don't know about you boys, but that has my tongue wagging like a hungry ol' dog."

"Better your tongue than your tail," Jake joked.

Sam and Johnny burst into laughter.

"It sure smells good," Jake and Johnny agreed.

They tied the horses next to the front porch. Johnny offered to feed and water the horses before taking them to the corral.

"I'll help." Jake wanted to avoid the conversation with Sam as long as possible.

Sam sensed Jakes' hesitation about going inside. He knew that learning you have a father you had no idea about was a lot to take in. It still felt surreal even to him. He nodded and headed inside the cabin. Johnny and Jake took care of the horses in silence. Johnny's mind was on Anna while Jake pondered the events that unfolded.

After the horses were fed and watered, they led them to the corral and placed them with the rest of the horses.

"Do you think Sam is telling the truth? I mean, about being my father?" Jake leaned against the rail fence.

Johnny fastened the gate and locked it before turning to face

Jake. "Well, you do have his beady eyes and crooked smile." Johnny laughed and then cleared his throat when he saw the serious expression upon Jakes face. "I believe he thinks he is," Johnny added.

"Why did Ma tell me my Pa died before I was born?" Jake whispered.

"I'm sure she had her reasons." Johnny propped his foot on the fence rail.

"I reckon she did." Jake picked up a rock and threw it across the field. "Looks like Ma has some s'plaining to do." Jake bent down to retrieve another rock.

"Explaining," Johnny corrected.

"What?" Jake asked as he tossed another rock.

"Never mind." Johnny was about to change the subject when he caught the whiff of a foul stench. "Do you smell that?" He strained his eyes, trying to see through the darkened woods. The moonlight shined brightly in the sky, lighting up the field.

"It stinks to high heaven. What is that? Jake glanced around the perimeter.

"If I had to guess, I would say it smells like a bear." Johnny loaded his gun that he had removed from his horse along with the saddle before placing him in the corral. "We best be getting back to the cabin."

"Yeah, I guess we should." Jake nervously glanced around before hurrying toward the cabin. Johnny followed close behind. Their eyes constantly scanned the area while they listened for any noises. They made it to the cabin and Jake rushed up the steps and ran inside. As Johnny neared the vicinity, he scanned the area with his eyes darting through the trees trying to adjust to the now darkened woods. He stopped at the foot of the steps when he caught a movement out of the corner of his eye. He turned to see Adam entering the outhouse. Daniel, with gun in hand, had followed Adam to ensure his safety. An uneasy feeling grew in the pit of Johnny's stomach. Just as Adam stepped out of the outhouse, Daniel threw an arm over his shoulder. "Son, walk quickly, don't run." Daniel warned.

"Why?" Adam glanced back over his shoulder but saw nothing.

"I smell a bear." Daniel gripped his gun tightly.

Johnny saw a movement behind a copse of trees. He stepped forward and yelled a warning. "Bear! Bear!" His voice was shrill.

Daniel turned to see the bear standing on its hind legs behind them. Adam backed up, tripped over a tree stump and fell. The bear roared and swiped its huge paw at Daniel, who jumped backwards to avoid the impending strike. His gun flew out of his hand as he tripped over Adam and landed on his back. The bear now loomed over them, growling and slobbering. Daniel felt its hot breath; the putrid smell was nauseating.

"I love ya, son," Daniel shouted. He rolled on top of Adam to protect him. The cabin door flung open upon hearing the commotion outside.

The noise from the men rushing onto the porch, guns in hand, distracted the bear long enough for Johnny to take aim. He pulled the trigger and fired. The bear dropped dead on top of Daniel and Adam. It was the biggest black bear anyone had ever seen. It took four men to roll it.

Upon learning it was Johnny who saved him and his son, Daniel gratefully threw an arm over Johnny's shoulder.

"I can't thank you enough." Daniel smacked him across the shoulder. "Let's get you in the cabin and fix you a huge bowl of venison stew."

"Sir, you're bleeding," Johnny said as he noticed blood oozing through Daniel's shirt sleeve.

"I suppose you're right." Daniel placed a hand over his upper left arm. "I didn't feel a thing."

Everyone rushed back inside. Nathaniel checked Daniel's arm. The sleeve was torn so he placed two fingers in the holes and ripped the rest of it off, revealing puncture wounds from a bite. Nathaniel cleaned the wounds by pouring water over them until all the dirt was washed away.

"It looks like that bear got you good." Sam bent over to get a better look. "The blood is oozing instead of spurting—that's a good thing." Sam reached into his coat pocket. "Here." He handed Nathaniel a flask. "Pour some whiskey over it. That'll take care of it."

"Would you like a swig before I pour some into the wounds?" Nathaniel held the flask up.

"No!" Daniel waved his hand and shook his head. "Just make it quick." He gritted his teeth and winced in pain as Nathaniel pour whiskey into the deep puncture wounds and then wrapped them in a makeshift bandage made from an old shirt one of the men tossed him. He tore it into strips before wrapping Daniel's arm.

"All that time spent hunting, and the bear came to us," James joked.

"It probably smelled the venison stew cooking and followed the scent," one man said.

Everyone agreed. They took a seat while Sam and Nathaniel served the stew and listened to each man tell of the day's events.

CHAPTER NINETEEN

SARAH COMES CLEAN

Sarah examined the book. She liked how Jimmy had taken the time to punch a hole through the printed pages and placed them in a binder, making it easier to flip through it.

"I love this story." Stacy stood.

"Me, too." Grams stared at the gently flowing river.

"I didn't want to stop reading, but it's getting late." Sarah held out a hand to her grandmother.

"Thank you, but I can manage on my own." She playfully swatted Sarah's hand. "Now that I'm twenty years younger than you thought, maybe you'll stop being so overprotective."

"Twenty years younger?" Stacy cocked her head.

"Yes, it seems that Grams is seventy-two and not ninety-two like I thought."

"Whoa, what a shocker." Stacy's eyes grew wide.

"Well, not to me." Grams stood up and folded her chair. "Sarah here has a bad habit of jumping to conclusions instead of asking a simple question." She winked at Stacy.

"Oh, I know that's right," Stacy agreed while giving Sarah the side eye.

"You two need to stop." Sarah rolled her eyes. "As for what

you're referring to—" She turned to face Stacy. "I'm working on it."

"What's there to work on? Just ask him." Stacy turned on her heel and headed for the car.

"I have no idea what you girls are talking about, but whatever it is, you best stop beating around the bush," Grams stated before picking up the lawn chair and making her way to the car.

Sarah knew she couldn't win between the two of them and she also knew they were right. "Fine, I'll ask him," she whispered to herself.

"Are you coming, or are you going to stand there talking to yourself?" Grams shouted just before closing the car door.

Sarah hurried to the car, placed everything in the trunk and headed home. Her mind was made up. She was going to confront Jimmy and see what he had to say for himself. She stopped at Serenity's Café and ordered a large ultimate deluxe pizza to go.

Upon arriving home, they noticed the work trucks were gone. The crew had finished for the day and left to enjoy their weekend with their families. Sarah couldn't help but feel disappointed. After unloading the car and putting everything away, they went inside.

Grams and Stacy took a seat at the breakfast table. It was always Sarah's favorite spot. The round table sat in the corner of the kitchen surrounded by windows. The pale yellow and white curtains had sunflowers along the edge. The matching tablecloth made the area appear sunny and cheerful.

"I have a craving for peach cobbler." Sarah took a baking dish out of the cabinet and placed it on the counter.

"I've never had peach cobbler."

Grams gasped, causing Stacy to look at her. "I can't believe you are from the south and have never had peach cobbler." Grams stood. "You do like peaches, right?"

"I love peaches." Stacy stood and strolled over to Sarah. "Can I help?"

"Sure but let me say that you're in for a treat." Sarah ran down to the basement and returned with a jar of Grams' home-canned peaches. "All set." Sarah opened the jar.

"What do we do first?" Stacy asked.

"Open a stick of butter and place it in the baking dish and slide it in the oven." Sarah pointed to the butter. "I've already preheated the oven."

Stacy did as she was told.

"I like to let the butter melt while I mix the rest of the ingredients." Sarah handed Stacy a bowl.

"What's that for?" Stacy set the bowl on the counter.

"I'm teaching you the way Grams taught me." Sarah placed self-rising flour, granulated sugar, milk, and a measuring cup on the counter. "There ya go, you only need one cup of each ingredient. Pour them into the bowl and mix well." Sarah put on a baking glove, opened the oven and removed the baking dish with the now softened butter. She stirred it around until it completely melted. Then she poured the peaches and the syrup they were canned with into the dish. She turned to find Stacy watching closely.

"It's mixed, but slightly lumpy." Stacy stared into the bowl.

"Oh, it's fine. It does that, but the lumps will cook out." Sarah smiled. "Just pour it evenly over the peaches."

"All I see is peach juice and butter." Stacy giggled.

"Trust me, by the time it gets done baking, you'll have a delicious dessert," Sarah assured her.

Before long, the sweet aroma of peach cobbler filled the air. While it baked, Sarah took Stacy to the basement to show her where the book was found. Once in the basement, Sarah noticed that Jimmy had placed new steps and a door leading outside.

"I guess the raccoon won't be coming back in anytime soon," Sarah mumbled.

"Did you say raccoon?" Stacy froze.

"Relax." Sarah chuckled. "That coon is long gone. Besides, Jimmy built a new door and steps."

"I'm telling you, he's a keeper," Stacy said in a sing-song voice.

"We'll see," Sarah replied. "Anyway, the original foundation are those huge stones placed around the bottom of the wall," Sarah continued.

"I take it that the book was found over there." Stacy pointed to the loose stone sitting next to an opening in the wall.

"Yes, it was in a hand-carved wooden box and then placed in a handcrafted steel box. Both of which are in my room."

"You'll have to show me later." Stacy walked over and ran her hand over the stone foundation. "Do you truly believe this is the house from the book?"

"I'm sure of it," Sarah said confidently.

"Amazing," Stacy whispered.

"If you think that's amazing, wait until you taste peach cobbler," Sarah said. "Come to think of it, it should be done by now." She sniffed the air, but the only thing she smelled was the musty old basement.

They headed up the basement stairs. Upon entering the kitchen, they were met with the sweet scent of freshly baked cobbler. Grams had pulled it from the oven and placed it on top of the stove to cool.

"Now that's more like it." Sarah closed her eyes and breathed in the decadent dessert.

"It sure smells better than the basement." Stacy stared at the golden-brown crust. "It smells and looks heavenly."

"She sure does." Jimmy followed Grams through the back door. He could hardly take his eyes off Sarah. She blushed and turned her head in the opposite direction.

"Now's your chance to confront him," Stacy whispered as she took the plate of cobbler from Sarah's hand. She scooped up a spoonful and then rolled her eyes as she took a bite. "Oh my gosh, this is so good."

"I knew you'd like it." Sarah scooped another serving into a bowl and handed it to Jimmy. "I hope you like peach cobbler."

"A woman after my own heart." Jimmy took the bowl. "I haven't had this since I was a boy."

Sarah watched as he closed his eyes and took in the aroma as though he were reliving a happy childhood memory. A curly strand of hair fell over his forehead. It was all Sarah could do to keep from brushing it back into place with her fingers. The plum-colored shirt he wore made his green eyes pop. Sarah stood transfixed as his eyes met hers.

Stacy brought them both back to reality when she spoke. "It's hard to believe something so simple to make is this delicious."

Sarah cleared her throat and took a step back. "It's Grams' recipe. I hope you like it."

"I'm sure I will." Jimmy held up a forkful and took a huge bite. He closed his eyes and savored it. "Yum, this is the best peach cobbler I've ever had." Before long, he stood there holding an empty bowl.

"It's now or never." Stacy took Jimmy's empty bowl and set it in the sink.

"Stacy, what are you doing?" Sarah spoke through gritted teeth.

"I'm helping you get to the bottom of things once and for all," Stacy replied. "Jimmy, Sarah needs to have a word with you." She placed a hand on both their shoulders and shoved them toward the back door.

"Stacy, stop. Now's not the time," Sarah argued.

"If you don't, then I will." Stacy stood her ground.

"Fine, but you and I will talk about with this later." Sarah glowered at Stacy and then followed Jimmy out the door.

Jimmy and Sarah stood quietly for several minutes before Jimmy broke the awkward silence. "Look, Sarah, I have no idea what all that is about, but—"

"Okay, Jimmy, I'm going to be straight with you." She paused. "Would you like to take a walk?"

"Sure, I guess." Jimmy hesitated when he stepped off the last step. "Listen, if one of my men offended you or your grandmother in any way, I'll—"

"No, it's nothing like that." She shook her head. "They've all been extremely polite."

"Then whatever it is, just tell me." Jimmy took her by the hand.

"Fine, are you trying to scam my grandmother out of her house?" Sarah blurted it out. Although she finally got it off her chest, she wondered why she didn't feel a sense of relief. Instead, she felt worse, and the expression on Jimmy's face didn't help.

"Wait! What? How could you think such a thing?" He began pacing. "I need to know where you got such a horrendous idea from." He ran his fingers through his hair.

"I overheard a phone conversation." Sarah bit her lower lip.

Jimmy stopped pacing, and his eyes bore right through her. "You mean you were eavesdropping?" He crossed his arms over his chest and stood with his legs shoulder-length apart.

"No, I wasn't." Sarah wished she could be anywhere but here. "You told someone that the old lady's house was worth more than the offer and you could get a lot more out of it," she said in her defense.

"If you think that I'm the type of person capable of scamming people . . . ." His eyes ignited with anger. "Especially someone as sweet as your grandmother!" He paused. "I don't know what to say, except I think we're done here." He turned to walk away.

"Jimmy, wait!" Sarah grabbed his arm, which he quickly jerked away and continued walking. "I was only looking out for my grandmother," she shouted, but it was too late.

Jimmy made it to his truck and was backing out of the driveway. He took one last glance at Sarah and saw tears spill over and run down her cheeks. She dropped to her knees on the ground and sobbed. It was all he could do to keep from slamming the truck into park and rushing to comfort her. He knew he let his anger get the better of him. He thought they had a special connection, but now he wasn't so sure about anything.

Grams and Stacy rushed outside when they saw Jimmy's truck pull angrily out of the driveway.

"Oh, Sarah, I'm so sorry." Stacy dropped to her knees beside Sarah. "This is all my fault." She hugged Sarah and cried with her.

"No. It's not your fault," Sarah managed between sniffles. "I should've confronted him from day one."

"Let's get you in the house before Ol' Sourpuss sees us."

Grams pulled a tissue from her apron pocket and handed it to Sarah before taking her by the arm and helping her.

"Who's Ol' Sourpuss?" Stacy inquired as they stepped onto the back porch.

"Stick around. You'll find out soon enough." Grams opened the back door and held it for Sarah and Stacy.

"Is she the neighbor you were telling me about? You know, the one who is trying to steal the pie recipe?" Stacy asked as they made their way into the living room.

"The one and only." Sarah chuckled and then blew her nose on the tissue. "Look at me." She motioned to her face. "I'm blubbering like a baby over a guy I barely know." She grabbed another tissue from the box on the coffee table. "I'm such an idiot," she grumbled as she plopped down on the sofa.

"You're not an idiot," Grams soothed. "You're falling in love for the first time." She took a seat on the sofa next to Sarah.

"Grams!" Sarah gasped. "I am not in love with him. I mean, we only just met like a few weeks ago." Sarah's voice trailed off.

"Who are you trying to convince?" Stacy motioned to herself and to Grams. "Us or yourself?"

"How about we just change the subject and read some more from the book," Sarah suggested.

"That's a great idea." Stacy started toward the kitchen. "I'll reheat the pizza," she shouted over her shoulder.

"I'll pour us a glass of sweet iced tea." Grams followed Stacy into the kitchen.

Stacy walked to the kitchen sink, turned on the faucet, and splashed water on her face. Grams placed an arm over her shoulder and whispered to her.

"Don't blame yourself for anything that happened this evening," Grams said softly. "If they're meant to be together, then things have a way of working itself out." Grams poured herself a glass of lemonade and then patted Stacy on the arm. "Let's go find out what happens to Anna and Johnny."

Grams and Stacy met Sarah in the living room. She sat on the sofa with the book open on her lap. They were all anxious to get back to the story.

"All right dear, you may begin." Grams took a sip of her drink and waited.

Sarah began to read.

CHAPTER TWENTY

New Friends

Early the following morning the men packed up and headed home. They were anxious to get back into town to check on Ben and let everyone know the bear was no longer a threat. Daniel, James, Adam, and Johnny decided to stay with Nathaniel a few days longer to hunt for deer. They didn't want to go home empty handed. No one dared to keep any bear meat since it was infected. Sam skinned it and made a bear skin rug he planned to give to Ben as a gift. Before leaving, everyone gathered in a circle and said a prayer for Ben in hopes he survived through the night and for a full recovery.

After the others left, Nathaniel, Daniel, and the boys headed over the mountain to hunt deer. Johnny hunted with Nathaniel, while Daniel hunted with his sons James and Adam. Several hours later, just before sunrise, shots rang out through the mountains. Nathaniel and Johnny each got a deer.

An icy chill filled the air and snow flurries began to blow. They tracked them down and hurried to field dress them before the weather got much colder. Using their horses, they easily dragged the carcasses to the cabin where they finished skinning and cutting up the meat.

"I wonder how Daniel and the boys are faring?" Nathaniel asked as he placed the slabs of meat in one of the many sacks Gracie made for him for this purpose.

I'm hoping they all get one." Johnny finished placing the last of his meat in the sack Nathaniel handed him. After tying it shut, they carried both sacks outside.

"It would be a real shame for someone to come back empty handed," Nathaniel said as he studied the huge Maple tree that stood next to the cabin. "Do you think you can climb that tree and tie these bags to that huge branch while I hold them up?"

"I believe so, sir." Johnny had no problem climbing the tree and shimming onto the huge branch. Nathaniel rolled a huge block of wood underneath the branch and then stood on it to put him closer to the branch so he wouldn't have to hold the sack of venison too high over his head. The plan worked like a charm. Johnny wrapped the rope from each sack around the branch several times and tied it tightly to the branch,

"That should hold it." Johnny said proudly as he climbed back down the tree. "It's high enough that no animal can reach it from the ground and hanging low enough that none can get to it from the branch."

"At least not before getting caught first," Nathaniel agreed.

Two more shots rang out over the mountainside. "Hopefully, that's a good sign." Johnny stared in the direction of the shots.

Forty-five minutes later, Daniel and James appeared at the edge of the woods. Both were grinning. There was no mistaken which two made a kill. Adam came trudging behind looking tired and forlorn. Johnny couldn't help feeling sorry for him. He knew how much it meant for Adam to get his first deer. After all, this was his and James' first deer as well.

Johnny helped James prepare his venison while Nathaniel

helped Daniel with his. They once again placed the meat in a sack and hung it in the tree, all except a strip of tenderloin they cleaned, sliced, and fried for dinner. Nathaniel had just enough flour to make biscuits.

"Oh, boy, there's nothing like fried venison on a hot biscuit." James broke open a biscuit and placed a few slices of meat on it and took a bite.

"It doesn't get any better than this." Adam finished off his and made another.

"Sorry you didn't get a deer this time, son. Maybe next time." Daniel rubbed his son's head.

"It's alright, Pa. We still have tomorrow." Adam finished off his meal. To everyone's surprise, he took his plate to the wash tub then washed and dried it.

"Thank you, Adam. I appreciate that." Nathaniel tipped his hat at him.

Not to be outdone by Adam, James and Johnny washed and dried their own dishes. Johnny even went so far as to wash Daniel and Nathaniel's as well as the frying pan.

"Well, that's a nice end to a wonderful day, don't you agree?" Nathaniel looked around the room and smiled as the boys huddled in the corner playing a game of marbles.

"The women folk are sure gonna be surprised when we come home with all this deer meat." Nathaniel leaned back in his chair and stretched his legs. By the way, how many points did yours and James' deer have?"

"Mine was a six-point and James got a four-point." Daniel smiled. "I couldn't let the boy out hunt his old man. How about you and Johnny?"

"Mine was a six-point same as yours, but Johnny there, got himself an eight-point," Nathaniel said proudly as though

Johnny were his own son.

"Nice job, Johnny." Daniel stood and shook Johnny's hand. "You got the biggest buck." He leaned close to Johnny. "At least, this time." He slapped Johnny across the shoulder. "You're a decent young man and you'll make some woman happy one day." Daniel turned to walk away.

"What about Anna, sir?" Johnny stood.

Daniel stopped and turned to face him.

James and Adam's eyes grew wide. Adam scrambled to collect all his marbles and shoved them in the pockets of his britches.

Johnny's heart leapt into his throat as Daniel smiled playfully at Nathaniel before turning to face Johnny. "Sir, I-I would like to come calling on Anna," Johnny stuttered. "That is, with your kind permission sir."

Daniel cleared his throat. "What are your intentions toward my youngest daughter, my baby girl?" his voice boomed.

"Purely respectful, sir. I-I would never allow her to come to any harm." Johnny could feel his insides quaking.

"What does Anna think about this?" Daniel questioned.

"I don't know, sir. I haven't asked her." Johnny felt as though he were sinking through the floor as beads of sweat popped out on his forehead.

"Calm down, son. I was only funning with ya." Daniel pulled Johnny in for a huge hug. "How can I say no to the young man who saved mine and my son's lives?" He released Johnny and mussed his hair. "You're a fine young man, Johnny Carlin."

"Thank you, sir."

That night everyone went to bed with joy in their hearts and a smile on their faces. Each person had something to thank God for.

"What is it with Adam?" Johnny whispered to James. "He's been smiling all evening."

"I noticed that too." James whispered back while watching Adam at the same time. "Who knows, maybe the cold weather froze his brain." James snickered.

Johnny wasn't convinced. He decided to watch Adam like a hawk. Something wasn't right with him, and Johnny wanted to know what it was.

Daniel and Nathaniel kept the fire going all night, keeping the cabin warm and toasty. Everyone slept like logs. Everyone except Adam. He rose at the crack of dawn, grabbed his gun, and snuck out on the back porch. A dusting of snow covered the porch and the ground. A chill shot through his bones as he lay on his belly on the porch, gun ready and aimed toward the dark woods. He said a little prayer and waited.

In the cabin, Johnny dreamed peacefully of Anna. James softly snored on the pallet next to his, while Daniel and Nathaniel slept soundly across the room.

A loud gunshot echoed through the cabin, startling everyone. They all scrambled, trying to get up. Nathaniel's long legs became entangled in his blankets, tripping him and causing him to fall into Daniel.

"What in tarnation is going on?" Daniel shouted as he staggered.

The back door to the cabin flew open and an excited Adam came rushing in shouting. "Pa, Pa! I got it Pa! I knew he would come back."

"Calm down, son, and tell me what's going on," Daniel said.

Johnny and James were both standing against the wall trying to figure out what was happening.

Nathaniel finally freed himself from his blankets and stood

next to Daniel, just as confused as the rest of them.

“Come see, Pa.” Adam raced out the door onto the back porch. He stopped and pointed to the right. “There he is,” he shouted proudly.

Daniel could hardly believe his eyes. He turned to see if anyone else was seeing what he was seeing.

“Lord a mercy, is that a ten-point buck, or is my eyes deceiving me?” Nathaniel never took his eyes off the deer.

“No, that’s a ten-point as sure as I’m standing here.” Daniel stared in disbelief.

“Well, don’t just stand there, help me with it!” Adam shouted excitedly.

Everyone raced through the cabin and out the front door where they all helped Adam skin and clean his massive prize buck. Adam never stopped grinning the whole time.

Once back in town, everyone ran to shake Johnny’s hand for shooting the bear and saving two lives, but everyone became distracted by the massive set of antlers tied to Adam’s horse. Sam and Jake were the first to notice.

“What do you have there?” Sam pointed at the rack. “Is that several racks put together?” He expected Adam to say yes. His eyes widened in disbelief when Adam removed the rack and handed it to him.

“I got him this morning.” Adam sat a little taller in his saddle. “Shot him from the back porch of the cabin.” He grinned.

“Well, I’ll be.” Sam held the antlers up for all to see. “If that ain’t the biggest rack I’ve ever seen, and this young man here brought it down.”

A reporter for the newspaper, a thin little man with a mustache that appeared too big for his face, shoved his way through the crowd. “Hello, I’m from the *Virginia Gazette*.” He adjusted his tricorne hat and loosened his ascot tie. “Do you mind answering a few questions?” he asked Johnny and Adam.

“How’s Ben?” Daniel took off his hat, preparing for bad news.

“He’s still kickin’.” Sam looked toward heaven. “Thanks to the good Lord above and the Shawnee. Doc says Ben should be all right.”

“He's a stubborn old coot.” Burl stepped next to Sam.

“That he is, but we wouldn’t have him any other way.” Daniel turned his attention back to Adam and the reporter.

Nathaniel was drawn to the commotion across the street. A buckboard carrying a family of slaves, a father, mother, and child who appeared to be around six years old were chained in the back of the buckboard. Nathaniel’s blood boiled as he pulled from his pocket the paper he took off the mercantile wall and read it. “It says the sale doesn’t start for another two hours.” he said loudly.

“Did you say something?” Daniel asked, all the while proudly watching the reporter speaking with Adam.

“I’ll be right back.” Nathaniel left to find the person in charge of the sale. He grabbed two boys by the scruff of the neck when he caught them harassing and throwing dirt at the family.

“Where’s your Pa and Ma?” Nathaniel shouted.

“What’s going on here?” The mother ran out of the mercantile, her eyes wide as she looked from her sons to Nathaniel.

“You’ll do good to teach them some manners.” Nathaniel shoved the boys toward her.

“Aw, we weren’t doing nothing wrong,” the oldest of the two boys shouted.

“Yeah, they’re just slaves and we were having fun,” the youngest boy replied.

"Boys, you're lucky if I don't tan your hide myself." Nathaniel stepped toward them. They ran and hid behind their mother. She stretched out her arms to shield them.

"Don't touch my children," she screeched.

"Your children are acting like heathens." Nathaniel glared at her. "They were throwing dirt on these people and their child." He motioned to the family in the buckboard behind him.

The boys' mother peeked around Nathaniel to see who he was referring to. "Well, boys will be boys," she said sarcastically as she gathered her skirt in her hands and stuck her nose in the air. "Besides, you heard them. They were only having fun, with, with . . . ." She leaned toward Nathaniel and whispered, "The slaves."

"Woman, it's no wonder your children haven't any manners, when their own mother doesn't have the brains that God gave a goat."

"I've never been talk to in such a manner in all my life." She looked toward the tavern doors when they swung open. Her husband staggered out to see what the fuss was about. "George, are you going to stand there and let your wife be insulted like this?" she shouted at her husband.

"Nope, I ain't gonna stand here." He hiccupped. "I'm a-sittin' back down and enjoying my drink." He motioned toward the tavern.

"George, you get back here!" she bellowed.

"Bah." George threw his hand in the air, turned, and staggered back into the tavern.

Nathaniel guffawed as the woman huffed. She grabbed her children by the hands and stormed down the street. "You'll do well to teach them boys some respect." Nathaniel shouted after her. A noise behind him caused him to whirl around. A chubby man half Nathaniel's height stood next to the buckboard, running his hands over his long scraggly beard.

"Hello, there. Are you the person in charge of the sale of these here slaves?" Nathaniel leaned against the buckboard. He hated the word *slaves* but knew he couldn't allow the slave trader to know that.

"Indeed, I am, sir. The name's William Barris, Will, for short." The man held out his hand toward Nathaniel. "Who wants to know?" Nathaniel begrudgingly shook hands. "The name's Nathaniel. How much for the lot of them?"

Will stood straight and began to pace back and forth next to the buckboard. "Well now, let's see." He stopped and smacked the father on the shoulder. "This here is a mighty fine specimen. He's strong as a bull and—"

"Spare me the details," Nathaniel said impatiently. "He's clearly worn out, his wife looks ill, the child is sickly, and from what I can tell, he is possibly going blind. I'll give you two hundred dollars."

The child gave Nathaniel a sly grin. He hugged his mama tightly. "Mama my eyes hurt. Where's Poppa? I can't see him."

Will rushed over to the boy and waved a hand in front of his face. The boy never flinched. Will cursed under his breath and paced nervously for a few minutes before turning to Nathaniel. "The auction isn't scheduled to start for another hour and a half. I can get a hundred and fifty each. That's . . . Umm . . . ." Will counted on his fingers. "Four hundred and fifty dollars."

"All right, then you do that, but I guarantee that no one here is willing to pay that amount for two sick adults and a half blind child," Nathaniel bluffed. "You can try to take them to Richmond for the main auction, if they survive the trip, let alone the night."

Johnny stood by observing, He tried his best not to burst into laughter as he watched Nathaniel bargain with the slave trader. Johnny stepped next to the slaves and pretended to be a potential buyer. He gave them all the once over.

"You interested in buying, sir?" Will sounded hopeful.

"Nah, they appear to be on their last leg, and the boy may not survive the winter." Johnny placed his hand on the boy's chin, looked him in the eyes, and winked. "The boy can't half-see. No sale here." He walked away. stopping in front of the saloon doors. "What'd you do? Win them in a poker game?" Johnny faked a laugh.

"Dag nabbit!" Will yanked off his hat and slapped it against his leg. "I should have known that game was rigged."

"Well, it was nice talking with ya. You have a good day." Nathaniel tipped his hat and pretended to lose interest in the purchase. He turned to walk away.

"Wait!" Will shouted. "Two hundred, ya say?"

Nathaniel nodded.

"Fine, give me the money and get them out of my sight." Will spoke through gritted teeth, He snatched the money from Nathaniel's outstretched hand. He pulled the papers of ownership from his pocket. "How do you spell your name?"

Nathaniel patiently spelled his name while Will filled out the paperwork and signed it. He quickly unlocked the shackles. The boy jumped to the ground and hugged Nathaniel's leg, while the parents kept bowing their heads saying, "Thank you, master."

Now that they were in Nathaniel's possession, he began to lay down the rules.

"I only have three rules that I expect you to follow. The first and most important rule is that you are not my slaves, and I am not your owner. You are flesh and blood created in the image of God the same as anyone. You'll be treated like family, fed three meals per day, and paid a decent wage for helping on my farm. I would appreciate it if you would call me by my name, Nathaniel, and my wife's name is Gracie. You'll meet her soon." Nathaniel rubbed his sweaty palms down his pant leg. The family stared in disbelief. They were unsure if they heard correctly or if this is some kind of horrible prank.

"Uh, may I ask what your names are?" Nathaniel asked the father.

"My name's Amos, sir." He nervously shook Nathaniel's outstretched hand. "This right here is my wife, Hattie Mae, and our son, Isaiah." Amos leaned in. "The boy's not blind, sir."

Nathaniel burst into laughter. "Yes, sir, I knew that, but ol' Will didn't."

Amos chuckled while Hattie Mae fidgeted awkwardly with her rag of a dress and kept a tight hold of her son's hand.

"Well, now, Amos, let's get you and your family home. Right after I've fetched my wife. I haven't seen her in two days.

"That's a long time to be without family, sir." Amos put his arm around Hattie Mae's shoulder and gave her a little squeeze. "Everything's gonna be all right," he said softly in her ear.

She smiled halfheartedly. She wasn't fond of things that seemed too good to be true, and this was one of them. The white folks never treated any of her people with love and kindness. Why should she believe this man to be any different? The question played over in her mind, only to be quickly replaced with the words Nathaniel spoke: *You are created in the image of God, you are family.* "God, please let this be real," she whispered.

Nathaniel fetched his horse and wagon. He motioned for Amos and Hattie Mae to sit upon the driver's seat. A confused look crossed Amos's brow as he helped his wife on board.

"You have driven a horse and wagon before, haven't you?" Nathaniel asked.

"Oh, yes, sir," Amos replied and took his seat. Nathaniel lifted Isaiah and sat him between his mama and poppa.

Johnny handed his reigns to Nathaniel. "Here, take my horse. I'll ride with Adam."

Isaiah stood. "May I ride with you?" He stretched his little arms toward Nathaniel.

Nathaniel rubbed Isaiah's head. "It's fine with me, but you need to ask your Ma and Pa if it's all right with them." He looked from Amos to Hattie Mae. They weren't sure how to react. They'd never been asked for their permission to do anything. They both smiled and nodded. They knew this new way of life would take some getting used to.

Before long, Daniel's house came into view. The women rushed onto the porch anxious to hear of their adventure. When the cart rolled to a stop, Gracie raced to Nathaniel's waiting arms. He spun her around.

"I have a surprise," he said excitedly. He helped Issiah off the horse. The little boy ran to meet Gracie.

"Hello, and who might you be?" she asked, her eyes wide and mouth agape when Amos and Hattie Mae climbed out of the wagon and stood next to it.

Hattie Mae shifted from one foot to the other, keeping her eyes to the ground.

"This is Amos, Hattie Mae, and their son Isaiah," Nathaniel announced. "I, uh, I purchased them."

"Nathaniel, you know how I feel about owning slaves," she

said softly. It just isn't right."

"They're no longer slaves." Nathaniel stood next to Amos. "I didn't purchase them." He paused. "I purchased their freedom."

"Freedom, sir?" Amos choked back tears.

"Yes, sir, Amos. You and your family will never be slaves again." Nathaniel smiled proudly.

Hattie Mae swiped at tears that spilled over and ran down her cheeks. Gracie placed an arm around her to comfort her.

"Now, don't you fret, Mrs. Hattie. You're among family and friends here." Gracie pulled a handkerchief from her apron pocket. She handed it to Hattie Mae.

"Thank you, ma'am." Hattie Mae gently took the handkerchief and dabbed her eyes.

"You may stay with us until you and your family can make it on your own." Gracie looked lovingly at Nathaniel and whispered, "Thank you."

"Hello, Mrs. Hattie Mae. I'm Mary Lou, Daniel's wife," she introduced herself. "Let's get you folks in from the cold." Mary Lou and Gracie each locked arms with Hattie Mae and walked with her toward the house.

Hattie Mae nervously glanced back at Amos. She wasn't used to being treated kindly by white folk. *God, if I'm dreaming, please don't let me wake up.*

"I hope everyone's hungry," Mary Lou announced as they stepped onto the front porch. "We cooked enough to feed an army."

As they walked through the front door, Amos, Hattie Mae, and Isaiah's nostrils were met with the delicious aroma of home cooking. Their stomachs did a somersault. They followed everyone into the dining room where Anna and Virginia had just finished putting the last of the food on the table. Amos, Hattie Mae, and Isaiah kept their distance and stood against the far wall.

"Hello, I'm Anna. If you folks would care to follow me, I'll show you where you can wash up for supper." Anna led them to a room off from the kitchen. She filled two wash pans with warm water and placed clean towels and soap next to the pans. "I'll find you something to wear, ma'am." She left the room, returning a few minutes later with two dresses draped over her arm. "These are for you." She handed the dresses to Hattie Mae. "The green one is from my sister Virginia and the blue one is from me."

"Oh, my goodness! I've never had such beautiful clothes." Hattie Mae held a dress up against herself. "Thank you, miss."

"You're very welcome." Anna smiled and then turned to Amos. "My brother James is fetching you a change of clothes as well." James knocked and stepped in with a white button up shirt and britches for Amos.

"Ma said these might be a little big on Isaiah, but he's welcome to them." James lay the clothes on the chair next to the wash basin, nodded and left the room, followed by Anna.

While Amos cleaned himself, Hattie Mae sponged Isaiah off then dressed him. The clothes were too big, but she was grateful to have them and they were clean. She folded the sleeves and the pant cuffs. Then she pulled a piece of twine she had her hair tied back with and fastened it around Isaiah's waist to hold his britches up. "Where's my little Isaiah?" she asked, pretending not to recognize her son.

"I'm right here, Mama." Isaiah giggled and ran out of the room before Hattie Mae or Amos could stop him. Amos quickly changed and hurried after him.

Hattie Mae closed her eyes and listened for the sound of a

strap across the backs of her husband and son. She braced herself for the screams that would soon follow. To her surprise, her ears were met with joy and laughter coming from her precious little boy and her loving husband. She finished sponging off and slipped into the blue dress before dropping to her knees and praying. "Dear heavenly father, please let this be real. Thank you for watching over my family and for placing us with good people." She stood and headed to the dining room. Amos' eyes lit up when he saw his wife in her new dress. He reminded himself to tell her how beautiful she looked when they were alone.

While all eyes were on Hattie Mae, Isaiah swiped a piece of bread from the table and crammed it into his mouth. He couldn't help himself. He was so hungry. Hattie Mae rushed to him and pulled him away from the table. Using her body to shield her son, she bent over him to protect him. "I'm sorry, master," she cried out. "The boy hasn't eaten in three days. Please forgive him and punish me instead." She kept her head to the floor.

Everyone sat in stunned silence. Gracie burst into tears and ran to Hattie Mae. "What have they done to y'all?" She gently took Hattie Mae and Isaiah by the hand and led them to the table. "No one will lay a finger on you or your family ever again." Pain and anger resonated in her voice.

Hattie Mae reluctantly took a seat at the table with Isaiah on one side and Amos was offered the seat on the other side of her. They sat in awkward silence for several minutes. They were used to sitting in the slave's quarters or the kitchen with very little if anything to eat. Ma stood and made each of them a plate with plenty of everything, from roast chicken, vegetables, bread, and apple pie for dessert. Everyone ate their fill.

As dessert was being served, Gracie lovingly took Nathaniel by the hand and announced, "Honey, the barley grew."

Nathaniel tilted his head quizzically. "What does that mean?"

Ma covered her mouth to stifle a laugh.

"It means that come spring, you—I mean we—will be welcoming a new addition to our family. I'm with child!" she shouted and stood up. Her face glowed.

Nathaniel leapt. "Is it true? I'm going to be a father?" He grabbed her and lifted her up, hugging her tight. "Oh, sorry, are you all right?" He gently sat her down.

"I'm fine. I just need to find a midwife."

"Excuse me, ma'am." Hattie Mae fidgeted. "I delivered a lot of babies in my time. Exactly fourteen." She dropped her head and stared at her hands.

"Oh, Hattie Mae, that's perfect," Gracie shouted. "You'll be close by when birthing time comes."

Hattie Mae was taken aback when Gracie hugged her. After dinner, she began to clear the table and prepare to wash dishes only to be stopped by Anna and Virginia.

"You're our guest. Just rest while we clean up." Virginia took the stack of plates from Hattie Mae's hands.

"I-I'm not used to anyone waiting on me or my family." Hattie Mae wrung her hands. "I mean, it just don't feel right."

"If it will make you feel better, you may help us." Anna smiled.

"Thank you. It's the least I can do for such a wonderful meal." Hattie Mae finished clearing the table and helped clean up.

"Well, I believe we should get going." Nathaniel placed his arms around Grace's waist. "I'd like to get home before dark."

They said their goodbyes and headed home. Once home,

Gracie showed Hattie Mae the house and the room they'd be staying in, while Nathaniel walked Amos across the property pointing out the boundaries as they came to them. They made their way back toward the house, stopping on a beautiful flat piece of ground. "What do you think of this spot?" Nathaniel stood with his hands on his hips.

"Well, sir. I believe it would make a lovely garden spot." Amos stared at the area.

"That it would," Nathaniel agreed. "I was thinking of building a house here."

"This is a perfect spot for a new house, sir. And I would be happy to help build it for you." Amos turned to face Nathaniel.

"Deal." Nathaniel stretched his hand toward Ames, who took it and gave it a firm shake. "You can't break a deal, Amos." Nathaniel refused to turn loose of his hand.

"Oh, no, sir. I would never." Amos stared at him wide-eyed.

"Good, because we're building this home for you and your family." Nathaniel slapped him across the shoulder. "What do ya think?"

"I... I... uh. Well, sir, I don't know what to say." Amos tried to hide his trepidation, but it was no use. Nathaniel noticed right away.

"Don't you fret, Amos. There are no strings attached." Nathaniel smiled warmly. "I'm doing what I feel is right and good in the eyes of God, and you seem like an honest man."

"Thank you, sir, I appreciate that, but I promise to work hard and repay you for everything, even if it takes the rest of my life."

"Let's not worry about any of that right now." Nathaniel looked back at the empty field. "We'll start building this spring, and over there—" He pointed. "That is where we'll plant a huge garden and split the bounty." Nathaniel laughed when Amos could no longer contain his excitement and let out a loud "Wahoo!" that echoed through the hills. In fact, it was so loud Gracie and Hattie Mae came running to see what the shouting was all about.

Amos grabbed Hattie Mae in his arms and spun her around. "We're going to have our own home, Hattie!" Amos shouted. He stopped spinning and set her down. "Right here in this very spot." He motioned with his arms outstretched wide.

Nathaniel thought he would burst with happiness for Amos and Hattie Mae. He strolled over and stood next to Gracie and placed an arm around her. Neither one could stop smiling as they watched Amos and Hattie Mae hug each other and weep tears of joy.

"You did the right thing." Gracie stared at her husband with tear-filled eyes. "I want our son to grow up to be just like you,"

"A son? Are you sure it's going to be a boy?" Nathaniel squeezed her hand.

"According to the saying, if the wheat grows it's a girl; if the barley sprouts, then it's a boy." She stared lovingly into his eyes.

"That's what you meant when you said the barley grew." Nathaniel chuckled.

Gracie nodded and swiped at a tear with the back of her hand. Nathaniel leaned down and gently kissed her lips. "How about we go inside and let Amos and Hattie Mae discuss their future alone?" Nathaniel glanced over his shoulder at Amos and Hattie, who were in deep conversation, oblivious to anything else going on around them. Gracie and Nathaniel walked hand-in-hand toward home.

CHAPTER TWENTY-ONE

FIRST KISS

Sarah closed the book and sat running her fingers over the pages. "What a beautiful gesture." She averted her gaze. "Too bad things aren't like they were back then," she said sadly.

"What do you mean?" Grams asked.

"Men were more manly then, more loving and protective." Sarah stood, hugging the book to her. "It seems the men and women fought for what they wanted and never gave up on each other." She handed the book to Grams and walked out onto the back porch.

A few minutes later, Grams stepped next to Sarah. "Do you want my honest opinion?" Grams stared at the stars in the night sky. When she got no reply, she continued. "I believe you're developing feelings for Jimmy, and you don't know how to handle that."

"I can't possibly have feelings for someone I've only known for a few weeks," Sarah stated.

Grams rolled her eyes. Before she could respond, Sarah said, "Seriously, Grams. We've never even kissed."

"Ah, Phooey." Grams brushed her hand in the air. "Kissing has nothing to do with it." She sat on the patio swing and patted the seat next to her.

Sarah plopped down beside her.

Grams stared at the evening sky. "I know a couple who talked on the phone for several months before they ever met face-to-face. Four months, to be exact, and they fell in love during those long, late-night conversations. The feelings grew stronger after they met for the first time."

"What happened to them?" Sarah questioned.

"We got married." Gram stood. "Not right away, but we did marry, a year later."

"Wow! I didn't know that, but this is different." Sarah looked away. "I mean, we haven't spent that much time together."

"It still doesn't change what the heart feels and wants," Grams said soothingly. "Your heart wants Jimmy." She paused. "And I believe he feels the same, just give him time."

"I need to have a word with Stacy." Sarah glanced toward the kitchen door.

"Take it easy on her. She's looking out for your best interest." Grams watched Stacy as she paced the kitchen floor. "She loves you like a sister, and a friendship like that comes once in a lifetime."

Sarah held out a hand to her grandmother. "You're right about that. She's the best friend anyone could ask for." They made their way back into the house.

Stacy was deep in thought, staring out the kitchen window. Sarah rushed over and hugged her.

"I'm sorry for meddling into your business." Stacy stepped back. "It won't happen again," she said sincerely.

"You were doing what you felt was right. Don't you dare change." Sarah playfully punched Stacy on the arm.

A tap at the back door startled them. Sarah turned to find

Jimmy standing there, a forlorn look upon his face. Her heart leapt into her chest. She raced to him, stopping within inches of him. “We need to talk,” she said softly.

“I agree.” Jimmy took her by the hand and led her outside toward the flower garden.

The sun had just begun its descent, casting a warm, golden hue across the sky. The flower garden was awash in a symphony of colors with vibrant blooms swaying gently in the evening breeze. The air was filled with the scent of lavender, honeysuckle, and roses mingling together in a sweet perfume that wrapped around them like a tender embrace.

In the heart of the garden stood a weeping willow tree, its long, graceful branches cascading down like a curtain of emerald lace. Beneath its sheltering boughs, the world seemed to stand still, as if time itself were holding its breath.

They stood close, their hands barely touching, fingers brushing with the lightest of touches. The rustling of the willow's leaves created a soft, soothing melody, harmonizing with the distant chirping of birds settling in for the evening.

“This has always been my favorite spot since I was a little girl,” Sarah admitted.

“I can see why.” Jimmy looked up into the tree’s branches. “I’m sorry I got angry and left the way I did.” His gaze met hers.

“No, I’m the one who should apologize.” Sarah shook her head.

Jimmy placed a finger on her lips. “Just hear me out and I’ll explain everything.”

“I’m listening,” she whispered.

“I got angry when you accused me of being a scammer.” He ran a hand through his hair while Sarah waited patiently for him to continue. “There’s an old lady who lives across town.

Her husband passed away a year ago." Jimmy closed his eyes and breathed deeply before continuing. "She was pressured by her friends and family to sell her home cheap. I knew that with a few repairs she could get a lot more out of the house should she choose to sell it." He paused and began pacing.

"What does that have to do with you?" Sarah asked.

"I couldn't stand by and watch this sweet lady get swindled out of her home—or, in your words, scammed by her so-called loved ones."

"I heard you say that you could get more out of the old lady's house than what was offered." She took a step back. "What did you mean by that?"

"I made a deal with the lady." He took Sarah's hands in his. "I told her that I would do all the repairs for free if she would let me sell her house for double what she was offered. She just needed to pay for the materials."

"How can you make such an offer? Did she accept?" Sarah asked.

"No, at least not on those terms." Jimmy stared lovingly into her eyes. "The lady, eh, Ms. Greer, agreed to allow me to do the repairs and remodel the house, which tripled the value, on the condition that I sell it for her and allow her to pay me and my crew for the work."

"Oh, Jimmy, I'm so sorry I jumped to conclusions without knowing the facts." Her face reddened.

"I probably would have thought the same thing had the shoe been on the other foot," he said reassuringly.

"I don't usually make assumptions like that." She paused. "I guess I'm just overly protective of my grandmother." She looked back toward the house.

"That's one of the many things I love about you." He paused, taking in the way her eyes sparkled when the lights in the garden hit them just right. The atmosphere was alive with a quiet magic, a sense of something sacred about to unfold.

Her eyes, wide with a mixture of anticipation and nervous excitement, met his. The golden light played across their faces, highlighting the soft curve of her lips and the warmth in his gaze. He reached out, tucking a stray lock of hair behind her ear, his touch lingering as if savoring the moment.

There was no rush, no need to hurry. The world beyond the willow's embrace faded away, leaving only the two of them cocooned in the gentle whisper of the leaves. Slowly, almost imperceptibly, they leaned in closer, drawn together as if by an invisible force.

Her breath hitched as his hand cradled her cheek, the warmth of his palm grounding her in the moment. The distance between them closed, and she felt his breath, soft and warm, against her lips. Her eyes fluttered shut as her heart pounded in her chest, each beat resonating in the quiet stillness.

When their lips finally met, it was like the first touch of spring after a long winter. Gentle, tentative, and filled with a sweetness that took her breath away. The kiss was soft and slow, a tender exploration, as if they were discovering a new world together. The petals of the flowers seemed to lean in, as if listening to the silent promise that passed between them.

In that kiss, time ceased to exist. There was only the softness of his lips, the comforting weight of his hand on her back, and the delicate flutter of her heart echoing the rhythm of his. The world around them faded into a blur of color and light, and all that remained was the profound, simple joy of being there together beneath the weeping willow sharing their first kiss in the heart of the garden.

He pulled her into his arms and held her tight. She laid her head against his chest and listened to the gentle beating of his heart. They both closed their eyes, not wanting this moment to end. After several minutes, he broke the silence.

"I stopped by this evening to tell you that I sold the house for triple the amount offered. Ms. Greer paid us our commission along with a huge bonus despite my protests,"

"That's wonderful," she replied, her head still resting against his chest.

"I'm taking my crew out to celebrate and would love for you and Stacy to join us," he said excitedly. "Your grandmother is welcome to come too," he added.

"So, you forgive me?" She hesitated. "I'm so ashamed of the way I behaved earlier."

"It's water under the bridge. Forgive and forget is my motto, so what do you say?" He placed a finger under her chin, tilting her face up to meet his gaze. "Next time, just ask and I promise to tell you the truth—no secrets, no lies."

"I will, if you promise to do the same." She stared longingly into his eyes. She knew at that moment that he was the one she wanted to spend the rest of her life with. She cleared her throat and looked away, hoping he couldn't read her mind. After all, they had just shared their first kiss. This was one summer she would never forget, and it was nearly over. She prayed he felt the same as she. She didn't want to think about that right now. "Tonight's a night worth celebrating." She reluctantly pulled herself from his arms. "I'm going to invite Grams and Stacy."

"I'll come with you." He placed his hand over hers, taking a mental note of how small and soft her hand was compared to his. They walked hand-in-hand into the house and found

Grams and Stacy in the living room in deep discussion about the old book.

“Oh, there you two are. I thought you got lost.” Grams teased.

“Jimmy has invited us all out to celebrate with him and his crew,” Sarah announced.

“What are we celebrating?” Stacy asked.

“We’re celebrating you and Robbie leaving tomorrow and the peace and quiet that comes afterwards,” Sarah joked.

“Ha, ha, aren’t you full of yourself.” Stacy grabbed a throw pillow off the couch and hit Sarah across the backside with it.

“We finished a job across town and received a bonus after the house sold,” Jimmy replied.

“How nice.” Grams clasped her hands together. “You young’uns go ahead and enjoy yourselves.” She shooed them with the back of her hand. “I’m going to catch up on a series I’ve been watching every week.”

“Maybe I should stay here.” Sarah sat on the couch next to her grandmother. “We bought pizza and were getting ready to eat.”

“I’ll be fine. Now, you get off your tail and go have some fun for a change.” Grams stood and pulled Sarah, then gave her a swat on the behind.

Sarah’s cheeks grew crimson as Jimmy and Stacy burst into laughter. After the initial shock wore off, Sarah giggled, hugged her grandmother, and said, “All right, you win. We’ll be home in a couple hours.”

Grams watched Jimmy’s truck pull out of the driveway. “Whew, I thought I’d never get the house to myself.” She hurried to the phone and dialed a number. A male voice answered on the second ring.

“Hello?”

“Hello, David., Or should I call you Dr. Brown?”

"Florence, is everything all right?" Concern resonated in his voice.

"Everything's peachy. Listen, I'm home alone and I have a pizza and sweet tea here. I would love it if you would join me for dinner."

"Florence, what are you up to?" he asked sternly

"Why do you always think I'm up to something?" she said defensively.

"Because you usually are, and it always has something to do with Gladys."

"Oh, posh." She swiped her hand in the air even though he couldn't see. "This has nothing to do with that old battle axe. Can I not invite an old friend over for a visit?"

"Sure, you can, but knowing you and Gladys have an ongoing feud, I have the right to wonder why." He chuckled

"Oh, all right. I was supposed to have dinner with Sarah, but she went out with her friends and I didn't want a good pizza to go to waste," she huffed. "See? This has nothing to do with Gladys."

"In that case, I'd love to," he answered cheerfully. "I'll be right over."

"Good. See you in a few." Grams hung up the phone and did a little dance, feeling as giddy as a teenager. She hurried to her bedroom and dabbed a little perfume behind her ears and on her wrists, then checked her appearance in the mirror just as the front doorbell rang. She went to answer the door, hoping Mrs. Stevenson wasn't being her nosy self. Instead, he found Doc Brown standing there dressed in a yellow polo shirt and a pair of khakis. Her breath caught when she saw him. He reminded her of the first time he showed up at her door to take her to the Spring Formal when they were sixteen.

"Hello, Florence. You're looking as lovely as ever."

"Glad you came over, David. Come in." She held the door open wide and glanced across the street. She turned to face her guest when she heard him snicker.

"Florence, are you checking to see if Gladys Stevenson is watching?"

"Actually, I was doing just that," she admitted with a sly grin. "Ol' nosey britches tends to keep tabs on me for some reason." She shut the door.

"Remember the time she told your father that we were at the river skinny dipping?" He chuckled at the memory.

"Oh my. I forgot about that." Her eyes widened. "My father was furious with her when he showed up at the river and found us fishing with your parents."

"Those were good memories despite Gladys always trying to get us into trouble." He thought for a moment. "Come to think of it, where would Gladys get such an idea?"

"Uh . . . I'll get the food and drinks." She turned to leave the room.

"Florence, you sly devil. You told Gladys that to get her in trouble, didn't you?" He tilted his head, looking at her over the rim of his glasses while trying his best to feign seriousness.

"Who, me? Now, would I do such a thing as that?" She pretended to be innocent.

He shook his head. "All these years, and I'm just finding out the truth." He chuckled.

"She deserved it after all she put us through, and she hasn't changed one bit," she said in her defense.

"You know, this neighborhood would be boring without you and Gladys around to liven things up." He took a seat on the couch while she went to the kitchen and returned carrying two glasses of sweet tea. The pizza still sat on the coffee table where Stacy had left it. They ate and talked about old times. Before they knew it, time flew by and Stacy, Robby, Sarah, and Jimmy came walking through the back door.

"Grams, are you all right?" Sarah rushed to her side when she saw Dr. Brown there.

"Calm down, Sarah. David and I were having dinner and reminiscing about old times," Grams said with a smile.

"David?" Sarah looked from Dr. Brown and back at her grandmother before it dawned on her what her grandmother had said. "Oh! Oh, my goodness. I'm sorry for interrupting." She turned to leave the room.

"It's fine, Sarah. I was just leaving." Dr. Brown stood. "Florence, I had a wonderful evening. We should do it again soon, my dear." He took her hand and gently kissed the back of it.

"I'd like that." She walked him to the door. He placed a kiss on her cheek and headed home.

She closed the door and began to clean up, hoping to avoid any questions.

Sarah was dying to ask, but she could see her grandmother would rather not talk about it. Stacy excused herself and followed Robby outside. Jimmy and Sarah said their goodbyes. on the back porch.

"That was some kiss you gave me earlier." Jimmy placed his hands around her waist, pulling her to him.

"Yeah, it was." She laid her head against his chest and listened to the beating of his heart.

Jimmy stroked her hair. "It's all I could think about the whole night."

"I'll take that as a good thing." She snuggled in closer to him.

“That’s a very good thing, but you know what’s even better?” he teased.

“Whatever could that be?” She playfully grabbed his shirt collar with both hands.

“This.” He leaned in and kissed her passionately on the lips.

Sarah’s mouth parted as she kissed him with just as much longing. She stepped away when she saw her grandmother through the kitchen window getting a bedtime snack.

“Now, that’s what I call a kiss,” Jimmy said breathlessly.

“That was an awesome kiss.” Sarah blushed at her awkward words.

“I’ll see you tomorrow.” Jimmy tilted his head.

“I can’t wait.” Sarah kissed him one last time before sending him off.

After the men left, Sarah and Stacy headed for the living room. Grams’ show had just ended. She turned off the television and placed the remote on the coffee table.

“Is anyone in the mood to hear more of the story?” Grams handed the book to Sarah.

“I can’t wait to find out what happens next.” Stacy plopped down on the sofa.

Sarah took a seat between the two of them and began to read where they’d left off.

CHAPTER TWENTY-TWO

PATRICK PROPOSES

Anna awoke early the next morning. She brushed her hair, gave it a twist, and pinned it on top of her head before heading into the kitchen. She realized she was the only one up. She slipped on her shoes and raced to the barn, determined to milk the cow and gather the eggs before James and Adam got out of bed. She grabbed the milk bucket and hurried to the barn.

Little did she know that Adam saw her entering the barn and he woke James to warn him.

"James, James, wake up," he said in a hushed tone.

"What's the matter?" James asked groggily.

"I just spied Anna entering the barn with a milk bucket."

"So. What of it?" James rolled over with his back toward Adam.

"So, she's doing it again." Adam shook him. "Get up!"

James rolled over to face Adam. "Think about it, Adam. She's milking the cow. Next, she'll gather the eggs and, if we're lucky, she'll shovel out the barn and lay fresh hay."

"That's our job, and she's taking over." Adam raised his voice.

"Would you be quiet?" James placed a hand over Adam's mouth. "The more of our chores she does, the less we have to do."

"But James, she's—" Adam started.

"The quicker we get done, the more time you have to spend with Elizabeth." James lay back down, pulling the covers over his head.

Adam sat there grinning as he lay back in bed and listened for Anna to return with the milk, only to head back out to gather the eggs, From time to time, he peered out the window to get a visual on what she was doing. Just as James had said, she was cleaning the barn and laying fresh hay.

Adam lay there wide-awake waiting for her to finish before getting ready to head to the fields to hoe the garden. He headed out when he saw her on the way to the creek to clean up. James was right behind him. Both were smiling all the way.

Anna saw the smiles on their faces and the happy mood they were in. She smiled to herself. If her brothers were in a wonderful mood, their work would go quickly and smoothly, giving Pa and Ma a much-needed break. Which also made their day more enjoyable.

Today was the day that Patrick was asking for Virginia's hand in marriage. Anna wanted it to be as perfect as possible, for Virginia's sake.

She quietly rushed about the kitchen and mixed wheat flour, water, and salt to make fried bread, a recipe Ma learned from her Shawnee grandmother. Next, Anna fried slices of ham and eggs. The smell wafted throughout the house. Before long, Pa, Ma, and Virginia wandered into the kitchen, their stomachs rumbling from the aroma of the food.

"Anna, everything smells wonderful." Virginia sniffed the air,

"How long have you been up?" Ma stepped next to her and

gave her a little squeeze.

"Long enough to milk the cow, gather eggs, and clean out the barn before making breakfast." Anna smiled proudly.

"What's gotten into you?" Pa looked at her suspiciously.

"I couldn't sleep, so I decided to make everyone's day a little better by helping. Is that so wrong, Pa?" Anna faked innocence.

"No, not at all." Pa kissed her forehead. "Thanks. I'm sure James and Adam appreciate it very much, as do the rest of us." He strolled outside with a cup of hot coffee and yelled for James and Adam to come to breakfast. They both waved to him from the fields before sprinting to the creek to clean up before breakfast.

Virginia stepped close to Anna and whispered, "Thank you for everything." She knew what Anna was up to and hoped it would make things easier when Patrick arrived.

James and Adam were halfway home when a couple of horses trotted up the road toward the house. Patrick took the lead followed by Johnny. James and Adam waved to them before entering the house.

"Patrick and Johnny are here," Adam announced.

Anna dropped a cup of cider, spilling it all over the floor. "I'm sorry, but did you say Johnny?" She cleaned up the spilled cider before rushing to the front door to see for herself. There was Johnny riding alongside Patrick.

Virginia ran her hand over her hair, making sure none was out of place.

"You look beautiful, dear." Ma gave her an approving nod.

Pa waited on the front porch while Patrick and Johnny dismounted their horses. "Howdy, boys. What brings you fellows out here so early in the morning?" He gave Johnny a knowing wink.

Patrick, on the other hand, had no idea what he was in for. "Good morning, sir." Patrick stretched his hand out to Pa.

Pa took his hand and gave it a firm squeeze, refusing to let go. He drew his eyes down into a scowl. "If you're looking for work, I may be able to find something for ya, but if either of you get a notion in your head about one of my daughters, ya best start saying your prayers."

Virginia turned three shades of red, but Patrick turned white.

Pa held him up for fear he was going to pass out.

Patrick tried speaking, but no words came. "Breathe, son, breathe."

Pa rubbed his huge hand across Patrick's shoulder. "I know why you're here. I was jesting with ya," he said soothingly.

Patrick let out the breath he didn't realize he held in. "Sorry, sir. I, I, I don't know what came over me." He sucked in a huge gulp of air—along with a fly that had been buzzing around. He leaned forward coughing and gagging.

Virginia, Ma, and Anna rushed out onto the porch to find out what was going on. Virginia just knew her father was strangling Patrick for sure.

Pa pounded on Patrick's shoulders yelling, "Cough it up, boy. Cough it up."

Johnny, along with James and Adam, were doubled over, laughing hysterically.

Virginia ran down the steps and threw her arms around Patrick.

He clamped his hands over his mouth. Unable to stop himself, he began to retch.

Lucky for Virginia she stepped aside just in time and stood there bewildered.

Johnny wiped the tears from his eyes and tried his best to

stop laughing.

"My goodness, if the thought of marriage makes you vomit, you better think twice before having wee ones," Anna stated.

This time Pa doubled over with laughter. "Anna, he, he . . . ." Pa continued to laugh. "He swallowed . . . a . . . horsefly."

"Yeah, a . . . big one," Johnny shouted and doubled over again, causing Pa to bellow.

Pa stood straight and tried to act serious. "Go ahead, son. Tell me why you're here."

Patrick began to studder. "I, I want to marry your horsefly." Patrick's eyes grew wide and his face crimson. "I, I mean your daughter, sir."

It was too late. The whole family, including Virginia, were now losing control.

"Welcome to the family, son." Pa slapped him across the shoulder.

Everyone erupted into laughter. After Patrick thought about it, he joined in and found himself wiping tears from his eyes. Once the laughter subsided, Anna wondered why Johnny was there. He stepped toward her and placed a hand over his mouth before speaking.

"What's wrong?" she asked.

"I want to ask you to the Autum Harvest Dance, but I didn't want to risk swallowing a horsefly." He chuckled. "Sorry, Patrick." He turned back to Anna. "Anna, will you go to the Autum Harvest Dance with me?"

Anna felt like screaming and wrapping her arms around his neck, but she kept her composure as she turned to face Pa and Ma.

"Anna he's waiting for an answer." Pa smiled approvingly.

Anna turned to Johnny and shouted, "Yes!" She lowered

her voice. "I mean, I would be honored." She looked at the young men. "Would you like some breakfast? I made plenty." She glanced at Patrick. "I'm sure it tastes better than an ol' horsefly."

She was shocked when Patrick placed a hand to his stomach and looked ill.

"Anna, that's not funny," Virginia stated.

"What's the matter? I was only asking him to breakfast." Anna stared dumbfounded at them.

"Come on, Anna, I would love some breakfast." Johnny locked elbows with her and stifled a laugh. He sure didn't want to get that started again.

Over the next few months, Johnny and Anna were inseparable. They continued meeting at Anna's favorite spot by the river, where they had a picnic, fished, or swam. Sometimes they just cuddled and talked about the future.

When Monday arrived, Pa took Anna and Adam to school in town, which also doubled as the church on Sunday morning.

Pa stopped to speak with a few gentlemen at Faraday's Blacksmith shop. Anna made her way to the mercantile during recess. She wanted to see what new fabrics Mrs. Collins had ordered. On the way she saw Hattie Mae sitting in the carriage.

"Hello, Hattie Mae. It's nice to see you again," Anna said cheerfully.

"Howdy, Anna. How are you this fine afternoon?" Hattie Mae adjusted her skirt, hoping Anna would notice it was new.

"That's a beautiful dress you're wearing, Mrs. Hattie," Anna stated.

"Why, thank ya kindly. I made it myself. Do you truly like it?" She stood so Anna could get a better look.

"You made it?" Anna stared at the dress in awe.

"Yes, ma'am, I sure enough did," she said proudly. "It took me two days to complete it."

"Mrs. Hattie, if I can get enough fabric to make both of us a new dress, would you make me one for the Autum Harvest Dance?"

"I'd be honored," she said excitedly. "Try to find a purple color. It'll bring out the green in your eyes."

"Thank you. I love purple." Anna could hardly contain her excitement as she entered the mercantile, only to race back out shouting for Mrs. Hattie to come in and help her choose the fabric.

Hattie Mae looked around nervously as Anna took her by the hand and begged her to come inside. Mrs. Collins stepped into the doorway and motioned to Hattie Mae.

"Come on in, Mrs. Hattie. It's perfectly fine. And if anyone has anything to say about it, I have something underneath my counter that can change their minds real fast." She glared at Mrs. Worthington as she hurried past.

Hattie Mae reluctantly climbed down from the carriage and entered the store. She followed Anna to the bolts of different colored fabrics. Anna held up a lovely lavender print. "How about this one, Mrs. Hattie?"

Hattie Mae studied the color and then gasped when she saw a beautiful purple on the bottom row.

"There, Miss Anna." She pointed. "That's the one."

Anna picked it up and held it against her. "It's the most beautiful shade of purple I've ever laid eyes on." She turned to Mrs. Collins. "How much for enough fabric to make two gowns for the Autum Harvest Dance?"

"Well, Mrs. Hattie, I overheard the deal you made with Anna —that she would get enough material for you a new dress in exchange for making her one. I'll make the same deal. If you're willing to make a dress for me, you can choose any color you like, and I'll give you enough to make yourself a new dress to pay you for your trouble."

Hattie Mae grinned a huge toothy grin. "I am a blessed woman indeed. I'll make as many dresses as you like in exchange for enough fabric to make a dress for me." Hattie Mae could hardly wait to go home and tell Amos what blessings had been bestowed upon her. Gracie appeared from the back of the store and was thrilled to find Hattie Mae and Mrs. Collins getting along splendidly. She was even more excited to find out about the deals she had made with Anna and Mrs. Collins. Anna offered to work for the fabric, but Mrs. Collins insisted on donating it to see what kind of designs Hattie Mae could come up with on such short notice.

"After all, she only has five days to come up with two dresses," Mrs. Collins reasoned.

Anna left class early and rode home with Gracie and Hattie Mae. She wanted to help make the dresses—or, at least help cut out the patterns to give Hattie Mae a head start. Using an old dress as a pattern, Anna and Gracie cut the material while Hattie Mae sewed it together. Her fingers moved like a well-oiled machine. She showed Anna and Gracie the beautiful stitching taught to her by her own mother. Before long, Gracie and Anna joined in on the sewing of the dresses. Carefully following Hattie Mae's instructions, Anna caught on quickly and, before long, she no longer needed to ask Hattie Mae what to do.

Anna skipped class all week and went to Gracie's to work on the gowns. Friday morning, she went to school and got her homework for the week. She explained everything to her teacher, Miss. Cornwell, who thought it was a reason worthy of being excused. She offered to give Anna the weekly quiz explaining to her that if she passed it, she needn't do the homework, but if she failed then she only needed to study the subjects she failed. Anna agreed and left the school forty-five minutes later, relieved at having passed the entire test.

Gracie picked her up and they drove to her house to find Hattie Mae already hard at work. She had just put the final additions on a gorgeous purple gown with a black velvet and lace bodice. She held it up to get Anna's opinion. Anna gasped, "Oh my goodness, that's the most beautiful dress I've ever seen. It's fit for a queen."

Well, Queen Anna, this one is for you." Hattie gave her a cheeky grin.

"For me?" Anna's breath caught in her throat. "Thank you, Mrs. Hattie." She took the dress and held it against herself. "I'm going to try it on right now."

Gracie showed her to her bedroom just off from the living room. Anna slipped out of her day dress and into the gorgeous purple gown. It fit perfectly. Hattie Mae's heart filled with pride as she watched Anna's face light up as she danced, twisted. and twirled around the living room. She ran to Hattie Mae and hugged her. "Thank you so very much," Anna whispered in her ear.

"It was my pleasure." Hattie Mae's eyes began to well.

"Hattie's right." Gracie stared in awe at Anna in her new gown. "Purple does bring out the green in your eyes."

"I can't wait for Johnny to see me in it." Anna held out the skirt and twisted it from side to side. "I started working on an old dress several months ago, only to give up when I couldn't figure out what to do with it."

"Stop by anytime and I'll teach you everything I know about sewing." Hattie Mae went back to sewing on Mrs. Collins' dress. It wasn't going to be as extravagant as Anna's, but it was what Mrs. Collins asked for. A green print dress, not too plain, but not too fancy, either. Hattie Mae has been sewing long enough to know exactly what each person had in mind.

The following day, Gracie and Hattie Mae waited outside the mercantile for Anna to get out of school. One of the boys rang the bell, signaling school was over. Children of all ages raced out, anxious to get home. Anna strolled toward the mercantile when she saw Gracie waving at her.

"Hello, Gracie, Hattie Mae." Anna nodded. "Did you finish Mrs. Collins dress?" She lowered her voice.

"I sure enough did." Hattie Mae patted the folded material laying on her lap. "We wanted you to be here when I give it to her." Hattie Mae stepped down from the carriage. The three of them walked into the mercantile. Mrs. Collins stepped out of the back room upon hearing the bell ring over the entrance door.

"Why, if it isn't my three most favorite ladies." Mrs. Collins clapped her hands together. "What can I get for you today?"

"Oh no, missus. We have something for you." Hattie Mae held out the bundle of folded fabric.

Mrs. Collins took it and unfolded it to find a stunning green print dress that was more lovely than she ever imagined. She gasped upon seeing it.

"Lord a-mercy, Mrs. Hattie Mae, you've out done yourself." She turned toward the backroom and yelled, "Henry, come here and look at this."

A thin man not much taller than she appeared. She held up the dress for him to see. His eyes grew wide as he examined the stitching and the material.

"Why, isn't this the material I just finished making myself?" He stared wide eyed at his wife.

"The very same." She then motioned toward Hattie Mae. "This here is the lady responsible for the incredible handiwork."

"You made this cloth?" Gracie ran her hand over the fabric.

"Yes'm, we sure did. Right back there in the backroom." Henry pointed.

"Wow! Our very own Virginia cloth made right here," Anna said as she stared in awe at the bolts of fabric on the shelf. "What made you decide to make your own cloth?" she asked.

"The English Crown had no right to tax Americans." Henry's eyes narrowed. So, we're fighting back by making our own cloth, and you, Mrs. Hattie Mae, proved that we could make clothing just as beautiful from our own homespun cloth." He leaned over the counter. "I would appreciate it if you ladies kept this between us."

Hattie Mae's eyes sparkled as she filled with pride. "I'm much obliged for the opportunity." She lowered her voice. "I would appreciate it if you kept my secret." She looked around the store. "I don't need no trouble, and I likes my privacy, so's I can sew for my Amos and Isaiah."

"Say no more, Mrs. Hattie, we fully understand." Mrs. Collins glanced at the customer entering the mercantile, "People would hound you day and night wanting something sewn," she whispered.

"Mrs. Hattie, may I ask one favor?" Henry whispered while keeping an eye on the customer, making sure he wasn't listening.

"Yes, sir, you sure enough can," Hattie Mae whispered back.

"If you would be so kind as to make me a couple shirts, I'll pay you for your trouble." Henry side-eyed his wife. "I know you can sew just fine, dear, but you've been so busy working."

Mrs. Collins held up her hand to hush him. She smiled at Hattie Mae. "It sure would help us both if you wouldn't mind."

"Well, sir, ma'am." Hattie Mae nodded. "Would you mind paying me in cloth as with the dresses?" Hattie Mae's voice cracked. "If it's not too much to ask." She wrung her hands.

A grin spread across Henry's face a mile wide. "That's even better, missus." He pulled out two bolts of cloth, the one beige and the other a light blue, and handed them to his wife. "Here ya are dear. Cut enough fabric to make two shirts of each color. One each for me and one of each color for Mrs. Hattie Mae, or any fabric of her choosing." He turned and headed over to help the customer.

"These colors will do just fine," Hattie Mae said excitedly. "I'm making my son and husband something nice." Her eyes welled with tears. She looked toward heaven and whispered, "Thank you, Lord, for all the many blessings."

The next day, Anna rushed off to help Hattie Mae work on dresses. As she rode through the quaint little town, she heard the laughter of children mingled with the rustle of leaves. The air, fragrant with the scent of late summer, reminded her that autumn was around the corner and with it came the Fall Harvest Dance. Her excitement grew as she reached the end of town and drew closer to Hattie Mae's. She found her on the front porch rocking in the chair Amos made for her. Anna adjusted her apron as she approached Hattie Mae's cottage. The clinking of her basket reminded her of the sewing circle they had planned for this afternoon.

"Good day, Mrs. Hattie," Anna called out, stepping onto the

porch of the neat modest home where the smell of freshly baked bread wafted through the air. Anna's stomach rumbled at the delicious aroma even though she wasn't hungry.

"Ah, Anna, girl! How wonderful to see you," Hattie Mae replied, her voice warm and inviting. She continued sewing on the dress sprawled over her lap. "Have you seen Gracie? She was to come help us with the stitching."

Anna's brow furrowed as she looked around, half expecting Gracie to come waddling across the yard, the sound of her laughing at herself as she held onto her huge pregnant belly.

"No, not since this morning. She was feeling poorly. Perhaps, she simply took a nap and overslept." Anna nervously fidgeted with her apron string. "The baby isn't due for another two weeks, right?"

A frown replaced Hattie Mae's gentle smile.

"Oh, lord a mercy, that baby is gonna come when he's good and ready." Hattie Mae's color drained from her face. "She went to pick apples some time ago. Hattie Mae laid down her sewing and looked toward the sky. "Lord, child, she should've been back by now"

"I'll check the house." Anna stepped backwards down the steps.

"She may be peeling apples or making supper." Anna whispered a prayer: "God, please let Gracie be all right."

"Wait! I'm coming with you." Hattie Mae rushed into the house and grabbed a cloth sack that she referred to as her birthing bag. Without a word, they hurried to Gracie's house only to find it empty. "Follow me." Hattie Mae took the lead and headed out the back door. "Gracie said she found an apple tree abundant with apples behind her house. Pray we find her there." Hattie Mae trudged through the overgrown weeds, thorns reaching out and snagging the long black skirt she wore. Anna followed close by her side, only she wasn't so lucky as thorns tore at her skin. She paid no mind to the blood trickling from the wounds and running down her legs.

"Gracie! Where are you?" Anna yelled, her eyes darting all around.

There was no response—only the soft rustle of leaves stirred by the gentle breeze carrying with it the sweet fragrance of apples. They continued their search, their footsteps quickening with each step as they entered the dense perimeter of the trees.

As they neared the woods, Anna's heart sank. The tranquility of their surroundings felt sinister now, and dread curled in her chest.

A faint sound—a soft desperate cry for help—reached her ears.

"I think I heard her!" Anna exclaimed, her pulse racing. "This way."

"Gracie, we're coming, child," Hattie Mae shouted.

They hurried toward the sound, breaking through the last line of trees to find Gracie collapsed against the gnarled roots of an old oak. Her face was pale and glistening with sweat.

"Gracie!" Anna rushed to her side, kneeling in the dry grass, the smell of earth mingled with the scent of apples that had spilled on the ground at Gracie's feet. "What happened? Are you hurt?"

"I, I'm fine," Gracie gasped, her breathing labored. "I didn't expect to run into a bear." She squeezed her eyes tight as a wave of pain washed over her. "It scared me, so I quietly backed away and then I felt the pain begin."

Anna's eyes widened as the realization sunk in. "You're in

labor?"

Hattie Mae knelt beside them, urging Gracie to lie back against the soft ground. "We need to help her, Anna. Just breathe, Gracie. You can do this."

The urgency of the moment transformed all fear into determination. Anna reached for Gracie's hand. "Just keep breathing. I can't allow you to take a chance and have your baby here." Anna stood "I'm going to get the wagon and get you home to your bed." She turned and sprinted like the wind before either one could protest. She raced back through the thorns, not feeling a thing as once again they tore at her legs. She scurried until she reached Gracie's backyard, then darted into the house through the back door and snatched a pillow and quilt off the bed. Just as she turned to dash out of the room, she ran into Nathaniel. Relief washed over her.

"Nathaniel, thank God you're here." She felt her eyes well with tears that threatened to spill down her cheeks.

"What's wrong? Where's Gracie?" he shouted, his eyes wide with fear.

"The wood . . . the baby is coming . . . Hattie Mae's with her," Anna said between breaths.

"Take me to her." They hurried out the door to the wagon. Anna's horse was still hitched to it. They climbed aboard with Nathaniel in the driver's seat. Anna held tight to the pillow and blanket she planned to place in the wagon for Gracie to lay on. She finished telling Nathaniel what happened just as Gracie and Hattie Mae came into view.

A broad smile spread across Gracie's face when she saw her loving husband. "Nathaniel, darling you're here." Her face registered fear as the birthing pains grew stronger.

"Are you able to stand?" Anna shouted as the wagon stopped.

"There's no time for that." Nathaniel jumped down to the ground with a thud. He rushed to his wife and scooped her up in his big strong arms. "Sorry, honey. I know it hurts, but I'm taking you home." He kissed her forehead. Gracie wrapped her arms around his neck and laid her head against his chest. Anna folded the quilt and put it in the back of the wagon making a soft pallet for Gracie to lay on. Nathaniel placed the pillow under her head. He chose to ride in the back with his wife.

Anna drove with Hattie Mae sitting next to her. They made it back to Nathaniel and Gracie's. Nathaniel gently and lovingly lifted his wife into his arms and carried her into the house. He laid her on the soft bed then placing a gentle kiss on her lips. He turned to leave the room, but stopped when Hattie Mae called his name

"Nathaniel, boil some water and set the pan next to the bed with a clean dry cloth."

Nathaniel nodded and headed to the kitchen.

"Anna, hand me my bag." Hattie Mae pointed to her bag she left on the floor by the bed.

Anna quickly grabbed it and handed it to her.

Hattie Mae rummaged through it until she found what she was looking for. She pulled out a piece of cloth and placed it in the palm of her hand. "Good, there is just enough," she said softly. "Take this to the kitchen and make a cup of tea and bring it to me." She handed it to Anna.

"What is it?" Anna asked, clinching the pouch tightly in her hand.

"It's black snakeroot. It helps with the pain. Hurry, child." Hattie Mae's patience was wearing thin. She didn't have time for questions. She'd seen too many women and babies die during childbirth.

Anna nervously ran to the kitchen and did as she was told.

Nathaniel stared into the cup as Anna poured hot water over the dried plant. "Snakeroot." He nodded his approval.

"Black Snakeroot," Anna corrected. "You've heard of it?"

"Yes. The Native Americans use it for various things, including childbirth, to help ease the pain." He took the cup from her hand. "I'll take it to her." Nathaniel smiled down at a nervous Anna.

"Thank you." Her voice cracked when she spoke.

"Perhaps you should go tell a few of the ladies as well as your mother that Gracie's childbirth has begun."

Anna nodded and then raced out the door to the awaiting wagon. The horse was still hitched to it. As she sped through town, she saw Mrs. Collins cleaning the mercantile windows. She slowed down slightly and shouted, "Gracie's birthing time has begun."

Mrs. Collins ran inside the mercantile, shouting for her husband. "Henry! I must leave. Gracie's having her baby!"

Henry waved a hand in the air, then returned to folding the newly made cloth and putting it on the shelf.

Anna headed home to get Ma. After all, Gracie and Ma were best friends, so it was only right that she be there for the birth, Anna reasoned in her mind. She whispered a silent prayer: "Lord, let us make it back in time." She sped down the road, leaving a trail of dust swirling behind her. She felt relieved as she saw the house come into view.

"Whoa, boy." She pulled back on the reins as she stopped in front of the house.

Ma came running out, fear etched on her face. "Anna, what's wrong?" She ran down the steps to the wagon.

"Gracie's baby is coming. We must hurry." Anna was

trembling.

"Scoot over. I'm driving." Ma climbed into the driver's seat. "Did they give her anything to help with the pain?" Ma asked calmly.

"Black Snakeroot," Anna replied.

"That's good. It's also known as black cohosh. Your grandmother used it for a lot of different ailments. Lest you forget, she was Shawnee."

"Does that make me Shawnee?" Anna asked.

"A little," her mother answered. "I'm half Shawnee and half Irish." Sadness overshadowed her face. "Some people are cruel not only to the Irish and Shawnee, but also Black folk. They have it much worse, which is why we oppose slavery." She turned to look at Anna. "You mustn't speak of our ancestry." She stiffened in the seat and stared straight ahead.

Anna knew the conversation was over. They made it to Gracie's and went inside. The living room was full of ladies from town, all there to show their support. Anna followed her mother to Gracie's room. Gracie's face lit up when she saw them.

"Mary Lou, you came." Gracie held out her hand to her dear friend. Mary Lou sat beside her and held her hand.

"I wouldn't miss this for the world." Mary Lou squeezed her hand.

"Is my baby going to be all right?" Gracie asked just before screaming out in pain.

"You and your baby will be fine, right, Ma?" Anna stepped forward.

"Yes, they both will be," her mother answered. "I've been thinking, you ladies have a sewing circle." Mary Lou stood. "Well, I say we form a prayer circle and pray for Gracie and her baby."

The ladies agreed and everyone formed a circle and began to pray.

The birthing pains grew stronger and were now nonstop. Hattie Mae could be heard instructing Gracie to push. One last scream from Gracie, and the baby was born.

Hattie Mae cleaned out the baby's mouth and shouted as he began to cry. "It's a strong healthy boy." The whole house exploded in cheers. Ma bathed the baby, wrapped him in a warm blanket, and handed him to Gracie.

Everyone congregated in the kitchen to allow the new parents time with their newborn son. Half an hour later, Nathaniel strolled into the kitchen with his baby boy in his arms. "Everyone, meet Joshua Alan Wright." Nathaniel proudly held up his son. The ladies doted over the baby before leaving the family alone to rest.

Hattie Mae said her goodbyes and walked toward home. She felt blessed to have been part of a miracle from God. She considered every birth a miracle. Her job was over—at least until the next birth. *Now back to stitching dresses.* She smiled to herself as she entered her home, not only feeling blessed, but free.

CHAPTER TWENTY-THREE

AUTUMN HARVEST DANCE
October 1765

The day of the Autumn Harvest Dance finally arrived. The whole town had been preparing for this day all year. Anna surprised Ma with a new dress she had personally cut and sewn with Hattie Mae's help. She would never forget the look on Ma's face when she handed her a beautiful dark blue gown trimmed in white lace.

"Oh, Anna! It's lovely." Ma hugged the dress to her. "I don't understand . . . where . . . ."

"I made it especially for you," Anna stated. "Do you like it?"

"Like it? I love it." Ma hugged her. "Thank you, sweetie."

"I made this for Pa." Anna held out a blue button up dress shirt. "Do you think he'll wear it?"

"You bet I will." Pa stepped up behind her just as she held up the shirt. He happily took it and put it on. "Would ya look at that? It's a perfect fit." He kissed Anna on the top of the head. "I might turn a few heads wearing something as nice as this." He winked.

"Yes, you will, and that's why you're not getting out of my sight," Ma teased. She held the new dress against her and spun around. "I'm gonna put this on right now." She hurried to her bedroom, returning several minutes later wearing the dress with her hair pinned on top of her head. Long ringlet curls framed her face, and a few hung down her back. Pa almost fell out of his chair when he glanced up and saw her descending the staircase. He took her hand and helped her down the last two steps.

"Have you ever seen anyone as lovely?" He twirled her around, pulled her into his arms, and gently kissed her lips. "Darlin', looks like the only one who'll be turning heads tonight will be you."

"Anna, I can hardly wait to show off my new dress to the other ladies." She turned to find Anna gone. "Well, I suppose she is getting ready as well. I'll go see if she needs help." Ma went back upstairs and gently knocked on Anna's bedroom door.

"Anna, it's Ma, may I come in?

"Come in, Ma. It's open," Anna shouted from behind the closed door.

Ma opened the door and stepped in. Anna stood at the window watching for Johnny. She turned and heard her mother let out a loud gasp.

"Anna, that has got to be the most beautiful gown in all of Virginia." Ma stepped closer. "You look like royalty."

"Do you really think so?"

"I know so." Ma began combing Anna's long dark blond hair.

Anna decided to wear it down. She pinned part of it up at the back of her head with a bow that matched her gown. It lay in gorgeous curls down her back. A few curls spilled over her shoulders and bounced as she walked.

"Do you think Johnny will like it?" She took her mother by the hands and looked into her eyes. She had never seen her mother's eyes shine the way they were at that moment. She wanted to remember everything about this night for the rest of her life.

"He would be a fool not to." Ma rushed out of the bedroom and looked over the railing. "Now's your chance to find out. He's here." Ma acted as giddy as a schoolgirl.

Johnny had ridden up in a carriage he'd decorated with wildflowers and threw fresh hay in the back.

Pa met him on the porch and invited him in. "First lesson where women are concerned, son." Pa slapped him across the shoulder. "They'll always leave you waiting for one thing or another."

"I don't mind one bit, sir . . . ." Johnny's voice trailed off as he caught sight of Anna descending the staircase. He gulped and swallowed the lump forming in his throat. He wondered if he was dreaming. He had never seen such a vision of loveliness. "She's like a goddess on Earth," he said breathlessly.

"That she is," Pa agreed. "She gets it from her mother." Pa pointed at Ma, who was a few steps behind Anna.

Johnny took Anna by the hand and led her to the awaiting carriage. "I love the way you decorated the carriage," she stated. "And you look very handsome," she added.

"Thanks," Johnny replied. He couldn't stop staring at her.

Anna began to fidget uncomfortably. "So, do you like my gown?" She tried to draw his attention to the dress. "Hattie Mae made it for me. Isn't she remarkable?"

"Uh huh." Johnny nodded.

"Uh . . . Johnny, don't you think you should watch where you're driving?" She held tightly to her seat.

"Why?" Johnny asked, not taking his eyes off her.

"Because the road is over there!" she shouted.

"Oh, sorry." He grabbed the horse's reins and guided them back onto the road.

Pa and Ma were watching the whole scene and burst out laughing as they passed them.

Johnny's face reddened. He cleared his throat and quietly rode the rest of the way to Mr. Tuckers' barn where the dance was being held. The barn was newly built and finished last month. The men from town pitched in for the barn raising while some of the ladies prepared food—the same as they did when Pa was building the new house they were now living in. That's one thing about country folk. They all pitch in to help one another.

They pulled into the huge field leading to the barn. Anna was giddy with excitement and could hardly wait to show off her new gown. Especially to the rich girl Sally McAllister. Anna had nothing against Sally—she didn't really know her. Sally always dressed nicely, and her hair was always perfect.

Anna wanted to look lovely even if it was only for one night. She felt like royalty when she walked into the dance. All eyes were on her. Several young men raced to ask her to dance. She gracefully turned them down and saved all her dances for Johnny. Everyone had a wonderful time. Anna received a lot of compliments from the ladies inquiring about who made her gown and the price. She smiled and told them she would talk to her friend and let them know if she was interested in sewing for them. She could hardly wait to tell Hattie Mae, but tonight was the night she had waited for since she'd first met Johnny three years ago, and it was everything she'd dreamed of and more.

She was thrilled for Sally when the boys huddled around her waiting for a turn to dance with her.

After that night, Johnny and Anna were inseparable. They spent every free moment together, usually at their favorite spot by the river.

It had been a year since Patrick and Virginia were betrothed. They married last month—September twenty-fourth, seventeen-sixty-six. Pa gave them the old house as a wedding present. Hattie Mae out done herself on the wedding gown—there was even a write up about it in the paper. After seeing the gown in the newspaper, ladies from all over the county began inquiring as to who made it. Everyone wanted a homespun gown of their own. No one—except Anna, Gracie, and Mr. and Mrs. Collins at the mercantile—knew who made all those dresses. Each of them honored Hattie Mae's wishes and kept her secret.

Anna finished her chores and then saddled her horse. She was going to visit her sister Virginia. It had been a few weeks since she'd last seen her, and she figured what a better time than this beautiful August day. *The weather is perfect for a nice horseback ride.* She strolled into the house in search of her mother.

"Ma! I'm going to visit Ginny. Would you like to come?" She crossed her fingers hoping she'd say yes.

"Not today," she replied. "Tell Virginia that I love her, and I'll visit soon."

"Yes, ma'am." Anna turned to leave.

"Wait! Take these to your sister." Ma handed Anna a basket of eggs and kissed her cheek. "Give her that for me as well."

The ride to the old homestead was pleasant. Anna loved the feeling of the wind in her hair as she raced the horse through the field where she stopped and picked flowers. She was especially excited when she found a crab apple tree. She gently placed several in the basket with the eggs and filled the oversized pocket on her apron.

"There. That should be enough to make cider," she said as she fed a couple to her horse. "You love apples, don't you, Chestnut?" She stroked the horse's nose before mounting him.

She headed back down the old dirt road. She was in no rush to get there. She allowed the horse to walk most of the way. She took in the sights and sounds all around her, from the birds singing to the wildflowers gently swaying in the breeze. Two deer ran out of the thick foliage and leaped across the road, disappearing into the dense forest. A rabbit scampered across the road, stopping to nibble on clover before going on his way. Anna loved these outings with just her riding Chestnut and the beauty of nature. Soon, the old homestead came into view. Virginia was hanging clothes out to dry. She waved. A huge smile spread across her face upon seeing Anna.

"Anna!" she shouted. "I'm so happy you're here." She hugged her.

"Ma said she'll come visit soon, and she said to give you this." She kissed her sister's cheek, then followed her into the house. "Oh, she also sent eggs." Virginia took the basket and set it on the kitchen table. "I picked the apples for you and these." She handed her the flowers before emptying her pocket of the remaining apples.

"How are you and Johnny doing?" Virginia placed the eggs on the shelf.

"I'm not quite sure." Anna took a seat at the kitchen table.

"What do you mean, you're not sure?" Virginia sat in the chair across from her.

"It's just that Johnny has been secretive, even distant, lately." A worried look crossed her face.

"Well, let's not jump to conclusions. Remember when Pa was acting the same way?" Virginia reasoned.

"Yes, I remember, but I saw Johnny with Sally more than once."

"Do you think that he and Sally are . . . . Well, you know."

"I don't believe so." Anna looked distraught. "They were only talking and Johnny smiled at me when he realized I saw them."

"He smiled at you!" Virginia slammed her hand on the table, causing Anna to jump. "He's got some nerve."

"Calm down, it wasn't that kind of smile," Anna reasoned. "He smiled like, like, I can't explain it, but it wasn't like he was doing anything wrong."

"Listen, Anna, you can either wait and see what happens, or . . . ." Virginia placed her hand over Anna's. "You could ask him."

"That's the problem. I don't want him to think I don't trust him." Anna stood and began pacing, pondering what to do. "I know, I'll do what Ma did." She stopped pacing. "I'll ask Sally."

"Do you truly think she'll be truthful?" Virginia placed the apples in the wash pan and poured water over them to clean them.

"The eyes will tell. If she can't look me in the eyes when she answers, then I'll know something's not right." Anna helped Virginia with the apples.

"You must tell me what you find out." Virginia transferred the apples to a bowl and set them on the table.

"I shall tell you as soon as I know." Anna bit her bottom lip. "Thanks for listening, Ginny."

"I'm here for you no matter what." Virginia dried her hands on her apron. "Take Ma a message for me."

"Sure, what would you like me to say?"

"Tell her that I'm going to need a small bundle of wheat and barley." Virginia grinned sheepishly.

"Are you serious!" Anna placed her hand on Virginia's stomach. "You're having a wee one!"

"Possibly." Virginia's eyes welled. "I'll know by the end of the week." She paused. "Providing Ma sends me the stuff."

"Sends it?" Anna squealed. "We both know Ma will bring it herself." They giggled and hugged one another.

"It seems we'll both have news to tell on our next visit." Virginia rubbed her belly. "Hopefully, it'll be good news.

"Yes, it seems so," Anna stared at her sister's stomach. "I can't wait to get home and tell Ma." Anna gave her sister one last hug before racing out the door. She mounted her horse and let out a loud, "Yee haw!" before riding off down the old dirt road leading home. Her thoughts were full of becoming an aunt, having a new addition in the family, and what it felt like having a child with the love of your life.

Sadness washed over her. She fought back tears as she stretched her hands out at her sides, closed her eyes, and enjoyed the cool breeze blowing over her face and through her hair, something she often did when she rode her horse.

"Stop it, Anna," she scolded herself. "This could be one of the happiest moments in Ginny's life, so no bad thoughts. Right, Chestnut?" She patted her horse on the neck. The horse whinnied as though he agreed.

They turned down the road leading home. Anna nudged Chestnut into a gallop, excited to tell Ma Ginny's news. However, once she removed the horse's saddle and gave him water, she decided it was best if Ginny told Ma herself. She had a sure-fire plan to get Ma to ride to Virginia's right away. She rushed into the house, sneaked into the pantry, and filled two pieces of cloth, one with barley and one with wheat. She tied them off the way Ma did for Gracie. One short string on the barley and a long string for wheat. She placed them in her apron pocket before searching for her mother.

"Ma! Ma where are you?" she shouted as she entered the kitchen. She saw her mother hanging clothes on the line out back. She raced up to her.

"You're home early." Ma placed a sheet over the line.

"I need you to come with me to Ginny's." Anna hoped her mother wouldn't ask questions, but she knew better.

"What's the matter with Virginia?" Ma's voice quivered as she followed Anna toward the house

"Don't panic. She's all right for now." Anna tried her best not to worry her.

"What do you mean, for now?" Ma untied her apron and hung it on the hook next to the back door. "You're frightening me."

Anna could see it was useless to keep it a secret and suspected this was why Virginia told her to inform their mother. "Fine, I was hoping Ginny could tell you the news—after all, it's her business."

"Anna, just tell me what it is." Ma was agitated.

"Here, Ginny needs this." Anna pulled the two little bundles from her apron pocket and handed them to her mother.

"Is that . . . . Are you jesting?" Ma took them from her hand.

"No, I'm not jesting, and yes, it's wheat and barley seeds." Anna grinned. "The short string is barley."

"Oh, my heavens." Ma placed her hand over her mouth. She handed the bundles back to Anna, who then placed them back in her apron pocket. "I might be a grandmother," she whispered.

"I might become an aunt." Anna stared at her mother.

"Let's get going." Ma headed out the back door and toward the barn. "The sooner we get this to Virginia, the better."

"Good morning, Lily Belle," Ma said gently to her horse as she placed the saddle on her. "We're going for a little ride." Lily Belle whinnied and bobbed her head up and down.

"Well, it seems that Lily Belle is more than happy to go, aren't ya girl?" Anna patted her on the neck.

They mounted their horses and off they went. By the time they reached Virginia's house, everyone was worn out, including the horses. Anna swung her leg over and jumped to the ground. Ma had already gotten off her horse and was anxious to see Virginia.

"I'll take care of the horses." Anna reached in her apron pocket, pulled out the two bundles, and handed them to Ma.

Her mother took them and hurried to find Virginia.

By the time Anna finished with the horses and walked into the house, she found Ma and Virginia in an embrace. "I'll be back to find out the news in three days," her mother said.

"*We'll* be back," Anna corrected her.

"Yes, of course. I wouldn't come without you." Ma hugged Anna. "We might be getting a baby." Ma's eyes grew wide with excitement.

"You'll be the first to know." Virginia laughed.

"You mean after you and Patrick find out," Anna said.

"Oh yes, of course." Virginia knitted her brows. "What if he passes out? Maybe I should wait and tell him along with everyone else."

Ma and Anna both chuckled. "I believe it best if you tell Patrick first. I have faith that he'll be just fine," Ma assured her.

"I suppose you're right." Virginia nodded.

Speaking of Patrick, here he comes now." Anna stood looking out the back door.

"Ma, would you and Anna mind coming back when I check the results.? Virginia clasped her hands in a pleading gesture.

"Of course we will. Right, Anna?" Ma nudged her.

"I'll be there with bells on." Anna hugged her sister just as Patrick walked through the door.

"Hello, ladies." He tilted his hat. "Is everything all right?" he asked Virginia.

"Everything's perfect," she replied. "Ma and Anna brought eggs and apples, and they were just heading home." She hugged her mother.

"See you in a few days," Ma whispered in Virginia's ear. They said their goodbyes and Patrick was none the wiser.

The ride home was a joyous one. Ma and Anna were both in a wonderful mood thinking of the possibility of a new baby on the way. They took their time and enjoyed much needed mother and daughter time. The day couldn't have been more perfect. A gentle breeze blew stirring up the lovely scent of flowers growing in the field nearby. Anna closed her eyes and tilted her head toward the sky.

Her mind wandered to Johnny. She couldn't bear the thought of losing him. Especially not to the likes of Sally. She shook the thoughts from her head as the warmth from the sun kissed her slightly tanned face. She daydreamed of what it would be like to marry Johnny and bear his children. She was brought back to reality when her mother cleared her throat before speaking.

"So, how are you and Johnny getting along?"

Anna opened her eyes and dropped her head. "I suppose we're faring well."

"You suppose? Has something happened that makes you

doubt so?" Ma stopped her horse and Anna followed suit.

"It's just that he's been spending an awful lot of time with Sally lately." Sadness filled Anna's eyes.

"Have you spoke to him about it?" Concern shone on her mother's face.

"I'm taking my cue from you." Anna sat up straight. "I'm going to ask Sally."

"That's a brilliant idea." Ma nodded. "If his meetings with Sally are purely innocent, then he doesn't have to know you ever doubted him."

"What if he's not innocent?" Anna looked away.

"Johnny loves you very much," Ma said softly. "I've seen it in his eyes when he looks at you. Have faith." She winked.

"I suppose you're right." Anna felt her body relax. She was happy that she'd confided in her mother about it. "I'm still going to speak to Sally about it." She nudged her horse with her heels. He obeyed and slowly began walking. Her mother rode alongside her.

"Race ya!" Ma shouted, and off they went at a full gallop. They turned down the road leading to home and raced to the barn. Ma unsaddled Lily Belle. She brushed and watered her before turning her loose in the field. Anna did the same with Chestnut.

They stopped by the clothesline and removed the day's wash, folded it, and put it away before cooking dinner. There wasn't enough time to cook stew, so they had eggs and porridge instead.

Everyone was so hungry by the time they came back from the fields that no one complained. Anna noticed Ma had a glow about her and smiled to herself. She knew it had to do with hopefully becoming a grandmother for the first time. Anna loved that she, Ma, and Ginny held a secret. Her only hope was that Ginny truly was with child.

CHAPTER TWENTY - FOUR

GINNY'S NEWS
JUNE 1767

Three days after Virginia took her test, Patrick was working in the field cutting hay. Ma and Anna arrived earlier than expected. Virginia was thrilled to see them coming up the road. She was excited they'd be there when she checks the results—although she wasn't sure who was more anxious to find out, her or Ma.

Ma and Anna tied the horses to the front porch banister and raced into the house.

"Did you check yet? What's it going to be?" Anna could hardly contain her excitement. "I just know you're having a baby."

"Whoa, slow down and breathe." Virginia laughed.

"Well, move along." Ma gently nudged Virginia.

"All right, I'm going, I'm going." Virginia giggled. "I don't know about the pair of ya." She deliberately walked slowly toward the bedroom looking over her shoulder, teasing Ma and Anna.

"Oh, for goodness sakes," Anna said. "If you don't hurry, I'll check it myself."

Patrick rushed in just as Virginia was about to check the results. "Are we having a baby? Is it a boy or girl?"

"Oh, Patrick, I'm happy you're here. Come find out with me." Virginia took him by the hand. They disappeared behind the bedroom curtain.

Ma and Anna waited. "Oh no!" They heard Virginia exclaim.

"What is it? What's the matter?" Patrick's tone changed from excitement to worry.

"I'm not quite sure." Virginia stepped into the kitchen holding the two bundles. Patrick followed. Virginia's hands were trembling as she held bundles of seeds in front of her. "Ma, does this mean what I think it does?"

Ma stepped closer to get a better look. "Oh, my goodness! I've never seen such a thing." Ma hugged her and they both began to sob.

"What does it mean?" Patrick and Anna shouted in unison.

"Well, I can't be sure, but it looks like you're having a baby . . . ." Ma paused and nodded at Virginia.

Patrick hugged Virginia. He lifted her off the floor and twirled her around. "Does it reveal what it's going to be?" He set her back on her feet.

"If the test is correct . . . ." Virginia gazed into his dark brown eyes. "We're having a boy and a girl."

Anna squealed as she jumped up and down. "Twins! You're having twins!"

Patrick blanched. "Tw, twins? Did you say twins?" Ma helped him to a chair at the kitchen table.

Virginia rushed to his side. "Patrick, are you all right?"

He looked lovingly at Virginia with tear-filled eyes. "I'm going to be a father." He leapt from his chair, grabbed Ma, and spun her around. "You're going to be a grandmother! What do you think about that?" He let her go and did a little silly dance with Anna. "You're going to be an aunt."

Virginia cleared her throat, her face aglow and her eyes sparkling with joy.

Patrick stopped and turned to face her. He gently hugged her. "You're going to make a wonderful mother." He kissed her cheek.

"What's all the shouting about?" Everyone turned to find Pa standing at the kitchen door.

"Daniel, what are you doing here?" Ma's expression turned from surprise to joy.

"I came to see if Patrick needed help repairing the barn roof." Pa stared at Patrick. "I heard shouting and ran to make sure everything's all right."

"Yes, sir, things couldn't be more perfect." Patrick stepped next to Virginia. "Honey, I'll let you have the honor of telling him." Patrick did a little playful bow.

Pa waited patiently.

"We're having a baby—er, possibly two babies." Virginia hugged Patrick.

Pa tilted his head. "What do you mean, two babies?" He paused and thought for a moment. His eyes grew wide. "You mean you're going to have a baby?" He took Virginia by the hand and stared at her face as though he was waiting for her to laugh and say she was jesting.

"That's what I just said, only maybe there are two babies." A happy tear ran down Virginia's cheek.

"Wahoo!" Pa shouted. "We're having twins! I'm going to be a grandfather." He danced a silly jig around the kitchen, causing everyone to burst into laughter.

"I'll need to get fabric to make some baby blankets and some gowns for the pair of them." Anna hugged her sister. "I'm so elated for you, Ginny."

"When will they arrive?" Patrick asked.

"According to my calculations, they should be here just before Christmas," Virginia answered.

"That's perfect and gives everyone plenty of time to prepare." Ma hugged Virginia and Patrick. "I must get home and get busy."

"I can't wait to tell James and Adam." Anna rushed out the door. "I'll see you and Pa at home," she shouted as she jumped on her horse and raced down the road. With all the excitement, she forgot about Johnny and Sally, at least for a short period of time. It didn't help when Adam unknowingly teased her about that very situation.

"Maybe one day you and Johnny will have children. That is, if Sally doesn't take him first," he teased.

Anna's face paled. She burst into tears and ran from the room. She couldn't bear to face anyone. Her mind was made up. She decided it was time to find out the truth. She saddled Chestnut and made her way into town.

Upon arriving in town, she saw Sally speaking with a young lady before they both disappeared through a side door of the brothel. A few minutes passed before she reappeared and then hastily retreated toward the mercantile.

"I don't know what you're up to Sally, but I'm going to find out," Anna whispered to herself. She waited until Sally stepped inside the mercantile before dashing across the street. After making sure no one saw her, she hurried to the side door of the brothel and lightly tapped on it. She was about to knock louder when the door slowly cracked open, and the same young lady Sally was with peered out. Anna noticed right away the girl couldn't be much younger than herself.

"Hello, sorry to bother you," she said sweetly. "I saw you

speaking with my friend Sally and—"

"Sally, she is your friend, *oui*?" the girl asked in strong French accent.

"Yes, she is my friend." Anna barely had the words out before the girl opened the door wide, a huge smile spread across her face. She stepped out gently, closing the door behind her. "Sally is . . . . How do you say? . . . . A good person." She struggled for the right words.

"Would you mind telling me why she was here?" Anna asked.

"She is helping me." She dropped her head. "Please, I can't tell you any more than that."

"If I knew what the problem is, maybe I could help too," Anna coaxed.

The girl said nothing. She continued staring at her hands.

"At least tell me your name before I go." Anna took a step back as though leaving.

The girl said nothing.

"Well, if you don't want to talk about it, I wish you good luck."

"Wait! Juliette. My name is Juliette." Her eyes darted toward the street. She stepped back into the doorway when she saw a man ride up on a horse and stroll into the sheriff's office.

"Is that who you're hiding from?" Anna pointed.

"No, no. I'm not hiding from anyone," Juliette lied.

"Well, that's the second—possibly the third—lie you told me in the space of about five minutes." Anna crossed her arms.

"What! I do not lie," Juliette said defensively. "Why do you say such a thing?"

"The only thing French about you is your name—if that's truly your name." Anna glared at her.

"Fine! I'm not French," Juliette said angrily in an accent

just as country as Anna's. "I thought an accent might make me sound older, more sophisticated." She flipped her hair and rolled her eyes up.

"How old are you?" Anna looked her in the eyes.

"I'm fourteen, but I don't have to tell you anything else," she answered defiantly.

"Then you can explain it all to the sheriff and to Sally." Anna turned and started walking away.

"Please wait." Juliette grabbed Anna by the arm, stopping her.

Anna turned to face her.

"It's true that I'm not French." Juliette glanced around the perimeter. "Please step inside and I'll explain everything." She held the door open.

Anna stepped inside with one hand behind her on the doorknob in case she had to make a hasty retreat.

"My parents were killed when their carriage lost a wheel and rolled down a steep ravine." Tears flooded Juliette's cheeks. The memory proved too painful, yet she did her best to continue. "We weren't rich, but my parents were well off and had set aside a nice amount of money for me."

"How did you end up here?" Anna's tone softened.

"My uncle took me in. At first, I was grateful." She averted her gaze. "He became mean and abusive." She pulled the oversized dress she wore off her shoulder revealing old scars as well as a few new ones. "They're from the strap he carries with him at all times." She pulled the dress back over her shoulder only to have it fall off again.

"How did you and Sally meet?" Anna asked softly.

"My uncle stopped here in town for supplies on our way to Pennsylvania. He was to meet a man there. He planned to sell me to him." Juliette fidgeted with the belt hanging loosely on her dress.

"How awful!" Anna's heart went out to Juliette.

"Oh, he never actually sold me to any of them." She placed a hand over her mouth as though she'd said something wrong.

"So, this is something he has done more than once?" Anna was appalled that anyone could be so cruel as to sell their own family, or anyone, for that matter.

"Yes, we traveled all over. He would sell me to different men. I'd get them drunk so I could run away and meet my uncle at a designated area." She dropped her head in shame. "He said he'd kill me if I told or ran away."

"He is a disgusting, pathetic pig." Anna stomped her foot angrily. "How did you manage to get away from him?"

"The last man he sold me to, didn't drink anything but water or tea. When he tried to have his way with me, I told him I needed to freshen up and go to the outhouse, only I ran past it and kept on going."

"Did you tell Sally the truth?" Anna asked.

"Yes, and she brought me food and clothes." Juliette smiled. "She's very nice for a rich girl."

"Yes, I suppose she is," Anna said softly.

"She's paying for my trip to Missouri," Sally said with a little bounce.

"Missouri? Do you have family there?" Anna questioned.

"Yes, my grandparents." She bowed her head. "They were my mother's parents."

Hmmm. Could this be the big secret between Johnny and Sally? Anna wondered. She decided not to question Sally about it. At least, not yet. "I'll help all I can, and don't worry, I won't tell a soul." She opened the door and peeked out making sure the coast was clear. She stepped out and Juliette gently closed the door behind her. Anna headed for the mercantile, hoping she didn't run into anyone along the way. She didn't have time to stop and talk to anybody. She was determined to find out if Juliette told Sally the same story.

The bell rang as she opened the mercantile door and stepped in. It was the one time she wished the bell wasn't there. She hoped to sneak in and out without anyone seeing her, but the bell alerted Mrs. Collins of a potential customer.

"Hello, Anna." Mrs. Collins poked her head around the corner from the back room only to disappear again. "What can I do for you today?" She reappeared with a piece of folded, pink-colored fabric. "What do you think of this?" She held it up for Anna to see.

"It's lovely." Anna examined the cloth. "Have you seen Sally?"

"She was just here." Mrs. Collins folded the cloth and placed it on the shelf. "I saw her heading in the direction of the blacksmith's."

"Thank you. I'll stop by before going home to look at the new cloth." Anna opened the mercantile door, almost bumping into Mrs. Worthington. "Good morning, Mrs. Worthington." Anna tried to step around her.

"Have you ever seen the likes of some people? No shame, no shame at all," Mrs. Worthington grumbled.

"I'm sure I have no idea what you're talking about." Anna stepped past her. "Have a lovely day."

"Mildred, Mabel." Mrs. Worthington waved a hand and hurried toward the two ladies who were looking in the window of the mercantile.

"What a gorgeous dress." Mildred stared at the dress hanging in the window.

"It is lovely." Mabel agreed. "I wonder who made it?"

Anna rushed past them with her head down, smiling proudly. She loved hearing the compliments on Hattie Mae's work. She didn't see Sally anywhere, so she turned around and went back inside the mercantile to talk to Mrs. Collins about the new homespun cloth. She wanted to get some to make baby items for Virginia. The first thing she picked up was the pink cloth she saw Mrs. Collins place on the shelf.

"This is very pretty. Ginny's going to love this one." Anna unfolded it to get a better look. "I'll take some blue as well." A commotion outside caught her attention. She looked up to see Sally rushing past the three ladies. Mrs. Worthington was speaking loudly but Anna couldn't make out what she was saying. She could tell by the look on Sally's expression that it was directed at her.

Anna slammed the cloth on the table. "I'll be right back." She marched to the door and flung it open.

Mrs. Worthington, Mildred, and Mabel were gossiping about things they knew nothing about, and that's what infuriated Anna most.

"Why look at the little trollop." Mrs. Worthington motioned toward Sally. "I wonder what her father will think when he finds out she has been frequenting the brothel?"

"That's not true," Sally said defensively.

"Oh, the nerve of her, talking back to her elders," Mildred remarked.

"Disgusting girl," Mabel added.

"Do you know what I find disgusting?" Anna stepped out of the mercantile.

"Now, here is a sweet girl. You could take a lesson from this one," Mrs. Worthington said with a tone of haughty disdain.

"You know what I think?" Anna stormed up to Sally and

stared into her tear-filled eyes before turning to face the three gossiping ladies.

"Go ahead, Anna, put her in her place," Mildred stated.

"She's what we call a soiled dove," Mabel added.

"The most disgusting thing I've seen today are you three vultures attacking an innocent girl!" Anna shouted angrily.

"How dare you speak to us that way," Mrs. Worthington huffed.

"No, how dare you, you foul gossiping pigs. You know nothing about Sally." Anna threw her hands in the air.

"I will not stand by and allow a child to speak to me that way." Mrs. Worthington stepped forward. "I'll tan your hide myself." She sneered.

"Don't you touch me!" Anna stood her ground. "All right, ladies, since you love gossip so much, let's talk about you." Anna glared at Mrs. Worthington.

"Me?" Mrs. Worthington placed her hand to her chest. "You know nothing about my life."

"I know that you told everyone that your husband died, when he actually ran off with a lady from the brothel." Anna crossed her arms over her chest.

"That is a vicious lie!" Mrs. Worthington shouted.

"Mabel, you've been known to sneak out behind the barn and have a little nip of brandy and oft times must be carried in the house because you're too drunk to walk." Anna ignored Mabel's angry outburst. She turned her attention to Mildred. "I have it on good authority that you have been sneaking in the barn with Carl Higgins while his wife attends church on Sunday mornings."

"You vile, lying girl," Mildred seethed.

"How dare you spread such lies and slander on our good

name!" Mrs. Worthington screeched, her face red with anger.

"Calm down, ladies." Anna held up her hands in a gesture for them to stop speaking.

"Don't tell me to calm down after spewing such vulgarity!" Mrs. Worthington stepped toward Anna with her fists clinched by her sides.

"How does it feel hearing horrendous rumors about you?" Anna smirked. She knew she'd gotten her point across from the expressions on each of their faces. "Now you know how Sally feels." Anna glanced at Sally and then back at the three gossips.

"I never thought . . . ." Mildred's voice trailed off as she hung her head in shame.

"I have never gotten drunk in my life." Mabel refused to make eye contact with either of her friends. "I wouldn't want that rumor to spread," she added.

"Come to think of it, I don't know anyone by the name of Carl Higgins," Mildred said softly.

"I hope you understand that I made all that up just now." Anna's eyes darted back and forth between the three ladies. "I had to make you realize that gossiping and lies destroy people —good, innocent people."

"I'm truly sorry, Sally." Mrs. Worthington spoke first. "I hope you can find it in your heart to forgive me for such atrocities."

"Same goes for me. I'm sorry too." Mabel could barely look Sally in the face.

"I apologize for my part in all this." Mildred gave Mrs. Worthington a sideways glance. "I'm so ashamed of myself."

"It's forgotten." Sally kept looking back toward the brothel. "If it's all the same to you ladies, I would rather not speak of this again." She turned around and walked away before Anna could stop her.

“Excuse me, ladies.” Anna gave a little nod and then ran to catch up with Sally. “Sally, wait!” she shouted.

Sally stopped when Anna stepped in front of her. “Thank you for what you did back there with those old prunes.” Sally motioned with her head.

“You’re welcome,” Anna replied. “I couldn’t stand by and do nothing. Besides, they deserved it”

“I’m thrilled that my cousin chose you, and I’m forever grateful that you came to my defense.” Sally smiled and continued walking.

“Did you say, cousin, as in you and Johnny?” Anna couldn’t believe her ears.

“Yes, his father is my uncle.” Sally’s face registered confusion. “I thought you knew that.”

Relief washed over Anna. She was glad she hadn’t revealed her suspicions. She thought it was best to change the subject. “I met Juliette,” she blurted out.

“What did she tell you?” Sally looked worried.

“She said she ran away from her evil uncle. By the way, he’s at the sheriff’s office, probably lying through his teeth about everything.” Anna bumped into Sally, who’d stopped suddenly.

“Why would he be at the sheriff’s?” Sally wondered. “Did Juliette say anything else?”

“Only that you’re helping her, which I think is wonderful, especially after seeing the scars on her back and then seeing her uncle carrying the strap he used on her.”

“I saw the scars,” Sally said sadly. “For the life of me, I’ll never understand how anyone can be so cruel to another human being.”

“Well, I’d like to take his strap and show him what it feels like," Anna said through gritted teeth.

As they approached the brothel, Sally nervously glanced around. "Wait here while I speak with Juliette." Sally rushed off before Anna had a chance to answer.

Anna paced back and forth wondering what Sally and Juliette were talking about. A few minutes later, the man Anna assumed to be Juliette's uncle stepped out of the tavern, which just so happened to be part of the brothel. Anna grew anxious when he stood watching her. She felt his eyes boring into her back each time she turned around.

"You wouldn't happen to be waiting on someone, would you?" He never took his eyes off Anna.

Anna stopped pacing. "Are you speaking to me?" she asked nonchalantly.

"Do you see anyone else around?" he answered sarcastically.

"Yes, it just so happens that I am waiting on someone."

"Who would that be?" He ran the strap through his hand.

Anna was relieved to see her father and Nathaniel standing in front of the blacksmith's. They were slowly walking in her direction.

"I asked you a question." The man stepped toward her.

"Who I'm waiting for is none of your concern." Anna tried to sound brave.

"You ignorant little ingrate," he said, seething. "No one talks to me in that manner." Two large strides and he was in front of Anna. He grabbed her wrist and drew back the strap.

Before he could strike her with it, Johnny appeared. He grabbed the strap, knocking the man off balance.

The man hit the ground hard on his back.

"If I ever catch you near my girl again, you'll regret it!" Johnny yelled.

Daniel and Nathaniel came running.

"What's going on here?" Daniel shouted.

"Pa, this man grabbed me and tried to hit me with his strap." Anna hugged Johnny. "I don't know what he would've done if it wasn't for Johnny." Anna spotted Sally and Juliette sneaking out of the side door of the brothel. She needed to create a distraction. "I was so afraid." Anna pretended to cry.

Her pa stood over the man like a giant bear protecting its cub. He jerked the strap from the man's hand and tossed it aside. He then grabbed him by the shirt collar and lifted him off the ground.

Juliette saw the whole thing. She raced over and stood looking up at the man.

"Juliette, please tell them I'm a good man," he begged.

Juliette thought he appeared quite small compared to Daniel and Nathaniel.

"Juliette!" he yelled. "For God's sake, tell them I'm your uncle."

By now, a huge crowd had gathered. Juliette stepped forward, looked him dead in the eyes, and replied, "You're no uncle of mine." She turned to the crowd. "What kind of man sells his fourteen-year-old niece to different men?" She turned back to face her uncle, seething with anger, her fists clenched at her side. "What kind of man does this to his brother's only child?" She pulled the dress off her shoulder, revealing the scars.

"I'll tell you, he's a low life filthy scoundrel. That's what," Mrs. Worthington shouted angrily.

"Oh, mercy, the poor child," Mildred cried out.

"I say give the girl the strap and let her have at him," Mabel yelled.

"Yes! Give the girl the strap. Let her give him a taste of his own medicine," someone hollered from amongst the crowd.

"Where's the sheriff when you need him?" an old man shouted.

"He rode off a few minutes ago," another man answered. "He said something about cattle rustlers," he added.

"Well, well, look here, boys. If it aint Byron Walker, the sidewinder who took my money and skedaddled." A dirty, unkempt man shoved his way through the crowd followed by his three sons. The Chapmen brothers.

"Hello, Daniel." Mr. Chapman nodded.

"Hello, Tim. "It's been years since I last saw you," Daniel responded.

"Yup, maybe we'll talk later." Tim motioned toward Byron. "I have some business to attend to."

Andrew nervously stepped back behind his brothers, unsure if Anna had said anything to her pa about what happened at the river. He relaxed a little upon realizing that Daniel hadn't a clue. He slipped through the crowd and made his way up behind Anna, causing her to jump when he spoke in her ear. "Anna, I'm sorry for how's I acted at the river."

Anna had much more to worry about than the likes of Andrew. She gave him a half-hearted smile. "Are you just saying that because my pa is right here?"

"No, I'm truly sorry." The look in his eyes told Anna he was serious. "Pa says that after today, we're turning over a new leaf." A confused look crossed his face. "Whatever that means."

Byron's shouting caught his attention. Anna was happy for the distraction.

"Get him, Pa." Gene, the oldest of the three brothers, grinned and spit tobacco juice on the ground.

"We'll teach ya's not to mess with us Chapmans." Andrew

stepped next to his father. “Right, Pa?” He shoved his hands in the pockets of his britches and rocked on the heels of his bare feet.

Andrew was the youngest of the three. Gene and David, the middle brother, grabbed Byron, tied his hands behind his back, and threw him over the back of the horse like an old rug. He was kicking and screaming the whole time.

“Someone stop this madness. Sheriff, help!” he pleaded.

“Wait!” Juliette took hold of the horse’s reigns to steady him. “What are you planning to do to him?” she asked, her voice shaky.

“Well, now, we were going to take him off somewhere and teach him a lesson,” David answered as he picked up Byron’s strap from off the ground.

“Please don’t hurt him.” Juliette’s heart went out to her uncle.

“Listen to the girl,” Byron shouted. “Just let me go, and me and my niece will be on our way.”

“How could you feel sorry for him after the things he put you through?” Mrs. Worthington stepped to the front of the crowd.

Juliette hung her head, unable to look at anyone. “Because I know how it feels to be beat with that strap.” Tears slowly found their way down her cheeks. “I don’t ever want anyone, not even my uncle, to feel that kind of pain.” Her gaze fixed on her uncle. “I loved and trusted you, Uncle Byron, but not anymore. I won’t be going anywhere with you.” She walked away.

“Juliette! You get back here, or it’s the strap for you,” he screamed furiously.

“Men, do what you must.” Mrs. Worthington threw her hands up in disgust.

“You heard the lady.” Gene led the horse out of town followed by his father and brothers.

The crowd dispersed, some shaking their heads while others grumbled about what an awful man Byron is. Sally and Johnny waited for Juliette to fetch her things from the brothel.

"I'll be right back." Anna raced off before Johnny could respond. She hurried to the mercantile. After explaining everything to Mr. and Mrs. Collins and what she planned to do, Mr. and Mrs. Collins looked at one another with a broad smile on each of their faces.

"Henry, are you thinking what I'm thinking?" Mrs. Collins gazed at her husband.

"I'm thinking Anna's right." He walked to the back wall of the shop and came back with a gorgeous green print dress. "That little girl needs a fresh start in life." He folded the dress and handed it to Anna.

"Thank you so much." Anna backed toward the door. "I have material at home, and I will make a new one in exchange for this one."

"Consider it a gift for the girl," Mrs. Collins shouted after her.

Anna rushed down the street and made it in time as Juliette was coming out the door. "Here, take this." She shoved the dress in Juliette's arms.

A look of surprise crossed Juliette's face.

"A gift from Mr. and Mrs. Collins at the mercantile."

Juliette glanced down at the rag of a dress she wore. "I was in such a rush to leave town that I forgot to change clothes." She paused at the brothel door. "In all honesty, I forgot I have new clothes." She dropped her head. "I'm not used to having anything but rags. Thank you both." She nodded at Sally and Anna.

She entered the door and returned wearing the dress Anna

gave her. She combed her long brown hair and pulled it up with a white ribbon.

"You look stunning." Sally clapped her hands together and gave a little bounce.

"I hope you don't mind that I chose to wear this dress," she said shyly.

"Not at all. You'll have plenty of opportunities to wear one of the dresses I gave you." Sally locked arms with Juliette, and they walked to the awaiting carriage. "This is my private carriage, and I'd like you to meet Alexander, my driver," Sally announced, smiling warmly at Alexander. He stood tall and attentive beside the carriage.

"Oh, no, miss," Juliette protested. "You've done so much for me already. I can't accept." She glanced uncertainly between Sally and Alexander.

"You can, and you will," Sally insisted, taking Juliette's hands. She then looked up at Alexander. "I trust you'll get her there safely."

Alexander tipped his hat. "Yes, ma'am."

"Wonderful." Sally clasped her hands together with a satisfied smile. "There shall be a huge bonus waiting for you upon your return."

Alexander's eyes widened and a huge smile spread across his face. "Thank you, ma'am." Juliette felt a little apprehensive, yet excited. She was going to Missouri to live with her maternal grandparents. Sally insisted on paying for the trip. Juliette reluctantly accepted her offer.

"Thank you for everything." Juliette took Sally by the hands. She glanced from Johnny to Anna then back to Sally. "You've all taught me that not everyone is cruel, and there are still kind souls in this world."

"I'll miss you greatly." Sally hugged her.

"I'll miss you as well." Juliette turned to board the carriage.

Johnny stepped forward to help her. "Allow me, my dear lady." He bowed playfully, causing Juliette to giggle as she took her seat.

Anna loved this side of Johnny. Her heart swelled with love and pride as she watched him stroll back to her side and place an arm around her waist.

"You look lovely in your new dress." Anna stepped up to the carriage window. "It was made by a friend."

"Thank her for me, and Mr. and Mrs. Collins too. Tell your friend she does beautiful work." Juliette ran her hand over the material.

The driver tipped his hat at Juliette. "Time to go, miss." He climbed aboard the carriage.

"I'll never forget you Sally," Juliette said as the carriage pulled out.

"Nor I you." Sally waved.

"Goodbye, Johnny. I wish you the best." Juliette hung her head out the carriage window. "Good luck to you, Anna," she shouted before ducking back inside the carriage.

Johnny, Anna, and Sally watched until the carriage turned the bend.

"I do pray she arrives there safely." Sally gazed at the empty dirt road.

"I'm sure she'll be fine." Johnny took Anna by the hand and the three of them slowly walked back to town.

"I have to get back to work. I have a cabinet to finish." Johnny kissed Anna on the back of the hand. "I'll see you later." His smile lit up his eyes, sending a chill through her. She loved it when he looked at her that way. She watched him mosey up the road, and then she headed to the mercantile. She wanted to get a better look at the new fabric.

Mr. and Mrs. Collins were extremely busy, so Anna purchased white material instead. She could hardly wait to get home and start sewing baby items.

Anna assumed Juliette was the big secret between Johnny and Sally. She learned differently on her sixteenth birthday when Sally presented her with expensive imported paper she used to make a journal.

"I heard you love to write, so I had this made especially for you." Sally handed her the gift wrapped in cloth.

Anna opened it and squealed with delight. "Thank you so much." She hugged Sally.

Johnny handed her a steel handcrafted box which she thought was the gift. "Thank you, Johnny, I love it." She hugged him.

"You're welcome, but that's only part of the gift." Johnny chuckled. "The real gift is inside."

Anna unlocked the steel box to find a handcrafted wooden box with all her favorite things carved into it. There's a girl with a book by the river, wildlife, fish leaping out of the water and wildflowers on each end.

"This is gorgeous." She examined the box. "Did you make this?" She ran her fingers over the artwork.

Johnny stood with his hands in his trouser pockets smiling proudly. "Yes. The girl is you at your favorite spot by the river." He pointed to the girl on the box. "It opens by pressing the center of the flower on the sides." He placed a finger on each flower and pressed them. The lid popped open, revealing an empty compartment.

Anna's eyes lit up. She hugged the journal to her before

placing it inside the wooden box. “I’ll forever cherish these gifts. Thank you both.”

CHAPTER TWENTY-FIVE

SARAH'S SUSPICIONS

Sarah laid the book beside her. "I wish we could go back in time when things were simpler."

"Well, I must say that was a long read." Grams stretched. "Let me add that, times back then weren't simpler. People grew accustomed to that way of life." Grams stood up. "It's all they knew."

"I would love to hear the rest of the story, but my bladder is screaming." Stacy stood and rushed off to the bathroom.

"I think we all need to take a break." Sarah placed the book on the coffee table. "Grams, do you believe in reincarnation?"

"Lord, girl, what kind of question is that?" Grams' expression softened. "The Bible says in Ecclesiastes that when you die, the body returns to dust, but the spirit goes back to God who gave it."

"Does it say what He does with it afterwards?"

"No, I don't believe it does." Grams eyed Sarah suspiciously. "Why do you ask?"

"It's something Jimmy said. Plus, he and Johnny are so much alike."

"What did he say?" Grams inquired.

"He has a recurring dream of dying in the Revolutionary

War, vowing to come back to his wife and children." Sarah frowned. "He also said that if God wants to recycle souls, that's his business." Sarah placed her hand in the back pocket of her jeans shorts and smiled. "You should have seen the look on his face when I told him John the Baptist was the reincarnation of Elijah."

"Well, I never thought about it." Grams eyes darted to the family Bible on the coffee table. "I do know that was a prophecy from the Old Testament that was fulfilled in the New Testament." Grams knitted her brow.

"So, what are you thinking?" Sarah shifted from one leg to the other.

"Jimmy is not my grandfather reincarnated! I don't believe in that stuff." She crossed her arms. "I'm getting ready for my doctor's appointment." She turned and left the room.

"I never thought about that," Sarah whispered. Her phone vibrated in the back pocket of her shorts. She felt butterflies in her stomach when Jimmy's name appeared. She sucked in a breath and released it before answering. "Hello."

"Hello, gorgeous. Are you busy?" he asked in a chipper mood.

"Grams has a doctor appointment today, but I'm free afterwards."

"Call me when you get home and let me know how it went," he said.

"I will. Besides, we need to talk." Sarah bit her bottom lip, hoping he didn't ask questions. She was relieved when one of his crew members distracted him.

"Okay, hun. Talk to you later." He hung up before Sarah could respond, but she didn't mind. All she could think about was how she was going to tell him. Her grandmother was taking longer than usual to get ready. Sarah tapped on her bedroom door. "Grams, are you all right?"

"I'll be right out," she answered from behind the closed door.

Jimmy gave his crew the day off. Bill, the oldest of the group, was at the hospital waiting for the birth of his first grandchild, and Jimmy was doing an estimate on a house across town.

Sarah and Grams arrived for her appointment. After a battery of tests, they were ready to leave.

"Your doctor will receive the results, and he'll let you know how they turned out and what the next step will be," the receptionist said with a straight face.

"Can anyone give me an idea if the tests are good or bad?" Grams whispered as she leaned toward the receptionist.

"I said you'll get the results when you see your doctor," the receptionist snapped.

Sarah knew the receptionist's attitude wouldn't sit well with her grandmother. She tried to intervene before her grandmother lost her temper. "Grams, let's hurry home and see what happens next in the old book." Sarah placed an arm around her shoulder and tried to usher her out, but Grams stiffened.

She stared the receptionist in the eyes. "You should get up and move around, stretch a little." Grams gave her a little smirk.

"Why would I need to do that?" The receptionist glared at her.

"Hopefully, it will loosen your bowels. You've given everyone here a constipated look, and personally, I think you're full of—"

"Grams! It's time to go." Sarah's face grew crimson as she grabbed her grandmother by the hand and pulled her away from the desk. A few patients covered their mouths and snickered while one teenage boy gave Grams the thumbs up and yelled, "Way to go, Grandma!"

Once outside, Sarah burst into laughter. "What am I going to do with you? I can't take you anywhere."

"I was going to say she's full of herself. What'd you think I was going to say?" Grams grinned mischievously.

"Never mind. Let's go shopping and then grab a bite to eat on the way home," Sarah suggested.

Several hours later, they returned home and were unloading the car when they noticed Mrs. Stevenson racing across the road toward them, waving her arms and yelling the whole way.

"Florence, Florence, I need to talk to you." She placed a hand to her chest trying to get her breath.

"Here we go," Grams said in a low tone, placing a hand to one side of her mouth.

"Behave yourself," Sarah whispered and forced a smile before turning her attention to Mrs. Stevenson. "Well, if it isn't our lovely neighbor."

"What do you want now, Gladys?" Grams ignored Sarah's disapproving look.

"I turned in my application for the Cherry River Fall Festival baking contest," she said smugly.

"That's wonderful. We wish you the best of luck." Sarah placed a hand on her grandmother's back and attempted to usher her toward the house, only Grams wasn't having it. She never was one to let sleeping dogs lie, as she always put it. She refused to budge until she had her say where Gladys was concerned.

"Listen, Gladys, I don't think you should enter your pie with the ingredients you stole from me." Gram fidgeted with her purse strap. "I just wouldn't feel—"

"Are you accusing me of stealing your recipe?" Gladys

interrupted her. "How rude! I'm shocked and ashamed of you, Florence."

"I know you stole it, Gladys. I'm trying to warn you, if you'd shut up and listen." Grams tried to tell her of the extra salt she put in the ingredients, but Gladys wouldn't listen.

Her statements became increasingly pugnacious. "You're jealous and worried that I'm going to win this year." She pursed her lips.

"Fine! Have it your way, Mrs. Prissy Britches, "Grams sneered. "Come on, Sarah, let's go." She adjusted her purse on her arm and snatched a bag from the car before storming off.

"There's no need for name calling," Gladys huffed and briskly walked home.

Once inside, Grams decided to retire to her room for a nap.

Sarah called Jimmy and invited him over. She wanted to get a few things off her chest before proceeding any further. She went to her room to freshen up.

Stacy came rushing in without knocking, which was something she often did, so it came as no surprise to Sarah. "I'm going back to Florida this weekend. Do you want to come with me?" she blurted out and crossed her fingers.

"So soon? Is something wrong?" Sarah set the hairbrush on the vanity.

"I'm picking up Max and we're moving here, to West Virginia."

"Are you serious?" Sarah's eyes grew wide. "That's fantastic."

"We're leaving early tomorrow morning."

"We, do you mean you and Robbie?"

"Yes. I've sold the business, and Robbie is going with me to help pack." She checked her appearance in the vanity mirror.

"That's fantastic, Stacy." Sarah hugged her. "I was dreading seeing you leave for Florida."

"Me, too. Stacy stared out the window. "I love it here. The mountains, the rivers—"

"Robbie." Sarah nudged her.

"It's just that he's so sweet, handsome, and charming." Stacy blushed.

"Oh my gosh!" Sarah squealed. "You're in love."

"Yeah, well, I don't think I'm the only one bit by the love bug." Stacy nudged her back.

"I'm not sure Grams is in love quite yet." Sarah put a finger to her cheek. "At least, I don't think she is."

"Very funny. You know I was referring to you and Jimmy."

"Me, in love with Jimmy?" Sarah placed a hand to her chest. "Surely you jest."

"I think you've been reading too much of that book." Stacy playfully shoved her onto the bed.

"Maybe, but it's such a wonderful story." She stood. "As a matter of fact, I'm going to read some to Grams later this evening."

"I take that as a no, you're not coming to Florida with us." Stacy frowned.

"Think of it this way." Sarah stepped toward the bedroom door. "You and Robbie will have a nice pre-honeymoon," she teased and raced from the room, leaving Stacy standing there, her mouth agape.

Stacy shook her head and followed Sarah downstairs. Jimmy and Robbie had arrived and were seated at the kitchen table eating blackberry cobbler. Grams placed a large scoop of vanilla ice cream on top of each.

"This is delicious," Jimmy said in-between bites.

"I can't believe you've never had blackberry cobbler," Robbie said before shoving a huge bite into his mouth.

"Wow, first peach cobbler and now blackberry. Is there anything else you haven't tried?" Sarah stepped into the kitchen.

"Well, actually there is." Jimmy wriggled his eyebrows mischievously, causing Sarah to blush profusely. "Not in front of Grams," she whispered and nodded toward her grandmother, who was standing in front of the sink with her back turned.

"I'm referring to your grandmother's famous apple pie," he teased.

"Sure, ya were." Sarah picked up an empty bowl from off the table and placed a scoop of cobbler in it.

"Would you like a scoop of ice cream, dear?" Grams placed a hand on the freezer door and was about to open it when Sarah shook her head.

"No, thanks. I like it just the way it is," she answered with her mouth full of the delicious dessert.

"Here, try this." Sarah handed Stacy a slice.

Stacy took a bite and nodded. "This is good, but I like peach cobbler best."

"You and me both," Grams said.

"I agree, it's my favorite too." Sarah placed the remaining cobbler in the refrigerator then turned to Stacy. "When did you say you're leaving?"

"Tomorrow." Stacy gave her an inquisitive look. "What do you have in mind?"

"I was hoping we could go to the swimming hole for an evening swim." Sarah stepped behind Jimmy and placed her arms over his shoulders. "What do ya think?"

"I'm in." Jimmy stood and kissed her on the lips. "Come on,

Robert, it looks like we're going to the river."

"Sounds like a plan." Robert took Stacy by the hand and pulled her onto his lap.

"Are you coming with us, Ms. McMillan?" Jimmy inquired.

"No, and you can call me Florence." She removed the dish towel she had flung over her shoulder. "You young'uns enjoy your swim. I have a date." She untied her apron and hung it on the hook by the kitchen door.

"Oh, my. Who's the lucky guy?" Stacy asked.

"That would be Doc Brown," Sarah answered before Grams had a chance to.

"That's right, and I had best be getting ready." Grams hurried from the room.

Sarah and Stacy went upstairs to change into their swimsuits, and then they pulled a pair of shorts and tee shirt over top.

"We'll take my car." Sarah nodded toward Stacy's car. "Since yours appears packed for your trip."

Jimmy and Robert agreed and then left to get ready themselves. Twenty minutes later, the four of them were on their way.

CHAPTER TWENTY-SIX

THE SWIMMING HOLE

The sun was shining brightly in the cloudless blue sky by the time they reached the banks of Gauley River. The clear water gently flowed over smooth, round stones. Golden trout could be seen swimming along the bottom of the river, darting back and forth as though performing a little dance. Sarah wondered if that was where the name "river dance" came from. She laughed inwardly. Her thoughts were interrupted when Stacy stepped next to her.

"Ah . . . ." Stacy stretched her arms toward the sky and tilted her head back. "It's a perfect day for a swim."

"It sure is." Jimmy stepped up behind them. He placed a hand around Sarah's waist and stood staring at the water. "A penny for your thoughts." He kept his eyes on the water.

"Gosh, my grandfather used to say that when I was a little girl." Sarah looked at him in surprise.

"Mine still says it." Jimmy turned to see Robert goofing around.

Robert playfully picked up Stacy and acted like he was going to toss her into the river. Stacy freaked out, wrapped her arms around his neck, and wouldn't let go.

"If I'm going in, you're coming too, Robbie!" Stacy kicked her legs, trying to escape.

Robbie kissed her nose before putting her down.

“It looks like love is in the air.” Jimmy nodded toward Robbie and Stacy.

“I’m thrilled for them both. They deserve to be happy,” Sarah replied.

“So do you.” Jimmy hugged her.

"Oh, man. I totally forgot about the stuff in the car!" She quickly gave him a kiss on the lips and then made her way to the car. Jimmy followed behind her. She grabbed a beach bag with snacks, towels, and a blanket.

"Oh, by the way, I stopped at the U-Save on the way back to your house and got some drinks," Jimmy said as he opened the back door.

"Drinks?" Sarah asked, confused.

"Yep, drinks," Jimmy replied, pulling out a six pack of soda. "What did you think I meant?" He took her hand.

"I was worried you meant . . . ." Sarah hesitated. "It's just that my ex-boyfriend used to get violent when he drank." She looked down at her feet. "That's why I don't like alcoholic drinks." She avoided eye contact.

Jimmy gently touched her face and lifted her chin. "My dad was an alcoholic, too, and I never want to make a woman feel scared like my mom,” he confessed, leaning in to kiss her softly.

"I guess there's still a lot we don't know about each other, huh?" Sarah whispered.

"Hey, get a room!" Robbie shouted but then got elbowed in the stomach by Stacy. "Ouch! Did you all see that?" Robbie doubled over, pretending to be hurt. "Look how she treats me," he joked.

Stacy laughed, "You guys better turn your heads so there are no witnesses when I kick his butt."

"Come on, Jimmy, these girls are tough," Robert said, motioning for Jimmy to follow him.

Jimmy grabbed the bag from Sarah and raced Robert to the grassy area under the tree.

"Nice purse, boss," Robert said, pointing at the bag.

"Thanks, it matches my eyes," Jimmy replied, holding the bag up to his face. Robert burst into laughter. "So, should I call you Robert or Robbie?" Jimmy asked as he spread out a blanket and neatly arranged the snacks.

"Most people call me Robbie, but you can call me whatever you want, boss," Robert said.

"You can stop calling me boss. It's Jimmy, okay?" Jimmy said, playfully slapping Robbie on the shoulder.

"Okay, boss—I mean, Jimmy," Robbie said, then walked over to the riverbank.

Sarah and Stacy quietly watched. “You two are adorable together!" Sarah playfully nudged Stacy.

“Yeah, so are you and lover boy over there.” She nodded toward Jimmy and Robert standing by the river, trying to decide where to jump in.

“I think that’s a good spot.” Robert pointed straight in front of them.

“I believe over there’s a little deeper and safer.” Jimmy pointed to the right.

“Let’s show them how it’s done.” Sarah ran to the opposite side of the tree and untied a rope swing. The guys watched in surprise as she gripped the rope tightly and then with a loud shout, “Wah-hoo,” she swung out and let go, splashing into the water with a grin. As she resurfaced, she called out. “You’ve got to try it." Her laughter rang through the air, water glistening on her sun-kissed skin.

Stacy was next, her heart racing with excitement. The men cheered her on as she bravely pulled back on the swing, laughing nervously. With a deep breath, she swung out, feeling the exhilaration of flight, and then with a loud scream, she dropped into the river, bubbles bursting around her as she made a splash. Within a few seconds her head popped out of the water. "That was incredible," she yelled. "Come on Robbie, try it."

Jimmy could sense Robbie's apprehension and decided to show him how it was done. "Come on, man. We can't let the girls show us up." He brushed past Robbie. He reached the swing, gripped the rope, and quickly swung out. He let go and did a twist before plunging into the water.

"Way to go, Jimmy." Sarah cheered as she swam to him. She placed her arms around his neck and gave him a congratulatory kiss.

"Whoa, what will I get if I do a double twist?" Jimmy teased.

"This!" Sarah dunked his head under water.

Jimmy tickled her before resurfacing.

Her laughter echoed across the river, mixing with the sound of birds chirping from the nearby trees.

"Come on, Robert!" Jimmy yelled. "You can do it."

"Just do it!" Sarah shouted.

Stacy noticed Robbie looking a little unsure, so she tried to lighten the mood. "I'll catch you." She stretched her arms out.

With a determined look on his face, Robbie pulled back on the rope and yelled, "Look out below." He swung high over the water and let go with a shout, "I'm going to die." He landed on his stomach with a loud smack.

"Oh, that's gotta hurt." Sarah scrunched her face.

"Robbie! Did you die?" Stacy asked. She swam to him as his head poked out of the water.

"I sure feel like I did." Robert grimaced and rubbed his stomach.

"I know how that feels. Been there and done that," Jimmy sympathized.

"I don't know what you call it in Florida, but here in West Virginia, we call that a belly smacker." Sarah glanced at Stacy.

"Poor baby." Stacy kissed Robbie's cheek.

"Oh, it hurts," he whined. "How about a kiss right here." He pointed to his lips, to which Stacy obliged.

"You're fine." Jimmy chuckled and splashed water on Robbie.

Robbie and Stacy swam after Jimmy as he ducked underwater and headed toward Sarah.

The four of them swam and splashed around, their laughter a testament to the joy of the moment. Stacy and Robbie challenged each other to races, their competitive spirits making the fun even more lively. Meanwhile, Sarah and Jimmy floated lazily on their backs, holding hands as they gazed up at the cloudless sky, feeling the gentle tug of the current as it carried them along.

After a while, they all gathered near a large, smooth rock in the middle of the river. Robbie climbed up first, extending his hand to help Stacy up, and then Jimmy did the same for Sarah. They sat together, legs dangling in the water, the sun drying their skin as they talked and joked. The conversation flowed as easily as the river, with stories, shared memories, and dreams of the future.

As the afternoon wore on, the sun began its descent, casting a golden glow over the landscape. The river, now shimmering with shades of orange and pink, seemed to slow its pace as if to savor the moment with them. Reluctantly, they decided it was time to head back, but not before one last splash in the water.

With their hearts light and their spirits lifted, they made their way back to the shore, water droplets sparkling on their skin like tiny diamonds. They gathered their things, the sound of their laughter still ringing in the air as they walked away from the river, already reminiscing about the perfect day they had shared.

"What do ya say we make this a tradition? We'll meet here every summer?" Sarah stopped walking.

Jimmy took her in his arms and looked lovingly into her eyes. "I think any place with you is perfect." He kissed her gently on the lips. "We've started a tradition that we can pass down to our kids."

Stacy smiled at Robbie, whose face turned pale.

"Oh my gosh. I meant someday when Sarah and I have children. Not now, silly."

Everyone burst into laughter, including Robbie.

As they left the river behind, they knew this day would be one they'd remember for a long time—an afternoon of sun, water, and the simple joy of being together.

CHAPTER TWENTY-SEVEN

THERE GOES THE NEIGHBORHOOD

When Sarah arrived home, her grandmother and Dr. Brown were ending their evening. She had never seen her grandmother kiss any man other than her grandfather, but it filled her heart with joy to know that her grandmother found love again at her age.

Grams walked the doctor out on the front porch to say her final goodbye.

Sarah couldn't help but wonder if she deliberately did it for Mrs. Stevenson to see, and see she did. She pursed her lips, crossed her arm and began tapping her foot in disapproval.

Grams smiled a huge toothy grin, threw up her hand and waved. "Hello, Gladys. It's a hot and steamy day out today." She watched Dr. Brown as he strolled down the street. "Well, it was." Grams placed a hand over her mouth and snickered as she turned to go back inside the house.

"Florence McMillan, just you wait until the ladies at the church auxiliary hears about this," Gladys shouted from across the street.

Grams stopped dead in her tracks and turned to face her. "Gladys Stevenson! You and your church auxiliary group ain't nothing but a bunch of gossiping old hens."

"That's not true," Gladys huffed.

Grams spotted Mrs. Johnson at the end of her driveway pretending to check her mail.

"Hello, Mrs. Johnson." Grams waved. "The mail hasn't run yet, so ya might as well come over here where you can hear better." She motioned to her.

"I'll have you know that I can hear just fine. I mean, I wasn't listening," Mrs. Johnson snapped.

"I'm sure you can hear everything," Grams retorted. "Especially now that you have hearing aids." She smirked.

Mrs. Johnson's eyes shot daggers at her. "Mind your business." She slammed her mailbox shut.

"I could say the same to you and nosy britches over there." Grams motioned across the street at Gladys.

"At least I'm not an old floozie." Gladys marched across the road pointing and shaking her finger at Grams.

Sarah heard the arguing and stepped outside to see what was going on. She made it just in time to see her grandmother pick up the water hose and spray Mrs. Stevenson.

"Take that, Gladys," Grams shouted, grinning the whole time.

Gladys tried to run, but Grams chased after her, soaking her from head to toe. Mr. Stevenson stepped out of their front door and doubled over laughing as his wife angrily raced past him.

"It's not funny," she screeched.

Sarah bent the water hose, cutting off the water. She held it tight to keep it from spraying. "Grams, let's get you in the house before someone calls the law."

It was too late. A patrol car rolled to a stop in front of Sarah and her grandmother. The officer slowly exited the car and made his way toward them. Jimmy pulled his truck into the driveway and got out. "Sarah, what in the world is going on?" He stopped walking when the officer held up his hand.

"Mrs. Stevenson started running her mouth against my grandmother," Sarah shouted to Jimmy as she pointed the hose vigorously toward the Stevenson's house. Unbeknownst to Sarah, the kink straightened in the hose, spraying the officer. He jumped back, trying to dodge the water, but Sarah was going off on a rant, shaking the water hose back and forth while speaking to Jimmy. She didn't hear the officer or Jimmy's warning until Grams jerked the hose from her hand, accidentally spraying Sarah.

Jimmy gently took it from her hand and then turned the water off.

"Oh, my goodness!" Sarah placed a hand over her mouth. "I'm so sorry, officer." She blushed.

"Same old Sarah that I know and love." The officer dried his face with a handkerchief he pulled from his shirt pocket.

"Lord, as I live and breathe." Sarah stepped closer to the officer. "If it ain't Jeremy Walker." She hugged him. "How the heck have you been, and how long have you been a deputy?"

"I've been in law enforcement for five years." He put his thumbs in his pants pockets and rocked on his heel. "Actually, I'm the new sheriff." He smiled proudly.

"Sheriff Walker. That has a nice ring to it." Sarah motioned for Jimmy. "This is my boyfriend, Jimmy."

"It's nice meeting you, Jimmy." They shook hands. "I must say, you have your hands full with this one." He nodded toward Sarah.

"Do tell." Jimmy placed his hands on his hips. "You have my full attention." He winked at Sarah.

"There's nothing to tell," Sarah interrupted.

"One time when Billy Hanson was tying helium balloons to a kitten's legs Sarah punched him square on the nose, grabbed the kitten and ran away."

"You punched him? How old were you when this happened?" Jimmy's eyes flashed intrigue.

"I was ten years old, and he deserved it," Sarah said in her defense.

"All right, the reason I'm here—" The sheriff turned to face Grams. "One of your neighbors called and said you assaulted her."

"Jeremy, how's your folks doing?" Grams stepped next to Sarah.

"They're fine. I was just on my way to see them." He stared at Sarah. "When the call came in about a dispute, I recognized the address." He dropped his head when Gladys Stevenson bounded toward them, yelling and arms flailing.

"Officer! I want her arrested." She shook her finger at Grams.

"Don't make me turn the hose on you again." Grams glared at her.

"Did you hear that, officer?" Mrs. Stevenson shouted. "She just threatened me . . . again."

"All right ladies, calm down." He placed the handkerchief back in his pocket.

"Ya see how she is." Mrs. Stevenson wriggled her finger back and forth in front of the officer. "I see she assaulted you with the water hose, too."

"Calm down, ma'am. She didn't do this," Jeremy stated.

"I see how it is." Mrs. Stevenson crossed her arms over her chest. "She bribed you." She bobbed her head. "Uh-huh, that's what she did."

"I've heard enough out of you." Sheriff Walker raised his

voice in frustration. "How about I haul you both to jail, and you can let the judge sort it out?" He playfully winked at Sarah. A slight grin tugged at the corners of her mouth.

"Well, now, sheriff, I don't think that's necessary. Do you, Florence?" Mrs. Stevenson gave Grams a sideways glance.

"No. I see no need for such drastic measures." Grams forced a smile as she stepped next to the sheriff. "Besides, Gladys can't help that she's a hot-headed nosy body." She patted the sheriff on the arm.

"What did she call me?" Gladys crossed her arms over her chest.

The sheriff rolled his eyes. "Ms. McMillan, did I hear you say something?"

"Nope, nah, uh, not a word." Grams took a few steps back. "Now if we're done here, I would like to get back to our book." She headed toward the house, stopping halfway. "Are you coming, Sarah?"

"So just like that, she gets off scot-free." Gladys placed her hands on her hips and glared at the sheriff.

"Well, we can do this one of two ways." The sheriff glared back. "I can arrest you both." He held up his hand when Mrs. Stevenson opened her mouth in protest.

"Arrest me! For what?" she shrieked.

"Now hold on for a cotton-pickin' minute and I'll tell you." His nostrils flared. "I can take you in for trespassing, harassment, and defamation of my character. Should I go on?"

"Defamation of character?" A confused look crossed her face.

"Yes, you accused me of accepting a bribe, which is an outright lie. I suggest that you go home and mind your own business." The sheriff turned toward his car.

"Give the old biddy what for," Grams shouted from her front

door.

Sarah gently pushed her inside the house. "Have a nice evening, Jeremy." She smiled and waved.

Luckily, Mrs. Stevenson was halfway across the street and was out of earshot. Jimmy walked the sheriff to his car. "Well, sheriff, it was nice meeting you. I'm glad I don't have your job." Jimmy laughed.

"After today, maybe I should rethink my career options." He shook his head and took his seat in his patrol car and drove off.

Jimmy hoofed it across the yard and up the front steps, taking them two at a time.

Sarah met him at the door. "Sorry you had to witness all that," she apologized.

He peered through the window, making sure Grams wasn't within earshot before turning back to Sarah. "I found the whole situation hilarious," he said in a low tone. "Are they always like this?"

"Ever since I can remember." Sarah nodded. "My grandpa used to say he was going to invite his friends over for coffee and a show." She crossed her arms and shook her head.

"You miss him, don't you?" He hugged her.

"More than you know," she answered.

"What do you say we take a nice long drive?" He stepped back to see her reaction.

"That sounds nice. I'd like that." She turned toward the front door. "I'll let Grams know." She stepped inside the house and yelled. "Grams! Jimmy and I are going for a drive. Be home in a few hours."

Grams peeked around the kitchen door. "It's about time. You two have fun." She suspiciously ducked back into the kitchen.

Sarah walked into the kitchen. Her grandmother had her

back to her and was talking to someone on the phone.

"No, David, I have no idea what Gladys's problem is. I don't just go around spraying people with the water hose willy nilly," she said softly. "She got what she deserved."

Sarah tiptoed out the front door, confident that her grandmother would be on the phone for several hours. "Let's go." She jogged down the steps with Jimmy on her heels.

"Will you grandmother be all right until we get back?"

"She'll be fine. She's on the phone with Doc Brown and will probably be talking with him long after we get home."

"That's wonderful, let's go." Jimmy raced Sarah to his truck. They always cherished their picnics by the river but today felt especially magical. They chose to drive down the country roads and enjoy each other's company. It was a perfect afternoon; the sun was warm but not too hot. The gentle breeze carried with it the scent of blooming flowers. Sarah rolled down the window and smiled as the wind swirled through the cab of the truck. She loved the way it felt blowing through her hair.

They turned down an old dirt road and drove until they came upon a huge lake. They exited the truck. Jimmy spread a blanket on the ground, the checkered pattern unfurling neatly on the soft grass. They lay on it, staring at the huge puffy white clouds as they slowly drifted by.

"Look!" Sarah pointed. "That one looks like a dog." She stared at the sky.

Jimmy followed her gaze. "That one looks like your grandmother with the water hose." They burst into laughter. Jimmy sat up and pointed. "Whoa, that one looks like you in the morning." He chuckled. "See? Your hair is standing straight up."

"Oh, really." Sarah sat up, her eyes twinkling mischievously as she straddled him, her body leaning close so she could feel his breath catch in his throat as she cupped his face, with a tenderness that made the world around them seem to disappear, she kissed him, deeply and passionately.

When they finally pulled away, they were both breathless and smiling. Sarah noticed the clouds had disappeared, leaving a clear blue sky. Nature itself became a silent witness to their shared moment of love and intimacy.

"That was some kiss," Jimmy whispered breathlessly.

"Yes, I agree." Sarah placed her head on his shoulder.

"I want you, but I want it to be special. Not here, not now." He stood with an outstretched hand.

Sarah took his hand and allowed him to help her up. "I want it to be a special moment too, and you're right, this isn't the right time or place."

They drove home feeling a deeper connection and a love like neither has felt before.

Jimmy dropped Sarah off and left to do an appraisal on a garage for a man in town. Sarah found her grandmother sitting on the couch still talking on the phone with Dr. Brown. She hung up as Sarah stepped in.

"How was your drive?" Grams inquired.

"It was lovely, but on the drive back all I could think about was the old book." Sarah stepped around the sofa and picked up the book from the coffee table

"I can't wait to hear more of the story." Grams patted the cushion next to her. Sarah took a seat, opened the book, and began to read.

CHAPTER TWENTY-EIGHT

1768 – WINTER STORM

On a frigid day two days before Christmas 1768, Virginia sat by the fire with her sister Anna. The warmth of the flames contrasted with the bitter cold that seeped through the walls as a relentless snowstorm raged outside. Virginia, nine months pregnant, rested her hands on her swollen belly, feeling the familiar but unsettling twinges of discomfort that had been growing stronger throughout the day. Her due date was the next week, and though she tried to remain calm, the uncertainty of what lay ahead weighed heavily on her mind.

Her husband, Patrick, was a banker and, despite the treacherous weather, he had gone to work that morning. Virginia had insisted he go, certain there was still time before their children would arrive.

Before arriving at the bank, Patrick stopped and spoke to the midwife, Hattie Mae, making sure she would be on standby. The two of them knew this day was coming, but neither expected it to coincide with the worst storm of the season.

As the day wore on, the contractions grew stronger. Virginia tried to hide her discomfort from Anna, but there was no mistaking the pain etched on her face. Anna, ever attentive, finally asked, "Is it time?" Virginia could only nod, her breath catching as another wave of pain swept over her.

Knowing they needed help, Anna rushed to the door, intending to fetch the midwife. But when she opened it, the wind nearly knocked her back, and the snow was blinding. She couldn't see more than two feet in front of her. Panic crept in as she realized how dire the situation had become.

Just then, the sound of a horse and buggy struggling through the snow reached her ears. Could it be Patrick?

Anna's heart leapt with hope as she peered through the swirling snow. To her relief, she saw the familiar figure of Hattie Mae, the midwife, climbing down from the buggy, and she brought Ma and Pa with her. Without wasting a moment, Ma and Hattie Mae rushed up onto the front porch and into the house, bringing with them a gust of icy air and a sense of calm.

"Ma, Hattie Mae, thank God you're here!" Anna exclaimed, her voice trembling with relief.

"Help your Pa tend to the horses," Ma said as she hurried to check on Virginia.

Hattie Mae followed, her face serious but calm. "Let's get her settled. We have work to do."

While Hattie Mae and Ma tended to Virginia, Anna hurried to help Pa take the horses to the barn.

"Anna, what are you doing out here?" Pa shouted over the howling winds.

"I came to help you with the horses," Anna yelled. The frigid air burned her lungs and the blowing snow stung her cheeks. She covered her face with her scarf and stumbled into the barn. She gripped one of the horses' reins and led it to a stall. Pa unhitched the other horse and placed it in a stall of its own before heading back out to brave the weather.

The storm was so fierce they almost lost their way back to the house, but determination and the thought of Virginia kept them going. By the time they returned, Hattie Mae was already preparing for what would be a long and difficult labor.

Hours passed, and the storm showed no signs of letting up. Virginia's pain was intense, but Hattie Mae's calm presence plus Ma and Anna's unwavering support kept her grounded. Just when it seemed the storm might defeat them, the door burst open and Patrick stumbled in, snow-covered and exhausted but filled with determination.

He hurried to Virginia's side, taking her hand. "I'm here, my love," he whispered, his voice thick with emotion.

"Your hands are so cold." Virginia rubbed his hands between hers before screaming in pain as the contractions grew stronger.

Hattie Mae nodded to him, her expression softening. "You made it just in time."

Patrick's face went pale as he stood. "I-I'll be waiting with your pa in the parlor." He gently kissed his wife on the cheek. The floorboards creaked as he nervously paced for what felt like an eternity.

"You're wearing a path through the floor." Pa chuckled. Although his nerves were worn to a frazzle, he hid it well.

"How did you do it, sir?" Patrick continued pacing. "You've been in this situation four times."

"Breathe and pray, son. It's all you can do." Pa stood and patted Patrick on the back. Patrick's pace picked up speed, each step a testament to his mounting anxiety.

Try as he might, Patrick just couldn't stay away. He rushed back into the room. Taking Virginia by the hand, he knelt by her bedside.

The labor was arduous, but Virginia was strong. With each push, she drew on the strength of her husband's presence and her sister's comforting words. Finally, after what felt like an eternity, the first cry of a newborn filled the room. A boy. Patrick's eyes filled with tears as he cradled his son, his heart swelling with love.

But the night was not over. There was still another life to bring into the world. Virginia, though exhausted, gathered her strength for one final push. And then a second cry, softer but just as strong, announced the arrival of their daughter.

Tears streamed down Patrick's face as he looked at his two children, a son, and a daughter, safely delivered despite the storm that raged outside. He whispered, "God has blessed us, Virginia. Despite this horrible storm, there is light."

The storm howled outside, but inside the house, there was nothing but warmth, love, and the joyous wonder of new life.

Early the next morning, Anna awoke to the sound of babies crying. She swung her legs off the bed and stretched her arms above her head. She loved the tiny cries of her niece and nephew whose names she had yet to learn. Virginia was worn to a frazzle after giving birth, and Anna was so busy seeing to it that Patrick and Hattie Mae took breaks while she tended to her sister that she forgot to ask what the babies would be named. *No matter, I'll find out soon enough.*

She stood, picked up a robe hanging on the bedpost, and put it on. Anna made her way to the kitchen. Patrick and Hattie Mae were already up. Hattie Mae had just finished making breakfast and Patrick was on his way to take a plate of food to Virginia.

"Good morning. I trust you slept well, judging by the way you snored," Patrick teased.

"I beg your pardon!" Anna gasped. "I do not snore."

"Yes, you do. Adam has been right all along. You sound like an old bear." Patrick chuckled.

Anna was shocked. This was a side of her brother-in-law she'd never seen. "Well, now, it seems becoming a father has brought out your playful side."

"No, it's always been there. You're just never around when I'm home." He took a bite of a hot hoe cake Hattie Mae fried and placed the rest of it on the plate Patrick was taking to Virginia. "Hattie Mae, I do believe you make the best fried bread in the country."

"That's one thing I agree with you on. Hattie Mae is good at everything she does." Anna took a piece of bread and smeared jam over it before taking a bite. "You should see all the dresses we made," Anna said proudly.

"I know what a wonderful seamstress Hattie Mae is. She made Virginia's wedding dress. Remember?" Patrick turned and headed for the bedroom, anxious to get back to his wife and babies.

"I'm coming with you." Anna raced after him.

Patrick stepped aside and, with a playful bow, he motioned her in. "Ladies first."

"Much obliged," she replied as she stepped into the bedroom.

Pa and Ma were already up and cuddling their new grandbabies. Virginia watched as her heart swelled with pride.

Anna strolled over to Pa since he was closest to the door and peered down at the baby boy.

"Hey, little one," she said soothingly. "Aren't you a handsome little thing?"

"He looks like his father, don't ya think?" Virginia said proudly as Patrick made his way over and kissed her on the forehead.

"Yes, they both are beautiful," Ma agreed as she stared at the tiny baby girl sleeping peacefully in her arms.

"May I?" Anna asked as she reached for her nephew.

Pa stood and placed the baby boy in her arms. "There, have a seat." He moved aside, offering her his chair. "I need to check on the horses as well as the weather."

"Thank you, Pa." Anna sat on the chair and turned her attention to the baby in her arms. "What are their names?" she asked.

"Patrick Lee Junior and Patricia Mae," Virginia replied.

"Does Hattie Mae know you named one of the babies after her?" Ma placed Patricia against her shoulder and patted her back.

"Not yet. Patrick and I planned on telling her together." Virginia reached for baby Patrick, who had begun to wake and fidget. A tiny cry escaped before Anna could place him in his mother's waiting arms.

"Well, I do believe it's a beautiful name." Ma cradled the baby in her arms. "They both have lovely names, and I can hardly wait to see the look on Hattie Mae's face."

"Well, wait no more." Patrick walked to the door and opened it. "Ahem, Mrs. Hattie Mae, would you mind coming in here?"

"Be right there, Mr. Patrick," she responded.

Patrick held the door for her. A few minutes later, Hattie Mae strolled into the room drying her hands on her apron. She stopped upon realizing everyone was staring at her. Her eyes grew wide with fear.

"Is everything all right?" she asked, concerned.

"Everything's wonderful, thanks to you." Virginia motioned toward the babies.

Anna stood. "Have a seat, Mrs. Hattie." She motioned at the chair.

"Thank you." Hattie Mae scooted back in the chair when Anna placed baby Patrick in her arms.

Ma handed Patrick his baby girl and, with one swift motion, he placed her in Hattie Mae's left arm.

"We'd like you to meet Patrick Lee Junior and Patricia Mae," Virginia announced.

Hattie Mae's eyes filled with tears and spilled down her cheeks. "Lord a-mercy, child." She placed a kiss on the baby girl's forehead. "You're the first child named after me. What a blessing indeed." She then placed a kiss on top of baby Patrick's head. "God has surely blessed you with these two."

"That he has, and he blessed us with you and your family too." Virginia dabbed her eyes with the sleeve of her gown.

Hattie Mae placed the babies in Virginia's arms. "I best be getting home. That is, if your Pa thinks it's safe to travel."

"If you must go, fare thee well," Virginia replied and then turned her attention to her mother. "Ma, must you go too?"

"Don't you fret." Ma pulled the quilt over Virginia and the babies. "I'll be staying for a few days."

"As will I," Anna announced. "You'll have your hands full with these two little ones." Anna stroked the cheek of each baby. "Not to mention the big baby you call your husband."

"I'll not forget that remark!" Patrick shouted from the doorway.

Anna jumped as Patrick winked at Virginia.

"It's nice seeing the pair of ya frolic so." Virginia smiled proudly at Anna.

Pa stepped through the front door with news that the sun was peeking through the clouds, and he was ready to start the long trek home. He knew Ma wouldn't leave until Virginia was back on her feet. Hattie Mae, on the other hand, was quite anxious to get home to her own family. Pa helped load her things. They said their goodbyes with Pa promising to return for Ma and Anna by the end of the week.

The next morning, Virginia woke feeling refreshed and grateful for the much-needed sleep. Anna and Ma had been tending to the babies, allowing her to rest. Sitting up in bed, Virginia expressed her gratitude. "Thank you both so much for staying and helping with the babies."

Ma, cradling Patrick, responded, "It was our pleasure." Anna, holding Patricia, nodded in agreement. Ma placed the babies in Virginia's arms after kissing her forehead. Virginia smiled down at them, her heart full of love. Understanding her need for privacy, Ma and Anna quietly slipped out of the room. Time seemed to fly and before they knew it, their stay had come to an end.

Pa kept his promise and returned by the weekend. After a tearful goodbye, Ma kissed her grandbabies and hugged Virginia.

"Woman, you act as though you'll not see them again." He rolled his eyes.

"Well, with this weather, I may not see them 'til spring," Ma sniffed.

"Well, we best be going." Pa kissed the babies on the top of their heads. "See you soon, wee ones." He hugged Virginia and slapped Patrick on the shoulder. "Patrick, my boy, take care of them."

"I will, sir." Patrick looked lovingly at Virginia.

Anna hated leaving so soon, yet she understood it was necessary. Patrick and Virginia required some quality time together as a family. She and Ma donned their wool mittens, cape, and bonnet while Pa put on his coat. And then they set off.

CHAPTER TWENTY-NINE

1769 – THE RIVER

Winter gave way to spring and summer soon followed, bringing with it hot days and warm nights. Johnny asked Anna to accompany him for a ride to the river, which she gladly accepted.

The sun hung low in the sky, casting a golden glow over the riverbank as Johnny and Anna made their way to their favorite spot beneath the grand Maple tree. Its sprawling branches provided a canopy of emerald leaves that rustled slightly with the gentle summer breeze. The rich scent of earth and wildflowers mingled with the cool, crisp air, creating an atmosphere of serene beauty.

Johnny spread out a handwoven blanket on the soft grass, the vibrant colors of the fabric contrasting with the deep green of the foliage. He'd carefully packed a wicker basket with fresh bread, ripe peaches, and a wedge of sharp cheese. As Anna sat down, her eyes sparkled with delight at the simple but thoughtful spread. She brushed a strand of hair away from her face and gazed at Johnny, her heart fluttering.

The river's clear waters meandered gently past them, its surface shimmering with flecks of sunlight that danced with every ripple. The soothing murmur of the current provided a tranquil song, punctuated by the distant chirping of crickets and the melodious calls of warblers hidden among the branches. They watched a deer on the other side of the river lumber to the water's edge to take a cool refreshing drink. Johnny flinched when something hit him on top of the head. He turned to Anna. His gaze followed hers toward a branch above them. A squirrel had lost its grip on an acorn and watched as its treat fell toward the ground. Johnny happened to be in the way.

"First you, now a squirrel. Did you teach him that?" Johnny teased.

A confused look crossed Anna's face. "What are you talking about?"

"Every time we meet, I always get something flung at me, usually at my head." He chuckled.

Anna threw back her head and laughed. “I'm not telling. That’s our secret.” She stared at the squirrel. “Shush.” She placed a finger to her lips.

Johnny watched Anna with an expression of quiet admiration, his green eyes reflecting the warmth of the moment. He took her hand, his touch tender and reassuring. The world seemed to fall away, leaving just the two of them in their secluded paradise.

“Anna,” Johnny began, his voice soft but filled with earnestness. He reached into his pocket and pulled out a small mahogany box. The corners of his lips lifted into a hopeful smile. “There’s something I’ve been meaning to say.”

Anna’s breath caught in her throat as she looked at him with wide, curious eyes.

Johnny opened the box to reveal a delicate silver ring, its centerpiece a single, glistening emerald surrounded by small diamonds that seemed to capture the essence of the river's clear waters.

"I've known for a long time that you're the one I want to be with forever," Johnny continued, his fingers trembling slightly as he held out the ring, "I can't imagine my life without you by my side. I love you, Anna."

Anna's eyes filled with tears as she gazed at the ring, then back at Johnny. She felt as though her heart was going to burst with joy.

"Anna, will you marry me?" Johnny's voice cracked and was barely above a whisper, but it carried the weight of his love and devotion.

A breathless silence hung between them for a moment. The squirrel sat motionless in the tree. Across the river a deer stood majestically on the hill watching. It was as if the entire forest was holding its breath in anticipation.

Anna's lips curved into a radiant smile; her heart swelled with joy. She nodded. "Yes, Johnny," she said, her voice choked with emotion, "I love you so much. Yes, oh, yes, I'll marry you." She threw her arms around his neck and hugged him.

With a look of pure happiness, Johnny slipped the ring onto her finger. The emerald gleamed brilliantly, a symbol of their love and the future they would build together. As he pulled her into his embrace, the river continued its gentle song. The squirrel barked and climbed higher into the tree as though announcing the news. The deer stomped the ground as if congratulating them before racing off into the woods. Even the maple tree seemed to stand witness to their vow, its leaves rustling softly in approval.

"I'm so eager to share the news with Ma, Ginny, and . . . ." Anna's eyes grew wide as she stepped back. "Does Pa know?"

She pressed a hand to her chest.

"I spoke to him last night." Johnny took Anna by the hand, running his thumb over the ring. "He gave us his blessings." He kissed the back of her hand and pulled her into his arms. Anna lay her head on his shoulder and stared at the ring.

The moment was perfect, timeless—a fleeting but eternal memory etched into the fabric of their lives.

CHAPTER THIRTY

WEDDING DAY
August 8, 1769

Johnny and Anna's wedding was the talk of the town. Anna's best work to date was the dress she stitched with Hattie Mae's assistance. The train's floral embroidery was stunning. A broad satin belt cinched her waist. Ma styled Anna's hair. Her face was framed by curling ringlets as she pinned them to thc top of her head. Virginia assisted her in putting on the dress. When she was ready, she turned to Ma, who gasped softly.

"Oh, my goodness. You look . . . simply stunning." Ma took her hand gently. "I'd love to give you a proper hug, but I don't want to ruin your beautiful hair." She leaned in and placed a quick kiss on her cheek before turning away to dab her eyes with a handkerchief.

"Look at you, my little sister, all grown up and about to get married." Virginia wrapped her arms around her for a warm embrace. "I love you, and you're going to be an amazing wife and mother." She brushed away a tear that threatened to fall down her cheek.

"I love you, too, Ginny." Anna twisted back and forth in her wedding gown. "Do you truly believe I'll make a good mother one day?"

"The best mother in all of Virginia—well, next to me and Ma." Virginia giggled.

"'Tis true. You and Johnny are going to be very happy." Ma quickly wiped the moisture from her eyes.

"I love you, Ma, and I don't care If I muss my hair." Anna pulled her mother to her and hugged her tightly.

Pa rapped on the door. "You ladies ready? The house is full, and everyone is waiting for the bride."

"Coming, Pa." Anna turned toward the looking glass. After a quick check to make sure her hair was in place, she turned to the door. Ma opened it, and Pa sucked in a breath upon seeing Anna. Sally ducked and hurried past him into the room. "Pardon me for being late."

"You look truly lovely." Pa stepped back to get a better view. "I'll be waiting at the foot of the stairs." He rushed off. Ma followed, and Pa locked arms with her and walked her down the stairs. He stopped and waited for Anna while Ma took her seat along with the rest of the guests in the parlor.

Ginny and Sally, dressed in their bridesmaid's gowns, took the lead. Upon their reaching the bottom of the staircase, Anna stood on the top step. She slowly descended the stairs as Hattie Mae hummed a beautiful unknown tune. Pa looked handsome standing at the foot of the beautifully decorated staircase, smiling proudly.

The wedding went off without a hitch. Adam hugged Anna before taking Elizabeth to the dance floor where they danced the night away. Anna felt as though she would burst with joy as Johnny held her in his arms and they twirled around the room.

"I shall never be as happy as I am this night." Anna gazed into

Johnny's eyes.

"Nor I, Mrs. Carlin." He gently lifted her in his arms, kissed her lips, and then carried her outside where he sat her on the porch swing. "I can't believe we're man and wife." He kissed her hand that was intertwined with his.

"I must admit the death do us part scares me." She dropped her head. "I can't bear the thought of ever losing you."

"I solemnly promise that if anything happens to me, I'll move Heaven and Earth to come back to you." He placed a hand onto her cheek. "Even if it's in the next life."

"That's not funny, Johnny Carlin." She pulled away from him. "Oh, goodness, I'm now Anna Carlin." She gasped at the sudden realization.

"Listen, Anna, I'm not joking." His expression was serious. "If God sees fit to allow me to come back to you, so be it."

"You're talking nonsense." She turned her head away from him.

"I reckon what God does with a soul is his business." He placed a finger underneath her chin and turned her head to face him. "I'm not going anywhere; we're going to have a long happy life together." He placed a kiss on the end of her nose.

"I pray we will." She laid her head on his shoulder. "We should go back inside."

They met James and Sally on their way out. The couple were laughing and didn't see Johnny and Anna.

"Land sakes, James and Sally!" Anna exclaimed. "Are the two of you . . . ."

"We're sorry we didn't say something sooner, but . . . ." Sally searched for the right words.

"This is your special day." James kissed Anna on the cheek.

"We wanted to wait until after your wedding to make

our announcement." James looked lovingly at Sally. "We're betrothed." Sally laid her head on his shoulder as she flashed an engagement ring.

"That's wonderful news!" Anna squealed and hugged them both.

"Congratulations, James." Johnny shook his hand and patted him on the shoulder. "You couldn't ask for a better woman."

"Thank you, Johnny. I appreciate that." James took Sally's hand as they strolled through the flower garden.

"Looks like tonight's magical for everyone." Anna hugged Johnny tightly. "Come on, husband. Let's get back to our guests." She tugged on his arm.

"After you, wife." He bowed playfully upon opening the door.

"There you are." Virginia met them as they were coming in the door. She had a baby on each hip. The twins were now eight months old, and both squealed with delight upon seeing Anna and Johnny.

"There's auntie's beautiful girl," Anna said as she took her niece who was leaning toward her, talking baby babble while kicking her legs excitedly.

"Here, you might as well get some practice." Virginia handed Lil Patrick to Johnny. "Ma sent me to find you. We're setting the table now." She motioned for them to follow her to the dining room.

Dinner consisted of beef roast, a whole hog cooked on the spit, potatoes, various vegetables, and desserts. There was more food than anyone could eat. No one left on an empty stomach, nor empty handed. Ma insisted the guests take some food home with them so it didn't go to waste, and everyone was grateful for it. She packed two baskets full of a little bit of everything.

"Here." She handed the baskets to Jake. "Please take these to Martha Winters and her sister's family on Panther Mountain."

"Yes, ma'am." He gladly accepted it. "I'm sure they'll be happy to get it."

"I'll go with ya, son." Sam rubbed his head. Jake nodded and headed toward the back door.

"Come on, Pa. We need to deliver this here food before it gets ruined." His cheeks tinted pink when he realized he'd just called Sam "Pa" for the first time.

Sam proudly puffed out his chest and left with his son.

Anna smiled at Johnny and whispered. "Told ya today is magical."

Anna and Johnny moved into a small log cabin on the outskirts of town. He built it as a wedding gift for Anna, although he planned to build a bigger house soon in western Virginia.

Rumors of war weighed heavily on everyone's mind. Johnny had enlisted long before he asked for Anna's hand in marriage. The very thought of losing a loved one to war scared Anna more than anything.

They quickly settled into married life. Anna loved being a wife, and with the help of Ma, Ginny, and Hattie Mae, the little log cabin was transformed into a cozy home. Each day when Anna finished with the housework and laundry, she rode her horse to visit Gracie and Hattie Mae. On warm days, they sat on Hattie Mae's front porch and stitched gowns. On cold days like today, they did their mending and sewing inside. Some of the dresses went to the mercantile store to be sold, and the rest were hung in a huge closet that Amos built for Hattie Mae. Anna has been meeting for their stitching circle since she was fifteen, and now at the age of twenty, they continued what they'd started five years ago.

"How many gowns do you think we've stitched?" Hattie Mae asked, not looking up from her sewing.

"I counted them this morning." Gracie dropped her fabric to her lap and sat straight.

"Well, how many are there?" Anna asked.

"Ninety-six. Can you believe that?" Gracie answered excitedly.

"Does that include the twenty-four dresses I took to the mercantile?" Anna asked.

"Goodness, I forgot about those." Gracie's eyes grew wide. "One hundred twenty. I can't believe we stitched that many dresses."

"I can." Anna held up a callused finger. The three of them burst into laughter.

"What do you suppose we do with all these gowns?" Hattie Mae finished the dress she was working on and held it up. It was pale blue with white lace trim.

"Now that you mention it—" Anna laid her sewing aside and stood. "I saw an announcement posted in the mercantile yesterday. The House of Burgesses are giving a ball at the Capitol for the entertainment of his Excellency Lord Botetourt.

"What's that have to do with our gowns?" Gracie wondered.

"I say we have a meeting with all the ladies. Those who are interested in showing up at the ball may do so in one of our very own homespun gowns." Anna smiled proudly.

"Is that in protest against the taxes?" Hattie Mae knew the answer before asking the question.

"We'll show them we can make gowns just as lovely with our very own Virginia cloth." The more she thought about it, the more excited Anna became.

They got the word out, and by the end of November, women from several counties attended the meeting. Before they knew it, they had ninety-eight women willing to show up at the ball in a homespun gown provided by Hattie Mae, Anna, and Gracie.

"All right, ladies, we shall meet here at my house the morning of the ball," Gracie announced.

"That will give each of us plenty of time to get dressed and leave in order to make it to the ball on time," Anna added.

The ladies of the town were abuzz with excitement as the ball approached. It was the event of the year, and every woman wanted to make a lasting impression. Sewing gowns was a true art form, and Hattie Mae, Anna, and Gracie took great pride in creating their own unique designs. With delicate fabrics and intricate details, the ladies poured their hearts and souls into their creations. Each stitch was carefully placed, each bead meticulously chosen. The gowns were works of art, and the three ladies were the artists. As the night of the ball arrived, the women in their dresses, along with their husbands or their betrothed, headed for the Capitol, which was illuminated for the occasion. As they approached the Capitol lawn, they twirled in their gowns, each one more beautiful than the last.

The streets were filled with whispers of admiration and envy. A reporter for the *Virginia Gazette* was there to report on the night's events. Anna heard whispers from a couple of women stating the ladies claimed their gowns were a gift and no one knew who'd made those lovely dresses or where all the fabric came from.

As they danced the night away, Anna and Gracie smiled at each other, for they knew the truth. They could hardly wait to tell Hattie Mae all about it, for this was truly a night to remember.

The following week, Johnny came home from town and laid a copy of the Virginia Gazette on the table in front of Anna.

"Thought you might be interested in this week's edition." He winked.

Anna eyed him suspiciously as she picked it up. Her eyes widened and she let out an excited squeal. "Have you read it?" she held up the paper and began to read aloud.

DECEMBER 14, 1769, THE VIRGINIA GAZETTE

On Wednesday evening the Honorable Speaker and Gentlemen of the House of Burgesses gave a ball at the Capitol for the entertainment of his Excellency Lord Botetourt; and it is with the greatest pleasure we inform our readers that the same patriotic spirit which gave rise to the association of the gentlemen on a late event was most agreeably manifested in the dress of the ladies on this occasion, who, to the number of near one hundred, appeared in homespun gowns; a lively and striking instance of their acquiescence and concurrence in whatever may be the true and essential interest of their country. It was to be wished that all assemblies of American ladies would exhibit a like example of public virtue and private economy, so amiably united.

"It appears the women's efforts to protest the taxes on goods imported from England worked." Johnny kissed her on top of the head.

"It seems we accomplished what we set out to prove by not wearing clothing that was either imported or made of imported material." She stood and hugged Johnny.

"I need to go back to town for a few supplies. Come with me." He placed the dipper in the bucket of cold water and took a huge refreshing drink.

"Do you mind dropping me off at Gracie's?" She rolled the paper up and slipped on her shoes and coat before stepping out into the cold morning air.

The buckboard rolled to a stop in front of Nathaniel and Gracie's house. Anna kissed Johnny before jumping down with a thud onto the frozen ground. "See you in an hour." She waved him off.

Gracie was thrilled to see Anna and even more so when she read the paper. "We should show this to Hattie Mae."

"I agree. Let's go now." Anna opened the door only to quickly shut it when a blast of cold air blew in. "I do believe it's getting colder out." She shivered.

"Well, then, we must hurry." Gracie threw her cloak around her shoulders and tied the hood underneath her chin. "Nathaniel and Joshua will be home soon and will be famished, I'm sure."

They ran the short distance to Hattie Mae's house and knocked on the door. Amos opened it with his usual friendly smile. "Come in out of the cold, ladies." He stepped back to allow them entrance.

"Thank you kindly, sir." Anna replied and bowed playfully.

"We can't stay long." Gracie glanced around the room for Hattie Mae. "We have some exciting news."

"Lord a-mercy girl, you're not pregnant, are you?" Hattie Mae placed a hand on Anna's stomach.

"Oh, goodness, no," Anna replied. "At least not yet." She laughed and held up the newspaper and began to read. When she finished reading, she looked to see Hattie Mae's reaction and was shocked when Hattie Mae danced a jig across the living room floor. Everyone laughed and joined in until they were all out of breath.

"Shew, I don't know about anyone else, but I needs to sit down." Amos took a seat at the kitchen table.

"Well, folks, I must say that was fun, but we must take our leave now." Gracie placed a hand on her chest trying to catch her breath.

"Yes, it was quite unexpected and enjoyable." Anna handed the paper to Hattie Mae. "This is for you, and I shall purchase another." She turned to leave.

"Thank you, ladies. Come visit again soon." Amos held the door.

"Good day." Anna stepped out the door in time to see Johnny coming up the road. He stopped next to Anna, jumped down, and helped her take a seat. She waved goodbye to Gracie as they rode off.

"I figured you might want to visit with your Pa and Ma for a bit before the weather turns," hc shouted over the noise of the horses' hooves and the buckboard's wheels rolling over the frozen ground.

"I'd like that very much," she shouted back.

Their visit with Pa and Ma went well. They made plans to return the next week for Christmas. The whole family would be there. Anna could hardly wait to spend the holiday with family and friends. She had a feeling this was going to be the best Christmas ever.

CHAPTER THIRTY-ONE

A CHRISTMAS TO REMEMBER
December 1769

The following week everyone gathered at Pa and Ma's on Christmas Eve. It was a wonderful time of year when family and friends came together for a delicious meal, sang Carols, roasted chestnuts over the fire in the hearth, and enjoyed each other's company. This year was different. After dinner, they opened the handmade gifts, each one special in its own way. Pa sat in the rocking chair next to the hearth and handed out gifts. The children sat on the floor at his feet giggling excitedly.

"Let's see, what do we have here?" Pa held up a gift wrapped in cloth. He smiled at Joshua and Paddy as he handed each a gift. Their eyes grew wide when they opened it.

"What is it?" Joshua held it up to show his father. Nathaniel gently took it from his hand.

"Well, son, this is a whirligig." Nathaniel saw the blank expression in his sons' eyes and began to explain. "A whirligig is a simple whirring toy made of a circular disc of bone, a spare button, or clay. A string is threaded through the hole in the center. He pulled the string tight then released it causing the whirligig to spin, making a buzzing or a whirring sound.

The whole room grew silent as all eyes were on the children who stared in awe at the whirligig. Nathaniel handed it back to Joshua, and he and Paddy sat down and played with their new toy.

Pa handed Patricia a doll made from corn husk. It wore a bonnet and a dress with an apron. Patricia squealed and hugged the doll to her while Virginia's heart swelled with pride as she watched both her children enjoying their Christmas gifts. The men each received a hand-stitched shirt and socks. The ladies were given a basket of assorted fruits and nuts. Adam gave Elizabeth an engagement ring, and Johnny made a new flail for Pa.

"Thank you, Johnny." Pa gave the flail the once over. "I needed a new threshing tool, and this one is sure going to come in handy." He shook Johnny's hand.

Anna stood next to Johnny. He lovingly placed a hand around her waist. "May I have everyone's attention please?" Anna asked and clapped her hands. The room grew silent once again. "As you know this year will soon be over, and the year of our Lord Seventeen Seventy is just around the corner."

"For lands sakes, Anna, get on with it," Adam shouted playfully.

Anna grabbed the tea towel she had draped over her shoulder and threw it at him. "Oh, all right. There's going to be a new addition to our family come summer," she blurted out.

"You're with child?" Virginia bounced happily in place.

"No, she's getting a goat," Adam teased as he threw his arm around Elizabeth. She playfully elbowed him in the gut.

"Adam, should I tell Elizabeth some of your most embarrassing moments growing up?" Anna raised her eyebrow and glared at her brother.

"Oh, do tell." Elizabeth stepped forward.

"Come on, little sis. Ya know I was jesting, and I love ya." Adam hid behind Elizabeth with his hands clasped in a pleading gesture, only to drop them at his sides when Elizabeth turned to look at him. Everyone burst into laughter.

"To answer your question, Ginny, I am with child." Anna placed a hand on her stomach. "I'm going to drive you mad with questions."

"I'd be more than happy to answer each and every one as best I can." Ginny grinned.

Ma and Pa hugged Anna and Johnny. "Did y'all hear that?" Pa shouted. "I'm going to be a grandpa . . . again."

Anna turned to see Hattie Mae with a huge grin. "Sorry, Hattie, I didn't mean to fib to you last week. I had to be sure before making the announcement."

"Don't you fret, child. I figured that if you didn't know already, you'd find out soon enough." Hattie Mae snickered.

"How'd you know?" Anna asked.

"Well, child, ya had a special glow about ya." Hattie Mae placed her hands on her hips and leaned forward. "When you've delivered as many babes as I have, ya just know."

James picked up the guitar and began strumming it. Sally sang in her angelic voice. Ma grabbed Anna by the hand and danced a little jig. Pa joined in, and before long, everyone was laughing and dancing.

Nathaniel noticed Isaiah standing next to the door watching. He whispered to Amos as he passed by, "Give me a few minutes and then come to the barn." He approached Isaiah and cleared his throat. "Isaiah, would you help me with something?" Nathaniel stepped out the door. Isaiah quietly followed. When they reached the barn, Nathaniel opened the huge barn door and waited for Isaiah to catch up. "Someone needs to learn to take care of their horse." Nathaniel nodded toward a beautiful Pinto standing in the middle of the barn.

"Yes, sir. Do you want me to find out who he belongs to and return him?" Isaiah approached the horse and gently stroked its back. He didn't see his Ma and Pa peeking around the barn door.

"I already know his owner." Nathaniel smiled at Amos and Hattie Mae.

"If he lives nearby, I'll take the horse to him tonight, sir." Isaiah continued petting the horse.

"I was hoping you'd say that." Nathaniel stepped next to him. "Because the horse belongs to you."

Isaiah swallowed hard. "Did you say he belongs to me, sir?"

"That I did." Nathaniel ran a hand down the horse's nose.

"It's our Christmas gift to you."

Gracie stepped around Amos and Hattie Mae, who both watched the scene unfold with tear-filled eyes. Neither could speak for the lump forming in their throats.

"Thank you, both. I'll take good care of him, I promise." Isaiah couldn't stop grinning. He noticed his ma and pa standing in the doorway and motioned to them. "Come see my horse."

Amos and Hattie Mae were speechless. They were overjoyed to see their son happy. Hattie Mae clasped her hands, looked toward heaven, and whispered, "Thank you." She knew this was going to be a Christmas to remember.

CHAPTER THIRTY-TWO

TOWN MEETING
March 1770

Winter soon turned into spring, bringing with it the spring thaw and news of the Boston Massacre. Some believed that was the start of the American Revolution. Anna was huge with child and although she was thrilled, she couldn't help feeling nervous about the future and the possibility of war breaking out.

Nathaniel left to attend a town meeting where they discussed taxes and impending war. He hadn't mentioned it to Gracie. He didn't want her to worry unnecessarily. He told her he was going to pick up the supplies she'd asked for.

Isaiah overheard Nathaniel mention it to Daniel. Isaiah, twelve, was curious about the topic, so he hid in the back of Nathaniel's buckboard while Amos and Hattie Mae were busy entertaining Gracie and her son, Joshua. No one noticed Isaiah sneak out.

The meeting, held at the church, was already underway. Nathaniel strolled in and took a seat in the back row. Isaiah followed close behind a man and then darted behind the bench Nathaniel sat on. It was clear that everyone there was willing to go into battle against British troops. No one was happy about the taxing of paper and paper products, material, and tea, just to name a few.

Sam, who sat three rows in front of Nathaniel, leapt and spoke loudly. "I volunteer to go to battle and fight for my country." He turned and looked around the packed church. "Nathaniel, my boy, I know you'll fight alongside me," he shouted.

Before Nathaniel had a chance to reply Isaiah stepped forward and yelled. "I volunteer to take Nathaniel's place." He stared straight ahead.

Nathaniel grabbed him by the arm and pulled him down on the bench next to him. "What are you doing here?" he demanded.

"I,I wanted—" Isaiah stuttered.

"The boy stays here." Nathaniel stood and announced.

"A slave can take the place of his owner, and the boy volunteered," one man shouted from across the room. "What's so special about the boy?"

"Nothing. I need him to work on my farm," Nathaniel lied. A hush fell over the crowd. "Sending the boy in my place is the coward's way out." Nathaniel shook his head. "I refuse to allow it."

"Should there be war, and I'm certain there will be, the boy will fight." Mayor Morris slammed his fist down on the pulpit.

"I'm not listening to this dung. If he goes, I'm going with him." Nathaniel shoved Isaiah out of the church. Once outside he took him by the shoulders and reprimanded him. "Do you realize what you've done?"

"I'm a man now," Isaiah said defiantly. "Mrs. Gracie and Joshua need you." He softened his tone.

"You're a twelve -year-old boy." Nathaniel loomed over him

like a massive giant. "You're all your pa and ma have in this world."

"I know, and you're all Mrs. Gracie and Joshua have." Isaiah dropped his head. "You're family."

Nathaniel placed a hand on Isaiah's shoulder. "You're like a son to me and I'll die before I'll allow anything to happen to any one of you." He rubbed Isaiah's head. "Let's get you home."

Amos and Hattie Mae were extremely unhappy to hear the news. "No, Isaiah! Why would you do such a thing?" Hattie Mae fell to her knees at Isaiah's feet.

"It's all right, Ma." He took his mother by the hand and helped her. "With God watching over me and Nathaniel by my side, I'll be fine." He dried her tears with his shirt sleeve. "I'll fight alongside you both."

Amos offered his services to protect his son.

Nathaniel shook his head. "I need you to stay here and watch over the womenfolk and my son." He placed a hand on Amos's shoulder. "I vow to keep your son safe if you vow to protect my family."

Amos knew he meant it. He dropped his head and nodded. "I promise. I'll die before I let anything happen to them." He trusted Nathaniel, but prayed war would never come.

Over the next few months, Johnny and Anna kept busy tending to their garden and preparing for the baby's arrival. It was grueling, hard work, but it kept their minds off things and rumors of war. Anna worked tirelessly on the house and chores. She stitched baby quilts, clothes, and napkins made from fabric with a regular pattern of stitches to increase absorbency. Wool or woolen twill pilchers were triangular covers worn over cloth napkins to provide extra moisture protection for the baby's bottom. She was thrilled when Ginny and Gracie brought her baby items they saved after their children outgrew them.

Early one morning in July, Johnny eased out of bed being careful not to wake Anna. He made his way into town to his father's shop. He needed to add a few final touches on a hand carved cradle. He planned on surprising Anna with it.

"There, it's finished." He stepped back to admire his work.

"It's perfect, son." Johnny's father Jacob examined his handiwork. "Your work has exceeded my expectations."

"Thank you, Pa. I can't wait to see the look on Anna's face when she sees it." Johnny lifted the cradle and carried it to his buckboard. He stopped and turned to his father. "Would you like to come with me?"

"I'd love to be there when she first lays eyes on it." Jacob Carlin climbed aboard and took a seat. Johnny could see the excitement in his father's eyes.

A few minutes later they rolled to a stop in front of the barn. Johnny unhitched his horse Ebony and led her to the field behind the barn. There he turned her loose and let her roam free. She loved it and Johnny loved watching her run and play, although he didn't have time for that now. Today he was anxious to get the cradle in the house before Anna woke up. He and his father placed the crib in the parlor while deliberately making noise so Anna would get up to find out what all the commotion was about.

She awoke and swung her legs over the side of the bed and yelled, "Johnny, is everything all right?" She struggled to stand. Her stomach was huge with child as she was due any day. She managed to hobble to the bedroom door, then she held onto the door frame and peeked around it but saw nothing. She made her way into the parlor. Johnny and his father were standing in front of the cradle to hide it. "Hello, Jacob. It's nice to see you." Anna smiled at her father-in-law.

"Hello, Anna girl. How's my favorite daughter-in-law and grandchild?"

"I'm your only daughter-in-law and we're both doing fine." Anna smiled and placed a hand on her back. "What brings you out so early?"

"He wanted to be here when I gave you this." Johnny stepped aside so Anna could see the cradle.

"Oh, my goodness!" She placed a hand to her stomach. "Johnny, it's gorgeous." She strolled over for a better look. "I love it." She hugged them both. "It's just in time; the baby is due in a week."

"I know, love. That's the reason I've been leaving earlier than usual." He turned to his father. "Sorry, Pa. I'll finish the cabinet this week."

"You just take care of this beautiful wife of yours." Jacob placed a hand on Johnny's shoulder. "The cabinet can wait a few days longer."

Anna removed a small quilt draped over the rocking chair and placed it in the cradle. "Excuse me, but nature calls." She hurried to the back door.

"You waddle more than the duck," Johnny teased.

"You're lucky your pa is here, or I'd throw something at you." She waddled out the door.

"I'm safe, because you can't bend over far enough to pick up a horse biscuit." Johnny laughed.

His pa shook his head. "Horse biscuit, you say? Why on earth would she pick that up?"

While Johnny explained to his father Anna's habit of throwing horse biscuits, Anna grabbed a pail of leftover breadcrumbs hanging by the back door and fed it to the chickens.

"I didn't forget you, Myrtle." She tossed some crumbs on the ground for the duck. "Sorry, but that's all there is until after breakfast," she said soothingly. She took a step toward the outhouse when she felt a twinge of pain. "Oh, no, little one." She rubbed her stomach. "I was hoping you'd be born on your father's birthday next week." She turned and hurried to feed the horses. When she didn't feel any more pain, she chalked it up to her imagination. Twenty minutes later, another pain hit. She knew then it must be time. She hurried across the yard and up the steps and through the back door. She could hear Johnny talking about the cradle he'd made. He was proud of himself and the hard work he'd put into it. She listened to Johnny and his father talking while she debated telling him when another pain hit, this one stronger than the others.

"You should be proud, son; you worked hard on it," Jacob said.

"Yes, I know, I worked my finger to the bone to make sure it was ready in time." Johnny stood triumphantly next to the cradle. "I think—"

Another pain hit and Anna panicked. "Johnny" She burst through the door, a wild look in her eyes. "It's time!" she exclaimed, clutching her belly.

"What! You mean the baby is coming now?" Johnny stepped toward Anna and placed his hand on her stomach. Panic washed over him like a bucket of cold water; he began pacing the floor, his mind racing faster than Anna's contractions. "Wait, what do we do? Should I get your mother? Should I get Hattie Mae? I can't leave you alone." He babbled as he picked up the cradle and raced to the bedroom with it.

Anna, half-laughing and half-grimacing, couldn't help but shake her head at the sight of him—her strong, tough husband transformed into a whirlwind of panic-stricken chaos.

"Jacob, would you mind fetching Hattie Mae?" Anna watched as Johnny raced from the bedroom, fear written all over his face. "When he calms down, I'll have him fetch Ma."

"It's a good thing you're not having twins." Jacob chuckled, but then a serious look crossed his face. "You're not, are you?

"No, there's only one." Another pain hit. Anna grimaced as she walked him out the front door.

Twenty minutes later, Hattie Mae, Amos, and Isaiah pulled in front of the house. Johnny was calm and sitting on the front steps.

"Kicked ya out of the room, did she?" Amos chuckled.

"She kicked me out of the house." Johnny put his hands on his hips. "She asked me to bring her some horse dung."

"Horse dung. What for?" Amos knitted his brow

"So, she could fling it at my head." Johnny began to unhitch the horse. Amos covered his mouth, trying not to laugh.

Hattie Mae, on the other hand, squeezed her lips tight trying her best not to laugh, but it was no use. Her whole body shook as she began to laugh. "Lord a-mercy, I best be getting in there." She grabbed her bag and headed into the house. She tapped on the door of Anna's room and poked her head in. "Mrs. Anna is it safe to come in?" she teased.

"Hattie Mae, am I glad to see you. Please come in." Anna rubbed her belly as the pains continued.

"All right, child, how long since the first pain hit?" Hattie Mae sat on the bed next to her and placed her bag on her lap.

"Early this morning. I was feeding the chickens when the first pain struck—the horses with the second."

"Hmmm. Sounds like they were coming every twenty minutes. Interesting." Hattie Mae opened her bag.

"That's right. About twenty minutes apart." Anna grabbed her stomach as another contraction hit. "What's interesting about it?" she asked.

"Out of all the babies I've delivered, you're the second one who seems to be progressing quickly."

"Who was the other person?" Anna wondered.

"Me. Isaiah wasted no time coming into this ol' world. And he's been in a rush ever since." She giggled.

Hattie Mae had a way of making everyone feel safe and calm during times such as this, and that's what Anna loved most about her. Anna's eyes grew wide upon realizing what Hattie Mae had said. "Wait. Are you saying that I'm going to give birth today?" Anna winced when another contraction hit, this one stronger than the others. "I thought it was going to take hours —or days.

"No, ma'am. It seems your little one is as anxious to meet you as you are him." She closed her bag and set it on the floor. "I won't be needing that today."

"Him? So, you think it's a boy?" Anna clenched her teeth as a wave of pain hit.

"Did I say 'him'?" Hattie Mae placed a hand to her cheek. "It's a figure of speech, child. Could be a girl." She strolled around the bed and peered out the window. "Your ma and pa's here." She waved to them. "Virginia and the children are with them."

Ma jumped down from the carriage and ran up the steps and into the house. Virginia sent little Patrick and Patricia with Isaiah to play a game of hoops. Hattie Mae met her at the door.

"How is she doing?" Ma asked.

"You made it just in time. You will meet your newest

grandchild in, oh, I'd say, three hours, maybe less."

"How long has she been in labor?" Virginia stepped through the door.

"According to my calculations, about two hours." Hattie Mae leaned toward them and whispered, "She's wasting no time." The three of them rushed into Anna's room when she let out a loud scream.

Hattie Mae dipped a cloth into a pan of cold water that Johnny had prepared and set it on the stand next to the bed. "Here ya go, Mary Lou." She handed it to Ma. "I'll let you do the honors."

Ma took the wet cloth and dabbed Anna's forehead with it. The contractions were coming one after the other.

Virginia sat on the bed next to her. She chose not to speak, knowing how irritating noise could be when you're in pain. After an hour, she stood and began pacing the floor.

Anna reached for her hand and Virginia gently took it. "Please get Johnny. I need him here," Anna begged.

Virginia nodded and ran to find Johnny. She found him pacing in the barn. He stopped upon seeing Virginia. "Is she all right? Is the baby here?"

"No, not yet. She's asking for you."

Johnny broke into a run. Virginia checked on the children, who were playing in the barn while the men talked. "It won't be long now, Pa," she shouted over her shoulder as she ran back to the house.

Johnny entered the room just as Anna screamed out in pain. Tears filled his eyes as he took her hand. "I'm so sorry, Anna. I'll never put you through this ever again."

Anna shook her head. "Don't say such things. You're about to meet our baby soon." She grabbed her stomach, gritted her teeth, and writhed in pain.

"How soon? She's only been in labor for four hours." Johnny looked from Anna to Hattie Mae. "I thought labor took longer, days, even." He stood.

"Not this time. That baby is already coming, and I mean now." Hattie Mae glanced up from the foot of the bed.

Johnny panicked, grabbed a clean cloth, dipped it in the pan of clean water and placed it on Hattie Mae's forehead. "Just breathe, woman, just breathe."

Hattie Mae drew her eyes down at him, laughed, and said. "Son, I think you should go tell the menfolk the baby is coming."

Johnny dropped the cloth and then kissed Anna on the cheek. "I'll be in the barn," he said and hurried out the door.

Just as he reached the barn, he heard Anna let out a loud scream, and then the sound of the baby crying. "It's here! The baby is here!" he shouted and ran back to the house to meet his first-born child. He ran to the window and shouted, "What is it? A boy or a girl?"

Anna grinned and shouted back, "It's a boy. You have a son." She burst into tears when Johnny rushed into the room and embraced her.

Ma took the baby and bathed him before handing him to Johnny.

Virginia hugged her sister before leaving the room and noticed James, Sally, Adam, and Elizabeth were sitting in the parlor. "How long have you been here?" she asked.

"We just arrived as you and Johnny ran into the house," James replied.

"Can we go in?" Adam stood with his hat in his hand.

Pa, Amos, and Jacob walked through the front door as Johnny

carried his son out for all to see. "Everyone, I have a son. Meet Thomas Alan Carlin."

He handed the baby to his father, who nervously held him for a brief second before handing him to Daniel. "Here ya go, Grandpa. I'm afraid of breaking him." Daniel handed him back to Johnny.

Johnny took the baby to Anna so she could feed him before anyone went in to visit them. Gracie, Nathanial, and Joshua walked through the door and were shocked that Anna had already given birth.

"Anna, I'm so sorry I wasn't here for the birth." Gracie sat on the bed next to her and apologized profusely. I thought it would take longer than—how long was it?"

"Four and a half hours," Johnny announced as Anna placed the baby in Gracie's arms.

"Four hours! That hardly seems fair." She snickered and gazed down at the baby. "He's so handsome."

"Wow, my baby sister had a baby," Adam said from the bedroom doorway. "May I hold him?" He reached for the baby. Gracie stood, and Adam took her seat on the bed.

"Don't be teaching him any of your ornery tricks." Anna giggled.

"Me? You're the one who was always sneaky and spiteful." He laughed. "If he is rotten, he gets it from you." James chuckled as he stepped in to meet his newest nephew.

Elizabeth and Sally walked to the doorway and waited for the room to clear before going in to speak with Anna and meet the baby.

After everyone left, Anna and Thomas settled down for some much-needed rest. Johnny made dinner and brought it to her in bed. As he lovingly stared at his little family, he thought, *Life doesn't get any better than this.*

CHAPTER THIRTY-THREE

GRANDMA COMES FOR A VISIT

The year was seventeen seventy-one. A year had passed since Thomas' birth. The whole family gathered to celebrate his first birthday. Anna didn't think her life could be more complete than it was right now. She looked forward to Christmas, it would be the first Christmas that Thomas would get to open his gifts. Although Christmas was more of a celebration of family and friends coming together and celebrating the birth of Christ, it was everyone's favorite time of the year.

Anna loved it when they gathered around the fireplace after dinner and sang songs and sometimes exchanged gifts. This year, she wanted to make it the best one yet. She'd received a letter from her grandmother in Pennsylvania announcing she was coming for a visit. Anna invited her to stay with them. She gladly accepted the invitation and would be arriving in September. She chose to travel when the weather wasn't too hot or too cold. The plan was for her grandmother to spend the winter with Pa and Ma before joining Anna for the remainder of her visit.

Anna spent the next two months preparing for her grandmother's arrival.

"Anna, if you keep scrubbing the house, there isn't going to be anything left." Johnny placed his arms around her waist. "What do you say we take a trip to the river?"

Anna glanced around the house looking for something that needed cleaning. "Well, I suppose it wouldn't hurt to take a break." She kissed him on the lips. "Let's go!" she said excitedly.

Johnny saddled the horses while Anna grabbed a bar of soap and kept Thomas busy. They mounted their horses and off they went. Johnny and Anna hadn't been back to that spot since the day he proposed. He helped Anna down the riverbank while she held Thomas tightly in her arms. Johnny dove in and swam to the center of the river and back while Anna gently eased into the cool water with Thomas. He squealed with delight and smacked his hands on top of the water, splashing Anna in the face. Johnny joined in on the fun of splashing Anna while Thomas tilted his head back and giggled.

Anna held Thomas up and blew raspberries on his tummy. He squealed and kicked his feet. She remembered the soap she shoved into her skirt pocket. She pulled it out and lathered Thomas up with it before rinsing him off. Johnny held the baby while Anna lathered herself up before diving under the water and resurfacing in front of Johnny. Thomas giggled and lunged for her. She caught him before his head went under water.

"All right, little boy, it's time we get you home." She handed the soap to Johnny, who quickly lathered up with it then ducked under the water before getting out.

"That was refreshing. We should do it again tomorrow." He took Thomas and waited for Anna to reach the top of the riverbank before handing him back to her.

"Yeah, and maybe we can stay longer." She mounted her horse. Johnny set Thomas on the horse in front of her. She rode slowly, waiting for Johnny to catch up.

August seemed to fly by, and before they knew it, it was September, and Anna found herself waiting for her grandmother's arrival. Her pa went to town to pick her up. After all, she was his mother, so it was only fitting that he picked her up and spent time with her.

Anna went to Pa's to visit as often as possible. Winter made it a little more difficult to visit, but winter soon turned into spring. Anna had just finished planting her garden when Pa and Ma pulled up with her grandmother.

"Grandma! I was just thinking about coming to visit." Anna washed her hands in a basin of water she left sitting next to the porch.

"Nonsense, girl. I spent six months with your Pa and Ma." She handed Anna her bag. "I promised to stay with you, and I intend to keep that promise." She allowed Pa to help her down from the buckboard. He then retrieved her bags and placed them in the house.

"Mother, are you sure I can't talk you into coming back home with us?" Pa gave her a hug.

"Daniel, I love you and Mary Lou very much. I enjoyed my time with you."

"We enjoyed having you, Eleanor." Ma placed an arm around her shoulder and walked with her into the house.

"This trip will be remembered." Grandma took Thomas in her arms and gave him a hug. "It was pleasant to spend time with James, Adam, and their lovely ladies after getting snowed in with Virginia, Patrick, and their kids. I missed Anna and this little feller the most." She put Thomas down and gave him a head rub.

Anna's heart swelled with pride at hearing her

grandmother's words.

Pa grabbed Thomas and spun him in circles before hugging him tight. "I missed my big boy." He did a double take at Anna. "Are you putting on weight?" Pa asked.

Ma turned to Anna, her eyes growing wide. "Anna are you, uh, with child?" she whispered.

"Yes, four months. I'm due in October." She rubbed her belly.

"I'm so happy for you." Ma glanced at Pa. "Did you hear that, Daniel? You're going to be a grandpa again!"

"Wahoo!" Pa shouted. "The more the merrier."

"Wahoo!" Thomas giggled and walked around the house repeating the new word he'd learned.

"We must be going. I have a few things I need to pick up in town." Pa kissed his mother on the cheek before hugging Anna and Thomas.

"Tell Johnny we said congratulations, and we'll see you all tomorrow." Ma hugged each of them before leaving with Pa.

Grandma settled in nicely, and before long she and Anna had a routine worked out. They rose early and cooked breakfast together. Then, Anna worked in the garden while her grandmother kept Thomas busy. Later, Anna sat on the porch, reading aloud to her grandmother from the book she'd been writing since she was fourteen. However, the entries ended abruptly with the arrival of her grandmother's visit. Her grandma was her biggest supporter in her writing endeavor and encouraged her to finish her story.

"I feel blessed to be a part of your life story," her grandmother said.

The summer seemed to fly by. Anna made it as memorable for her grandma as possible, from picnics at the river to stitching a beautiful new dress for her grandmother's birthday. They made soap and smoked meat to store for winter. One weekend, they made homemade apple butter. The whole family pitched in and helped with peeling apples and stirring them with a huge wooden paddle Pa made. James played guitar and Grandma sang a song Anna hadn't heard before called "Springfield Mountain." The song told the story of a man named Johnny mowing a field of tall grass. A snake bites him on the heel and they carry him home to his Sally dear—only Grandma changed the girl's name to Anna. By the end of the song, Anna was in tears.

"I do believe that's the saddest song I've ever heard," Anna dried her eyes on her apron.

"I'm sorry," her grandmother said. "I didn't mean to make anyone cry."

"It's fine, Grandma. It's just part of being with child, I suppose." Anna sniffled.

"I have no excuse." Sally dried her eyes with a handkerchief

James played a happy song, while Sally sang with Grandma to lift everyone's spirits. By the end of the evening, everyone was smiling and ready to go home. Thomas had fallen asleep in Ma's arms.

Grandma announced, "I'm dog tired." She stood up and excused herself. She moved slowly toward the house, adding, "I'm going to bed. Goodnight, everyone." The next morning, she was back to her old self. Anna invited her to ride into town with her and Thomas.

"Thank you, but if you don't mind, I'd rather sit on the porch and enjoy this lovely weather. "She tilted her head back as a warm gentle breeze blew around her.

"We won't be long," Anna said, kissing her grandmother's cheek. "I want to see if the mercantile has any new material."

True to her word, they soon returned and met Johnny on the front porch. Thomas had fallen asleep, so Johnny carried him into the house and put him to bed before heading out to help Anna.

"Your grandma has the spirit of a wildcat," Johnny said as he lifted the supplies from the buckboard.

Anna tilted her head. "What makes you say that?"

"I was going to surprise her with breakfast," he explained. "But she chased me out of the kitchen, threatening to clobber me with a frying pan." He shook his head and chuckled.

Anna stared wide-eyed and speechless.

"Now I know where you get your ornery streak from," he teased, kissing her cheek.

Anna covered her mouth and giggled. "I suppose you'd better keep her away from horse biscuits then." They both erupted into laughter.

"She confessed that she loves being here with us and wants to help choose a name for the baby." He placed a hand on her stomach. "That's wonderful news." Anna smiled and turned on her heel when she heard someone calling her name.

"Anna, Anna! I need to have a word with you." Mrs. Worthington came racing up the road stirring up dust behind her. The carriage came to a stop and Mrs. Worthington nearly fell headfirst off the carriage seat.

"How may I help you, Mrs. Worthington?" Anna inquired.

"You bought material at Collins Mercantile this morning, did you not?"

"Yes, Mrs. Worthington, I did." Anna drew her eyes down and glanced at Johnny. "What about it?"

"Well, it's mine and I want it." Mrs. Worthington crossed her arms.

"Sorry, Mrs. Worthington, but I—"

"You should be sorry," Mrs. Worthington interrupted. "Go on, give it here." She held out her hand.

"Mrs. Worthington," Johnny said, "I'm sure there's more material like it at the mercantile that—"

"Stay out of it." She pointed at Johnny. "This is between me and Anna."

Anna's grandma was listening, and she'd had enough. She sprinted down the steps faster than Anna had ever seen her move. She pointed her finger at Mrs. Worthington and shouted, "How dare you come here acting all high and mighty!" Her face glowed red with anger.

"This has nothing to do with—"

"Hush your pea pickin' mouth." Grandma interrupted her for a change. "Now, from what I understand, Anna made a purchase today and now it belongs to her." Grandma crossed her arms over her chest and tapped her foot. "Who do you think you are, coming here and demanding that she give anything to you?"

"I, I, I hid that material until I could come up with the money to purchase it," Mrs. Worthington stammered. "The pattern and color were an accident, and now they can't figure out how they made it."

"Well, that's too bad." Grandma softened her tone. "I hope they figure it out for you."

"No need. I came for that material and I'm not leaving without it!" Mrs. Worthington shouted.

Grandma got into a fighting stance with her fist out in front of her. "Come down here, you old crow. I'll knock you into next week."

"You wouldn't dare!" Mrs. Worthington screeched.

"Try me." Grandma stepped forward and smacked one of the horses on the behind, scaring it and causing it to lurch forward. Mrs. Worthington fell back into her seat with her skirt flying up. Her bonnet fell over her face as the horses raced back down the road.

"I know where you get your temper from." Johnny placed a hand at the side of his mouth and whispered to Anna, who playfully backhanded him in the gut.

"Let's get you inside where it's a little cooler." Anna locked arms with her grandmother and helped her into the house.

The rest of the day was filled with laughter as Ma and Pa came to visit and were informed of the altercation between Grandma and Mrs. Worthington. As the day wound down, Grandma once again began to feel weak and tired. She went to bed earlier than usual and woke up feeling refreshed and wearing her new birthday dress.

"What day is it?" she asked.

"It's Sunday," Anna replied.

"Sunday, huh? Take me to church." She headed toward the front door.

"Uh, all right, but I haven't been to church in a month of Sundays." Anna wiped Thomas with a wet cloth after he finished his breakfast.

"Where's Johnny? He needs to come with us." Her grandma peered out the window and then went out the front door when she saw him coming from the barn.

Anna picked up Thomas. "Looks like we're going to church." She changed his clothes before getting herself ready.

A few minutes later, Johnny strolled in with Anna's grandma. He followed Anna to the bedroom and whispered, "So, I guess we're all going to church today."

"I suppose so. I've been meaning to get back in church anyway, but what made you decide to go?" Anna peeked out the bedroom door making sure her grandma wasn't listening.

"I saw the way she glared at Mrs. Worthington. I'm not taking any chances." He shook his head. "I'd rather take on a bear." He chortled.

Once they reached the church, Anna noticed that Mrs. Worthington's carriage was there. She cleared her throat and motioned at it when Johnny looked at her. He looked toward heaven and whispered, "Lord, get us through this day without incident."

They slowly strolled inside. Anna and Johnny took a seat next to Ma, Pa, Virginia, and the twins. Anna thought her grandmother was going to sit with them, but nope, not a chance. She marched herself up the middle aisle and plopped down in the front row seat next to none other than Mrs. Worthington.

"What's she doing?" Anna whispered to anyone who heard her.

"She'll be fine. We're in church," Pa answered and then whispered a prayer, "Lord, what did I ever do to you? Please keep your hand over my mother's and Mrs. Worthington's mouths for their own sakes."

Johnny snickered softly and whispered to Anna, "Who knew that church could be this entertaining?"

Anna covered her mouth and cleared her throat to stifle a laugh.

Mrs. Worthington was speaking with Mildred when she turned and saw who sat next to her. The smile immediately left her face.

"Uh-oh, here we go." Johnny sat a little straighter in his seat while Anna chewed her bottom lip.

"Well, now, Eleanor, did you come to ask me for forgiveness?" Mrs. Worthington smirked.

"Forgiveness, from you? Nope." Grandma's eyes stayed focused on the minister.

"You owe me an apology, ya know," Mrs. Worthington whispered with a smug look on her face.

Finally, the service was almost over when the minister asked if anyone wanted to come to the altar. The whole church grew quiet. Grandma stood.

Johnny grinned and scooted to the edge of his seat. Anna moved to the edge next to him. They quietly waited.

Grandma made her way to the altar and turned to face the congregation. "Hello, everyone. My name is Eleanor McCullough. Some of you may know my son Daniel and his family." She glanced at Mrs. Worthington, who sat tight-lipped, bobbing her head from side to side. Grandma tried ignoring her. "The reason I'm here today is because I need salvation and I will ask God for forgiveness, but before I do, I want to get a few things off my chest. I want to apologize to my son and my grandchildren for living so far away."

"With her attitude, they're probably grateful," Mrs. Worthington said in a low tone to Mildred, but not low enough that Grandma couldn't hear it.

"All right, I've had enough. I need salvation like everyone else, and some need to get off their high horse and stop pretending to be godly." She kept her eyes straight ahead. "My granddaughter Anna purchased material to make me a nice dress. It is to be my burial dress when I die, which won't be much longer now."

"What's she doing?" Ma asked Pa

"I have no idea, but I believe she's teaching Mrs. Worthington a lesson on kindness." Pa looked at Anna and shrugged.

"One of the members of your congregation came to her home yesterday and accused her of stealing the material and demanded that she give it to her. Mind you, this woman hadn't paid for it, but she stated that she'd hid it to purchase at a later date. Now, I ask you, who do you say was in the right?"

"Anna was in the right." Mrs. Collins stood. "I had been searching for that material and couldn't find it. That is until Anna came in with Thomas. He was to pick the color for your new dress."

"I'll bet he found it and chose that one." Grandma smiled.

"That he did!" Mr. Collins shouted. "Who is the culprit that is hiding things in my store?" he asked.

Mrs. Worthington's smug smile disappeared, and she scooted lower in her seat. Grandma knew she could ruin her, but instead she answered, "Mr. Collins, I'd rather not let the cat out of the bag, especially not in church." Grandma smiled at Anna. "I just wanted to get my point across, and I believe I have. Now if you don't mind, Pastor, I need salvation. I don't have much time left on this old Earth and I'd like to make things right with God."

Mrs. Worthington's jaw dropped. She, like everyone else, thought Grandma was jesting. Anna was the first to stand, tears streaming down her face as she made her way to her grandmother.

"Grandma, please say it isn't true," she begged.

"I'm sorry, child, but it is true. That's why I'm here in Virginia with my family." She looked up at her son Daniel as he scooped his mother in his arms and cried like a baby.

"You should have told me, Ma," he cried in her ear.

"I'm telling you now, son, and I would like it if you were to get saved along with me." She wiped the tears from her eyes. "Don't do it for me. You must do it for yourself, and you have to want it, to mean it, son."

Pa nodded. "I've thought about it a lot since the bear attack and yes, I want and need it."

There wasn't a dry eye in church that day. Even the preacher cried. Fourteen people received salvation including Ma, Virginia, Anna, and Johnny. Everyone left with peace and an overwhelming feeling of love in their hearts.

Grandma passed away two weeks later. The whole town showed up for her burial. One week later, Anna gave birth to a beautiful baby girl. Instead of being happy, all she felt was sadness. She cried every time she looked at her baby, wishing her grandma could have held on long enough to meet her. Ma stayed for two days after the baby's birth, praying that Anna would snap out of it. Not even Johnny could get through to her.

"I don't know what to do." Johnny hugged his baby girl. "Here, it's time for the baby to be fed." He handed Ma the baby. "Maybe you can get through to her." He picked up Thomas and held him tight.

Ma carried the baby to Anna and gently placed her in her arms. "She needs fed, and she needs a name. It's been two days."

"Grandma told me to wait, and a name would come to me. It hasn't." She held her baby and sobbed. "I need to know grandma is all right."

Ma sat on the bed and ran the back of her finger down the baby's cheek. "Pray about it. Ask God to allow her to let you know somehow."

"Do you believe He will?" Anna wiped the tears from her eyes.

"I'm sure of it. You just have to recognize it when it comes."

Ma leaned forward and kissed them both on the cheek before leaving the room.

That night before drifting off to sleep, Anna prayed, asking God to allow her grandmother to give her a sign that she's all right.

Ma said a silent prayer herself, as did Johnny.

The next morning the sun shone brightly in the October sky. Something felt different to Anna. She couldn't figure out what it was. Johnny had gotten up early to care for the animals and Ma brought the baby in and placed her in Anna's arms. Johnny stood at the bedroom door, silently praying.

As Ma turned to leave Anna averted her gaze out the window and gasped. She sat straight up in bed and hugged the baby to her. "Ma! Johnny!" she shouted. "He did it! He answered my prayers."

Ma and Johnny looked at one another before rushing to Anna's bedside to find out what she was talking about. "Look out the window. It's the rose Grandma planted. She said it wasn't supposed to bloom until next year."

Ma and Johnny peered out the window at a single red rose blooming on the hillside next to Anna and Johnny's bedroom window.

"Well, I'll be, a single red rose blooming in Autumn." Ma stared at it in disbelief.

"That's it! I have a name," Anna said excitedly. "I want you both to say hello to Autumn Rose." Tears streamed down Anna's face.

Johnny sat on the bed next to her while Ma went to check on Thomas, who was still sleeping soundly in his bed. She lifted her eyes toward heaven and said a loud, "Thank you, God, and thank you, Eleanor, for coming into our lives when we needed you most."

CHAPTER THIRTY- FOUR

1775 - WAR HAS BEGUN

In the eerie stillness of a moonlit night, Johnny slept peacefully next to Anna. The children slept soundly in their own beds. The only sound was the crackling of the fire slowly burning in the fireplace. As the embers died down, the silence was shattered by a thunderous knock at the door, its urgency sending shivers down Johnny's spine. As he stumbled to the entrance, his heart pounded with trepidation.

A messenger stood before him, his face grim and his voice heavy with news. “War has come, Johnny. The British are at our shores."

Anna gasped upon hearing the conversation, her knees growing weak, making it hard to stand. She sat back down on the edge of the bed before mustering the courage to stand when she heard the children stirring.

"Papa, who's here?" Three-year-old Autumn called to him as she climbed out of bed.

"Come, children." Anna knelt in front of them. Trying to put on a brave face, she hugged her children to her.

Time seemed to slow to a crawl as Johnny absorbed the gravity of the situation. The American Revolution had begun, and he was called to fight. With a heavy heart, he turned to his wife, Anna, and their young children.

"Forgive me, my love," he whispered, his voice thick with emotion. "But I must go. My duty to our country calls."

Tears streamed down Anna's face as she embraced her husband tightly. "I'll miss you, Johnny. Promise you'll come back to me, to us." She looked at the children, their little faces registering confusion.

"I promise, my love." He held her tightly, burying his face in her neck, breathing in the scent of jasmine in her hair and the warmth of her embrace.

Anna pulled away, rushed to the kitchen and retrieved her bible from the table. "Here, take this with you." She placed it in his haversack. "May God protect you."

Johnny kissed his children, their small hands clutching his own. "Be brave, my little ones. I'll return to you as soon as I can."

With a final, lingering glance at his family, Johnny stepped into the darkness. The moonlight illuminated his path as he marched towards the nearby town square where the militia was gathering.

As he joined Nathaniel and Isaiah, a surge of determination filled him. He had never imagined himself a soldier, but now he was ready to fight for the freedom of his people and his family. With a musket in hand, he marched off into the night, his heart filled with both fear and anticipation.

The battle was fierce and bloody. Johnny witnessed horrors he had never imagined, but he fought valiantly alongside his fellow soldiers. Days turned into nights as the conflict raged on, and Johnny's resolve only strengthened.

The dense woods of Virginia were shrouded in the heavy darkness of night with only the slivers of moonlight piercing through the thick canopy of trees. The Revolutionary War had dragged on, and the once vibrant wilderness now echoed with the distant sounds of skirmishes, the cries of the wounded, and the ominous silence of those who had already fallen.

Tonight, the moon shined unnaturally bright, casting an eerie glow across the woods. A disturbing calm filled the air, making everything feel strange and unsettling. Johnny, Nathanial, and Isaiah sat beneath a huge sycamore tree, listening to the silence that had fallen after the fighting ceased. Seeking to bring some sense of normalcy to the situation. Nathanial leaned toward Isaiah, his voice a low murmur. “Isaiah, tell us about your girl. What’s her name?”

A smile, the first in months, touched Isaiah’s lips. “Eliza, my beautiful Eliza.” He picked up a twig and began sketching in the dirt.

“I didn’t know you had a girl.” Johnny playfully nudged him. “How long has this been going on?”

“We've been seeing each other in secret for nigh on a year.” Isaiah smiled, a hopeful glint in his eyes.

“A year, eh? Do your parents know?” Johnny inquired, a hint of concern in his voice.

“They do,” Isaiah confirmed, “And when this war's done, I'm buying her freedom and we're getting married.”

“How old is she?” Nathanial inquired.

“Eighteen. Same as me.” Isaiah tossed the stick aside, his gaze hardening as he looked at Johnny. “Old Man Crowley owns her. He's a cruel man, and he'll get what's coming to him someday.” He leaned back against the tree, knees bent, his head tilted back and his gaze lost in the canopy above.

“When you marry Eliza," Johnny whispered, "I want to give you a piece of land as a wedding gift.”

"No, sir," Isaiah said quietly, head dropping. "I want to pay for everything I own. What good is a man if everything's handed to him?"

Johnny understood the young man's pride and didn't press the issue.

"All right, we'll come to an agreement on the land," Johnny declared, his voice firm. "But I'm determined to help build this house, and I won't be dissuaded." He punctuated his statement with a pointed finger.

"Okay, Johnny, I'll accept your offer," Isaiah replied.

Nathanial immediately chimed in, "I'll lend a hand as well." He extended his hand towards Isaiah. "We need to shake on it to seal the deal."

Isaiah grasped Nathanial's hand first, then turned and shook Johnny's, making the agreement official.

The sudden crack of gunfire shattered the silence, signaling renewed fighting. Musket balls whizzed through the air, thudding against trees as the skirmish intensified. Screams pierced the chaos as men fell wounded. In the ensuing confusion, the ranks dissolved, and Johnny lost sight of Nathanial and Isaiah.

The skirmish broke their regiment, scattering the men like leaves in a storm. Johnny sat with his back against a sturdy oak tree, his breathing labored, and his thoughts clouded with exhaustion and worry. He had managed to crawl to this spot, hoping against hope that his comrades were safe and that they might find him. His thoughts drifted to his family, his wife Anna and their two young children, images of them filling his mind as he fought to stay awake. He hugged Anna's bible to his chest and said a silent prayer for his comrades, his family, and himself.

A rustling sound nearby snapped him out of his reverie. He tensed, his hand instinctively reaching for his musket, though he knew he had no strength left to defend himself. The rustling grew closer, accompanied by the careful steps of someone trying to remain undetected. Johnny's heart pounded in his chest, and just as he was about to call out, he heard a familiar voice.

"Johnny," came the whisper, almost lost in the stillness of the night.

Johnny's heart soared with relief. "Isaiah!" he whispered back, his voice tinged with disbelief.

Through the dim light, Isaiah emerged from the shadows, his face drawn and tired but alive. As the moonlight filtered through the leaves, it illuminated Johnny where he sat, a sight that made Isaiah's cautious approach falter for a moment. Isaiah moved closer, dropping to his knees beside his friend.

"You're alive," Johnny said, his voice choked with emotion. He struggled, a smile breaking through the grime on his face. He embraced Isaiah, their bond as strong as ever despite the horrors they had faced.

But as Johnny pulled back, his eyes caught a glint of metal, the moonlight reflecting off it near a tree behind Isaiah. His instincts kicked in, and without thinking, he shoved Isaiah to the ground. The crack of a gunshot shattered the stillness, echoing through the trees.

Johnny staggered, a searing pain ripping through his chest. He gasped, falling to his knees as Isaiah scrambled to his side, panic and anguish contorting his features. Shots rang out all around them. An unknown soldier—one of their own—stumbled from behind a tree, clutching his own chest as he fell lifeless beside Johnny.

"No, no, no!" Isaiah cried out, cradling Johnny's head in his lap, tears streaming down his face.

Johnny's breath came in ragged gasps, the warmth of life quickly ebbing from him. He reached up, his bloodied hand gripping Isaiah's arm with surprising strength. "Isaiah. Listen. I need a favor," he whispered, his voice barely audible.

"Anything, Johnny. Just hold on," Isaiah pleaded, his voice cracking with desperation.

"Tell Anna—tell her I love her," Johnny rasped. "Tell my children . . . to be brave, to-to remember their father." His eyes searched Isaiah's, pleading for a promise. "Tell Anna that I will come back to her, if not in this life, then in the next life to come."

"I will," Isaiah swore, his voice breaking. "I promise, Johnny."

As Isaiah spoke, Johnny's gaze shifted over his shoulder. A young man, barely more than a boy, dressed in the uniform of the enemy moved toward them, musket in hand, his eyes wide with fear and determination.

"Run," Johnny urged, his voice a strained whisper. "Run, Isaiah!"

Isaiah hesitated for a heartbeat, torn between staying with his friend and the impending danger. Johnny's grip tightened, a final surge of strength. "Go! Now!" he demanded.

With one last, heart-wrenching look, Isaiah gently laid Johnny's head down and rose, the anguish in his heart threatening to consume him. He glanced at the young enemy soldier, then turned and ran, the shadows swallowing him as he disappeared into the woods.

Johnny watched him go, a sense of peace washing over him. The pain began to fade, replaced by a profound calm. He closed his eyes, the faces of his wife and children, the last images in his mind as the sounds of the night faded away.

As Isaiah ran, tears blurring his vision, he carried with him the weight of his friend's final words and the resolve to see them delivered. He would survive this war for Johnny's sake and make sure that his sacrifice would never be forgotten.

CHAPTER THIRTY-FIVE

TAKING A BREAK

Grams handed Sarah a tissue to dry her eyes while she did the same. "I admit, I didn't expect that." She sniffled.

"I know what you mean." Sarah blew her nose. "I'm not sure if I can handle reading anymore." She stood and stretched.

"I know it's hard, but I want to know what happens to Anna and those babies, not to mention what happens to Nathaniel."

"I suppose you're right." Sarah placed the book on the coffee table. "If you don't mind, I'm going to take a shower and then read more before bed."

"That sounds good to me," Grams agreed. "I'll make some sandwiches."

Sarah headed to her room to shower. She decided to call Stacy to see how her trip was going and update her on the book. She hung up after the fifth ring. She chose to send a text message before getting in the shower. After showering, she dried off and slipped on an oversized tee-shirt and a pair of shorts. She checked her phone and read the text message from Stacy.

We made it safely and will be meeting with the new buyers of my business in the morning. Talk to you soon. Love, Stacy

Sarah placed her phone on her nightstand and went

downstairs to check on her grandmother. She found her sitting on the couch and took a seat next to her. Sandwiches and chips were arranged neatly on a platter in the middle of the coffee table.

“Have you heard from Stacy?” Grams picked up a sandwich and took a bite.

"They arrived safely, and they have a meeting with a possible buyer in the morning." Sarah's gaze was fixed on the ground.

“Why so glum?” Grams sipped her lemonade. “Are you thinking about the book?”

“No, I was thinking about Jimmy’s dream, and the similarities between him and Johnny.” Sarah picked up a sandwich and bit into it. She picked up a glass of lemonade and took a drink.

“I’m sure it’s just a coincidence.” Grams placed the glass of lemonade on the platter. "However," she added, "some dreams do have a purpose." She looked Sarah in the eyes while crossing her arms over her lap.

“I’ll speak with Jimmy and find out if there’s more to the dream than what he’s telling me.” Sarah went upstairs to retrieve her phone. She called Jimmy. He answered on the second ring.

“Hello, love. What’s up?” He sounded chipper.

“I’m sorry to bother you, but I wanted to ask you about the recuring dream you have.”

“Sure. What do you want to know?”

“All of it, from beginning to end,” she said softly.

“I told you all of it, except last night there was something different about it.”

“Would you mind telling me about it?” She bit her bottom lip.

“The dream started out as usual, I was awakened in the

middle of the night. War had begun and I was called to fight. I kissed my wife and children goodbye and then, the next thing I knew, I was dying. Only last night, the dream changed. When I looked down, I was covered in blood. My clothes were red with it."

"That's horrible." Sarah gasped. "Did you die in the dream?" her voice trailed off as she asked the question.

"Yes, I'm sure I did," Jimmy said sadly. "I died, well, in the dream, that is. Beneath an apple tree in an orchard."

Sarah decided it was time to let Jimmy know about the book and the similarities between him and Johnny. She started from the beginning of the book, ending with the last page she'd read to her grandmother.

Jimmy quietly listened. After a few moments he spoke. "So, you're wondering if I am the reincarnation of Johnny?" he asked hesitantly.

"No, I told you I don't believe in that stuff, but it does seem strange that your dream matches Johnny and Anna's story from the book. Except you died in your dream, and Johnny didn't—at least, not yet." She sat on the edge of the bed. "What's strange is the feeling I've had from the moment I first met you." She paused. "It's as though I've known you my whole life." Her voice trailed off.

"I thought you said you didn't believe in that stuff," he teased.

"Everything about Johnny and Anna feels familiar. It's as though I'm reliving everything, reliving our past through this book," she confessed.

"Babe, do you realize you just said our past life?" Johnny asked. "Do you believe it now?"

"I don't know what to believe anymore."

"I'll be there in a second," he shouted to one of his men, then returned to his phone call. “I hate to run, but I need to get this job finished. I love you, and I’ll see you tomorrow.”

“I love you. See you tomorrow.” Sarah stood.

“I can’t wait to hear the rest of the story,” Jimmy said before hanging up.

Sarah felt relieved to hear Jimmy’s voice. She was glad to hear that his dream had changed and the similarities were just a weird coincidence.

She went back downstairs, anxious to get back to the book. Her grandmother was just as eager to hear what happened next.

CHAPTER THIRTY-SIX

ANNA RECIEVES NEWS
June 13, 1776

Pa was hired for a job in town, and this one was by far the biggest undertaking of his career. As a skilled carpenter, he typically took on small jobs here and there, but when he received a commission from Mayor Morrison, the task took on a special significance. The mayor's daughter was set to wed in a year, and he wanted to gift her an impressive house as a wedding present.

In the meantime, Virginia and the twins made frequent visits to see Anna and her children, coming by twice a week. Ma had made the decision to stay with Anna during this period, cherishing the time spent with her grandchildren. She planned to remain until Pa completed the house, contributing her support and love to the family while they anticipated word about Johnny.

The day seemed off. Anna couldn't put her finger on it, but it felt as though an ominous dark cloud hovered over her. She stepped outside into the bright sunlight and looked up at the seemingly cloudless sky. She shook her head and tried to forget the feeling of dread that washed over her.

Ma stood watching her with a look of concern. "Is something

wrong?" she questioned.

"No, nothing's wrong." Anna kept her back to her mother. She leaned forward, placing her elbows on the porch banister. "I was thinking of taking Ebony out for a ride," she said softly. "I think she misses Johnny." Ebony was Johnny's magnificent black horse, a gift from his father. Johnny loved that horse.

"I think it would do you both some good." Ma stepped next to her. "I'll take care of the children until you get back."

"I shan't be long. They'll sleep for several hours." Anna jogged to the barn to prepare the horse. "Hello, girl." She stroked the horse's mane as she saddled her. "You miss him, don't you?" She hugged Ebony. "It's okay, I miss him too," she said softly.

She put one foot into the stirrup and threw her leg over the horse, then adjusted herself in the saddle. She allowed Ebony to walk slowly out of the barn. Once outside, Ebony seemed to perk up, especially when she saw the open field. Just as they reached the edge of the field, Anna dismounted the horse to open the gate. Her thoughts were of Johnny when a messenger approached bearing a letter. Anna ripped it open and quickly read the note from his commanding officer that offered his condolences about Johnny's death. He stated Johnny had died courageously.

Anna read the letter multiple times in a daze, the words blurring, the world swaying around her. The horse seemed to sense her pain, his head nuzzling her shoulder as if offering comfort.

"I'm sorry, ma'am." The messenger, a young boy about the age of twelve, took a couple steps back before turning to run away, unable to bear the anguished look on Anna's face nor the thought of delivering such horrible news.

Anna, shaking from the news, mounted the horse. She didn't

bother closing the gate as they raced across the vast field, the horses' hooves kicking up dirt that sent dust swirling like tiny tornados. The wind whipped through Anna's hair, a cascade of golden dark blonde that flowed like silk. She didn't look back. She couldn't. Not yet. Not until the pain that clawed at her heart had subsided, even for a moment. Today, the world was a blur of green, gold, and purple as she raced through the field of wildflowers. Nothing, not even the afternoon sun shining brightly in the sky could break through the dark cloud of grief that filled her soul. Tears blurred her vision. Today, she was a whirlwind of grief, her soul torn apart by the loss of her one true love, Johnny.

She pictured Johnny with his eyes the color of the emerald, green river, her favorite spot, the place where he proposed, and his laugh that could chase away any dark cloud. "God! this can't be happening. Please, God, wake me up from this dreadful nightmare," she shouted.

As the horse approached the middle of the field, Anna stretched her arms out at her sides and let out a gut-wrenching scream that sent birds flying and deer scrambling. "Johnny!" she screamed as she tilted her head toward heaven. "You promised we'd be together forever." The horse slowed to a stop as Anna slumped over on her back, allowing herself to fall to the ground. She lay in a heap crying and thinking of her lost love, Johnny, who had sworn his love for her beneath the same sun that now felt cold and distant. Johnny, who was now nothing but a hollow echo in the vast emptiness of her broken heart.

She stood and once again mounted Johnny's horse. Now, she rode and rode, letting the wind cleanse her tears, letting the speed of the horse carry her away from the pain, even if only for a fleeting moment. She imagined Johnny's laugh echoing around her, the sound weaving through the wind, a phantom melody that brought a momentary flicker of warmth to her cold heart.

The sun dipped low in the sky, casting long, skeletal shadows across the field. Anna slowed the horse, her weary body protesting. The world around her, once a blur of motion, began to sharpen. She saw the wildflowers, the vibrant yellow and purple, whispering tales of life and renewal. Their beauty tugged at the edge of her grief, reminding her that life goes on, even without Johnny. She eased off the horse and slumped to the ground.

She sat staring at the weeds swaying in the breeze. She plucked a blade of grass, remembering how Johnny placed it between his thumbs and blew on it making a loud whistle. "Why can't life be like this blade of grass," she whispered. "Once cut, it'll grow back again new and alive." She angrily ripped it from the earth by handfuls and threw it, scattering it in the breeze.

"It's not fair!" she screamed. "We were supposed to grow old together. You promised, Johnny. You promised." Her legs grew weak. She fell to the ground and lay there sobbing uncontrollably. "God, please, say it isn't so."

She let Ebony graze, her black coat shimmering in the sunlight. As she lay on the ground, her back against the cool, damp earth, a single tear escaped, tracing a path down her cheek. It was a tear of pain, of loss, but also of hope. A hope that the memory of Johnny would be a beacon, guiding her through the darkness, a hope that she would find strength in his love, a hope that someday even the deepest sorrow could be replaced by the quiet balm of remembrance.

Looking toward heaven, she whispered, "I'll never forget you, Johnny. I'll love you, forever." And as the sun slipped behind the clouds, she knew she must return home to her children. She burst into tears at the very thought of telling them their father would never be coming home. She was grateful Ma was staying for a few days. She couldn't bear being alone when the children learned the sad news.

The cracking of a branch and an anguished male voice startled her.

She stood and looked up the hill in the direction the voice came from. She saw Isaiah at the edge of the woods but couldn't make out what he was saying. She made her way up the hill, leaving Ebony to continue grazing. As she drew closer, she heard Isaiah cry out. "Why, God? Why Johnny?" He pounded his fist against his chest. "Why didn't you take me?"

Anna eased up closer. That's when she saw it. Isaiah held a gun. "I'm sorry, Johnny, I can't keep my promise." He dropped to his knees. "I can't bear to face them." He began to sob. "God forgive me." He placed the gun to his head.

Anna gasped. She rushed toward him, knocking the gun from his hand. It went off, sending a single shot echoing through the treetops.

"Anna! What are you doing?" His eyes widened in surprise at seeing her there.

"No, Isaiah! What are you doing here, and what does this have to do with Johnny?" she demanded.

Isaiah dropped his head in shame and sobbed uncontrollably. Anna cried along with him. When their tears subsided, Isaiah spoke. "I was there." He choked on the words.

"You mean, with Johnny?" she whispered.

Isaiah nodded and swallowed hard. He explained everything

leading up to finding Johnny clutching something to his chest while sitting with his back against an oak tree.

"He was clutching his chest. Was he hurt?" Anna scooted up onto her knees in front of Isaiah, wanting to hear the last moments of Johnny's life.

"No. At least, not when I found him. I thought he was holding his gun, but now I think about it," Isaiah wiped the tears from his eyes with the back of his hand. "I believe he was holding a book."

"My bible," Anna whispered. "It had to have been the bible I placed in his haversack. Go on," she said softly.

"It happened so fast. We were happy to see each other. He embraced me before throwing me to the ground as a loud gunshot rang out." He began to sob yet again as anger surged through him. "It should have been me."

"But it wasn't. God spared you for a reason." Anna placed a hand on his shoulder as a gesture of comfort. "I need to know if he said anything before . . . before . . . ." Anna tried choking back the tears that once again escaped her eyes and trickled down her cheek.

"Yes!" He nodded. "He wanted me to tell you he loves you, and for the children to be brave and never forget him." Isaiah stared off into the distance.

Anna sat speechless; tears flooded her already soaked cheeks. "Have you been home to see your Pa and Ma?"

Isaiah cleared his throat and shook his head. "I was going to let them think the war took me too," he said sadly. "It should've been me."

Anna stood and stretched out her hand. "Let's go home."

He stared at her in disbelief as he took her hand and stood.

"He loved both of us, ya know." She forced a smile. "I'll take you home." she said as he followed her down the hill to the awaiting horse.

They rode in silence to Amos and Hattie Mae's. Once Isaiah climbed off the horse, Anna didn't waste time getting away from there. She wanted to get home to her children and her own mother. She slowed the horse to a trot as the house came into view. She ran her fingers through her tangled hair, straightened her clothes, and dried the tears from her eyes as best she could. She met her father as he was coming from the barn.

"Young'un, you look like you were caught in a windstorm." He jested, then felt horrible when she fell from the horse into his arms and sobbed.

"Johnny's gone, and he's never coming back," she said between sobs.

"I'm so sorry, Anna." Pa stroked her hair while trying to hold back his own tears. He cleared his throat as he released her. "Go inside with your Ma and children. I'll take the horse to the barn." He quickly brushed his hand over his face as he turned with the horse and walked away.

Anna's feet felt heavy the closer she got to the front door of her house. She took a deep breath and slowly opened it. The children ran to meet her, questioning her whereabouts.

"Ma, where were you?" Four-year-old Autumn hugged her waist. "I helped Grandma make dinner and was waiting for you." She made a pouty face.

"That's true, she refused to eat until you got home." Ma glanced up from her sewing, then quickly laid it aside when she saw Anna's tortured expression.

"Anna! What's the matter?" Ma rushed to her.

Anna tried her best to be strong for the children's sake, but it was no use. She fell to her knees, hugging her children tight. "Your Pa is . . . is . . . God help me, I can't bear to say it," she screamed. "He's in heaven," she blurted before losing her nerve again.

"No! It can't be true!" Ma stared in shocked disbelief. "Is there anything we can do?" she asked.

"You mean, he's with Grandma?" Autumn gazed at her mother with the same emerald green eyes as her father.

"Yes, my love. your Papa is with Grandma." Anna turned toward her son. "Thomas, he wanted you and Autumn to be brave and never forget him, and to know that he loves you both very much."

Overcome with grief and disbelief, six-year-old Thomas recoiled from his mother and yelled, "My pa is not dead! Stop saying such things!" unable to process the devastating news, he bolted out the door, seeking refuge in the familiar comfort of the barn, where he scrambled up to the hayloft. "God, please don't take my pa away. I promise I'll be a good boy. I'll help Ma with the chores; I'll never fight with Autumn again." He clasped his hands in prayer so tightly his knuckles turned white. "God, please send him home. Please." He lay down in the hay and cried until he had no tears left. Exhausted, he drifted off to sleep.

Daniel was still in the barn. He fell to his knees in prayer. He quietly sobbed upon hearing the anguished cries of his six-year-old grandson. "God, take this pain from my family." He climbed into the hayloft and lay beside his grieving grandson and silently grieved with him while he slept.

Anna found them both there sleeping soundly. She backed down the ladder and returned to the house to console her daughter whose four-year-old mind finally grasped what was going on. With her rosy cheeks and tangled curls, Autumn was a picture of innocence. But the life she had known had crumbled around her, leaving behind an unfillable void. She too had fallen asleep only to awaken screaming, "I want my Papa! Papa, where are you?" It was more than Anna could bear. She felt helpless as she sank to the bed, buried her face in her pillow, and screamed as loud as she could into it.

Her mother tried to console her, but Anna's mourning turned to anger. "How are we supposed to grieve properly without his body to lay to rest?"

"I understand, but it's impossible to find him with this horrible war going on." Ma held Anna and cried with her.

"We'll find him," Pa announced.

Neither Anna nor her mother had heard him walk in. He held Thomas in his arms, the boy still sleeping soundly. Anna reached for him, and her father gently placed Thomas on the bed beside her.

Thomas awoke and began to cry once more. She pulled him to her and held her grieving son.

Several nights later, Thomas awoke during the night. The walls of his bedroom seemed to close in on him, suffocating him with emptiness. Thomas' laughter had turned into silent sobs that echoed through the darkened house. His toys, once a source of endless joy, lay forgotten on the floor.

Each evening, he would sit by the windowsill, his tiny hands pressed against the cool glass, his gaze lost in the twilight, watching, praying to catch a glimpse of his father coming home. The once familiar stars now seemed distant and cold, their twinkling light failing to comfort his aching heart.

As darkness enveloped the town, casting long, ominous shadows, Thomas's imagination ran wild. He would envision his father's gentle smile, his hearty laugh, and the warm embrace that had always made the world feel safe. But now, those memories were all that remained, a bittersweet reminder of what he had lost.

One night, as the rain pounded upon the roof, Thomas felt a surge of desperation. He couldn't bear the weight of his grief any longer. Slipping out of bed, he made his way to his father's favorite chair in the living room.

As he sat down, his fingers traced the worn armrests, seeking some semblance of connection to the man he loved. Tears streamed down his face as he whispered, "Papa, I miss you so much." He sat for a while, drifting in and out of sleep. Finally, he stood and quietly walked to his mother's room and lay down next to her.

The next morning Anna awoke early and lay there staring at the ceiling praying aloud, "God how do I have a burial and say goodbye to my husband without his body?"

Thomas awoke when he heard her voice. "Ma, can't we pretend that Papa is coming home? I don't want to say goodbye." His eyes filled with tears.

Anna nodded and hugged him tightly. "Yes, son, we aren't saying goodbye just yet." She swung her legs over the side of the bed and slowly stood so as not to wake Autumn Rose. Days turned into nights as Autumn's tiny body trembled with grief.

One evening, as the moon cast its mournful glow upon her room, Autumn's piercing cries echoed through the silent house. "Papa! Papa!" she sobbed, her tiny voice laced with anguish. "Where are you, Papa? I need you!"

Anna, torn apart by her daughter's pain, rushed to her bedside. She held Autumn close, her own tears mingling with the child's. But no words could soothe the unbearable ache in their hearts.

As the night wore on, Autumn's cries intensified. She pleaded in the darkness, her tiny voice a beacon of desperation. The stars seemed to weep with her, their celestial brilliance dimmed by her sorrow.

"Why did you leave me, Papa?" she whispered, her voice barely audible. "I miss you so much."

CHAPTER THIRTY-SEVEN

WORD TRAVELS FAST

Ma was in the kitchen with Pa. Together they made breakfast. The aroma of the food along with freshly brewed coffee wafted through the house. Anna was glad to have company, especially when Virginia and Patrick brought Paddy and Patricia over every week to entertain Thomas and Autumn. Anna kept the news silent as long as possible, but after a while, word got out and family and friends came to offer their condolences.

"Are you sure he's dead? When did he pass?" Mrs. Worthington asked.

"Mrs. Worthington, what sort of question is that?" Virginia scowled at the woman.

"It's fine." Anna took Virginia by the arm and moved her out of the way. "It's been two months today, Mrs. Worthington."

"Why the secrecy?" she demanded.

Anna hung her head, fighting back tears. "There's no body. Therefore, no closure. So I clung to the hope that he might still be alive."

"Well, child, it's good that you can get over him so quickly and move on with your life." She wrinkled her nose. "Ya know, for the children's sake."

“I’m not over him.” Anna resented her for saying that. “I’m trying to stay strong for my children, but we miss him so.” She swiped at a tear.

“Are you sure he didn’t run off with another woman?” Mrs. Worthington prodded as she stepped closer, invading Anna’s personal space. “You said so yourself. There’s no body, no closure.” She glared at Anna. “I’ll wager that he’s entertaining another woman. And that’s why all the secrecy.”

Anger coiled tight in Anna's stomach as she pushed Mrs. Worthington backward, the older woman landing with a splash in the horse's water trough.

Stepping out of the house and unaware of the conversation she’d missed, Ma gasped at the sight of Anna shoving someone. “Mrs. Worthington!” she cried, rushing to help the woman. “I'm so sorry. Anna hasn't been herself lately.” She took Mrs. Worthington by the hand trying to assist her out of the trough.

“That's the problem with kids these days, Mary Lou.” Mrs. Worthington threw one leg over the trough while holding onto Ma's hand, struggling to get out. “No respect, that’s what it is, and I'm sure she gets it from her parents.” She continued to rant. “I tried to tell her that her husband ran off with another woman, but she won’t listen to reason.” She huffed.

Ma grabbed Mrs. Worthington by the head and shoved her under the water.

“Yup, she gets it from her mother,” came a male voice from behind Anna.

She angrily gritted her teeth as she bent down and picked up a huge piece of horse dung and turned to throw it at the person who dared insult her or her mother. She froze and stared wide-eyed at the man to whom the voice belonged. She tried rubbing her eyes to make sure she wasn't dreaming and smeared horse manure on her face.

"What is it with you and horse dung?" He laughed.

"Johnny, is that you?" she whispered. Her eyes began to well. "You're alive!" She splashed water from the trough onto her face, making sure she wasn't dreaming.

Mrs. Worthington, who was still struggling to get out, stopped when she noticed Johnny standing there.

"Last time I checked." He opened his arms. "I missed you and the children more than you'll ever know."

Anna ran to him. "Johnny, oh, Johnny, I missed you my love! But how, what happened?"

"I'll explain later. Let me look at you." He held her at arm's length. "My beautiful Anna." He kissed her passionately on the lips. She didn't want to let him go for fear of waking up and finding it was all a dream.

Ma stood by shocked and unable to speak. After a few moments, she said, "Johnny, it's a miracle from God." She hugged him before running to the barn to get Daniel and the children. screaming for them with every step she took.

"Daniel, Daniel!" She reached the barn and met Daniel at the door, a frightened look upon his face. "Come, children! It's a miracle from God." She picked up Autumn, grabbed Thomas by the hand, and ran toward the barn door.

Daniel followed, just as confused as the children. "What in heaven's name is going on?" he shouted as they stepped out of the barn.

"It's a miracle." She pointed.

Thomas was the first to speak. "Papa!" he squealed and broke into a run toward Johnny and Anna. Johnny caught him as he jumped into his father's waiting arms.

"Papa, Papa!" Autumn screamed, tears flowing down her

cheeks. "I knew you'd come home." She made it to Johnny just as he set Thomas down.

He picked up his baby girl and hugged her tight. Everyone stood with tear-soaked faces, including Daniel. He hugged his son-in-law.

"Welcome home, son." This time, he didn't bother hiding his tears, for these were tears of joy.

The whole town caught wind of Johnny's return from the dead and rushed out to see for themselves. After a while, the people slowly dispersed and went back home.

No one noticed the young man standing next to the tree taking it all in. That is, until Johnny turned and motioned to him.

"Everyone, I'd like you to meet my friend Edmund." Johnny patted Edmund on the back. "He truly saved my life."

"Hello, Edmund, it's nice meeting you." Daniel stepped forward and shook his hand, followed by Anna.

"Thank you, Edmund, for saving my husband and bringing him home to us."

Edmund nodded but said nothing.

"Can you not speak?" Thomas asked.

Johnny rubbed his son's head. "All in good time, son."

After dinner that evening, Pa built a fire. The whole family gathered around to hear Johnny's story. Anna sent Patrick to fetch Amos, Hattie Mae, Isaiah, Gracie, and Joshua to join them around the fire. It wasn't revealed to any of them about Johnny's return home. As they pulled in front of the house and climbed down from the buckboard, Isaiah hesitantly approached the waiting crowd. He hadn't noticed who was sitting in the chair in front of him with his back turned. That is, until Johnny stood and spoke. "Here, take my seat." He turned to face Isaiah whose eyes grew as big as saucers.

"Johnny, is that you?" Isaiah stepped back and rubbed his eyes.

"In the flesh." Johnny grabbed him and gave him a huge bear hug. "Thank you for keeping your promise. You'll never know how much it means to me."

"I don't understand." Isaiah scratched his head. "I heard the shot. You grabbed your chest and fell."

"The musket ball didn't strike my chest." Johnny reached into his haversack. "It struck Anna's bible." He held up the bible for all to see, the musket ball still lodged in its pages.

Johnny handed the bible to Anna. She gently took it from his hand and inspected it. "What stopped it from exiting completely?" She knitted her brow. "Wait! There's not one, but two musket balls!"

Everyone grew silent as Johnny told his story. "The fighting was all around us, men dropping like flies. After our regiment got separated, I was sitting under a tree holding the bible and praying. That's when Isaiah found me." Johnny turned to face Isaiah. "I saw the glint of a gun in the moonlight. I knew you were about to get shot, so I threw you out of the way. I was still clutching the bible when the shot rang out. It struck the bible, knocking me to the ground. My bayonet cut my arm, and the force from the musket ball broke my ribs. At some point, I was shot in the leg. It went straight through, missing the bone."

"Was that where all the blood came from?" Isaiah asked.

"Yes, and the broken ribs were the reason I had trouble breathing. I was sure I was going to die, especially when I saw young Edmund here slipping up behind you. I wouldn't be here if it weren't for God, or Edmund."

"I thought you was a dying." Isaiah wiped the moisture from

his eyes. "Wait! The young man sneaking up behind me was a British soldier, a Red Coat. It was you."

Edmund nodded. "Yes, sir, it was." He replied in a thick British accent. "I didn't want to fight any more than you did." He dropped his head. "I just wanted to go home," he said sadly.

"How old are you?" Ma asked him.

"I'm eighteen, ma'am."

"Just a young'un." Ma shook her head.

"Edmund bent down to try to help me," Johnny continued. "I thought he was going to stab me. Just as I held the bible up to protect myself, another shot sounded, striking the bible that I now held against Edmund's chest. God protected us both that night."

"How did you manage to get out of there?" Pa inquired. "I mean, Johnny had broken ribs and had been shot."

"I was still unsure of Edmund, and I didn't fully understand what had just taken place," Johnny continued. "An unknown American soldier lay dead next to me. As the fighting intensified, Edmund had to think fast to save us both."

Anna stepped toward Edmund. "What did you do?"

"I panicked. I looked down at my red clothes and knew I was a target. So, I changed uniforms with the American soldier who passed." He dropped his head and whispered, "God rest his soul."

"He dragged me through the group of American soldiers, who covered for us while he helped me to safety." Johnny playfully nudged Edmund. "Only he didn't stop going until we reached the river. There, we took a boat belonging to the British. We laid down in it and sailed downstream until the fighting could be heard far in the distance. We abandoned the boat and borrowed a horse and rode until we came upon a small house belonging to an old man and woman. They took us in, fed us, and nursed us back to health. We spent the next few months repairing their roof and fence and building a new porch to show our appreciation. Afterwards, we headed home."

"What about Nathaniel?" Gracie asked, her voice trembling.

"We saw Nathaniel a week ago, and he's fine. He wants you to know that he loves you, and Joshua and will be home soon." A sadness crossed Johnny's face. "An outbreak of smallpox took the lives of many of our men. Luckily, it passed by Nathaniel and his men. They chose to stay and fight alongside General Washington. I was sent home due to my injuries. I'll forever have a limp." He patted his leg and looked at Anna.

"I don't care about your limp." Anna hugged him. "What matters most is that you're alive and home safe with us."

"I should have stayed with Nathaniel." Guilt resonated in Isaiah's voice. "It's my fault he's there."

"No, it's not your fault. He chose to be there." Gracie placed a hand on his shoulder. "I'm happy to hear that he is fine and will be home soon." She forced a smile.

"Don't you worry, Gracie." Ma hugged her and spoke softly in her ear. "The same God who saved Johnny and Edmund is watching over Nathaniel."

"I know. I just miss him so, and it breaks my heart each time Joshua asks about his Pa." She sobbed.

The whole family, along with Amos and Hattie Mae, pitched in to ensure that Gracie and Joshua were well taken care of. During the winter months, Gracie stayed with Ma and helped around the house. Ma loved having her there and hated it when spring came and it was time for them to go home, but she understood that Gracie missed being in her own home.

"Mary Lou, Daniel, thank you for your hospitality. It means a lot to us both." Gracie stood by the buckboard with her overnight bag in her hand.

Joshua took it and placed it in the back of the buckboard.

"We enjoyed having you both." Ma hugged her. "I'll drop by to check on you soon."

"I'd appreciate that." Gracie turned toward the buckboard, and Joshusa helped her to her seat, then off they went. A sadness came over Gracie. She was glad to be going home but also knew she was going home to an empty house. A house that no longer felt like a home without Nathaniel.

Johnny and Anna took in Edmund until it was safe enough for him to go home. Edmund was a huge help, and the children loved him. Autumn mimicked his accent so perfectly that Johnny became concerned someone could become suspicious that they were protecting a British soldier and harm might comc to him.

Edmund settled into the American way of life well. One day while in town, he met a woman his age. She had two small children, a four-year-old son and a three-year-old daughter. Her husband had been killed in the war, and they were left alone. Six months later, they married, and the children thought of Edmund as their father. He loved them as much as he would his own. His wife Hannah ran to meet him as he was walking home from the fields.

"Edmund, I'm going to have a baby." He was overjoyed. He lifted her in his arms and spun her around.

He thanked God for giving him a second chance. A second chance at life, happiness, and a family of his own.

Summer turned to fall, and winter wasn't far behind. Hannah gave birth to a son she named Levi. Isaiah met

Edmund on his way to see Eliza, and Edmund filled him in on all the details about his marriage and his newborn son. Isaiah informed Johnny when he returned home that evening.

Johnny left long before daylight. He was on his way to speak with Eliza to see what she wanted. Did she feel the same for Isaiah? Did she want her freedom? *That's a dumb question.* He promised Isaiah a piece of property to build a home for himself and Eliza, after they married. Isaiah insisted on purchasing the property, so Johnny decided to purchase Eliza. He cringed at the very thought of purchasing another human being, but it was the only way he could get her away from her master. *Master*—that's another word he despised. There's only one Master, and his name is Jesus, Johnny said to himself. He hoped to make the purchase, set her free, and surprise Isaiah when he came in from the fields with his Pa. He smiled to himself at the thought of Isaiah and the love of his life finally getting the chance for happiness.

He was thrilled to find out that Edmund didn't live far from Eliza. He made up his mind to visit Edmund after picking up Eliza, that is, if he could strike up a deal with the old farmer who owned her. Johnny was excited to meet his friend's new family. He wished they lived closer so they could visit more often.

He made it to Crowley's farm. Old man Crowley was a mean old coot. It was said that he treated his hunting dogs better than he did his family. Johnny left his horse tied to a tree in the field and sneaked to the slaves' quarters out back, behind the old farmhouse. He tapped on the door of the old shed. The door cracked open, and a woman's voice whispered in the darkness. "Who's there?" her voice cracked.

"I'm looking for Eliza," Johnny replied.

"What cha want with her?" she asked.

"I need to ask her some questions about my friend Isaiah."

The door swung wide open. "Isaiah! Is he all right?" she said a little louder.

Johnny knew this must be Eliza and he could hear in her voice all he needed to know. She truly loved Isaiah and Johnny knew he made the right decision to purchase her freedom. "I've come to purchase your freedom so you and Isaiah can be married, if that's what you want."

Before Johnny finished speaking, she clasped her hands together and whispered, "Yes, oh, Lord, yes, sir, more than anything." She spun around in circles.

"I'll speak to Mr. Crowley and see if I can make a deal with him." Johnny froze at her next reply.

"Mr. Crowley isn't here. He went to the farm up the road. He wants to kill a man named Edmund; says he's a Red Coat."

Johnny's blood ran cold. He felt as though he was going to be sick. "How long ago did they leave?" he asked calmly.

"Not long before you got here. Maybe ten, fifteen minutes," she replied.

Johnny ran as fast as he could and jumped on his horse and raced up the road. He made it about halfway to Edmund's when he ran into old man Crowley and his two sons. They had Edmund thrown over a horse and were laughing and calling him names. They got their hands on a British soldier's uniform and had put it on Edmund.

Johnny pretended he had no idea what was going on as he stopped next to them. The moonlight shone brightly and illuminated everything.

"Where are you boys off too?" Johnny asked, keeping his voice steady and calm.

"The way I see it, that's none of your business," Crowley's son, who appeared to be the oldest, sneered.

"We snagged us a British soldier. See his red coat?" The youngest son laughed.

"Hush up, Elias, Isaac. You boys talk too much. Maybe this here stranger is going to get us into trouble." Mr. Crowley pointed his gun at Johnny and spit tobacco juice on the ground.

"Trouble over a filthy Red Coat? Why I'd like to be the one who pulls the trigger," Johnny lied.

"If'n anyone's pulling the trigger, it's gonna be me." Mr. Crowley pointed his gun toward the ground.

"Mind if I watch?" Johnny motioned toward Edmund.

"The more the merrier, I always say." Mr. Crowley led the way to a grove of trees just off the road.

Johnny got off his horse. "Allow me the honor of removing him from his horse." He quickly walked over to Edmund and whispered in his ear. "Hey, it's Johnny. I need you to speak in the best American accent you can."

"What's taking so long?" Elias shouted.

"What was you saying to him?" Mr. Crowley pointed his gun at Johnny, who had Edmund thrown over his shoulder.

"I was telling him to say his prayers." Johnny set Edmund on his feet. "Well, go ahead and start praying," Johnny shouted.

"No! Please, don't kill me," Edmund shouted in his best American accent. I'm an American and I have a wife and three small children."

Johnny held up his hand. "I thought you said he was a British soldier." He grabbed hold of Edmund. "He's no more British than I am."

Mr. Crowley grew angry. "Which one of you boys said he was British?" he yelled.

"I did, Pa, but I swear he talks like one." Elias shifted on his horse.

"No matter. Someone is dying tonight, and it ain't gonna be me." Mr. Crowley aimed his gun at Edmund.

"No!" Johnny screamed as he tried knocking the gun away. It went off, struck a tree, and then ricocheted off another before hitting Edmund. He fell back onto the ground, fighting for breath.

The Crowleys took off toward home, taking Johnny's horse with them. As they topped the hill, the sheriff and several men waited for them.

Johnny placed Edmund's head on his lap, praying and begging God to show mercy. "Please don't take him. Not now, not like this."

"Johnny, tell my wife and children that I love them, and I will return to them, if not in this life than in the one to come," Edmund said between breaths.

"Don't say such things." Johnny sobbed.

"What God does with a soul is his business. You taught me that." Edmund laughed and then winced in pain.

"It's not fair. You're young and have your whole life ahead of you."

Edmund looked at his chest. "There's so much blood. All I see is red."

"Edmund, you have a red shirt on." Johnny wiped tears from his eyes. He looked up and saw the sheriff speaking with the Crowleys.

Edmund closed his eyes; his body went limp. "I'll be right back." Johnny gently laid Edmund's head on the ground and climbed the hill on foot.

"Sheriff, arrest these men," Johnny demanded. "They shot

my friend, threatened to kill me, and stole my horse." Johnny walked over and took Ebony from Mr. Crowley.

"Arrest 'em, boys," the sheriff yelled.

Mr. Crowley aimed his gun at the sheriff, and one of his deputies shot him.

Elias grabbed his gun and yelled, "You shot my pa, you filthy swine." Just as he aimed his gun, the sheriff pulled the trigger. Elias rolled backward off his horse and lay lifeless on the ground next to his pa.

Issac surrendered and went peacefully. He apologized to Johnny for his part in everything. .

"Save it for the judge," the sheriff announced. He then turned to Johnny. "Would you like for one of my boys to stay and help you with your friend?"

"No, this is something I need to do alone; besides, if he doesn't survive, I have to take his body home to his wife and children." Johnny fought back tears that threatened to break free once again.

"I'll send the Doc out to check on him." The sheriff removed his hat and placed it on his chest. Johnny gave him directions to the general area of Edmund's home.

"I'm sure the doc knows where it is. Prayers for your friend." He watched as the sheriff and his men left with Isaac. He rode his horse over the hill to retrieve Edmund.

Edmund still lay on the ground the way Johnny had left him. His face was pale.

Johnny felt sick. "How am I supposed to tell your wife and children their daddy is gone?" He kicked a stick lying on the ground.

"How about you hold off on telling them," Edmund answered.

"Edmund, you're still alive." Johnny scrambled to his side. "How are you feeling?"

"Not as well as this morning." He tried sitting up, but the pain was unbearable.

"I thought you were dead."

"I need you to see something." Edmund reached down and touched his side. "What is that?"

Johnny looked down to see what he was talking about; his eyes grew wide in surprise. "Edmund, try not to move." Johnny took hold of the object and pulled it out of his side.

Edmund let out a loud scream.

Johnny tore off Edmund's shirt and checked him for wounds. The only one he found was where the stick had stuck him in the side.

"How did that happen? I thought I was shot?" Edmund's eyes filled with tears once again, only this time it was happy tears.

Johnny took him home, and after a checkup from the doctor, he determined that Edmund was a lucky man. He wasn't quite out of the woods yet, as he had to be careful that his wound didn't become infected, but, with time, it should heal fully.

Johnny left and stopped at Crowley's farm to deliver the news to the shooter's wife. He was relieved to hear that one of the sheriff's deputies had already paid a visit and took the bodies of her son and her husband to her.

She gladly sold Eliza to him for half of what he was willing to pay. He bought a horse with the rest of the money and helped Eliza up on its back. He took her straight to Amos and Hattie Mae's. Eliza slid off the horse and ran to meet Isaiah in the middle of the field. They got married a year later and moved into the house Johnny, Pa, and Amos helped him build.

Anna and Johnny's hearts went out to Gracie. Ma and Hattie

Mae took turns making sure she stayed busy to keep her mind off Nathanial as much as possible. It was the nights that were the hardest. Sometimes she prayed half the night; the rest of the time, she cried. She tried not to let negative thoughts enter her mind, but it became harder each passing day. She cherished the messages she received or the notes he sent whenever he could.

On this day, she didn't have the energy to get out of bed, but she had no choice when she heard Daniel calling her name. She knew it was Mary Lou's day to spend with her, but she just wanted to be alone today. Nathaniel's birthday was in four days, and once again she couldn't spend it with him. She made her way to the door, slowly opened it, and looked up into the face of . . . Nathaniel.

She squeezed her eyes shut, and when she opened them, Nathaniel was still standing there. He pulled her into his arms and kissed her passionately on the lips. Joshua ran to his father and hugged him. They were together as a family.

Nathaniel returned home a changed man. He had witnessed the horrors of war, but he had also discovered a newfound strength and a deep love for his country. As he embraced his family once more, he vowed to cherish every moment he had with them.

In the year of our Lord seventeen eighty-one, after a grueling siege, the British forces surrendered. Victory was declared, and the American Revolution had forever etched itself into everyone's memory, a testament to the sacrifices made by ordinary men and women for the sake of liberty.

Johnny and Anna built a fulfilling life together. They purchased property in Kanawha County, Virginia, which later became Nicholas County West Virginia, founded in January

1818. They raised their children, who eventually married and started families of their own, bringing nine beloved grandchildren into Johnny and Anna's lives. Anna cherished every moment spent with her grandchildren, particularly during the holidays. Thomas and his wife Clara contributed five grandchildren to the family, three boys and two girls. Autumn and her husband Christopher added another four, three boys and a girl. Johnny and Anna adored each and every one of their grandchildren. In fact, early on, Johnny had such a strong vision for their future family that he built the spacious house he promised Anna, a home designed to accommodate their growing family for generations to come.

In the year of our Lord eighteen-thirty, Johnny, at the age of seventy-two, was standing in the apple orchard he had planted forty years before. He was picking apples for Anna so she could make a pie for his upcoming birthday.

"Well, Jack ol' boy, what do you think?" Johnny rubbed his hound dog's head as he held up a bucket full of apples.

"Woof," the dog barked as though he understood.

An argument broke out somewhere amongst the trees. Johnny called out, "Who's there?"

No one answered.

As the arguing continued, Johnny made his way in the direction the shouting was coming from. "You have two seconds to get off my property!" he shouted.

Anna was hanging the wash out to dry and heard a gunshot. She dropped the basket of clothes and ran toward the orchard.

Isaiah was working in his field next to the orchard. He too heard the commotion and the gunshot. He raced to where he'd last heard Johnny shouting. He ran through the apple trees and collapsed at Johnny's side. His longtime friend lay on his back beneath an apple tree. He'd been shot in the chest. His breathing was labored as he fought to speak.

"Anna, my sweet Anna." Johnny winced in pain. "Please tell her I'll love her forever." He coughed up blood. "Tell . . . tell her." He trembled. "Tell her . . . I'll come back to her, if not in this life, then in the next life to come."

Anna made it in time to hear his words. She screamed. "Johnny, my love, please stay here with me." Tears flooded her cheeks. "Don't go." She fell to the ground next to him. "I'll love you forever." She kissed his lips one last time.

"Anna, this isn't goodbye." Johnny forced a smile. "I promise, I will find you, and we will be together again." With that, he closed his eyes and breathed his last breath.

CHAPTER THIRTY-EIGHT

SARAH AND JIMMY

Sarah closed the book for the last time. She sat staring at the pages. "Grams, did you notice something about the story? I mean, did something sound familiar to you?"

"I was trying not to think about that." Grams stood and stretched. "I think I'm going to bed before both our minds start going crazy."

"You noticed it too. The dream Jimmy had of seeing red all over him, the gunshot to the chest that Johnny received, and Jimmy's dream of being shot. It's all too much to be a coincidence, don't ya think?" Sarah stood, stretched, and decided not to press her grandmother on the issue. She chose to call Jimmy instead.

"Hello," Jimmy answered groggily.

"I'm sorry for waking you, but this is important." Sarah sat on the edge of her bed.

"What's up?" Jimmy yawned.

"I finished reading the book to Grams," she said hesitantly.

"How did it end?" Jimmy ran his fingers through his hair.

Sarah filled him in on everything. Jimmy quietly listened, taking in every word. When she finished speaking, she waited for him to respond.

"It's interesting, for sure," he finally said.

"Interesting? Is that all you have to say?" She couldn't believe her ears.

"Look, Sarah, it's just that I have been having this dream since I was a child. I'm used to it." He paused. "I would like to dig deeper into Johnny's history and find out if there are any other coincidences or similarities."

"Well, I just want you to know that I am going to publish the book and fulfill Anna's wish."

"I think that's a wonderful idea. I love you, and I'll see you in the morning."

The next few months flew by. Grams entered her pie in the Cherry River Festival baking contest and won, as usual. She had tried to switch pies with Mrs. Stevenson to allow her to win for a change, but Mrs. Stevenson saw her and switched them back—and accused Grams of cheating. And thus, the feud continued.

Sarah struggled to dismiss the dream and the book, but the more she tried, the more the uncanny similarities surfaced in her mind. Compounding this was the undeniable connection she felt, not only to Jimmy in the present but also to Anna in the past. That night, her subconscious pulled her back in. She found herself at her beloved spot at the river, but as she gazed into the water, her reflection wasn't her own. It was Anna's. "Anna, you look a fright," she heard her own voice, now Anna's, say. She splashed water on her face, then walked to her usual tree. Kneeling, she dug a deep hole beneath its roots, removed a golden locket from around her neck, placed it in a small metal box, and buried it.

Sarah jolted awake at 5:16 a.m., the dream's images still

vivid. She sat on the edge of her bed, wrestling with its meaning, unable to shake the unsettling conviction that she was Anna.

Sarah steeled herself, knowing what needed to be done. She dialed Jimmy's number, and he answered immediately.

“Hey, baby, is something wrong with Grams?” he asked, his voice laced with concern.

“No, she's fine.” Sarah began pacing, her anxiety rising. “I need you to come with me somewhere. Now.” She stopped, holding her breath, awaiting his reply.

"Care to fill me in on what's going on first?"

"I had a dream," she began, her voice tight. "I was Anna, an older version of myself, and I—she—buried a locket beneath the tree by the river." She paused, letting the information sink in.

“That was, what, two hundred fifty years ago?” Jimmy asked, disbelief in his tone. “Surely that can't be the same tree.”

“Actually, it is possible,” Sarah countered. “But it's not the tree that's important, it's what she buried beneath it, and from what I gather, it was about one hundred ninety years ago.”

“So, you want to search the area to see if this dream is real?”

“Yes. If we find nothing, then I'll chalk it up to coincidence.”

“And what if you find the locket? Will you believe my dream could be real?” he asked in a low tone.

“Let's just check it out and take it from there.”

Sarah roused her grandmother, recounting every detail of her dream.

“Please, inform me about everything you find, whatever it is,” Grams yawned, already drifting back to sleep. “Have fun, dear. I'm going back to bed.” She turned over, snuggling under the covers.

Twenty minutes later, they were driving. The truck rumbled to a halt near the ancient tree, and Sarah practically leaped out, rushing to the exact spot from her dream. "It's right there!" she exclaimed, pointing.

Jimmy grabbed a work shovel from the truck bed and began to dig. After several frustrating minutes, just as he was about to give up, the shovel clanged against something solid. "I think we might have something here," he announced, passing the shovel to Sarah. He knelt and carefully cleared the remaining earth with his hands, revealing a small, rusted metal box.

Sarah stood frozen, her jaw dropping in disbelief. She couldn't quite process that her dream was unfolding before her eyes.

Jimmy placed the box on the picnic table, retrieved a screwdriver from the truck, and carefully pried the lid open. Inside, nestled within the rusted metal, lay a gold locket, exactly as she had seen in her dream.

Tears streamed down Sarah's face as she gazed into Jimmy's beautiful green eyes. "I've missed you, Johnny," she whispered, wiping away the tears.

"I've missed you too, my lovely Anna," he replied, pulling her into a warm embrace.

"Welcome home, my love," she murmured, kissing him with a fiery passion that time and distance couldn't extinguish.

If you enjoyed this book, please consider rating and leaving a review on Amazon and Goodreads. You can also find other books by this author on the platforms listed below.

GUARDING ANGEL (Book 1 of 3)

ANGEL'S CALLING: Sometimes things aren't always as they seem (Book 2 of 3)

AVENGING ANGEL: Eye for and eye (Book 3, coming soon)

And my YA (young adult book)

ADVENTURE ON MARS: Fun with NASA

www.ingramcontent.com/pod-product-compliance
Lightning Source LLC
LaVergne TN
LVHW090548110826
845146LV00001B/58

* 9 7 9 8 2 1 8 7 1 3 6 7 6 *